T0283768

KEEPERS OF THE STONES & STARS

PRAISE FOR
ONE MAN GUY

"Feel-good, bubblegum romance . . . hand this one to those who've already gone through Levithan's *Boy Meets Boy* and Kluger's *My Most Excellent Year*."

—*BCCB*

"A sweet-spirited love story . . . The Armenian content adds flavor and texture."

—*Booklist*

"The story will appeal to both young people who are just discovering their own sexuality and readers who enjoy a good budding romance."

—*School Library Journal*

"Barakiva's debut is well-wrought and realistic . . . and it's entertaining."

—*Kirkus Reviews*

"Barakiva avoids stereotypes and clichés to create a sweet portrait of nascent adolescent love between two boys growing up and finding themselves (with some help from nearby New York City)."

—*Publishers Weekly*

"A kind and generous book about the loneliness of a young boy trying to navigate between a chaotic Armenian family and a school of bullying cliques. Alek Khederian deals bravely and inspiringly with the perils of learning to love your family, to love someone else, and most of all, to love yourself."

—Eleanor Bergstein, screenwriter of the film *Dirty Dancing*

PRAISE FOR
HOLD MY HAND

"Love abounds, heartache happens, and friendship endures in this hilarious and timely coming-of-age novel . . . Barakiva creates an engaging central couple whom readers will root for and smartly surrounds them with a flawless cast of three-dimensional supporting characters who round out the protagonists while standing out in their own rights . . . The novel is enriched with vividly textured Armenian cultural details. An honest and compelling teen romance."

—*Kirkus Reviews*

"Barakiva follows up *One Man Guy* with a highly satisfying sequel that continues to develop the authenticity and complexity of both Alek and Ethan . . . Alek's story also delves realistically—and with some humor—into the stand he takes when his Orthodox pastor proves to be homophobic . . . This story shows the ways people can disappoint one another, break one another's hearts, and get past such crises . . . A delightful and important addition to collections serving teens, whether or not the first book is held."

—*School Library Journal*

"A love sandwich of Armenian American culture and romantic anguish with extra kissing and a side of LGBTQ+ empowerment. So. Much. Fun."

—E. Lockhart, bestselling author of *We Were Liars*

ALSO BY
MICHAEL BARAKIVA

ONE MAN GUY

HOLD MY HAND

KEEPERS OF THE STONES & STARS

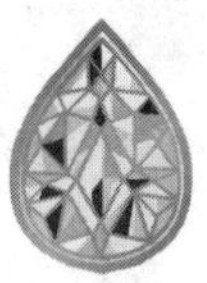

MICHAEL BARAKIVA

FARRAR STRAUS GIROUX
NEW YORK

Farrar Straus Giroux Books for Young Readers
An imprint of Macmillan Publishing Group, LLC
120 Broadway, New York, NY 10271 • fiercereads.com

Our books may be purchased in bulk for promotional, educational, or business use. Please contact your local bookseller or the Macmillan Corporate and Premium Sales Department at (800) 221-7945 ext. 5442 or by email at MacmillanSpecialMarkets@macmillan.com.

Library of Congress Cataloging-in-Publication Data is available.

First edition, 2024
Book design by Julia Bianchi
Printed in the United States of America

ISBN 978-0-374-31440-8
1 3 5 7 9 10 8 6 4 2

To my father, Haim Bar-Akiva (1930–2022),
who believed his children could do anything

(and speaking of children)

To my nephews Ayden, Austin, Benjamin
and my godchild, Jay

We are counting on extraordinary young people
like you to save the world.

KEEPERS OF THE STONES & STARS

PRÓLOGO

I know you have questions, and I know you want answers.

I am reticent, however, to give them. Not because I am withholding. But because I will not be able to satisfy your desires. Understand this: it is not my job to explain such things. Many of them remain a mystery, even to me, even now, all these years decades Passes later. And that is how it should be. You must be able to live with that, as I do. As I have. As I will. At least you have the privilege of your mortality. And yes, it is a privilege. A privilege that, like so many, can only be appreciated once it is gone.

But I am getting ahead of myself. As I often did. Do. Did.

So I will step back, so that I may take a great leap.

"Quien saltar quiere lejos, debe medir la distancia."

There are many ways to tell this story, but I will let Reed begin. It is one of the many courtesies I have granted him.

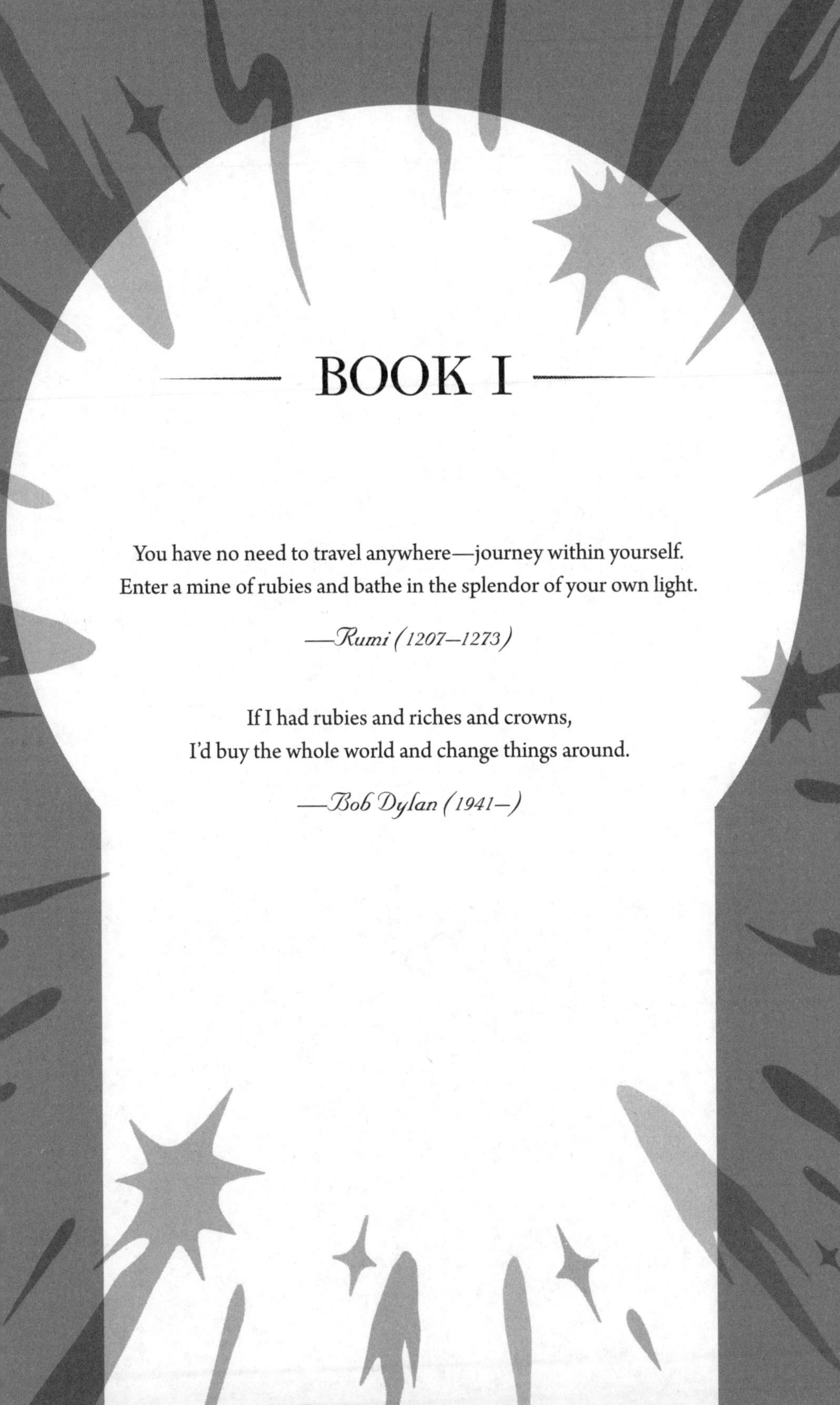

BOOK I

You have no need to travel anywhere—journey within yourself.
Enter a mine of rubies and bathe in the splendor of your own light.

—Rumi (1207–1273)

If I had rubies and riches and crowns,
I'd buy the whole world and change things around.

—Bob Dylan (1941–)

CHAPTER 1

RUNAWAY REED

DO NOT TRY TO FIND ME.

Was it too short? Too mysterious? Not mysterious enough?

The all caps were definitely extra.

Reed crumpled up and threw away yet another draft of his runaway note.

Midnight approached.

Get it together, Reed.

The minimalist approach wasn't going to cut it. At the very least, he needed his mom and Rose to know he was okay. That he'd be home in a few months. It needed to serve "don't worry about me" vibes.

Inspiration struck.

Reed grabbed his notebook and scribbled giddily. Like all good runaway notes, his would also contain a secret clue. To the other person he cared about most.

Dear Mom and Rose and everyone else,

Please don't think this has anything to do with you. Please don't think this has anything to do with what you did or didn't do, because the last thing I want is to cause you any pain. It's just that I've been called. To do something important. Something big. Something only I can do. I'm sorry I can't tell you more, but don't worry. I got this, and it'll all make sense after I'm there and back again in a few weeks. I see now that life would be so wonderful if we only knew what to do with it.

Sincerely,
Reed de Vries

Reed folded the note in thirds and slipped it into an envelope. He made space on his crammed nightstand by rearranging half-full glasses of water, burned-down candles, and errant sheets of music that seemed to multiply of their own accord. Earlier that afternoon, he'd thought about cleaning the junkyard of discarded artifacts that was his room but decided against it. Nothing that would call attention to itself. He put PJ, his red-pawed teddy bear, on the nightstand and propped his runaway letter up against him.

He wasn't taking much. He even left his wallet behind, as he'd been instructed. Mr. Shaw said he'd take care of everything. Even if he hadn't accidentally shorted his cell phone (could it really have been only) a few hours ago, that was obviously a no go now. The only thing he was taking, in fact, was the Stone itself. He grabbed the black velvet drawstring pouch that until recently had held his lucky set of scarlet carnelian dice and slipped it into his pocket. The journey to the other side of his room, to the wall with windows, never felt so significant. He raised the blinds to the far window and slid it open. May's humidity greeted him with a damp caress.

Now or never time.

He allowed himself one last look back: the crimson Maple Electric he'd gotten for his fifteenth birthday after his mom finally let him drop piano for guitar; the collection of reverb, delay, phaser, and flanger guitar pedals he'd painstakingly assembled; a menagerie of shells from a lifetime of beach-walking; pages and pages of sheet music; the backpack full of books he dutifully lugged to school every day; the closet door that didn't completely close, hiding a lifetime of T-shirts, jeans, and flannels.

It wasn't too late—he could still rip up the note, get back into bed, and pretend none of this had happened. If not for . . .

Reed slipped the black velvet pouch out of his cargo shorts pocket and tugged it open. The perfectly round ruby inside emitted a cherry glow, pulsing like a heart.

My precious, he chuckled to himself.

If not for that.

His calloused fingertips pressed the opening chords to "Adventure of a Lifetime" into his palm as if it were the fretted neck of his Maple Electric. Coldplay was more mainstream than Reed's usual jams, but if the tune fit . . .

Dm–G–Am

What would happen when he turned his magic on?

He returned the pouch to his pocket as a gust of wind blew in from the window, planting kisses on the back of his neck. Reed turned his back to his room and slid the screen up. He climbed through the portal and balanced himself in the frame.

Then he jumped.

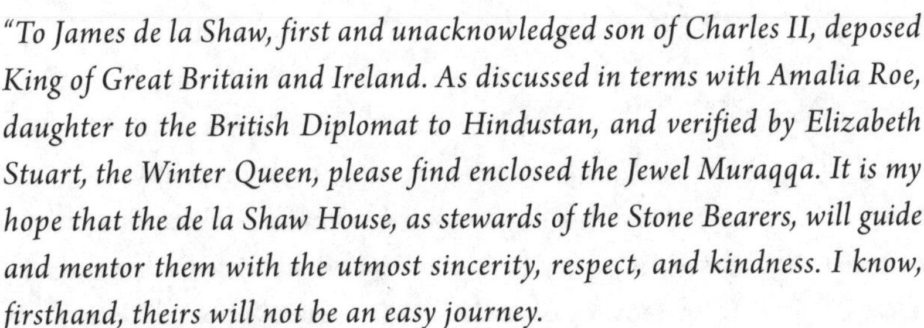

"To James de la Shaw, first and unacknowledged son of Charles II, deposed King of Great Britain and Ireland. As discussed in terms with Amalia Roe, daughter to the British Diplomat to Hindustan, and verified by Elizabeth Stuart, the Winter Queen, please find enclosed the Jewel Muraqqa. It is my hope that the de la Shaw House, as stewards of the Stone Bearers, will guide and mentor them with the utmost sincerity, respect, and kindness. I know, firsthand, theirs will not be an easy journey.

As per our compact, please find the agreed-upon shipments of cotton, silk, indigo dye, saltpeter, and tea, all tariff-free. We hope this is the beginning of a long and equitable relationship between the British East India Company and the Hindustan Empire."

Princess Zeb-un-Nissa
Daughter of Aurangzeb,
Third Son of Shah Jahan, King of the World
Pass One, 1653

CHAPTER 2

PRESIDENT REED

Just two days ago, the idea of Reed abandoning his life and embarking on an epic adventure to save the world would have seemed as unlikely as farting glitter.

He was a normal kid, growing up in the very normal suburbs on the very normal shore of the unfortunately normal New Jersey. He had very normal hobbies, which ran the gamut from geeky (Magic: The Gathering, Dungeons & Dragons, really all things sci-fi/fantasy) to almost cool (playing lead guitar in his band Ragna Rock, which just started getting its first paid gigs of bar mitzvahs and sweet sixteens). He was a normal five-foot-seven and weighed a normal (okay—slightly scrawny) 121 pounds. He spent the spring of his junior year practicing parallel parking with his mother in the office building lot down the street and tormenting his younger sister with tales of what high school would hold for her next year.

The only thing unusual about Reed was his flame-red hair. Reed's hair wasn't the strawberry blond of a Norfolk terrier, the rust of weathered cast iron, or the auburn of autumn. It was unmistakably fire-engine, pigeon-blood, thermometer-mercury red.

Strangers assumed he dyed it, especially since his mom and sister were standard milk-chocolate brown brunettes. But with an awe she saved for very few things, his mom told anyone who asked that it had always been that way.

Until two days ago, Reed's biggest concern was whether to run for Asbury Park High School Student Council president.

"You have to run!" Arno insisted as they walked to the boardwalk after school that cloudy Tuesday afternoon. "You've been talking about it since freshman year."

"I don't *hafta* do anything," Reed responded playfully.

Reed and Arno arrived at their familiar boardwalk stretch, an expanse nestled between the mini golf course and the convention hall. It was thinly populated with a handful of preseason beachgoers braving the heavy clouds, thick and full like swollen organs.

"Sit or stroll?" Arno nodded to *their* bench, directly across from *their* hot dog vendor, Louise, with her classic Jersey Shore Italian accent.

"Stroll," Reed decided.

"Let's pro/con Student Council. That's the best way to make decisions." Arno was a few inches shorter and rounder than Reed, with an olive complexion. His hair was almost as dark as his eyes, which were decades older than his sixteen years. "Pro: if you were president, it would be great for the school."

"Con," Reed countered. "I'd have to work with Principal Trowbridge and her legion of doom."

Although the summer season didn't officially start for another two weeks, a few of the ice cream, trinket, lemonade, and fried-food storefronts had already emerged from hibernation.

"Pro—isn't this exactly the kind of thing colleges look for?" Arno asked. "At least, that's what Mr. Shaw says." Both of them sighed jointly at the evocation of the impossibly dreamy college consultant who appeared last year like a deus ex machina.

"He specifically wrote about that on his blog," Reed conceded without admitting that his Google alert told him every time a new post dropped. "Did we ever find out where he's from?"

"The accent's British, right?"

"Yeah, but he could've picked it up at Oxford."

"Señora Perez-Walters told us he speaks Spanish like"—Arno searched for the words—"a chilango auténtico!"

"After he visited our French class, Monsieur Ouellette said he could pass for a native Parisian." Reed inflected "Parisian" with his best attempt at a French accent. "Which is just about the greatest praise he could bestow on any mortal."

"And his website says he also speaks Russian, Arabic, and Farsi." Arno sighed. "With that skin tone and those green eyes, he could be from anywhere from Spain to the Middle East."

"Is it wrong to crush on a teacher?" Reed asked with faux concern.

"He's not *technically* a teacher."

"Which is probably why we take him seriously."

They continued strolling down the worn wood of the boardwalk, narrowly avoiding a collision with a pack of unruly skateboarders.

"Okay—con." Reed picked up their thread. "If I ran, I'd have to give up GSA."

"What?" Arno exclaimed. "Really?"

"Student Council distributes money to the rest of the groups," Reed insisted. "It would be a total conflict of interest."

A flock of white birds flew above, V-shaped, like a spearhead.

"Okay—another pro," Arno started shyly. "I'd be your campaign manager."

Reed stopped walking. "Really?"

"That *is* a pro, right?"

"Of course!"

This was one of the moments when Reed suspected maybe, just maybe, Arno was crushing on him. Not that Reed had any definitive proof. Arno was so painfully private that despite how much time they spent together, Reed still felt like he barely knew him. Reed and Arno had hung out at Reed's house many times, but never at Arno's. He'd never even met Arno's parents, and only one of his four siblings in passing. Whenever they were together, the conversation moved with a healthy ebb and flow. Only afterward, when replaying it in his mind, did Reed realize how many questions Arno had asked him, and how few Arno himself had answered.

"I believe in you, Reed." The deep brown pools around Arno's pupils quivered. "And I believe that you'd make our high school a better place."

Reed had met Arno in the Gay Straight Alliance group at Asbury Park High. Reed, who'd come out unceremoniously in seventh grade, started the GSA chapter in his middle school shortly thereafter. He joined the high school chapter his first week of freshman year and had attended the biweekly meetings since. ("GSA: where the weekly meetings are not the only things that are bi," Reed would joke.)

Arno first showed up to GSA just after winter break. Many of the kids who joined started out identifying on the *S* part of the GSA rainbow and slowly made their way over to the *G*. But Arno didn't participate at that meeting, or the entire year. He just listened, intently, knitting needles bobbing up and down during discussions, presentations, and guest speakers.

As freshmen, they'd taken that pivotal step from making eye contact when passing in the hallway to actually saying, "Hey." Sophomore year, they sat next to each other the first day of Mr. Huff-Wells's humanities class and stayed in those seats for the rest of the year. When it came time to partner up for the final presentation, their eyes met as if they were the only two students in class. The friendship bloomed in those spring afternoons researching World War II espionage and evenings watching movies. Their final, interactive, multimedia presentation about Spanish double agent Juan Pujol García scored them both As. By junior year, they were running GSA, Reed as president and Arno as his VP.

"Do you ever . . . ," Reed started.

"Do I ever what?"

"Do you ever think"—Reed gestured to the boardwalk, the beach, the town where they'd both spent their entire lives—"there has to be more to life than this?"

"More what?" Arno asked.

"I just mean . . ." Reed searched for the words to articulate the phantom haunting him. "Are we destined to go to college, get a job, get married, maybe even have some kids, then retire, like our parents and their parents, never actually doing anything important, then disappear from the world like we were never even here?"

"It sounds so hopeless when you put it like that." Arno frowned.

"But isn't it?" Reed asked. "Unless we do something that tips the needle to good in some real way?"

"We?" Arno closed his eyes the way he did when he was thinking about something intensely. "You. Everybody knows you're meant for extraordinary things."

Before he could chicken out, Reed slowly slipped his hand into Arno's. His guitar-calloused fingertips found the ridges of Arno's knuckles.

Neither of them acknowledged this hand-holding, just as they hadn't acknowledged when it first happened a few weeks ago, or any of the times since.

Reed conducted a quick scan. Even in his hometown, with its famed history of welcoming LGBTQIA+ communities, he'd learned the hard way to always be vigilant.

First, was anyone radiating toxic hostile vibes in their immediate vicinity?

A bored hot dog vendor.

A few middle schoolers eating pretzels.

No toxic hostile vibes, check.

Second, were there any groups of guys within line of sight?

Any groups of guys, unless they presented as unequivocally queer, would automatically be cataloged as potential threats.

The skateboarders circled back around. Reed instinctively put his body between them and Arno, tightening his hold on Arno's hand as they passed. The wannabe hooligans certainly clocked them, but more with curiosity than hostility.

No dangerous groups of guys, check.

Third, what were their nearby escape and authority figure options? The stairs to the boardwalk were a trap: fleeing was harder on sand. The boardwalk stores were a potential refuge, especially that hipster coffee stand coming up. As for authority figures, they'd passed two police officers a few blocks back, but even with Reed's white privilege, he never really knew if he could count on cops in these situations.

Escape options and authority figures, good enough.

Satisfied they were not in clear or present danger, Reed initiated the stroll down the boardwalk, hand in hand with Arno.

The sharp smell of sea salt.

If, two and a half years ago, a future version of Reed had traveled through the fourth dimension and told him he'd be holding hands with Arno, Reed would've laughed him out of time. When they first met, Reed hadn't experienced any of the heart-fluttering, sweaty-palmed, self-conscious agony/ecstasy that had underscored his meet-cutes with either of his two ex-boyfriends. But Lucas ended up being a liar, and Anuvab, a bore. Arno, with his tent T-shirts, ancient eyes, and quiet calm, hadn't exactly inspired romantic swooning.

But since this new development of hand-holding, Reed found himself thinking about Arno in all kinds of ways and wondering—was Arno thinking about him? Of course, he didn't know. He didn't even know if Arno had ever had a boyfriend. Or ever kissed a guy. Or ever kissed anyone, for that matter.

"Besides, you're a shoo-in." Arno tugged on his two-sizes-too-large, faded mustard T-shirt. "Everybody loves you. And it's about time Asbury Park High had its first queer Student Council president."

"At least its first out one," Reed joked. "You know, with me gone, you'd be prez of GSA."

"What? No way." Arno's fingers tensed around Reed's. "I'm not executive material."

Reed chose not to acknowledge Arno's self-disparaging remark, just as he chose not to acknowledge their hand-holding. At least with the latter, Reed was scared that acknowledgment would dispel it, like an illusion.

"Come on." Reed tugged Arno toward the ocean. "I wanna feel the water on my feet."

Reed and Arno scrambled down the steps, yanking off sneakers and sandals, hands finding each other again the moment they were free. They ran over the lukewarm sand to the wet ribbon of shore. The next wave, ambitious, splashed their shins and ankles.

"Seriously, Reed. Here's the thing." Arno burrowed the sole of a foot into the wet sand. "If there were some other great candidate for Student Council, it would be different. But Raul is basically a fascist-in-training, and Jane is high seventy-five percent of the time. Which sort of means you have to do it, you know?"

"You're right, Arno." Reed pitched his voice above the waves. "But only if you'll help. Can I count on you?"

Words failed Arno. But actions did not. He arched up on his tiptoes and kissed Reed. Without thinking, Reed kissed him back.

Arno's feelings flooded into Reed—his desire, like a dog sprinting across a field; his hope, guarded like a fortified castle; his fear, as blinding as a spotlight. Reed welcomed them all.

One, two, then a multitude of raindrops fell from the nimbus clouds, dotting the sand and the ocean. The two boys kissed in the rain, the final chord of a melody that had taken its sweet time to resolve.

★

"At all costs, protect the Stones."

Hortense de la Shaw
Provost, Pass Five

CHAPTER 3

REED'S MENAGERIE

The afternoon shower had animated the ocean, prodding the waves into competition, until they curled and crashed up to Reed's and Arno's knees.

"Just Like Heaven" by The Cure. A much more sophisticated song than it first appears, with almost no chorus, an insistent rhythm guitar that allows the lead guitar a unique simplicity. And the title sung only once, at the abrupt end of the song. How often does that happen?

Reed didn't know how long they stood there, kissing. Time had lost its shape, twisty and gooey like saltwater taffy, until Arno realized he was about to be late for work.

"Arno . . ." Reed searched for the right words to express how utterly surprised, how utterly unexpected, how utterly delicious their afternoon had been.

"Yes?" Even in that simple word, Reed sensed Arno's fear about what the next words would be.

That meant Reed would have to be extra careful. But what could he say that was meaningful without being cheesy? "I see now that life would be so wonderful . . ."

". . . if we only knew what to do with it," Arno completed their favorite quote with obvious relief. He pulled away, sneakers in hand, throwing back a smile as radiant as the emerging sun before scrambling off to his job at the Empress Hotel.

The moist sand welcomed Reed's feet as he meandered up the shore, but not as much as Reed welcomed bathing in the sensation of getting to kiss the boy he didn't realize he'd been crushing on for weeks.

Would they kiss again? Should he call him tonight? Or play it cool and just see what happened when they saw each other in school tomorrow? Were they going to become boyfriends? Or was this going to be strictly a FWB sitch? And what about prom in two weeks?

Reed let himself mull the possibilities as he relived the warmth, the intimacy, the absolute perfection of the moment. He strolled the beach, occasionally stooping to pick up a shell. Many caught his eye, but few would be honored with an invitation to join his home menagerie.

The rain had dissipated, but every part of him was soaked, from his red hair splattered to his head like roadkill to the now-translucent white T-shirt clinging to his wiry (*okay, skinny*) frame. Every third or fourth wave erased the footprints he'd squished behind him, restoring the tabula rosa of the sandy shore.

The beachgoers who'd been caught in the storm emerged from the stores where they'd sought refuge, ice cream or fudge or lemonade or french fries in hand, glancing suspiciously at the sky. The weather had already betrayed them once.

Half an hour later, three seashells had passed Reed's standards: a swirl of white and gray that almost looked silver in the beams of the emerging sun; a long, thin spiral alternating streaks of white and pitch black; and a bulbous taupe affair that could've passed as a pastry in any bakery.

He wouldn't call Arno tonight—too needy. And texting wasn't an option since Arno was literally the only person their age who didn't have a cell phone. Besides, Reed didn't want to appear desperate. That meant he had until precalc tomorrow to figure out how he was going to play it. Decision made, at least for now.

He was about to turn back and go home when he felt . . . a tug was the best way to describe it. As if Rose were yanking on his shirt to get his attention. He squatted, following the pull to a flat, large shell. Unremarkable. Certainly not take-home-worthy. But nestled in the sand underneath . . .

Words couldn't do it justice. Neither could music.

A bloodred ruby, multifaceted and round like a disco mirror ball, dazzled in the sun's emerging light. Reed snatched the gem out of the sand.

Joy, like finishing a race

The moment his fingers came in contact

Hunger of watching your prey

with its warm, smooth, inexplicably dry surface,

Satisfaction of a job well done

emotions flooded him.

Anger, the moment before a volcano erupts

They attacked him from all sides,

Desire for one more kiss

pounding into him like juggernauts.

Helplessness of witnessing the inevitable

He fell out of his squat, back, down, landing on the wet sand with an unceremonious plop.

"It's contact with the Stone." The girl appeared from nowhere. She must've been younger than Rose—maybe ten years old?—with two side braids framing sparkling eyes.

Reed managed to squeeze out a "Huh?"

"Release the Stone."

Reed shoved the gem into his pocket. The moment his hand was free, the emotions evaporated, dispelled like demons onto another plane, leaving no trace behind but the tears he hadn't realized were running down his face.

"How did you know?" he asked the girl.

But she, too, was gone.

"We'll try again tomorrow, okay?" Mr. Tomasevic told Reed's chemistry class the next morning. His experiment to illustrate chemical bonds and ionization had failed, again, slipping the befuddled teacher's success rate lower than most baseball players' batting averages. He stared, confused, at the sugar cubes and stirring rods in his ancient, wrinkled hands. The stubbornly clear liquid refused to turn pink, taunting him with its transparency.

The clock's minute hand took its sweet time inching to 11:45. In a few minutes, class would finally end. In a few minutes, the bell would ring and Reed could sprint down the labyrinth of halls to Mrs. Bryant's precalc. In a few minutes, he'd see Arno for the first time since their first (*but please, God, don't let it be our last*) kiss. In a few minutes, Reed would ask him to junior prom. He was nervous, he was excited, he couldn't wait.

Reed performed the ancient ritual perfected by students the world over, of pretending to pay attention during the last few minutes of class while putting away his textbook and notes.

Last night, he'd written a 250-word essay about "Why He Wanted to Run for Student Council President." He had completed the online form, entered in his 3.7 GPA and extracurricular list, and gotten his mom's signature. All he needed was for Mrs. Bunge Bowers, Mx. Adelewitz, and Ms. Chung to send their teacher recommendations, and his application would be complete.

That was the first thing he'd tell Arno. And then, casually, *very* casually, he'd take the folded junior prom flyer out of his pocket and ask Arno what he was doing in two Fridays. Even though the early-price ticket period was over, even though he knew Arno's parents were all kinds of messed up and might not let him go with another dude, even though he had no idea how to procure or pay for a tux . . . he shook it all away. Drowning in a whirlpool of "even thoughs" never accomplished anything.

Besides, a vision of them leaning into each other, slow-dancing to "The Night Is Still Young," persisted in his imagination. The calloused fingertips of his left hand pressed the A–B–C# minor opening chords on the imaginary guitar neck of his palm. The certainty of that image gave him the courage to do anything and everything he needed to make it so.

The turtle of the minute hand finally arrived at the nine. Reed leaped to his feet and darted out the moment the bell rang, ignoring Mr. Tomasevic's lingering instructions about tomorrow's homework. He made it through the annex before hitting foot traffic. He raced his way down the breezeway and turned the corner, passing the library on the right, multimedia on the left, and into the main hall, which he decided against cutting across because of the science fair. He spent the rest of the trip in the Sisyphean chore of trying to smooth down his dreaded cowlick. He arrived at precalc in record time, buying him a precious two minutes.

Two minutes with Arno, who sat at his desk, dutifully reviewing yesterday's homework. Could he have any idea how beatific he appeared, the sun casting a saintlike halo behind him?

Reed faltered. *What if Arno says no?* Or even worse, what if he laughed? Maybe Reed should wait for a better time. A more romantic time. How was his breath? *Why'd I wear that stupid old T-shirt today instead of . . .*

Then, as if they were telepathically linked, Arno looked up, straight at Reed.

The smile that spread over his face was the only talisman Reed needed to banish his fears.

Reed ignored the throbbing Stone in one pocket and slipped his hand into the other. Junior prom flyer, check.

Okay. Now or never time.

"Reed de Vries?" A ruggedly handsome man in his early forties, with a touch of gray dusting his temples, approached him.

"Mr. Shaw?"

"Good day, Reed." Mr. Shaw's British accent was as smooth, crisp, and tidy as his signature button-down shirt and linen jacket. He held up an official-looking form with the school's insignia. "I've permission to pull you out of class."

"Is everything okay?" Reed turned back. "Does Mrs. Bryant . . ."

"Yes, and she does." Mr. Shaw adjusted his tortoiseshell glasses and made eye contact with Mrs. Bryant. She responded with a nod and held up a copy of the official-looking form. "All legitimate."

"Is this about my PSAT scores?" Reed scrambled. "Because I could retake them before . . ."

"As much as I appreciate the gesture"—Mr. Shaw laughed—"this is to do with something of actual import. I don't mean to alarm you, but time, as they say, is of the essence. Would you follow me?"

Daring one last look at Arno, who was throwing him some major WTFs, Reed followed Mr. Shaw out the nearest exit. They emerged into the faculty parking lot, a dismal corner formed in the amorphous space between the original building and the newer annex. The sun shone bright and unforgiving in the clear aquamarine sky.

Mr. Shaw's gray linen jacket hugged the white button-down shirt, open one button lower than most teachers would dare. His perfectly tailored chinos tapered at his sturdy calves, meeting his brown leather wing tips. He dressed at least two clicks better than any teacher at Asbury Park High: a royal failing to pass as a commoner.

He aimed his smartwatch at Reed and tapped it twice. The gizmo chirped like a bird on steroids. Mr. Shaw didn't bother to contain the ear-to-ear smile that splayed across his face. A dimple creased his right cheek.

"May I see it?" he asked with a child's eagerness.

Reed didn't know how or why, but he understood exactly what Mr. Shaw meant. Even though he had considered leaving it at home, the idea of being apart seemed as nonsensical as showing up to band practice without his guitar. "Should I just—I dunno—whip it out right here?"

"Of course, you're right. 'Urgency is the enemy of safety.'" Mr. Shaw looked about furtively. "I must ensure nothing—not even my enthusiasm—jeopardizes the mission."

He tapped his watch again. A car that called attention to the fact that no faculty member at Asbury Park High could ever own, let alone drive, a classic sixties James Bond convertible, complete with a front hood that swooped over the front tires, managing somehow to be both full of classic style and ahead of its time, pulled up next to them.

"Sweet." Reed whistled. "Is that a Tesla beta autopilot?"

"I am fortunate to have access to some technology that hasn't quite yet reached the mass market." He tapped his smartwatch again, and the doors hinged up and open.

"I don't know, Mr. Shaw," Reed joked. "My mom told me never to get into a car with a stranger."

"Good thing, then, that I'm not a stranger," Mr. Shaw quipped back. "But if you'd feel more comfortable calling her first?"

"JK, dude."

"LOL."

Mr. Shaw's response earned him a noticeable cringe from Reed but that didn't stop him from sliding into the leather luxury of the passenger side. Mr. Shaw climbed into the driver's seat just before the doors hinged close.

Mr. Shaw looked at Reed expectantly.

Reed withdrew his repurposed black velvet pouch. Remembering the mystery girl's instructions, he opened it and showed Mr. Shaw its cherry-glowing contents without making direct contact.

"It's been so long . . ." Mr. Shaw folded his fingers in front of his heart and let his eyes close. "Hear me, all Chancellors and Provosts back to the first Pass," he chanted. *Or was it a prayer?* "I vow to mentor the Five Stone Bearers and to teach them the Feat of Terminatio, which will seal the Pentacle Portal. Red, the first Stone, the Stone of the Leader, all this I say unto you." Mr. Shaw opened his eyes. "You must forgive me, Reed. But when you finally arrive at the moment to which you've dedicated your entire life . . . it's simply transcendent."

"Tell me I've been chosen!" Perhaps someone else would've been freaked out by the recitation, or the unexpected holy fervor. But a lifetime of J. R. R. Tolkien, Ursula K. Le Guin, George R. R. Martin, N. K. Jemisin, and other fantasy authors with initials in their names had prepared Reed exactly for this moment. "Tell me I've been chosen to go on an epic magical quest to save the world!"

"Righto!" Mr. Shaw exclaimed. "That Stone that you're holding is . . . okay, a few centuries ago, my family was entrusted with . . ." He took a few deep breaths. "Would you mind accompanying me to my office? I'm not exaggerating when I say the fate of the very world hangs in the balance."

Reed looked over his shoulder, to where Mrs. Bryant and precalculus and, most of all, Arno were waiting for him. "Is there any way this could wait, like, forty-five minutes?"

"I'm afraid not, Reed," Mr. Shaw said. "Remember what I said about time?"

"It's of the essence?"

"Exactly!"

"Then what are we waiting for, Mr. Shaw?" Reed yanked the velvet drawstring pouch shut and slipped it back into his pocket, past the folded-up junior prom flyer. Mrs. Bryant, precalc, even Arno would have to wait. "Time for me to meet my destiny!"

"Shall we?"

Reed nodded his consent.

"Please do buckle up." Mr. Shaw pressed a button, and the car's engine whispered to life. "Safety first!"

"Sapphire single-handedly fought her way through the Szeged witch trials, through all who stood in her way. Care must be duly taken to harness her considerable power."

Bayard de la Shaw
Provost, Pass Three

CHAPTER 4

REED SMELLS AN INFO DUMP

Reed drove with Mr. Shaw through downtown Asbury Park to the swankiest commercial high-rise in town. (*There wasn't, for the record, much competition.*) When they arrived, Mr. Shaw handed the keys, along with a crisp twenty, to the valet. "Good afternoon, Jimmy."

"Good afternoon, Mr. Shaw," Jimmy responded with an OG Brooklyn accent as he pocketed the tip with surprising nimbleness for someone whose fingers looked as if they had both broken things and been broken repeatedly.

Reed followed Mr. Shaw into the lobby of the building, full of swooping beige and off-white curves. The walls, the furniture, and even the doorways melted this way and that, undulating like a Dalí painting.

They walked through a lobby populated with suits, consulting their tablets or talking on their cell phones in hushed voices—the things important-looking people did to look important. In the far corner, a young receptionist sporting a smart black suit greeted them from behind a counter.

"Good afternoon, Mr. Shaw." The receptionist smiled and smoothed a stray strand of black hair behind their ear.

"Good afternoon, Satvi."

Satvi waved Mr. Shaw in but gestured for Reed to wait. A small orb of a camera took his picture before they nodded him through. The turnstile wasn't a standard bar affair: sliding panels, like angel wings, parted to let him enter.

Mr. Shaw and Reed passed the main elevator bank and continued to what was clearly the most special, fancy-schmancy elevator tucked in its own corner alcove. Mr. Shaw punched a series of numbers into the chest-level pad embedded in the wall. A long beep (F#?) rewarded his efforts, and the doors slid open. Up, the elevator whisked them, to the penthouse floor.

"All this is yours?!" Rather than opening into a hallway, the elevator revealed—well, "office" didn't do an iota of justice to the penthouse Stark Tower–Bat Cave love child.

"Have a gander, if you'd like." Mr. Shaw smiled.

"Holy . . ." The torus-shaped loft wrapped around the elevator like a life preserver. One half was dedicated to research: microscopes, gizmos, and tools piled up high on concentric tables.

". . . freakin' . . ." Bins filled with jewels sat on the most interior ring of tables, organized by color, like a serve-yourself candy store: rubies, sapphires, topazes, emeralds, amethysts, onyxes, and finally, diamonds.

". . . shit . . ." The dragon's hoard glittered in the light streaking through the entirely glass exterior wall of windows, which also doubled as monitors. Sometimes they collaborated to create one large image; other times they went their separate ways, running different feeds simultaneously. ". . . dude!"

"I made some adjustments, naturally," Mr. Shaw said with faux humility, "when I first leased this humble gaff last year, Red."

"You mean Reed."

"Do I?" Mr. Shaw tapped his smartphone, and the exterior window wall turned opaque pearl.

"Why'd you even set up camp in sweet ol' Asbury Park in the first place?" Reed asked. "You don't strike me as a Springsteen fan."

"It's true—I wasn't quite born to run." Mr. Shaw grinned. "I came here because of you, Reed. Father's algorithm allows us to discover the general vicinity of Red's manifestation. And the Muraqqa's protocol instructs to establish a presence as soon as possible so that trust exists when the first Bearer is chosen. That is the only reason someone of my pedigree allowed himself to be employed by the"—he involuntarily shuddered—"New Jersey public school system. The Stones manifested two weeks later than my calculations predicted but still well within the margin of error. So everything is still going rather swimmingly." He smiled. "Tea?"

"Righto," Reed said in his best approximation of a jolly chap who had all the patience in the world.

Mr. Shaw led Reed to the residential part of the penthouse. A zinc bar horseshoed around the elevator shaft, presenting bottles of every hue and shape. A low-backed leather chaise ran parallel in a larger arc, with slabs of granite acting as modular coffee tables. "Take a pew."

Reed lowered himself onto the leather chaise. The cotton-poly blend of his shorts, he suspected, was the cheapest material to ever grace its surface. "So spill the tea."

"But I haven't made it yet." Mr. Shaw tilted his head quizzically. "Besides, even if I had, why would I want to . . ."

"Never mind." Reed allowed himself a perceptible eye roll. "You were saying . . ."

"The truth is"—Mr. Shaw took a dramatic pause—"I am not actually a high school college counselor."

"I smell an info dump."

"You are a wise young man, Reed." Mr. Shaw produced the pot, cups, and saucers of a perfectly matching bone-white tea set decorated with cornflower-blue blossoms. "This info dump is the behemoth of bowel movements."

Reed crossed his legs and made himself comfortable.

"Centuries ago, my family was chosen by Zeb-un-Nissa, Blue Bearer in Pass One and Princess of the Mughal Empire, to act as mentors to the future Bearers of the Stones." Mr. Shaw filled an electric glass kettle at the bar, then plugged it into a previously hidden outlet. "My entire life has been spent preparing for this moment."

"Your entire life was spent"—Reed leaned against the low back of the leather chaise—"preparing to make tea for a hilarious, dashing, queer high school junior?"

"I wonder if you should first perform the Feat of Relinquo," Mr. Shaw mused, stroking his chin. "Perhaps the next Bearer whom Red selects will exchange snark for deference." He flipped a switch on the kettle. It lit up.

"Keep on dreaming, Mr. Shaw. You and I—we're stuck with each other."

"In that case, here goes." He was suddenly all business. "You have been chosen to unite the Five Stone Bearers and use the Feat of Terminatio to seal the Pentacle Portal and save the world on July 6, 14:51, UTC."

"That's so weirdly specific."

"'God is in the details,' said the atheist."

"Okay." Reed knew this was the moment when he was supposed to protest.

Oh no, Mr. Shaw, magic couldn't possibly be real. Or: *Someone absolutely normal like me couldn't possibly have been chosen for an adventure like this.* But he had no need for that facade. "What is the Pentacle Portal?" He wanted the facts. "Who are the Five?" The deets, the specs. "And how am I supposed to unite them/us?"

This was his destiny.

"Approximately four hundred years ago"—Mr. Shaw took a deep breath—"a cosmic event altered the path of the Ikeda comet. In its new orbit, the Ikeda passed closer to our planet than any other celestial body in recorded history. A mere three lunar distances, or 1.15 million kilometers, to be exact, when it reaches its closest approach every thirty-seven years."

"Closest approach—that's when two objects orbiting the sun are nearest each other?"

"With skills like that, it really is a wonder your PSAT scores aren't higher." The kettle's whistle climbed in half steps (D–D#–E–F), like a singer warming up. "Two extraordinary events are triggered by the Ikeda's aforementioned closest approach. The first is the opening of the Pentacle Portal."

"I'm guessing that's not a good thing?"

"You're guessing correctly. The Portal, unchecked, would release wild, chaotic, uncontrollable magical energies that would destroy our world."

"I'm hoping the second thing is better."

"Your wish, my command." Mr. Shaw bopped his head in a gesture of a djinni, earning another noticeable cringe from Reed. "A few weeks before the Portal opens, the five Stones manifest: a ruby, sapphire, topaz, emerald, and amethyst. They each bond to a young person and grant them extraordinary powers."

"So you're saying this ruby is going to make me a superhero?" Reed produced the black velvet bag holding his Stone. "Hot damn! I knew magic was real. And I'm not just talking about my MTG white/blue deck rocking four Azorius Guildmages."

"Very funny, Reed. But no, we are not discussing Magic: The Gathering." Mr. Shaw poured milk from a previously hidden minifridge into a mini porcelain pitcher. "Although I'm sure my red-green direct damage–megamonster creature deck would *obliterate* yours." He produced an elegant leather box from under the zinc bar.

"Is that where you keep the spell components?"

"This is where I keep my tea." Mr. Shaw swung the box's lid open. "And if you'd care to let me finish *without interruption,* I assure you I'll answer most of your questions before your imagination runs off in flights of fancy. Now, black or herbal?"

"Black, I guess?"

"Very good. I've got an excellent Lavender Earl Grey." He produced a cylinder of loose tea from the leather box, as well as a metal sieve filter and an actual silver spoon.

It took all of Reed's patience to stay silent as Mr. Shaw spooned tea into the filter. Getting superpowers was *literally* the best thing that could ever happen to him. A dream fulfilled. His mind raced with all the possibilities of secret identities, costumes, and sidekicks before he stopped himself and used the maddening silence to promise himself, right there and then, first and foremost, that he would use his powers only for good.

"What I'm saying," Mr. Shaw finally continued, "is that since Pass One in 1653, the Stones have granted their Bearers some *very limited* powers in the few weeks surrounding the Ikeda's closest approach." He snapped the cylinder shut. "And most important, all the Stones working in concert are capable of sealing the Portal itself."

"So the Ikeda awakens both the possibility of apocalypse and the tools by which to remedy it," Reed observed.

"That's very well put." Mr. Shaw nodded appreciatively, and Reed allowed himself to bask in the compliment. "Much of what we know is from Pass One, when Red granted Sarmad the gift of prophecy."

"He could look into the future? Very Destiny. And *Charmed*."

"In his True Dreams, Sarmad saw how to perform the Feat of Locatio, which leads each Stone Bearer to the next." The kettle piped soprano notes as the water finally reached a boil. "He found the Blue Bearer: Princess Zeb-un-Nissa of the Mughal dynasty, the Muslim descendants of Genghis Khan and Timur, who ruled India from the sixteenth century until the Brits took over."

"You are so casual about your colonial past."

"As are you about interrupting your superiors." Mr. Shaw poured a healthy swig of the steaming water into the teapot and gave it a few swirls. "Even at sixteen, Zeb-un-Nissa was a scholar of astrology and one of the greatest minds of the world. She had already identified the Ikeda on its new course when Sarmad found her."

Mr. Shaw placed the tea-stuffed filter into the pot, then slowly poured in the piping-hot water.

"Sarmad revealed how he and Zeb-un-Nissa would assemble the Five Bearers, enter the Pentagon Chamber, perform the Feat of Terminatio to seal the Portal, and save the world. Zeb-un-Nissa selected my family to inherit the honor of mentoring the Bearers. We've passed the great responsibility down from generation to generation. With obvious success since, well, you know, the world is still around to be saved."

Reed picked up the teapot to pour himself a cup.

"If you let it steep for another minute, it will achieve its full flavor."

"And what if I let it steep longer?" Reed asked.

"Then you'd risk bitterness," Mr. Shaw warned.

"We wouldn't want that, now, would we?"

"No, Reed, we wouldn't," Mr. Shaw replied with mock seriousness. "You see, time is always of the essence."

"So if what you're saying is true"—Reed returned the pot to the table and did some simple math in his head—"you were just a kid during the last Pass."

"Correct! As Novice, I got to see Father mentor the Five Stone Bearers in record time before they successfully sealed the Portal!"

"In that case, shouldn't you have a young Padawan watching your every step?"

"I should, but"—Mr. Shaw shifted awkwardly—"I have been unsuccessful in producing a Novice."

"Wait," Reed started, "are you saying that you're . . ."

"Oh no, lad," Mr. Shaw responded quickly. "I'm straight as an arrow. And trust me, at an all-boys prep school, I had plenty of opportunities to figure things out. What I mean to say is that I am biologically incapable of producing an heir." He hung his head in shame. "The first infertile Provost."

"But that means there's an opening!" It all made sense to Reed now. He wasn't *just* going to devote the next few months of his life to saving the world. He had the chance—the once-in-a-lifetime, magic-ticket, never-look-back opportunity—to dedicate his entire life to the greatest goal possible. "For me to be your Novice!"

"I'm not making any promises, Reed, you understand?" Mr. Shaw poured himself a few drops of the tea and tasted them appraisingly. "We must focus on the present Pass Eleven."

"Yessir! But . . ."

". . . but after the Portal is sealed, if I decide you pass muster, and you decide you're willing to dedicate your life to this cause, well . . ." Mr. Shaw filled Reed's teacup with the fragrant concoction before filling his own. ". . . you could be the first Novice outside our bloodline to be trained and entrusted with this enormous honor, responsibility, and burden of mentoring the next generation of Stone Bearers."

"We continue to theorize, without progress, about what cosmic event may have led to the alteration in the Ikeda's path. Gravitational perturbation? Collision with another astral body? Kepler's laws continue to guide us."

Livingston de la Shaw
Provost, Pass Four

CHAPTER 5

REED ANSWERS THE CALL

"You're right." Reed sampled the Lavender Earl Grey, trying his best to perch on the leather chaise in Mr. Shaw's penthouse as if he belonged there. "Worth the wait."

"I'm so glad you agree." Mr. Shaw added a splash of milk to his teacup before taking a sip.

"So to summarize"—Reed daintily placed his teacup down—"I've got just less than two months to assemble the other Bearers and learn the Feat to seal the Pentacle Portal before it consumes the world in a hellish fury greater than even my outrage at the DC Extended Universe."

"I accept your abridged version."

"Shouldn't we add something to up the ante a bit? Like maybe—I'm just spitballing here—making magic accessible to all?"

"I realize that engaging your facetious suggestions is probably a mistake, but if you were to succeed in such a foolhardy plan, you would destroy the world because magic and electricity are incompatible."

"Like oil and water?"

"Like sodium and potassium. They make each other go kablooey." Mr. Shaw illustrated an explosion with his hands. "The phenomenon of Disjunctis was first noted in 1877 by Algernon de la Shaw, the Pass Seven Provost. As technology reliant on electricity became more and more prevalent, Disjunctis has become more and more of an obstacle."

"Disjunctis?" Reed was already itemizing all the areas in his life that would be compromised without electricity: communication, transportation, gaming, music. Obviously not in order of importance. "Couldn't you come up with a name that doesn't sound like a dental condition?"

"All our terminology is Latin, Reed. What do you expect from a bunch of old white men?"

"I just wish it wasn't so The Series That Shall Not Be Named, you know?" Reed responded. "So assuming this all works out hunky-dory and I seal the Portal and become your apprentice, what would we do for the next thirty-seven years?"

"I'd train you to become the Provost for the next generation of Bearers, at which point I would become your Chancellor, as Father is mine. The curriculum would require a singular dedication the like of which you've never known: linguistics, combat, history, magic theory, astrophysics, and of course, diplomacy and international affairs. Because our noblesse oblige doesn't stop there. For four hundred years, since my family was tasked with becoming the guardians of—"

"—the galaxy?"

"—the Stone Bearers," Mr. Shaw continued without missing a beat. "The Shaws have eschewed direct power. We have served as advisers, guides, and mentors to many of the most influential courts and governments in history, including the Hapsburgs, the Qing dynasty, the Romanovs, and of course, the Mughals. We established centers of learning, as well as hospitals, libraries, and observatories. And it is of no shame for me to say that we were instrumental in negotiating the ends of the Thirty Years' War, as well as the First and Second Oirat-Manchu Wars and World War I."

"Okay, I get it. You do good but always"—Reed dropped his voice down to a gravely whisper—"in the *shadows*."

Mr. Shaw chuckled approvingly.

"Why don't you just use the Stones yourself?" Reed asked.

"I do not deny"—Mr. Shaw's eyes lit up as he put his hand out, palm up—"that my heart has greatly desired this. But it's not an option." Mr. Shaw dropped his hand and the Tolkien affect. "The Stones only bond to teenagers. Look, you can see here in Appendix A of the Muraqqa." Mr. Shaw scrolled through his tablet. "Every Provost documents the ages of all the Bearers. Thirteen to seventeen. No exceptions. And the experiments to manufacture Stones that can bond with adults have failed spectacularly."

"It must have something to do with the malleability of our brains." Reed scratched the side of his head. "And/or bodies?"

"That's one of our leading theories!" Mr. Shaw exclaimed. "One of our most formidable challenges is that we have so little time to gather data. Especially because we must use the Feat of Locatio to find Blue as soon as possible. Since all the Stones manifest at the same time, this period—after the Bearers are chosen but before they're contacted—is when they are most vulnerable."

"Vulnerable to what?" Reed asked.

"With great power . . ."

". . . comes great responsibility," Reed completed the Spider-Man mantra. "And I'm assuming without your sparkling mentorship, we Bearers can trigger some of the Stones' power and harm ourselves or others?"

"See how quickly you catch on?" Mr. Shaw nodded. "You lead us to Blue, they find Yellow, Yellow gets us to Green, and finally Green to Purple. You pick up a few power-ups along the way, and once all five Avengers are assembled, I teach you the Feat of Terminatio . . ."

". . . and we seal the Pentacle Portal," Reed concluded. "And then?"

"The Ikeda continues on its merry way, and the Bearers have a lovely window during which they continue enjoying their quickly receding powers. On the autumnal equinox, your gems will blink away, and you will resume your young adult life. And of course . . ."

". . . if you think I pass the mustard—"

"—muster—"

"—you invite me to be your magician's apprentice."

"Exactly!" Mr. Shaw tapped his tablet, and a map of Northeast America leaped onto the enormous screen. "So what do you say, young man?"

Reed bought himself a few seconds by taking another sip of his perfectly brewed Lavender Earl Grey.

Was he really going to say yes? Reed had always felt, always known, deep inside of himself, the same way he knew he liked boys, that he was destined for something greater. It was core to his being, central to his identity, at the very heart of who he was. But now that he was presented with the actual opportunity of it . . .

Who was he kidding?

"I grew up on superhero movies, Mr. Shaw. My final paper for freshman English was an in-depth analysis of Octavia Butler's Xenogenesis trilogy. My D&D character, a seventh-level rogue with three secret levels of sorcerer, is named Emma after *The Promised Neverland*, for God's sake. I've been preparing for this my whole life!"

"One last thing you ought to know, Reed"—Mr. Shaw's forehead furrowed in uncharacteristic seriousness—"before you accept and we begin to experiment."

"Let me guess," Reed quipped. "You have a girlfriend?"

"No," Mr. Shaw responded, "but why would that be relevant?"

"Just go on." Reed allowed himself another eye roll.

"The Feats exact a toll. Locatio, for example, makes it impossible for you to interface with electricity. And the Feat of Potentia—the one that grants you a special power—is accompanied by a Price that is impossible to predict."

"Seriously?"

"Fo' rizzle."

"Okay, first"—Reed cringed—"absolutely not no no way are you ever to say that again. And second, what if my Potentia sucks or the Price is something horrible?"

"You can just bequeath the Stone to someone else. That's what the Feat of Relinquo is for. Exit anytime you choose. No repercussions." Mr. Shaw leaned in. "Reed, I know an element of trust is required here, just as I acknowledge there's nothing I can say to make you trust me. Trust must be earned, through actions. Will you give me the opportunity to earn your trust?"

"Let's do this already!" Reed produced the Stone from his pocket. He carefully laid it in his palm, like a dormant scorpion that might strike at any moment.

Excitement, before the start of a race

Emotions flooded him,

Satisfaction, of being where you know you belong

tidal waves that threatened

Anticipation, of a life's dream

to drown him in their magnificence,

Concern, when facing a daunting task

leaving no trace that he had ever been.

"Clasp the Stone tight in your dominant fist; that's right." Mr. Shaw demonstrated. "Each Feat is unlocked through a series of forms. Here is the sequence to perform the Feat of Locatio."

Mr. Shaw drew his clenched fist into his heart, shifted his feet, bent his knees, then performed a complicated smorgasbord of martial arts/yoga/modern dance that appeared challengingly impossible, at best, to catalog let alone reproduce. He concluded by rotating his arm and shooting his hand out sharply straight ahead.

Reed copied Mr. Shaw's movements to the best of his ability, but his awkward aping culminated in a possible shoulder dislocation. His unexpected yelp came out much more soprano than he would've liked.

"Is something supposed to happen now?" he asked Mr. Shaw after holding the pose for a few very awkward moments.

"When you do it correctly, the location of Blue reveals itself on the map."

"And what'll we do if Blue is in, like, Nepal?" Reed asked.

"All the Stones manifest within a few hundred kilometers of one another." Mr. Shaw paced in a circle around Reed. "Finding Red was one of the Provost's more challenging obstacles until Father discovered the algorithm."

"Father?"

"Provost to the Pass Ten Bearers, Chancellor to me now." Mr. Shaw fanboy-sighed. "The most extraordinary man I have ever known. I wonder, all the time, how I will ever fill his shoes."

"That's the nice thing about not having a dad," Reed observed wryly. "No daddy issues."

"Nonetheless, Reed, I hope you come to count on me. The way I have been able to rely on Father."

"I know I will." Reed surprised himself and Mr. Shaw with his sincerity.

"Shall we try again?"

Reed nodded yes.

Mr. Shaw clicked his tablet. The window monitors shifted from their opaque pearl to a video of Mr. Shaw, dressed in martial arts whites, performing Locatio, while his British baritone narrated the sequence step-by-step. "The first Feat, Locatio, is designed to locate the next Stone in the series of the Five . . ."

They practiced for an hour, paying attention to details so minuscule that at times Reed suspected that Mr. Shaw was making them up.

"Your lats have to slide down in the next position," Mr. Shaw instructed.

"Excuse me?"

"Is it all right if I place my hands on your back?" Mr. Shaw asked.

"Go for it." Reed didn't know if he'd ever been conscious of the latissimus dorsi muscles spanning his midback until Mr. Shaw outlined them with his fingers.

After perfecting the movement of the fingers on his left hand, after repeatedly viewing the video, after landing the correct angles at which his fist should move through the air, and yes, after discovering how his trapezius shifted down his back, Reed still . . .

Felt . . .

Nothing.

"Again," Mr. Shaw instructed.

Moving his weight back on his heels, Reed initiated the sequence again, moving slower than felt natural, prioritizing precision over speed.

He cleared his mind. Of Mom. Of Rose and the ventilator she still used to treat her long COVID. Of Arno. Of Student Council. Of Ragna Rock. Of school. Of prom. Of everything. Of Arno.

Fist to heart, arm rotation, shift of feet, semisquat, twist, turn, shift, shift again. The sequence couldn't be longer than a minute, ninety seconds tops.

When Reed shot his gem-clenched fist straight up, completing the final form, did he feel—or was he just imagining it?—a tingle that started in his hand, made its way down his forearm, through his bicep, and into his shoulder?

The image of a perfectly square sapphire entered his mind, crystal cold. A face followed. Wide nose. Strong jaw. Beckoning him to . . .

Mr. Shaw's watch chirped three sharp, shrill notes, shattering Reed's concentration and the image in his mind's eye.

"Would you excuse me?" Mr. Shaw consulted his wrist. "I will return in a few minutes." He slipped his tablet into a cross-strap leather satchel and, passing the elevator, took the stairs.

Had something actually happened between him and the Stone in the moment before Mr. Shaw's watch chirped? Or was it just his imagination?

Just my A major *imagination,*

running away with D major *me . . .*

Reed slid open the glass doors to the wraparound terrace and stepped outside. The sun, a shiny coin in the ocean of the sky, had begun its descent. Although he recognized all the structures in Asbury Park, like the municipal building and abandoned carousel, this perspective made them look like a LEGO model.

He'd blown precalc entirely, obviously, and study hall as well. Was it just yesterday that he'd kissed Arno? And this morning when asking him to prom seemed like THE MOST PRESSING ISSUE? If he went back now, he'd at least get back for . . .

The elevator doors pinged open.

"Thank God I found you, honey." Reed's mom stepped through, her eyes awash in relief. "Quickly, Reed—we have to go. Something happened to Rose."

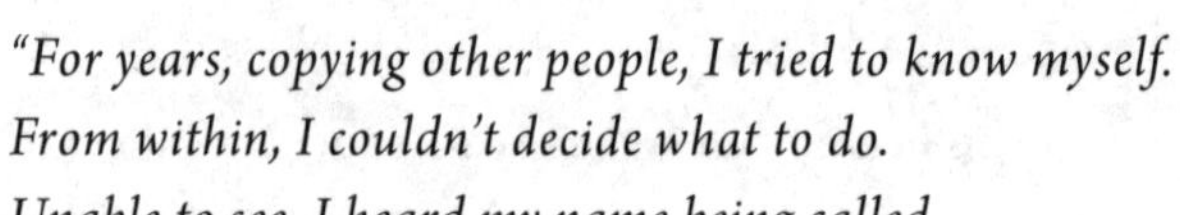

"For years, copying other people, I tried to know myself.
From within, I couldn't decide what to do.
Unable to see, I heard my name being called.
Then I walked outside."

Rumi, as quoted by Hortense de la Shaw
Provost, Pass Five

CHAPTER 6

REED'S FIRST CRISIS

"To Rose? What happened?" Reed ran across the penthouse, to his mom, grabbing his backpack along the way. *Medical emergency* was where his mind went first, between the long-term side effects from her COVID-19 and her underlying type 2 diabetes. But, of course, he couldn't rule out the possibility of a school shooting. *Or traffic accident, or kidnapping.* He raced through all the other horrific possibilities as he jammed the down arrow button three times for good measure. "Is she okay?" Reed reached out to his mom, but she kept him at arm's length.

"Don't—please. I'm not sure if I'm contagious." Tears threatened to escape her puffy eyes, almost as red as the piles of rubies in Mr. Shaw's penthouse. She tightened her grip on the black Berluti leather briefcase she bought herself for her forty-fifth birthday. "I don't want you to catch anything."

Something infectious? Another pandemic?

"Is Rose sick? In the hospital? Are you okay? What's going on, Mom?"

The elevator doors finally dinged open.

"I'll tell you all about it when we're there, okay?" Reed's mom stepped into the elevator car.

Before Reed could join her, the fire stairs door swung open. Mr. Shaw rushed out, panting like he'd just burst through the ribbon at the end of a marathon. "Reed, thank goodness!"

"Honey, we need to go." His mom's voice cracked. "Rose needs us."

Reed hesitated for a fraction of a second. If Rose was sick, could he actually do anything for her? And in the grand moral universe, wasn't saving the world more important than uselessly sitting by his sister's bedside?

But of course, there was no actual decision. Anything could wait if Rose needed him now.

"I'll call you soon." Reed stepped into the car, causing the closing doors to stutter. "Okay, Mr. Shaw?"

With an acrobat's grace, Mr. Shaw launched himself inside the elevator, landing in a perfect roll just before the doors slid shut behind him. As the elevator began its descent, he shifted his weight forward and—

—much to Reed's surprise—

—hurled an uppercut fist at Reed's mom.

"What the—" Reed cut himself off when Mr. Shaw's hand passed through his mom. She flickered, like an image with a weak signal, before disappearing in a shower of sparks.

"What did you do to her?" Reed winced as errant sparks sizzled his exposed forearm like hot oil. "What happened to my mom?"

The foul stench of melted plastic and burnt hair polluted the descending elevator.

"That wasn't your mother, Reed." Mr. Shaw gritted his teeth as he peeled off the molten machinery that had been his smartwatch, taking strips of his flesh with it. "It was just an illusion. A Glamour. Created by . . ."

The elevator reached the ground floor, and the doors pinged open. A punk girl around Reed's age awaited them, tapping her combat-booted foot impatiently. Her ripped jeans looked like they might fall apart without the legion of safety pins holding them together. The pink and purple spikes of her mohawk matched the spikes on her leather jacket.

". . . JoAnne!" Mr. Shaw finished. "JoAnne . . ." He faltered, emotions flashing across his face faster than Reed could clock them. ". . . it's so good to see you again." Mr. Shaw moved forward, putting himself between her and Reed. "How can I help you?"

"Bite me, Rupert." Her gamine features contorted into a sneer. "Now hand over the Red Bearer."

"Or what?"

"Don't try me, wannabe." Her pierced eyebrows furrowed. "You know I'll do whatever it takes."

"Like impersonating his mother and lying about his poor sister's welfare?"

"Rose is fine?" were the first words that Reed's scrambling mind could form.

"I didn't say she was fine." JoAnne addressed Reed. "Why don't you and me bounce, and you can find out for yourself?"

"JoAnne, I can't imagine what you've endured to be here, but let me help you," Mr. Shaw pleaded.

"No duh you can't imagine what I've been through." A smile twisted JoAnne's mouth into a sinister smirk. "Or what I've learned." A forced laugh escaped her throat. "So move aside. Your time is up."

"Actually"—Mr. Shaw held up his cell phone—"I've got all the time in the world." He pressed a button, and a tiny projectile shot out so fast Reed experienced it only as a blur.

But instead of striking JoAnne, it flew right through her, as if she wasn't even there.

Because, of course, she wasn't.

More sparks erupted as the projectile exploded midair where the illusion of JoAnne had been.

"Another Glamour? Lovely." Mr. Shaw ran through the lobby, ignoring Satvi behind the counter, who was already calling the police, as well as the handful of suits in the lobby so alarmed that they actually considered disengaging from their phones or tablets. "But remember, I know all about you, JoAnne. Your range limit means you must be in the building." He raised his voice. "Maybe even in the lobby, disguised as one of these normal folk." Those normal folk glanced at Mr. Shaw with concern. "I'll find you. If not today, then soon. And I'll make sure you get the help you need. Because nothing, especially not you and your parlor tricks, is going to stop me from assembling the Five and sealing the Pentacle Portal!"

"Luckily, Rudolpho appears immune to all manifestations of fire."

Hortense de la Shaw
Provost, Pass Five

CHAPTER 7

REED ANSWERS THE CALL FOR REAL

After JoAnne's attack, Reed called Rose's middle school from Mr. Shaw's penthouse.

"So nothing weird happened to you today?" he asked her once the school had gotten her on the phone.

"Besides you getting me pulled out of social studies, you mean?" Rose's voice crackled on the other end. "No, nothing *else* weird has happened."

"And you're feeling fine?"

"Oh my God, yes. No shortness of breath. No wheezing. Any other questions, *Doctor Dad*?" He could hear her eye roll.

"Rose, what's the name of your bard?"

"You know I don't play a bard in D&D when I deign to join you and your loser alt indie emo wannabe bandmates." Rose sighed. "My barbarian Silas is the tank that your rogue Emma with sorcerer levels I'm not supposed to know about desperately needs since she has around twelve hit points. Now, can I go back to class, or do I need to tell Mom that you're finally having a breakdown?"

"I love you, Rose."

"You are such a weirdo." She hung up.

A call to his mom at work confirmed she was also okay.

"So . . . ," Reed asked Mr. Shaw after he got off the phone with his mom. "Did you just forget to mention that we had an archvillain?"

"I confess—there is no precedent for this. I'm utterly gobsmacked. But I don't want to share any unverified information just yet, Reed." Mr. Shaw finished scrolling on his tablet and gave Reed his full attention. "For now, all we know for sure is: one, JoAnne can project Glamours. Two, she's dangerous. Three, she's most likely deranged. We'll have to proceed with great caution since she seems hell-bent on preventing us from sealing the Portal." Mr. Shaw slammed his fist down on one of the granite side tables. "It's difficult for me not to feel as if I've already failed you."

"Hey, Mr. Shaw—it's okay. Besides, that attack might've been the best thing that could've happened."

"Why do you say that?"

"This is like when the Empire kills Luke's uncle and aunt in Episode IV." Reed's resolution stacked itself up, brick by brick. "Any doubt I had is gone."

"You realize that JoAnne's presence changes everything." Mr. Shaw began packing a leather weekender bag. "We'll have to leave quickly, employing more subterfuge than I would like, to draw her away from your family. For all the obstacles that other Bearers and Provosts have faced, I don't think they've ever been up against anything quite like this! If only . . ."

"If only what?"

". . . we knew the location of Blue."

Instead of responding with words, Reed closed his hand around his Stone and drew it into his heart. Time slowed. His body executed the motions Mr. Shaw had taught him, but his mind focused on the sapphire that had revealed itself to him. He felt every part of him—relax? surrender? open?—to the cosmic energies of the Stone. That same tingle tickled his fist, made its way through his forearm, through his bicep, and into his shoulder. He was its conduit, a converter for its splendiferous power, invoking, summoning, channeling, until finally . . .

He opened his fist. Red slowly spun in his palm, a dreidel with all the time in the world. Then it picked up momentum until it twirled so fast it blurred. When it stopped, a scarlet beam shone at Mr. Shaw's map, directly on Washington, DC.

"The Feat of Locatio." Mr. Shaw ran his hand through the light, marveling. "It's even more glorious than I remember."

The plan they concocted was simple.

Later that night, his runaway note neatly tucked into an envelope and propped up by his red-pawed teddy bear PJ on the nightstand, Reed jumped out his bedroom window and landed safely two feet below on the sloped roof of the living room extension that had been his mom's fortieth birthday gift to herself. It easily held his weight, as it had earlier that afternoon when he'd practiced his escape route. He crouched, leaning against the house itself, listening for any sound of movement inside.

So far, so good.

He wasn't one of those kids who had ever had to sneak out: his geekiness and his mom's laid-backness had just enough Venn diagram overlap to have successfully maintained peace. Reed crawled forward on all fours, following the gentle slope of the roof extension as it angled toward the driveway. One hand, one knee. Other hand, other knee.

The crickets orchestrated his careful descent with a syncopated symphony. It wasn't exactly the heavy bass *Mission: Impossible* theme playing in his head (A–A–A♭–B♭–A–A–E♭–E), but that didn't stop the bass drum of his heart from trying to pound pound pound its way out of his rib cage. If even a fraction of what Mr. Shaw had told him was true, crawling down the rooftop from his bedroom window was a mere blip on the danger radar of his new life.

The tiles were slick from a spring shower, as unexpected and unwelcome as a pop quiz. He paused midcrawl. Nothing could be done about the salacious wet patches emerging on his jeans. He dried his hands against his hair, futilely engaging his true nemesis, a cowlick with an immortal's persistence.

The climb down might've been dangerous if he'd been encumbered, but Mr. Shaw had told him not to bring anything, not even his wallet. He moved slowly all the same. *Nothing would suck more than failing a Dexterity check and having to complete the adventure on crutches.* One hand, one knee. Other hand, other knee.

When he reached the edge of the extension roof, he allowed himself a short rest. Once he'd coaxed his pounding bass drum heartbeat down to a gentle timpani, he swung his feet over, toes finding the ledge of the window below. He lowered himself using the top of the window as handholds, hopping down the rest of the way, and landing on the ground in his best approximation of Black Widow's crouch.

The darkness softened as his eyes adjusted. The faint glow of the Kambaras' night-lights from their plum split-level colonial next door provided the only illumination. In the suburbs of New Jersey, midnight was dark.

Now what?

While he waited, doubt seized him.

This must be the craziest thing I've ever done in my life. I don't care how much of a DILF Mr. Shaw is—the idea of throwing my life away and trusting a stranger is . . .

"I knew I could count on you." Mr. Shaw's crisp British baritone pierced the night a moment before he and his green eyes emerged from the darkness on freakin' horseback, of all things. He looked like a centaur, his solid, muscular form melding into the steed beneath him.

"Horses?" Reed exclaimed. "Now don't I feel foolish for not taking any skill points in equestrian." He would never talk to a teacher this way. But unlike most adults, Mr. Shaw invited this kind of engagement. It was one of the reasons Reed trusted him.

"Trust me, anything's preferable to the hang-glide debacle of Pass Nine." Mr. Shaw dismounted his coal-black stallion like a pro and tossed Reed a spare helmet from the saddlebag of a white horse trailing behind. "Let me make sure you put that thing on correctly." Mr. Shaw walked over to Reed. "Is it all right if I make physical contact with you?"

"Sure." Reed threw in a half eye roll for good measure. He was all for establishing consent, but sometimes . . .

Mr. Shaw's rough, calloused hands swatted Reed's off the straps. Somehow, his former high school college counselor was always wearing the right amount of cologne. And the good stuff, too, that made it smell like spring. Not the musky junk that the jocks of Asbury Park High showered in.

"How's that?" He secured Reed's helmet with ease, giving the straps a satisfying tug.

"Perfectly snug."

"One foot in the stirrup"—Mr. Shaw led Reed to the white horse and formed a cradle with his hands—"then put your knee here. I'll boost you up the rest of the way. When you dismount, we'll do it the same way but make sure your foot is out of the stirrup first—that's how most newbies hurt themselves." Mr. Shaw ran his hands through the horse's thick mane. "Her name's Snowflake."

"A bit on the nose, isn't it?" Reed awkwardly jammed one foot into the stirrup.

"You've always got a rejoinder"—Mr. Shaw formed a cradle with his hands for Reed's knee—"haven't you?"

"It's a blessing, really."

"In Ancient Greek, one word meant both blessing and curse."

"The line is *so* thin."

Against Mr. Shaw's six feet of solid mass, Reed's own five-foot-seven, 121-pound scrawny frame felt all the more knobby-kneed and narrow-shouldered.

He mounted Snowflake successfully on his third attempt, knee and ego equally bruised. "You do know that I've never ridden a horse before, right?"

"It's only a fifty-mile ride, before we take to the water." Mr. Shaw patted Snowflake affectionately. "Challenging in one night, for sure, but we'll break it up with rests to stretch and water the flowers."

"Excuse me?"

"To use the loo. The men's. The bathroom."

"You Brits are so quaint, what with your sayings and all."

"Which is all to say, don't worry," Mr. Shaw continued, ignoring Reed. "Snowflake's been trained for a virgin rider."

Reed arched an eyebrow but resisted the slew of deeply inappropriate responses that presented themselves as Mr. Shaw remounted his horse. He maneuvered with the ease of a lifetime of riding, using just his sturdy knees and thighs, reins held loftily.

"Everything you need to know to become a formidable horseback rider in five concise minutes." Mr. Shaw demonstrated how much force to use when digging your knees into the horse's flanks, the easiest way to access the canteen looped around the saddle, different ways to position arms for balance, how to hold the reins, and the appropriate level of tautness. "It's absolutely fine to put pressure on them as long as you're not clutching."

"There's only one thing I ever clutch." Reed splayed his hand up to his imaginary pearls.

"Focus, Reed," Mr. Shaw admonished him. "All you really need to do is stay calm and loose and match Snowflake's rhythm. She'll do most of the work. She's been trained to follow Midnight, and horses have excellent night vision. It'll take us around eight hours, breaks included."

Reed nodded.

"You're sure you want to do this, right, Reed?" Mr. Shaw softened. "Because you can still back out."

Mom. Rose. Home. His band. School. And of course, Arno. He was tempted.

But how would he live with himself if he turned his back on what would be the greatest adventure of his life? "Lead on, O captain! My captain!"

"You're the Leader, Reed." Mr. Shaw gave his horse's ear an affectionate scratch. "I'm just the bloke who's spent his entire life preparing to help you achieve your destiny." Mr. Shaw dug his heels into Midnight's flank. Horse and rider turned.

In the moment before Snowflake followed, Reed caught a glimpse of—was it the same glowing-eyed girl from the beach?

"Everything all right, Reed?" Mr. Shaw called over his shoulder.

Reed turned back, but she was gone. Or maybe she'd never been there in the first place. "All good."

"Then let the great adventure begin!"

★

"The Chancellor's theory that each Stone governs a sphere of power is close to being proved beyond a reasonable doubt, as all four Green Bearers have hence far manifested a Potentia in the Travel realm. (See Appendix F.)"

Livingston de la Shaw
Provost, Pass Four

CHAPTER 8

REED RIDES

Reed felt like he was clinging to Snowflake for dear life. Maybe because he was.

He did his best to match his body to Snowflake's stride as they raced west across central New Jersey through Thursday's earliest hours. He had no idea how to guide her, but he didn't need to. She followed Midnight, alternating gallops with slower trots. By the time Mr. Shaw called their second break, Reed realized they were for his benefit as much as the horses'.

The inside of his mouth cracked like aged parchment. Until he proved dexterous enough to unscrew the tantalizing camo canteen while riding, he'd have to suffer through the dry.

He didn't bother dismounting Snowflake on their third break, going straight for that leprechaun-elusive canteen. Besides, he wasn't sure he'd have the strength to get back on, even with Mr. Shaw's help.

Those five minutes couldn't possibly have lasted the three hundred seconds he'd been promised before they were off again.

Just like the beast he clung to, Reed was sweaty. He was tired. His inner right thigh and crotch chafed from the denim of his jeans rubbing against the rugged leather of the saddle. His skeleton jostled with every bound like a pair of dice.

He was here for every moment of it.

Dawn's rosy fingers rippled across the Thursday morning sky, as if drawing back a curtain, by the time they embarked on what Mr. Shaw promised would be the final stretch of this leg of their journey. Who knows how much time had elapsed before they reached the bank of the Delaware River and finally slowed down. They traced the New Jersey–Pennsylvania border south, riverbank on their right and trees providing cover on the left.

“Up and down and up and down.” Mr. Shaw demonstrated how to match the horse’s trot, a slower but counterintuitively more difficult gait to master than the full-out gallop. Reed’s teeth rattled with each miss.

The first sliver of the sun appeared, growing into a shiny mound on the horizon. They stopped at a small, unassuming dock in the river attended by two androgynous servants in gray single-piece uniforms. Neither of them spoke as they helped Reed dismount. (Mr. Shaw needed no assistance.)

“I’ve had the servants’ tongues removed and eardrums pierced to ensure discretion,” Mr. Shaw whispered to Reed as they approached the dock, where a river barge awaited them.

“You what?” Reed asked, horrified.

“I’m kidding, of course!” Mr. Shaw stifled a yawn, the first sign of fatigue he’d shown. “But it does behoove us to speak as little as possible around them or anyone else. Nothing can compromise the mission.”

Two more equally anonymous servants in equally androgynous gray uniforms emerged from the barge. It was a simple affair: a backyard-size floating platform attached to a small house of a tugboat. “I’m not going to short anything, am I?” Reed asked.

“We’ve designed the barge proper to be entirely electricity-free, so as long as you stay off the tug, we’ll avoid a bout of the old Disjunctis.”

“It’s like you’ve been planning for this your whole life!” Reed hoped his glibness covered the fear he felt as the androgynous servants from the barge extended a plank to the dock.

“We can get started on the Feat of Potentia when we get onboard.”

“Mr. Shaw, we must be nearing seven AM.”

“Oh, I’m sorry, Reed, are you too fatigued to save the world?” Mr. Shaw crossed the plank and stepped off onto the barge with a tightrope walker’s confidence. “This is going to take work. Real work. And sacrifice.”

Reed tentatively stepped onto the plank, which was sturdier than it seemed but not nearly as sturdy as he would’ve liked. Two feet across and ten feet long. Plenty of opportunity to fall. “I’m so tired I can’t even think straight.”

“Sometimes that’s the best time to train. When your conscious mind is too exhausted to resist.” He called over from the barge. “Now arms out, head up, one foot over the next.”

Much to his surprise, Reed made it onto the barge without falling. His name, stenciled in red, appeared on the door of the first of five cabins.

The denial of sleep was made even more excruciating by the comforts of his cabin, an exercise in luxury straight out of Pottery Barn. The queen-size bed, draped in cream-and-earth-tone linens with matching pillows fluffed like marshmallows, beckoned him.

Reed changed into the perfectly sized cargo pants and three-button, short-sleeve crimson Henley that had been laid out for him.

A bit on the nose. Redheads never wore red, of course, but he forgave Mr. Shaw his limited, hetero imagination. *At least it's a blue-leaning crimson and not something orangey.*

He chomped down on some roasted almonds and dried fruit from the basket of goodies on the room's only table, chased it down with bottled water, and met Mr. Shaw on deck. His tablet was already open.

"Feat of Potentia, Red Bearer."

"Flame on!" Reed pumped his fist into the air.

"I can't believe that didn't work." Mr. Shaw's delivery was desert dry.

"No need to get snarky. Just do your thing and mentor me already."

"I thought you'd never ask." Mr. Shaw scrolled on his tablet until he found the appropriate section. "Stone clasped in the dominant hand. Feet facing me. Now, rotate your right foot ninety degrees out and your left foot forty-five degrees in that same direction. Keep torso facing forward! Okay, that's better. Passive hand straight out, shoulder height. Straight! Now move your fist from your heart to the sky and back to your heart. The movement has to be crisp! Look at the passive elbow—it's lazier than a donkey's bollocks. Sharp movements, you understand? That's better." Mr. Shaw spent the next ten minutes detailing the Feat of Potentia in all its nitpicky, painstaking glory.

Reed wasn't unathletic. He'd run cross-country since seventh grade and could hold his own in pickup soccer or basketball. But after fifteen minutes, beads of sweat formed on his brow and in the small of his back. His lower back, glutes, and IT bands, already sore from the horseback riding, ached as he moved through the unfamiliar forms.

"How . . . ," he asked between gulps of air, ". . . how will I know if it works?"

"Oh, you'll know." Mr. Shaw circled Reed, appraising him from all angles.

"And does the Muraqqa say how long it takes most Bearers to unlock their powers?"

"Usually a few days. Father and Rahalleh set a record in Pass Ten, when she did it on her first go. I still remember the way her face lit up. But Father was more goal-oriented than I, so I choose not to fixate on their accomplishments. 'Comparison is the thief of joy.'"

"Your pithy sayings are the thief of coolness."

"Try again." Mr. Shaw's sturdy hands adjusted Reed's shoulders.

Reed did his best to execute the movements exactly. But after an hour of holding his feet in place as his torso and hands moved, holding his hands in place as his feet traced patterns in the ground, pumping his Stone-clenched fist into the air, putting it up against his forehead, his mouth, his throat, his heart . . . he still . . . didn't . . . feel . . . a thing.

Except Mr. Shaw's frustration, that is. Even though his mentor didn't show it, Reed felt the emotion like a physical force, bludgeoning him with its bluntness. Between the toil and toll of the forms themselves and Mr. Shaw's mounting disappointment, Reed reached the point where he just had to . . .

"Enough!" His sweat stained his clothes. It dripped down his forehead, onto the floor, making meaningless constellations. "I'm done. That's all I got, Mr. Shaw. Guess I'm just a failure." Reed dropped against the barge rail, defeated.

"Reed." Mr. Shaw squatted down next to him. "I want you to understand something. During our time together, you will fail. And I, too, will fail. Failure is, in fact, necessary for growth. The trick is to fail intelligently, analyze that failure, learn from it, and move on. Understand?"

"Yes, sir," Reed said, feeling both more and less foolish.

"Now get to bed. You've earned it." Mr. Shaw stood and held a hand out to help Reed up. "We'll try again tomorrow, and tomorrow, and tomorrow, until we get it right."

"The ongoing scholarly debate of how the Stones tap into their Bearers' cognitive abilities, proposed by Provost Ignatius in Pass Eight, is both supported and contradicted by some experiments I've conducted, detailed below."

Broughton Shaw
Provost, Pass Ten

CHAPTER 9

REED'S POTENTIAL

The barge docked in Wilmington Thursday afternoon, awakening Reed from his much-earned slumber. A shower, two protein bars, and another horse ride trailing Mr. Shaw through White Clay Creek State Park found them in White Hall, a small town on the northeastern most point of Chesapeake Bay. Could it possibly still be Thursday? The blur of embarking on a second barge, identical to the first, disappeared into an even blurrier slumber.

He awoke before sunrise, showered, and changed into another crimson Henley/cargo pants ensemble. As he made his way up to the deck, he chowed down on the ham-and-cheese croissant that had appeared while he slept.

How incredibly bougie, Reed thought to himself with every buttery bite. *And far more practical than stew.*

"Feat of Potentia—Take Two!" Mr. Shaw was already waiting for Reed on the deck, groomed, coiffed, and ready to go. "Ready?"

"I couldn't be readier," Reed said. "I'm going to take this Feat of Potentia by the horns and show it who its daddy is."

"I shall refrain from commenting on your dubious mixing of metaphors."

"What's it called," Reed mused, "when saying you won't do something actually accomplishes it?"

They trained for hours on the deck of the barge, reviewing all the movements with a kind of specificity Reed assumed had been reserved for brain surgery.

"Would it help if I tried rotating my left foot out first?" Reed demonstrated.

"No. The movements should be followed exactly."

"And are you sure this worked for other Reds? Maybe—I don't know—maybe each Bearer has to access it differently?"

"Reed, I assure you, I have studied the Muraqqa since I was old enough to read. I was present as Novice when Father led Rahalleh through this very Feat successfully in the last Pass. This is the only way."

Drenched in his own sweat hours later, however, Reed felt as far from unlocking the Feat as he did to God. "Maybe we should just skip Potentia and go straight to Terminatio. That's the important one, right?"

"The Feat of Terminatio is a Synergia among all five Bearers, only possible once each has unlocked their Potentia. Besides, there's no skipping Feats, Reed. The Muraqqa is extraordinarily clear on this point—each Feat prepares you for the next. Like progression in yoga or learning major chords before minor."

But even Mr. Shaw's musical analogies didn't help. Reed's Stone still lay dull in his hand, unchanging, unhelpful, unresponsive.

"Why don't we return to this later?" Mr. Shaw tried his best to sound encouraging.

"Is that the lovely British way of saying we're giving up?" Reed asked sharply.

"I told you, Reed. Failure is inevitable. You must accept that to transcend it."

Reed persuaded Mr. Shaw to train again after dinner on Friday. They worked well into the night, unsuccessfully.

He woke up early the next morning—Saturday?—and made his way to the deck without bothering to shower, as wisps of pink floated up from the horizon. Mr. Shaw, unsurprisingly, was already there. As they trained, the barge continued floating down Chesapeake Bay, veering right into the Potomac River.

Mr. Shaw entered a deeply reserved state during the multihoured session. Reed couldn't tell what he was thinking or feeling. He didn't rise to any of Reed's quips nor engage him in the banter that had defined most of their previous interactions.

"What else can you tell me about the Feat of Potentia?"

"'For years, copying other people, I tried to know myself,'" Mr. Shaw recited. "'From within, I couldn't decide what to do. Unable to see, I heard my name being called. Then I walked outside.' It's a Rumi poem, and that's all the Muraqqa offers. Again, please."

Reed planted his feet and initiated the movements. He'd performed the short sequence so many times in the last two days that his body just clicked into autopilot. Right foot, ninety degrees. Shift. Left foot, halfway to follow. Torso forward. Hands raised. Elbows bent. Adjust. Focus.

Still nothing.

"Again, please." Mr. Shaw paced up and down the deck.

"You know, I wish you'd just tell me how sick of this you are rather than fronting like you're not."

"I'm sure I don't know what you're talking about."

Disgust like rotting meat

"I can smell it on you . . ."

Frustration of having to deal with an ignoramus

". . . reeking under that fancy cologne you splash on . . ."

The frenzied fear of a parent's disappointment

". . . so just tell me what you're really feeling."

"This is what I'm really feeling." Mr. Shaw spoke slowly and with deliberation. "I wish that Red hadn't chosen a git who would overegg the pudding."

"And I'm feeling how totally over I am of you and your stupid Britishisms." Reed seethed, his anger finally giving him permission to rip off the mask of good manners. "You don't teach me squat. You just sit there telling me to repeat these stupid-ass forms. That's not mentoring. That's Jazzercise."

All he could see was red. But this wasn't like the time he lost it when his mom accidentally threw away all his original Dungeons & Dragons books, including his mint condition first edition Fiend Folio. This time, he literally saw red, as a curtain of color washed over his field of vision, bleeding over Mr. Shaw, the barge, the surroundings.

Then, with a certainty that defied all logic, Reed found himself inside his Stone.

"I have yet to predict how Halley's comet will affect the Ikeda, but I have no doubt that this Pass shall be especially charged."

Broughton Shaw
Provost, Pass Ten

CHAPTER 10

INSIDE REED'S STONE

A prehistorically vast burgundy canyon, contained by crimson cliffs, surrounded Reed. This entire world, in fact, from sky to ground, was red. But the varying translucency created the mirage of different shades, from an almost transparent rose to an opaque, almost black, maroon. High, high above, where a sky should be, jagged planes of carmine met like tiles in a monochromatic mosaic. When Reed squinted, he could make out faces etched into the sky tiles, staring down at him.

"Hello?" Reed yelled.

He heard the word at the exact moment he spoke it, tinged with the identical attempt to mask his terror, lilting up in a call for help. Both calls echoed up the cardinal cliffs.

Reed turned.

A guy his age, lankily built, with knobby knees that bowed slightly and shoulders too narrow, topped with a dollop of flame-red hair, turned to him at the same time. The coin of disorientation flipped over and over until Reed realized he was staring at an identical version of himself.

"Are you . . ." Reed trailed off when his mirror image spoke simultaneously. They both took half a step back. Then another.

Reed backed farther away. His reflection mirrored him. Was that really what he looked like, so gangly, with that lopsided smirk and unruly cowlick? He continued his slow and steady retreat, his eyes on the equally receding figure, until he was backed up against the crystal cliff of the valley. By this point, Reed could barely make out his doppelgänger across the football field between them.

Okay, your back is LITERALLY against a wall. Now think, you idiot, think! You've been separated from the rest of your party, or maybe you're in a solo escape room scenario. Mission: find your way the hell out of here!

The double is an obvious clue. Maybe too obvious. Maybe not even a clue, but actually . . . a red herring!

Reed chuckled at his joke. Was it his imagination, or did he hear an echoing chuckle from Other Reed across the valley?

There was no sun inside this crystal prison. But every facet of the world, from the face-tiled sky to the crags to the ground, glowed cerise.

Reed placed a hand against the cliff. Despite the light it radiated, the surface was cool, perfectly smooth, and harder than rock. He tried to wedge his feet into the crevices and use the nooks as handholds, but the slippery surface prevented traction. Besides, without gear, he'd soon reach a point where any mistake would send him plummeting to certain death.

He circled the perimeter of the valley, looking for any irregularities that might reveal a clue. The cliffs betrayed no pattern in formation. Reed looked for a panel, a switch, a lever, a hidden anything that might open a secret something. Nothing. Not even something he could misconstrue as a clue.

He guesstimated that it took him one hour to walk half the circumference of the valley. Time was already losing meaning because the light showed no sign of ebbing or flowing. He fought the urge to freak out by checking in.

He wasn't tired. He wasn't hungry. He wasn't thirsty. He didn't need to "water the flowers," as Mr. Shaw had called it. But after continuing his fruitless search for what must've been hours, he was bored as hell.

Desperation moved him to engage the only other option. Red herring or not.

Reed turned around and headed back into the middle of the valley, so scarlet it was . . .

The opening chords to Taylor Swift's "Maroon" were pretty simple, actually: C–G–Em. So was the rest of the song. A–C–G–D progressions that showed how a song can be brilliant without being complicated. The bridge returned to the C–G–Em opening, in a clever and subtle inversion of itself.

Halfway there, Reed could make out his double, heading to meet him. Three-quarters of the way, he could make out the details in Other Reed's identical outfit—all clothes that had been provided for him by Mr. Shaw & Co.: the cargo pants, the three-button Henley. Their pants were the only things disrupting the space's carmine monochromaticity, as out of place as a lightsaber at a Star Trek convention.

Reed self-consciously smoothed out his maddening cowlick, using his double as a mirror. By now, they were close enough to touch. They put their hands up, slowly inching them forward. The moment before they would've met, he encountered a paper-thin force field that prevented contact. They moved their hands slowly against the invisible barrier, mirroring each other in the exercise that permanently drove Reed away from Drama Club.

Reed felt no warmth from the Other. Was he an illusion, like one of JoAnne's Glamours? Without electricity, he had no idea how to disrupt it.

They tried to punch their way through. The force field rewarded them with bruised knuckles.

"You must be the key, right?" he asked the Other, only to hear the question come back at him.

"Oh my God, you're such a loser." Did his lip really curl like that?

"Are you going to help me or what, dude?" The butch approach was neither convincing nor fruitful.

"Okay, I can wait, too." Reed sat cross-legged in his estimation of meditation. Whenever he opened an eye, he found the Other cheating a peek as well.

He got up and entered the Feat of Potentia, as Mr. Shaw had taught him. Seeing the movements on someone else's body certainly made his shortcomings perfectly apparent—the crook of an elbow, an unaligned knee. He spent who knew how many minutes—hours?—perfecting the movements. But even when he could perform the five-minute sequence in its Platonic ideal, nothing happened.

He dared his Other to touch him. He laughed. He spat, learning the gross way that saliva could pass through the invisible barrier between them as they wiped off their faces. He slipped off his sneaker and threw it at his antagonist, dodging the one coming at him just in time. The two Reeds circled each other to reclaim their original shoe. He repeated the experiment, this time daring to slip his foot into the Other's sneaker. It almost felt like progress, but ultimately, Reed suspected that the key to solving this puzzle didn't hinge on footwear.

"Please," they begged.

"Come on," they pleaded.

"Forget this." They gave up.

Reed still wasn't hungry. He still wasn't thirsty. He still didn't need to go to the bathroom. Then the true horror occurred to him. He could be stuck here for the rest of his existence, with nothing to do or be.

He would just be some dude, stuck in a crystal world, forever.

That's when he lost it. He charged at his opposite, and they both banged against that impossibly thin force field with their fists, yelling, screaming, snot driveling out of their noses.

"Fuck you, Red," he yelled at his double, getting yelled at back. "Fuck you, Ikeda comet; fuck you, Pentacle Portal and Pentagon Chamber; and especially fuck you, Mr. Shaw."

Is that what he looked like when he lost his shit, that destructive glint in his bloodshot eyes, more animal than human?

"The first real challenge I'm up against, and I fail?"

Was his voice really that whiny, that ineffectual, that pathetic?

"And what happens now?" the two Reeds yelled. "I spend the rest of my meaningless life here because I can't pass this stupid bullshit test?"

Raising his voice had made him feel so powerful in the past, as if he were drawing strength from lava in the earth below. But seeing himself do it revealed how much he looked and sounded like an overgrown child. Out of control. Pathetic.

He didn't remember dropping, but they were both on their knees now, panting, sniveling, exhausted.

Thank goodness, Reed thought, looking up at himself, *that Arno hasn't seen me like this. No one who did could ever really love me.*

He forced himself to look at his pathetic Other, spent from the tantrum, crumpled on the ground like dirty laundry. Useless. Discarded. Despicable.

Crawling, he and his Other inched their way to each other. They sat, legs folded underneath, one hand up, calloused fingertips separated by the invisible barrier.

Calm, after the storm had passed

Reed closed his eyes.

He inhaled.

He exhaled.

He breathed.

Focus, a tight laser etching a patch

He thought about how he'd just seen himself—how hideously ugly he'd been, two Hydes staring each other down, desperate for their Jekylls.

Acceptance of surrender to the inevitable

He looked unlovable. He felt unlovable. He was unlovable.

But that didn't mean he was incapable of loving.

Forgiveness, even when it hurt

He forgave his Other. And then, himself. For trying his hardest and still failing. For never being as good of a son or older brother or student or GSA president or person as he could be. For all the times he tried but came up short. For all his failures.

Hope with no expectation

He opened his eyes just in time to see his Other staring back at him without judgment.

It wasn't that he absorbed his Other self. Or that his Other self absorbed him. It was more like they simply united. Or was it reunited?

Then he was back on the barge.

"Empathy? My stupid-ass power is Empathy?" Reed leaned against the barge rail just a few moments after his Saturday afternoon temper tantrum meltdown. As Mr. Shaw had told him, he had no memory of what had happened or how he completed the Feat of Potentia. Whenever he tried to send his mind there, all he saw was an image of himself. But the Stone's power coursed through him like the caffeine buzz of a perfectly cold-brewed coffee.

"That's what I'd surmise." Mr. Shaw was typing furiously on his tablet keyboard.

"So, what—I'm supposed to save the world by telling how people really feel? 'Blue Bearer—you're saying you're not tired, but wait—let me conjure the extraordinary power of the Red Stone—I can sense . . . you are actually exhausted! Aha!'" Reed stared at the gem in his hand, accusingly.

"You know, Reed, I can't tell you how delighted I was when Red chose you. I thought, with your unique perspective, that you would bring some true leadership to the Five."

"What unique perspective?"

"You know . . ." Mr. Shaw trailed off.

"Oh, man up already," Reed dared him. "You can just say it. Because I'm gay?"

"Yes." Mr. Shaw gathered his thoughts. "When I learned Red had selected you, I thought, 'Here is someone who's in touch with himself, who could be a real Leader.' But you're succumbing to the same old-fashioned, heteronormative, patriarchal idea of heroism. You think shooting fire out of your eyes is going to make you a better collaborator? You think superstrength will help you inspire the other Bearers to accomplish the formidable tasks ahead of them?"

"Have other Reds had those powers?" Reed pouted.

"Empathy is a gift." Mr. Shaw pointedly didn't answer Reed. "It's a leader's greatest tool. Besides, you have no idea how your Potentia might evolve as the Ikeda nears closest approach. So consider yourself grateful—grateful that the Stone has chosen you, grateful that you completed the Feat of Potentia, and grateful that you've been blessed with something that will truly allow you to help others."

"Thanks, Mr. Shaw." A smile slowly spread on Reed's face. "Now, what was that you said about power-ups?"

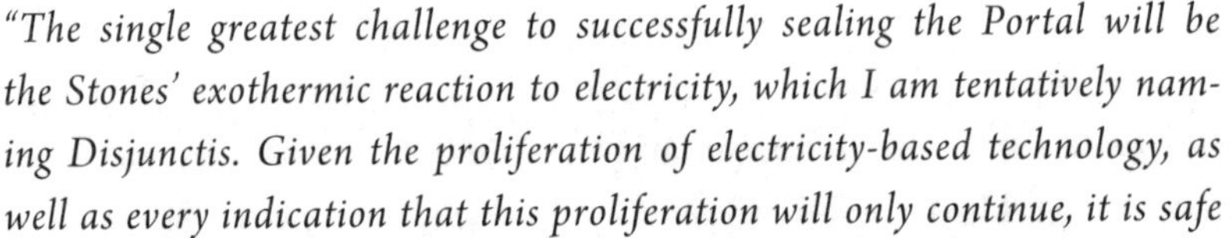

"The single greatest challenge to successfully sealing the Portal will be the Stones' exothermic reaction to electricity, which I am tentatively naming Disjunctis. Given the proliferation of electricity-based technology, as well as every indication that this proliferation will only continue, it is safe to assume that Passes Eight and onward will require enormous leaps of ingenuity from Bearers, Provosts, and Chancellors to successfully complete Terminatio. Making me wish all the more that I had a Chancellor to guide me."

Algernon de la Shaw
Provost, Pass Seven

CHAPTER 11

RED SPIES BLUE

The Blue Bearer stepped back, parried, lunged, parried again, feinted, then thrust his blade into his opponent's chest. A single tone (B♭?) beeped, and a red light blipped like Cyborg's eye.

Victorious.

Again.

Reed and Mr. Shaw had now witnessed the Bearer vanquish three opponents before noon in the high school fencing competition.

"That's our man?" Mr. Shaw asked hopefully.

Reed entered Locatio as subtly as possible, perched on the top of the college bleachers. His Stone, an agitated cardinal, chirped with excitement as he moved his thoughts to the fencing figure inside the mesh wire mask and padded armor. Wide nose. Strong jaw. His relationship with Red had changed since unlocking his Potentia. He couldn't say how, but now they were communicating back and forth, sending missives like eager pen pals. "I'm positive. That's the Blue Bearer."

"The Warrior."

Blue saluted his defeated opponent.

Reed and Mr. Shaw had arrived in the DC docks that Saturday night, where a rickshaw was waiting to take them to their hotel.

"Ah, the conveniences of city living." Mr. Shaw leaned back as their covered bicycle taxi made its way into the heart of town. They checked into their hotel suite: private rooms and bathrooms with an adjoining common space.

By the time the third card key shorted out, Reed accepted that Mr. Shaw would have to let him in and out of the room. "Next time, can we go to a hotel that uses actual keys?"

“No one uses keys anymore, Reed,” Mr. Shaw scoffed. “Besides, this way I can keep an eye on you.”

“Oh yes, hooligan that I am. Who knows when I might sneak out to the nearest board game store and enter a Pokémon tournament?” Red sent an urgent pulse to Reed. “We’re near Blue. I can feel it. Like a magnet.”

“We’ll find the Blue Bearer first thing tomorrow morning.” Mr. Shaw was already heading to his bedroom. “Tonight, we’ve earned some rest.”

Clothes were waiting for Reed in his room—Mr. Shaw had planned for everything. They slept, woke up, hit the breakfast buffet, and left the hotel with Red as their guide.

“We’re close.” Reed had never been to Washington, DC, before. As much as he wanted to take in the city, all his energy was spent protecting himself from the emotional barrage of passersby. “Just a few blocks, I’d guess.”

They wove their way through the Sunday morning crowds of mostly Black, mostly exquisitely dressed women, proudly parading hats like crowns as they walked to or from church. By the time they reached their destination, a college gymnasium, it was already 10 AM. Mr. Shaw paid for two tickets to the high school fencing competition. Red was positively atwitter now, chirping so loudly Reed couldn’t believe other people didn’t hear it.

“Whoa.” Standing outside the gymnasium proper, a wave of lightheadedness hit him

Hope Fear Anxiety Desperation Confidence

like he had just stepped off a dizzying amusement park ride

Hunger Fatigue Aggression Arousal

and was about to pass out.

Mr. Shaw slipped his arm underneath Reed’s shoulders and pulled him aside. “You all right there, lad?”

“All those people. It’s like—they’re all trying to get inside me.”

“Is Blue going anywhere?”

Reed checked in. “Nope.”

“Righto! Let’s take a spell to figure out how to protect yourself when you’re all chockablock like this.” The tablet was already in Mr. Shaw’s calloused, sturdy hand. “We’ll try a few things and see which one works. The most important thing you have to learn is how to take control of the Stone. If you do not assert yourself immediately now that you've unlocked the Feat of Potentia, it will become your master."

After experimenting with different movements, Mr. Shaw and Reed created a new Feat to help him keep others' feelings at bay.

"It's important to keep your feet parallel as you crouch back." Mr. Shaw demonstrated. "Your opposite foot can leave the ground, but the current foot has to stay planted."

"Why don't we call it the Feat of Sweet Sweet Relief?"

"I'll enter it into the Muraqqa tonight." Mr. Shaw smiled.

Like every gymnasium Reed had ever been to, the smell of perspiration hung thick, baked into the polyurethane wood floor, padded walls, and retractable risers. They discovered Blue mid-duel in one of the taped-out strips in the far-right corner of the cavernous space. Apparently, he was a draw—at least fifty spectators had gathered just to watch his bouts. And after three victorious matches, Reed and Mr. Shaw could see why. His natural strength rippled in every motion with relentless, measured strokes.

"The Stones have a way of finding the appropriate Bearers," Mr. Shaw confided. "You clearly have the makings of a Leader, and look at Blue wield that épée."

"That's the sword?"

"Épée is the heaviest of the three fencing blades. By the looks of him, he's going to be a fine Warrior."

"So Blue is always the Warrior?"

"Indeed, just as Red is always the Leader."

"What Yellow's deal?"

"Yellow, Illuminator," Mr. Shaw rattled off. "Green, Traveler. Purple, Mystic. It's impossible to determine what the actual Potentias will be, but they always manifest within the Stones' domains."

"So I'm just supposed to stroll up to Blue and tell him he's going to have to give up his life and join us to save the world?"

"Usually, the Provost makes first contact."

"Really?"

"This protocol was established after the debacle of Pass Five."

"I'm going to go out on a limb and say that I think this pitch is going to be easier coming from someone his age instead of a rando Gen Xer." Reed cracked his knuckles. "No offense."

"You think you're up for it?" Mr. Shaw asked. "It breaks protocol, but I don't see any reason why we can't try."

"I got this, Mr. Shaw." Reed nodded eagerly.

The Blue Bearer continued fighting with a surgeon's precision, an assassin's intensity, and a dancer's agility. After his final victory, his coach rolled over with a towel and bottle of water. The Bearer squatted down to the wheelchair to ask his coach a question. After a curt nod, they bumped fists and his coach wheeled away.

Blue stood up, put down his blade, and removed his helmet.

A waterfall of brown hair came cascading down. Blue unzipped the padded armor and let it drop to the floor.

"Tangled Up in Blue" by Bob Dylan. G–D–A–Asus–A–Asus. Seemingly simple verses, complex chorus, and a narration that shifts from first to third person as needed.

Blue was most definitely not a dude.

INTERLUDE A

MUGHAL INDIA, 1653

ZEB-UN-NISSA WRITES

Princess Zeb-un-Nissa sits at her inlaid desk and dips a quill into one of the inkpots before her, part of a dazzling array as colorful as the jewels woven into her hair piled high. The quill flies across a sheet of stout, glazed paper, pausing only when the feather's tip runs dry. She writes furiously, feverishly. In these states, she is simply a conduit, letting the words flow into her, through the quill, and onto the paper.

Three servant women clear the remnants of a royal lunch. The eldest, permanently hunched over like a crook, gathers hammered silver dishes of perfectly sliced guavas, bananas, and mangoes. The second woman, thick with middle age, collects the silken tasseled pillows. The third, the youngest, brushes the rug that covers the vastness of the chamber. The *swoosh-swoosh* of the broom sounds like small waves, crashing against the shore.

When Zeb-un-Nissa completes the first page, she impatiently dusts it with fine powder, gives it a gentle shake, then quickly blows it dry before launching into the next. It is not until she is in the middle of the third that her quill comes to an unexpected stop. She narrows the large pools of her dark brown eyes on the still-wet words she has just written.

"'To God, Who sinners can forgive and lead/Inscrutable Himself, yet Who can read/The hidden heart and comprehend its need. O Prophet, shining like a lonely' . . ." She taps her painted fingernails impatiently against the ivory and tortoiseshell inlay of her desk. ". . . a lonely *what*?"

"A lonely jewel?" The servant girl's whisper is barely audible above the *swoosh-swoosh* of her broom.

The other two servants freeze. Such audacity! The elder barely recovers in time to save the pyramid of plates she has carefully gathered from crashing down.

"A lonely jewel?" Zeb-un-Nissa makes sure her fingers are free of ink smudges before using her dupatta to wipe her brow. "That's close, but not quite right. But what about . . . a lonely *gem*! Yes, a gem, that's perfect!" She releases her tasseled silk shawl so that her quill may continue its flight, scrambling to keep up with thought. "'O Prophet, shining like a lonely *gem*,/The fairest of heaven's highest diadem,/Look on our need and intercede for us!' Thank you . . ."

". . . Sireli," the servant girl whispers. "I am called Sireli."

"Sireli?" Zeb-un-Nissa considers her. "You are new here, are you not? What an unusual name."

"It means *Beloved*." The servant girl dedicates herself to the task of carpet-brushing with even more devotion. The *swoosh-swoosh* comes more quickly now, as if a storm approaches.

"The root isn't Farsi or Arabic. Or Sanskrit, I believe. I shall consult one of my correspondents immediately." Zeb-un-Nissa produces a clean sheet of stout, glazed paper. "This would be a good matter for Nasir Ali. He will be so flattered that I am seeking his counsel; his response will be especially prompt. We shall solve this mystery of your name, Beloved."

"There is no mystery," the servant girl whispers. "It is Armenian. Like me."

The two older servants depart, pillows and uneaten fruit exiting with them. The quarters shrink with their absence. Somehow—she does not know how—somehow, Zeb-un-Nissa senses that something extraordinary is about to happen.

"I am drawn to you." Sireli sways, as if in a trance, and drops her broom. For the first time, she looks directly at Zeb-un-Nissa.

The bejeweled hilt of a dagger appears in Zeb-un-Nissa's hand, blade so sharp it whispers death. She will not be easy prey.

"Please don't call the guards! I mean you no harm." Sireli moves slowly, removing layer after layer of orange, yellow, and red servant robes, letting them drop to the floor in a pool around her, like the petals of a flower, until only the white small-clothes remain. "I am not what I seem."

The energy in the room changes dramatically, like the air pressure before a cloudburst.

"How did a boy gain entrance to the mahal?" Zeb-un-Nissa gasps, immediately adjusting her dupatta to cover her face as well as her hair. "Your life was forfeit the moment you entered the zenana."

"Please." His almost-black eyes burn with a sycophant's zeal against his pale olive skin. "I was drawn to you."

He opens his hand to reveal a perfectly round ruby. Its carved facets sparkle infinity in the afternoon sun.

"There are others like me, then?" A sapphire, as square as the ruby is round, floats out of a hidden pocket in Princess Zeb-un-Nissa's robes. It hovers in front of her, protectively. "Others who were chosen to bear a Stone?"

"You will not believe what I have seen," the boy whispers. "Or what we will accomplish together, you and I, Princess Zeb-un-Nissa, Jewel of Womankind."

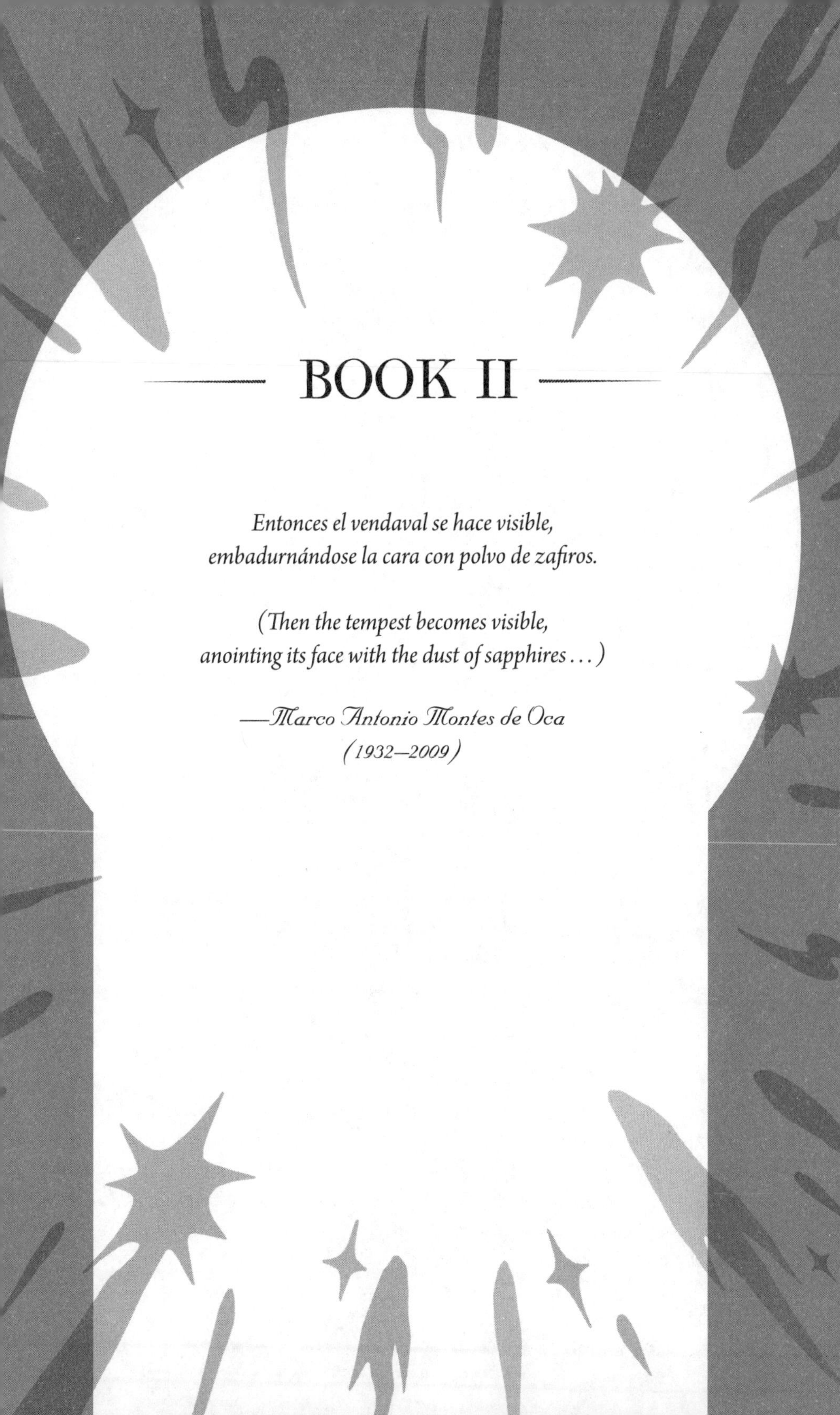

BOOK II

Entonces el vendaval se hace visible,
embadurnándose la cara con polvo de zafiros.

(Then the tempest becomes visible,
anointing its face with the dust of sapphires . . .)

—Marco Antonio Montes de Oca
(1932–2009)

CHAPTER 1

LA PRESENTACIÓN DE ALEJANDRA

Como todas las buenas historias, la mía es inesperada. Nací en la Ciudad de México, pero crecí por todo el mundo: Egipto, Francia, Estados Unidos. Supongo, que ésta es una de las razones por las que amo los idiomas.

Perdón—¿usted no habla español? No hay problema.

I can do English. I could also do French, and in a few years, my Mandarin should be strong enough. Don't be impressed—the United States is the only world power whose people can speak only one language. I think that is why so many of its citizens are narrow-minded. Learning other languages forces the imagination to expand. In Mandarin Chinese, for example, there is no past or future tense: the temporal meaning of verbs is changed by the addition of adverb or aspect particles.

I'll give you another example. In Spanish, the adjective comes after the noun. That might not sound important. Just an issue of syntax. But the effect is infinitely more poetic. The big house? Qué horrible. "The big house" does not inspire a single iota of poetry. But see what happens when the big house becomes la casa grande? Who would not seek solace in la casa grande? Even the words themselves carry poetry. "Big" just lies there, like a doormat. But grande—yes, roll the r*—it sings.*

I suppose it is because so much of English comes from German. And yes, while Germany is known for many things—philosophy, music, desserts—poetry is not one of them.

Unlike Spanish. There is a reason certain languages are Romantic.

Many people believe it is easy to learn another Romance language if you already speak one. They have never tried to learn French. If I had not spent those years in Dijon, I would still be stumbling over l'accent circonflexe and the irregular conjugations of common verbs. And the spelling! Why the French need all those extra vowels, I will never understand. Beaux *is a word that should not contain more than two letters. Hors d'oeuvres? Perdón, but really. Nothing should take longer to spell than it does to eat. The one thing that the French understand more than anyone, however, is form. That must be why fencing has Gallic parentage. Touché, en garde, flèche—these words are so French no one dares translate them.*

I will always remember the first time I felt the weight of an épée in my hand. I was in grade six. We were living in Cairo, before the pandemia, just before my father was posted to France. The grip fit in my palm like a gun in a holster. I wrapped my fingers around it and embraced the bell guard as it embraced me. The blade became an extension of my arm, an appendage I did not know I was missing until we were reunited. My citli—my paternal grandmother—had raised me on stories of our indigenous roots as pre-Hispanic warriors. Perhaps this is why I have never feared death. And why combat came so easily to me. It was in my blood.

There are three types of fencing blades. Since foils began as lighter practice weapons, used by duelers to train safely, you score a point only on the torso. Sabers, however, can score anywhere above the waist (except for hands but including the head) because they were originally used by cavalry. But my weapon, the épée, evolved from the French small sword, a thrusting weapon. The entire body is a target.

Women know this, even though we were not permitted to compete with the épée until the '96 Olympics. I do not know what I would have done if I had been a creature of an earlier era.

The fencing team at Friends is coed, like many high schools in the States. I had never fenced against men until we moved here two years ago. Most of the world is more like Mexico: girls fence with girls, boys with boys, and if you identify as neither or both or anything in between: ¡Buena suerte! You should see me explaining the concept of trans or ace to my uncles. They just roll their eyes and call it another fad from los Estados Unidos.

That reminds me. Nobody but the people who live in this country refer to it as America, and I will not, either. America is the continent, and the whole continent, for that matter. Most of the world teaches America as one continent, with-

out a North/South division. It is, after all, connected by land. Do not ask me why Europe and Asia are considered two different continents. I imagine it comes from European terror at being associated with brown people. But calling the United States "America" is as offensive as the phrase "Jalisco es México." A part cannot be the whole, no matter what they tell you in Guadalajara.

The whole concept of mestizo—how most Mexicans identify now, as a combination of indigenous and European—comes from the same terror. Those who ruled at the inception of Mexico (mostly the descendants of Spaniards, mostly white) perpetuated many of the colonial policies that they had rebelled against. The concept of mestizo, in fact, is designed to de-indigenize us. The irony, of course, is that the idea of indigeneity is celebrated in Mexico, while the indigenous themselves remain disenfranchised. With a truly fresa mother who thought of herself as white, and a father who was the first in his family to leave the rural community and attend college, I am keenly aware of these dynamics. They have been a defining factor of my life. Almost as much as fencing.

After fencing coed for almost a year, I have learned that men do not have much of an advantage. Yes, they tend to be bigger and stronger. It is foolish to pretend otherwise. But it does not make much of a difference in this sport. Fencing is the only combat sport without a weight class.

What most men have in reach, they lack in strategy. Or rather, I should say, most men confuse exertion with efficiency. (This is true of many things, not just fencing.) The trick, I have found, is to make sure to keep your distance—even more distance than their increased reach demands. I let them feint and thrust and jab until they are spent. I just wait, and once I see an opening, I pounce, like one of my Aztec Jaguar warrior ancestors. I have come to prefer dueling men. Not because they are superior. Because it is more satisfying to defeat them.

I had ended a day of many such victories when I first spotted him, with hair the color of flame. He lingered, waiting for a scrap of my attention. Was this how Sarmad first approached Zeb-un-Nissa, all those centuries ago? Was this how every Red Bearer approached, seeking an audience with the Blue Bearer? How every Leader approached every Warrior?

But, of course, I did not know such things at the time. I knew so little of the past and the future. And even of the present.

APPENDIX B

Pass Number	*Year*
Ten	1986
Nine	1951
Eight	1913
Seven	1877
Six	1840
Five	1803
Four	1765
Three	1728
Two	1691
One	1653

Larkin Shaw
Chancellor, Pass Ten

CHAPTER 2

LOS SEGUIDORES DE ALEJANDRA

I am accustomed to fans hovering after matches. Usually, they want a selfie. I have over forty thousand followers on Insta and even more on TikTok. I would not describe myself as an influencer, but when you have achieved my level of play, a degree of fame is natural. The vids of my winning points against opponents with thirty centimeters and twenty kilos on me get the most likes. Sometimes, I imagine my phone chirping with notifications during a match as I am tagged. Last year, a slo-mo clip of my winning flèche at State went viral and inspired a thread of TikToks: underscored with Beethoven's Third, with Beyoncé, with narcocorrido. Then an entire batch of duets and stitches. I received five thousand followers from that alone. Even if I choose against going to the Olympics, it is important to maintain a social media presence.

With all things, patience is key. Just because he approached me did not mean that I was obligated to acknowledge him or his inexplicably clenched fist. Instead, I finished my post-match ritual. Mask. Gloves. Blades. Jacket.

"Good match." Addyson kept most of the envy out of her voice. She was the only other fencer at Friends who was a worthy opponent. Besides my nemesis, Hikaru. But Addyson never resorted to cheap tricks, like he did.

"You too, Addyson. That foot touch you landed against Tilly? Buenísimo." I popped my mask off.

She blushed, her pale skin turning the rare pink of a perfectly cooked rib eye. "Thanks, Alejandra."

"You can call me Ale." Most people from the States shied away from my disyllabic hypocorism.

"Okay, Ale." She said my name tentatively, and it came out somewhere between "alley" and the French "allez." Close enough. "Catch you later."

The redheaded chico, apparently finding his courage, approached with the daily program in hand. "Hi, Alejandra Almada?"

I winced as he hammered the vowels of my name flat like gringos always do.

Most of the people who stay after a match are either girls who want to know how I beat all those chicos or those chicos who think they have a shot with me. (Spoiler: They do not.) But the chico with hair the color of flame did not belong to either category. He was slim, almost athletic, but clearly not a fencer. I could tell by the way he stood, one hand still clenched into a fist, toes slightly bent in, shifting from one foot to another—this was not someone who has danced with blades.

I popped open my water bottle and took a long swig.

Also, I could tell he was del otro lado. I know that is not a politically correct thing to say, and that it is impossible to tell just by looking at someone. But I always know. Not by how someone looks. But by how they look at me.

When most chicos look at me, I can see what they see. I am not saying they are all imagining me naked. Though I would not be surprised if they were. The way their eyes follow my curves, the way they must force their gaze up a few centimeters to my eyes when I speak. The thought passes across their faces as clear as a hot-air balloon across a San Miguel sky. Most girls have figured this out by seventeen. Or earlier.

But when this chico stood there, respectfully waiting, he did not look at me like a thing. That is how I know. Los del otro lado actually see you. That is why it is easier to be friends with them. Masuda, from Egypt. Timothée, from Lyon. They offer the best of both worlds: ease without competition.

"That was—um, that was amazing." His pigeon-toed feet shifted when he spoke, as if the ground were undulating beneath him.

"Gracias." I unwound the pronged cord connecting my blade to the scoring machine, snaked it out of my jacket, and handed it to one of our aides. Tony? Thomas?

The gym had almost finished its restoration. The tables were cleared and the chairs folded, stacked, and wheeled into closets. All that remained were for the blue pistes to be rolled up and put away. Did I remember something about a basketball game tonight, in the middle of our tournament? Not great scheduling.

"Almada, I'm uploading some videos." Coach Vassallo rolled past me. "Review matches three and six, then check out your in-progress analysis." He continued talking over his shoulder as he passed by in his wheelchair. "And check out Hikaru's matches—you two are going head-to-head on Wednesday."

"Claro, Coach." I gathered my stuffed duffel bag and turned to the locker room. I had forgotten the fist-clenched redhead was still there until he spoke again.

"I know you're probably really tired from—gosh, you were like Massacre Girl out there demolishing everyone, but if you have a sec, I'd really love to talk."

"Ping me on Insta." I started to go.

"Please!" His desperation filled his voice. "I was drawn to you because I'm supposed to lead the . . ." He opened his clenched fist. A Ping-Pong ball of a ruby lay inside, glowing pomegranate.

"What makes you think I would ever follow you?" I grabbed him by his shirt and pulled him close, a violent parody of a lover's gesture. "Now get away from me! ¿Comprendes? ¡Vete!"

He opened his mouth like he was going to say something, so I shoved him back.

I turned and left for the locker room, where he could not follow me.

We are discouraged from keeping anything superfluous on our body during competition. It is the only time I remove the turquoise earrings my citli gave me, the ones that have been in my indigenous family for generations, even before my mother's family (the Spanish invaders) arrived. Which makes it all the more unlikely that snuggled in my breeches' pocket lay my sapphire. Mi zafira.

I knew my sapphire was special the moment we found each other, just as I knew she was not a zafiro, but a zafira.

Now, she burned ice hot against my body, long after the chico had fled. The chico with a jewel as red as mine was blue.

"The expenditure of resources to make a monochromatic design style vogue is perhaps the most formidable accomplishment of our family. Success now ensures that Bearers will have access to the residences of heads of states for generations to come."

Hortense de la Shaw
Provost, Pass Five

CHAPTER 3

REED'S BODGE

When Mr. Shaw had suggested, the next afternoon, that they take a tour of the White House, Reed had no idea they'd be the only two people on the VIP experience.

"The White House was originally referred to as the Presidential Palace." The tour guide adjusted the badge clipped over the breast pocket of his navy jacket. The badge wasn't any straighter after the fidgeting, but the guide smiled, content, as if he'd accomplished something profound. "It wasn't until 1901, when President Theodore Roosevelt had the words engraved on stationery, that the white house actually became *the* White House." He removed his thick glasses, gave them a quick wipe, and returned them to their perch on his nose before waddling away. Reed and Mr. Shaw followed.

Reed had woken up that morning with his head throbbing as if it had just been used as the percussion in an especially aggressive rendition of "Carmina Burana" (Dm^{7}!–B♭!–Dm!–B♭!–Am^{7}!–Dm^{7}!–Am^{7}!). It hurt more than either of his hangovers.

He'd stayed in bed all morning, grateful to Mr. Shaw for excusing him from training—excusing him from everything, actually. When the pounding had softened to a gentle snare, he emerged from his bedroom and Mr. Shaw surprised him with news of their White House tour.

"The Library, one of the final stops in the first part of the tour of the East Wing, was bestowed that name by Franklin D. Roosevelt in 1935." The tour guide droned on about the room's previous functions as a storage and laundry room, before returning to the works currently housed in the rectangular room with built-in bookcases.

"How did you manage to swing this, anyway?" Reed whispered.

"My family makes a point of remaining on good terms with the rulers of all the major powers." Mr. Shaw traced his finger over a mahogany table, as if he were inspecting for dust.

"Even Putin?" Reed asked as they walked into the Vermeil Room. "Your family is even on good terms with him?"

"Of course." Mr. Shaw took the liberty of sitting on one of the ridiculously low, ridiculously long orange sofas facing each other. Reed suspected it was a liberty that few people on the public tours took.

Mr. Shaw was apparently oblivious to his transgression, as well as the tour guide's internal debate about whether to address it. "You have to start thinking about things in a larger framework, Reed. Regardless of your personal opinions about individual leaders, our job is to steward the entire world. It's infinitely grander than the reign of any one figure."

"The Vermeil Room is named after the over 1,500 objects of gold-plated silverware that the White House received in 1957." The tour guide apparently decided against confronting Mr. Shaw. "President and First Lady Eisenhower decided to use the gift to decorate this room, which had previously been a service space and a ladies' sitting room."

"Eisenhower bodged up Middle Eastern politics almost as poorly as you bodged the recruitment of the Blue Bearer," Mr. Shaw observed casually.

"Me? Really? Bodged?" Reed delivered each word at a higher pitch than the one before, his voice cracking on the final soprano note. "I don't even know what 'bodged' means."

"The context supplies the definition."

Reed made faces into the side of a teapot polished to a mirror's brilliance. His fun house reflection spread concave on its bulbous side. "So what do we do now?" If he were a little bolder, he would have inspected the equally brilliantly polished miniature teaspoons.

"Let's first review other stratagems that may have been more successful." Mr. Shaw ran a finger along the window panels of patterned silk in olive and gold. "Then we'll explore tactics to implement those stratagems. It's best practice." He scrunched up his nose at the window drapery, unimpressed by the quality of the material. "First, analyze what went wrong before deciding how to move forward. Remember, you will still need to recruit three more Bearers."

"Right now, it feels like anything would've been better than running away before she Swiss cheesed me," Reed said.

"I am still not hearing any thoughts as to what you could've done differently—only moping about what went wrong." Even with the air-conditioning blasting, beads of sweat accumulated on both their foreheads. "For example, you could've approached the Blue Bearer at a different time, or chosen a more private location."

"But you're the one who told me to go up to her then!"

"And you're the one who's going to have to stop blaming others for your mistakes. You must think for yourself, Reed, if you're going to become the Leader the world needs you to be."

Reed massaged his temples until the bass drum–pounding heading quieted down to a hissing snare. It wasn't like he had even used his Potentia on anyone yesterday. He'd just prevented other people's emotions from overwhelming him. Even in the relative safety of their hotel room, the wants, needs, and desires of passersby assaulted him: a concierge's pink bubbling anticipation of a midnight tryst, a couple's red-hot rage after a recent fight, the cleaning guy's burgundy boredom.

Reed stumbled on the stairs up to the State Floor.

Mr. Shaw steadied him. "All right?"

"Close enough."

"Running water and central heating were added in 1835." Their guide looked up, as if consulting notes only he could see. "With gaslights in 1848, electric lights in 1891 . . ."

"Hey, Mr. Shaw." Reed leaned against the sturdy oak banister. "How come being with you doesn't trigger my Empathy?"

"Part of Provost training included mental shielding, in case Bearers develop Potentia in the psychic domain. It's sometimes relegated to an elective, but"—Mr. Shaw's chest puffed with pride—"I insisted on studying every module, to serve my Bearers as best as possible. The Feat of Sweet Sweet Relief that we created to protect you is a variant of my training. As long as I meditate for an hour every morning, we can continue working together without my presence taxing you."

They arrived at the staircase landing and walked in quick succession through the monochromatically decorated Green Room and Blue Room.

"What else have you gleaned from your failure?"

"I didn't have to show her the Stone—that seemed to freak her out." Reed recalled how Red and Blue communicated when they were in proximity to each other, as if the Stones formed a circuit. "Also, Batman would've spent some time trailing her, and getting to know her, to choose an approach that was more specific to who she is. Like you did with me."

"Now you're thinking." Mr. Shaw followed the tour guide, who led them into the Red Room. "Although at the same time, it's important to remember that time is, as always, of the essence."

"I thought we still had, like, a month and a half." Reed gingerly sat on a coral chaise, underneath an electric candle chandelier. Why did he feel more powerful in this room, where everything matched his Stone?

"This phase—after manifestation, but before recruitment—is when the Bearers are most dangerous to themselves and others. So yes, we're still on schedule." Mr. Shaw pronounced "schedule" with the British "sh." "But no one'll be the worse for wear if we make good time assembling the Bearers."

"Excuse me—" Reed squinted to read the name on the tour guide's much-adjusted name badge. "—Mr. Akwala?"

"Yes?" The tour guide glared at Reed for interrupting his rehearsed speech.

"Why were these rooms decorated in a single color?" Reed asked.

"It was considered part of the fashion in nineteenth-century Europe, and since this country was quite young, many of its fashions and mores were borrowed from across the Atlantic. For example . . ."

Mr. Akwala covered the topics of silhouette, corset, pinched waistline, and tail-coat before finishing his dissertation on nineteenth-century fashion and allowing them a few minutes to explore the grounds.

"Funny, isn't it?" Reed followed Mr. Shaw, who walked with the confidence of a beloved houseguest. "Red Room, Blue Room, Yellow. It's almost like the rooms were decorated after the Stones."

"Not a coincidence," Mr. Shaw whispered conspiratorially.

"Really?" They passed an ornamental mantel clock that Mr. Akwala described as one of the first skeleton clocks, designed to display rather than conceal the gears and machinery inside.

"I brought you here to show you how the Stones have woven their way into history over the last few centuries. The color of your Stone plays an important role in the Feat of Teleportare, which you perform to journey to the Pentagon Chamber."

"So why don't you just teach it to me now?" Reed teleporting to concerts in any venue. Reed never being late again. Reed seeing parts of the world he'd never have access to otherwise. "And then my sore legs and I will never have to get on a horse again."

"I told you, Reed. The Muraqqa is very clear about the sequence of the Feats. Going out of order runs the risk of harming the Bearer. Like trying a muscle-up before a kipping pull-up."

"I can't believe you've been hiding your secret identity of CrossFit bro!"

"Is this another example of your attempt to deflect our serious conversations with—and I use the word loosely—'humor,' as you did when you were conducting your self-evaluation of your recruitment of the Blue Bearer?"

They emerged outdoors, into the Rose Garden.

"Why don't you just tell me what you think I should've done since you *clearly* have some ideas."

"Of course I could. That's how Father and most Provosts mentored the Bearers of yore. But I'm choosing to employ the Socratic method, because I believe that any insights you have will be more powerful if you unlock them yourself." Mr. Shaw put a hand on Reed's shoulder and got uncharacteristically sentimental. "I am really trying to do things differently, lad, you understand? At least as much as I am permitted to."

"Um, I guess so?" Reed responded.

"So I'll give you a clue: what are you planning to do differently with the Blue Bearer?"

Reed searched for an intelligent response.

"For example, will you use your Potentia to discern her true feelings to gain insight that may persuade her?"

"Can't we just, I don't know"—Reed shifted uncomfortably—"snatch the Stone away from her when she's not looking and give it to someone else? Someone who won't threaten me with physical violence?"

"Once a Stone chooses a Bearer, they're fairly impossible to separate." Mr. Shaw snapped a rose blossom off its stalk and slipped it into his lapel, an impromptu boutonniere that struck Reed of treason. "The only way is for a Bearer to willfully surrender their Stone using the Feat of Relinquo. Then they have the option of choosing a successor or letting the Stone select one."

"So maybe we can ask her to do that?" Reed and his pale skin took refuge from the burning sun in the shade of a crab apple tree in the center of a diamond-shaped flower bed.

"It's not without precedent. But we'll leave it as a last resort. And only if you know someone who is willing and worthy."

Reed decided against sharing the flash of Arno that sprang into his mind.

"Besides, the Stones don't choose their Bearers arbitrarily. Your natural inclination to leadership is clear, as is Alejandra's to combat. Isn't it exciting to consider how Yellow's illumination will reveal itself, or Green's traveling, or Purple's mysticism? And how these Potentias will evolve?"

"This is not your first mention of power-ups, O vague and mysterious mentor of mine."

"You feel it, don't you?" Mr. Shaw leaned in. "The closer the Ikeda gets, the more powerful your Stone."

"Then why do I still feel like Invincible *before* he gets his powers? When he is still very much vincible?"

"Reed, use your imagination. We are at the White House, which has been populated by some of the greatest leaders your country and this world have ever known—Kamala Harris, Barack Obama, Abraham Lincoln. They didn't just read people's emotions. They inspired them! They changed the course of history by altering how the masses considered their worlds. What you and your Stone can do with Empathy is limited only by your own imagination."

"That's all well and good," Reed whispered to Mr. Shaw as their tour guide rejoined them, wiping his wet hands on his uniformed navy pants. "But I would never, ever, use my power on another person to influence them against their will. So I guess we're going to have to think of some old-fashioned way to get her on our team. Okay, boss?"

"You know, saying 'never' is just an invitation for fate to thwart you."

"Is that supposed to be your version of 'do or do not, there is no try'?"

"Something like that." Mr. Shaw smiled somberly. "If history is any indicator, assembling the Five and sealing the Portal is challenging even under normal circumstances. In Pass Ten, Halley's comet reached closest approach within months of the Ikeda, and the results were unpredictable and dangerous. Disjunctis, of course, has made every Pass since Seven a unique and horrific challenge. Pass Three transpired against the backdrop of the Szeged witch trials in Hungary. But in my estimation, JoAnne is the most formidable obstacle we have ever faced. What is she doing now? What is she planning? Of course, I have no idea what the future holds. But I know you will face enormous obstacles, Reed. You, like all leaders, have to ask yourself if you are brave enough to venture down the difficult path."

"As it is impossible to predict what Potentias will be granted to the Bearers, we have decided to include mental fortification as part of the Provost's training, especially given Ruby's and Amethyst's tendencies to the metaphysical. Experience and observation conclude that Zazen meditation is the most effective, but we will continue to study other disciplines from the Orient as well."

Livingston de la Shaw
Provost, Pass Four

CHAPTER 4
LA MANIFESTACIÓN DE ALEJANDRA

This might sound like a paranoid fantasy, but I am sure

Advance

that even though we are plugged into the same wiring system,

Retreat

when I scored, it sounded like a

PING

"Point, Almada. En garde. Prête? Allez!"

Feint. Feint. Thrust.

and when he scored it sounded like a

PONG

"Point, Yoshida."

Practice on Wednesday was, as some of my girlfriends in the States like to say, a hot mess. My laser-sharp focus was butter knife dull. My responses were padded with sloppy fractions of seconds, weighing me down like lead woven into my lamé.

I could have pretended it was because I was preoccupied with my upcoming trip to CDMX. I had not been back for years. Not since my citli (indigenous grandmother) and mi abuela (mestizo grandmother) had quarreled so ferociously they both swore they would never be under the same roof again. My parents have never said this, but I believe it is the reason they accepted posts abroad. Easier to remove themselves than be caught between these two titans.

But truthfully, returning to Mexico did not cause me anxiety. Being home is the only way for me to remember who I was.

PONG.

"Point, Yoshida."

En garde. Long lunge. Beat.

It was not any of that.

Feint. Feint. Block. Thrust.

PING.

"Point, Almada."

It was all about the Stone.

Its cold fire pulsed through me, igniting and burning. Mi zafira had never behaved this way before. I had not told anyone about it—not Lucía, not M., not even Masuda when we WhatsApped last night. After he had gone on and on about his new boyfriend, I wanted to show him my jewel. But my petrified hands would not reveal it.

Flèche. Pass. Attack.

Miss.

PONG.

I hated the sound of that *PONG* almost as much as I hated the smile so smug it oozed out of Hikaru's mesh face guard. But I would show him. Just like I showed . . .

How could that gringo with red hair and an even redder Stone have possibly known? Mi zafira had been my secret since I found her last week on the class trip to the Endless Caverns.

Lunge. Riposte.

¡Maldición!

PONG.

"Match, Yoshida."

I stomped off the piste, hating every centimeter of that fourteen-meter strip almost as much as I hated myself.

"Almada, get your head in the game."

Coach Vassallo never barked at me like that. Letting him down hurt worst of all.

I needed to work harder. I would never make it to the Olympics like this.

When I was in the right headspace, I was unstoppable. A force majeure. But when I stumbled, I slid all the way down a slippery glass slope without traction, friction, or handholds. As unforgiving as my mother at her worst, like the day I explicitly defied her and got my navel pierced.

I kept my mask on until I had made it to the privacy of the locker room, then slammed it against a locker. A few times. I yanked off the rest of my gear—gloves, jacket, plastron, trousers, socks, shoes. After I had stripped down to tank top and shorts and was sure I was alone, I extracted my Stone. It was hard to believe we had been together for only one week. Already, life without her felt unimaginable. The square, princess-cut gem sparkled today like the turquoise of Puerto Marqués Bay on a perfect New Year's Day.

I found mi zafira last Tuesday on a trip that had started like any other. Mx. Buggeln's photography and imaging class had arrived at Friends an hour before first period to board the bus that would take us to the Endless Caverns in Virginia, two hours west. Our assignment had been to experiment with photography in low natural light.

I sat pressed between Lucía and M. I did not actively seek out the other native Spanish speakers in my class when I arrived at Friends. But speaking in another language, even one that I grew up with like English, takes a toll. The additional step between thought and word fatigues. We naturally gravitated toward each other.

Lucía did most of the talking, mostly about the boys she was dating. Her Spanish had the rhythms of Italian, like many Argentines, and she gesticulated animatedly when she spoke. She had always been boy crazy, she told us, even before she'd begun transitioning.

M.'s quiet compensated for Lucía's chatter. They were the first person I'd ever met from Ecuador. Their dad was a diplomat, like mine, and I found myself hoping to run into them at state functions. Their Spanish was so good they could have been from Mexico. Some of the so-called Spanish they speak in the Caribbean? Me mata. The United States should be tried at the International Court of Justice for what it did to the Spanish of Puerto Rico.

I would tell you what we talked about during the two-hour bus ride, but it does not matter. Our crushes, music, summer plans—all inconsequential now. Lucía played with her thick, curly hair. When she spoke, she would twist it up like a turban, then let it all come tumbling down. M. was moonier—happier to listen than talk. But when they did speak, their half-closed eyelids fluttered, like a butterfly's wings. The rest of the time, you got the sense that only half of them were here. The other half was somewhere else, somewhere infinitely more interesting. I wished I could be there with them.

Leaning on one another, we fell asleep in a pile, limbs intertwined. I woke up first, as our bus pulled into the Endless Caverns parking lot. I slung my camera bag across my chest but left my backpack and purse. This is one of the few things I like about being in the States. In Latin America, like southern Europe, when you leave something unattended, the chances of it being there when you return are as slim as Hikaru Yoshida fencing an entire match without resorting to foul play.

We filed off the bus and met our tour guide at the cavern entrance. Emmaline was a few years out of college, sporting flannel despite the season. Her eyes were set wide apart, amphibious. She passed out miners' helmets, with a light affixed on the front. We tightened them to our heads using a knob at the back. She led us into the caverns.

"The Endless Caverns are not actually endless." Emmaline's voice kept falling into inaudible as she gave us the history of the six-mile cave system, discovered in 1879 at the base of the Massanutten Mountain range. Then, realizing that those of us standing in the back of the group could not hear her, she yelled a few sentences before reverting to her natural mumble. Like being on a Zoom call with errant volume.

We followed Emmaline into the caverns proper, hunching down to enter the Yosemite Room.

Mx. Buggeln had chosen this location because the low light both created ambience and provided photographic challenges. Some of my classmates had brought tripods, but my hands were fencer-steady. I uncapped the Hasselblad my parents had presented as a peace offering when my father was reposted to Madrid. I accepted the gift only after persuading them to let me finish junior year at Friends as a boarder. We were still in negotiations for next year. As for college, they did not know I had decided to return to Mexico. I had been gone from home long enough.

I snapped on the Nikon lens.

Half of my class stayed in the Yosemite Room. I led the other half into the Curtain Room. It was dimmer here. More challenges, more opportunities. Each of the Shield formations stood like a statue from antiquity, water carving details over lifetimes. I flipped the aperture settings down to f/1.8 to shoot. A few moments later, I continued to the Cathedral Room with Lucía and M.

Unlike in museums, we could touch everything in the Endless Caverns. I traced the crevices, the ridges, the ripples of the geology, spun with the whimsy of candy, in the Cathedral Room. The formations connected ground and ceiling like the flying buttresses of every church in the center of every square in every town in Mexico. But because it was natural, it hummed holier than any architecture, this thing made by nature, free of humanity and its sins, smooth and grand and precipitous.

I went to the Blue Room by myself to work without the distraction of Lucía's chatter. The damp in the air, different from DC humidity, settled cold and heavy in my lungs.

The Blue Room was not blue, but the stalactite formations in the ceiling invoked a clear sky—long clean swaths of textured rock mimicking clouds. A ribbon of a river, far below, rustled under a grate in the ground.

The moving water inspired a long exposure. I usually resisted this kind of blurry picture. But when done correctly, it created a sense of motion that challenged the very idea of what a photograph could be. I did wish, now, that I had brought a tripod to help me angle straight down. I snapped, adjusted, snapped again. Just when I was contemplating resorting to the flash, the light in my helmet flickered off. A moment later, all the artificial lights in the Blue Room blinked off as well. Darkness enveloped me.

I immediately assumed the en garde pose. I did not have a weapon. But that did not mean I would be caught unprepared. I could be the weapon. If this was a trap, I would not be easy prey.

I waited for my eyes to adjust, but they did not. I had never been in that kind of absolute dark before—not even during Cairo's power outages.

Down here, buried meters below the earth's surface, I understood true darkness for the first time. It was so thick you could slice and serve it like a diabolical dessert. So dark it made the memory of light feel faint.

I tapped my helmet. The flashlight did not turn back on. I stood for a minute or longer—the lack of light distorted my sense of time. I waited.

My turquoise earrings tingled.

I sensed it a moment before the byzantium glow, like the cloak of the Virgin Mary, beckoned me. I walked slowly, carefully, groping around stalagmites and other potential treacheries.

My fingers wrapped themselves around the gem's cool, perfectly square surface. It burned cold. Then I must have hit my head, because I did not remember what happened next.

★

"It remains one of the Stones' most eccentric peculiarities that the Trial of Potentia is nearly instantaneous for some Bearers while others slip into subconsciousness, for as little as a few minutes or as long as a few hours. Zeb-un-Nissa mentions nothing of this in her initial pages, which we initially assumed was an intentional omission but have now concluded is simply another example of this phenomenon. Regardless, they have no memory of what transpired."

Broughton Shaw
Provost, Pass Ten

CHAPTER 5

EL INTERIOR DE LA PIEDRA DE ALEJANDRA

I was still in the Blue Room of the Endless Caverns. But it was different. The formations were infinitely more exquisite, stalactites stretching down like icicles, stalagmites sprouting up like a garden of spears. Where they met, they formed epic crystal hourglasses. But the oddest thing was that everything—the ground, the ceiling, every surface, every formation—was blue. Todo azul. Everything Blue.

Cerulean was the primary hue. Deep but bold. Majestic. In certain areas, like the base of the formations, the color shaded darker: royal blue, then navy, and almost midnight. The planes of the crystal ceiling up above tinted lighter, a cloudless spring sky in Provence. Each panel had a face etched into it. The two-dimensional etchings were drawn in simple, elegant, geometric shapes, like the Ancient Mayan designs appropriated by Frank Lloyd Wright.

Every shade of blue was present in the crystal world, from playful capri to royal blue to teal, turquoise, lapis: shades to rival every pair of jeans I've ever owned.

This Blue Room was mythically proportioned, spreading out in all directions. Of course, I had to stay alert. The low ceiling and crystal formations encouraged ambush.

I do not know how I was aware of the other creature in the crystal cave. I could not see it, and it was as silent as I had been. But I was as sure of its presence as I was of my own. It decided to approach me the exact moment that I decided to approach it. It synchronized its breathing to mine to avoid detection.

I acted swiftly and without hesitation.

I instinctively reached for my épée, and my right hand manifested my need, elongating into a pacific crystal blade. I turned around into a quick flèche, sprinting into the running attack.

I had often longed to experience real combat and felt an immeasurable satisfaction when my weapon-limb landed true, piercing the creature's heart . . .

PING

. . . just as an identical crystal blade penetrated my own chest.

PONG

I followed the weapon as it widened and turned into an elbow, just like mine. My gaze continued up the shapely tricep, over the dark shoulder and the cloth of the sleeveless lace blouse, then finally to my adversary's face. Thin lips contorted in triumph and terror. Perfect copies of my turquoise earrings. My own oval, wide eyes open, looking back at me.

Aiuchi. The Japanese fencing term when two opponents strike each other at the exact same time. When fencing with an épée, that meant a double touch: a point for both. But this was not a match. This was a mutual kill.

We stood like one of the blue crystals that made up the dream world, statues locked in a frozen moment of battle. My identical double and I. My opponent, my victim, my killer.

We both bled blue.

CHAPTER 6

LA BENDICIÓN DE ALEJANDRA

"¿Ale? ¿Ale? ¿Estás bien?"

I smelled pine.

M. stroked my face gently. Lucía, Emmaline, Mx. Buggeln, and the rest of the class blurred into my vision, staring down at me, like the statues of Easter Island. I was lying on the ground of the Blue Room. The light had returned. I had dreamed, but the memory evaporated from my mind like vapors from a mist.

I made sure none of them saw mi zafira, hidden in my clenched fist.

★

A week had passed since that day in the Endless Caverns. A quick locker-room shower cleared my mind after my humiliating defeat to Hikaru. I got dressed, put my gear back on, and reentered the gymnasium ready to compete. The only thing that mattered now was victory.

"Almada, you planning to show up today? Or should I send you home?"

I did not dignify Coach Vassallo's question with a response.

"All right then. Yoshida, number three."

"Again?" I asked before I thought to stop myself.

"What's the matter, Almada?" Hikaru strutted on the piste, taking en garde. "You need more time to towel off? Hate for you to play with a wet back."

The trick when someone says something so blatantly and intentionally offensive is to ignore them. Hikaru was just doing whatever he thought would give him an edge.

When looking at the pixelated world through my fencing mask, my opponents become anonymous automatons. Hikaru was not a privileged Japanese American heir to one of the largest technology firms in the world, who would use fencing to get into a top college, where he would peak, then spend the rest of his life trying to recapture his glory days. If he even finished college. So many tech bros dropped out like Zuckerberg en route to Silicon Valley.

"Vete al demonio, hijo de puta." I whispered the insult so that only Hikaru could hear it.

Sometimes you must do the thing you know you should not. Just to show you can.

En garde!

Mi zafira pulsed in my pocket, just as it had when that chico with red hair approached me on Sunday. Every morning, I thought about leaving it in my bedroom. But something about us being apart, about not having her on my body inherently and intrinsically felt wrong. Like the hard taco shells from los Estados Unidos.

En garde!

"Si vale la pena hacerlo, vale la pena hacerlo bien."

"If it's worth doing, it's worth excelling at."

In this match, I relented. I breathed the blue gem in, letting its energy wash over me. My heartbeat synced with its pulsing. It was a part of me, like the hair on my head or the blade in my hand.

En garde!

Flick. Defend. Counterattack.

I imagined azul washing over me, crawling through my blood, into and out of my organs, surrounding me in its cold nimbus. I imagined my blood flowing sapphire.

En garde!

"Sí adelante no vas, atrasarás."

"She who does not advance, goes backward."

Four pings and four pongs later, we were tied, each one point away from victory.

En garde!

"Quien saltar quiere lejos, debe medir la distancia."

"One must step back, to take a great leap."

I was outside his reach when I lunged. I should not have been able to strike him. But my desire for victory was so great that I willed my body to defy its constraints. The point of my épée wove through his last-minute parry, making contact in the soft flank where his liver would be.

PING!

"Welcome back, Almada." Coach Vassallo tossed me a water bottle. It was the closest I would get to a compliment from him. Not that it mattered. I did not need his approval. Only my own.

Hikaru slammed his mask down hard, pretty lips pouting in disbelief. I turned and yanked off my jacket, plastron, and chest protector. That was enough for today. I conjured the hot tub and my plan to soak in it until my skin wrinkled like fruit in a Christmas ponche.

"You were working some voodoo out there, Almada." Hikaru strolled over to my side of the piste. Even in practice, this was considered in very poor taste. He took a furtive glance to make sure no one was looking, then he flicked the tip of his blade against my arm. It was a cheap shot, designed to cut through my long-sleeve compression top, maybe even break the flesh and draw a few drops of blood. The kind of poor sportsperson behavior for which Hikaru was renowned.

I do not know which of us was more surprised when the tip of his épée blade bent backward and snapped.

"The fuck?" he said.

I worked my finger through the tear, just below the crook of my elbow.

It can't be. My blood turned to ice.

I poked and prodded and scratched in disbelief. How could my body have done this? Dread washed over me, turning to rage. This was a nightmare. A true horror.

I shoved Hikaru back and ran out of the gymnasium, ignoring the voices asking if I was all right.

What Hikaru could not see, what none of them could see, was that my arm was no longer flesh.

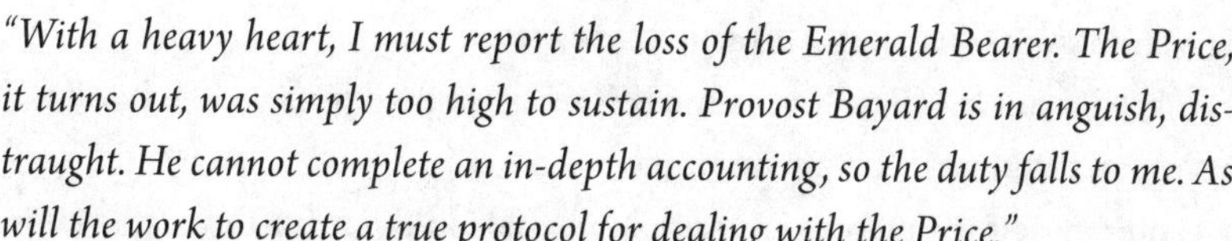

"With a heavy heart, I must report the loss of the Emerald Bearer. The Price, it turns out, was simply too high to sustain. Provost Bayard is in anguish, distraught. He cannot complete an in-depth accounting, so the duty falls to me. As will the work to create a true protocol for dealing with the Price."

James de la Shaw
Chancellor, Pass Three

CHAPTER 7

ALEJANDRA Y REED

The chico with red hair found me sitting on the steps of the Lincoln Memorial.

The May sun was a blazing gold doubloon. The humidity made my already sweaty practice clothes stick to me. A reminder that this country's capital was built on a swamp. I suppose I should not criticize—the Aztecs built Tenochtitlan on a lake. Then the Spaniards built Mexico City on Tenochtitlan.

"I told you to stay away," I told him.

The lights hummed orange inside the temple of the Lincoln Memorial, as the last sightseers trickled down the stairs after visiting the goliath statue of the slavery-ending president, sitting on his throne.

"I can help you." He wore cargo pants and a short-sleeve red Henley, again. Another affront.

My Blue Stone pulsed in the presence of his. I could not see his ruby, but I sensed it, just as I was sure he could sense mi zafira.

"I said vete." I had run through town, desperate, like a coyote wounded, refusing to look at the part of my body that had turned. My feet took me to three hospitals, but I could not bring myself to enter. I did not want anyone to witness my body's revolt. "Go!"

His shoulders collapsed, a broken marionette.

But he did not give up. "My name is Reed." He held up his pale, bony wrists, palms open, facing me. "I come in peace."

Despite myself, I laughed. We both knew he could not hurt me. The laughter defused me.

I must have looked a sight, in fencing pants and ripped long-sleeve compression top, my hair like the wrath of the gods, as mi abuela used to say. My muscles ached, a punishment for not stretching properly after practice: knees tight, shoulders clenched. Today, these pains were the least of my problems.

"Can I sit?" he asked.

I granted him the shortest of nods. He joined me on the steps, keeping a respectful three meters between us, like in the time of social distancing.

"How did you know I was here?" I asked.

"Our Stones give us these awesome powers, and one of them is that we can find each other! Actually, mine is drawn to yours, and yours will be drawn to Yellow, and . . ." He stopped his own torrent of words. "I'm getting ahead of myself. Are you okay? I sensed something . . . a great distress?"

"Were you spying on me?" My defenses shot up immediately.

"No, that's my power. Forty-five minutes ago, I felt . . ." He closed his eyes in concentration. "Anguish, like you had been betrayed. Confusion, in the face of an invasion. Fear, like the very fabric of your reality was coming undone."

I did not know how he knew all that, and I resented his knowing it. But his calm settled me. The truth was, I did not have many options. He offered an open face and heart as proof that maybe, just maybe, I could trust him.

I angled my body to hide my arm from the few remaining tourists. Then I rolled up my sleeve, forcing myself to look at the aberration. My forearm had elongated a meter's length and transformed to blue crystal. The azure planes reflected the setting sun, like the very sky itself.

I was gangly. Lopsided. Inorganic.

My sapphire arm had proved impervious to scratching, cutting, slashing, and piercing. I had always wanted to be invulnerable. But at what cost?

"Wow!" Reed's face lit up, like my Stone did around his. "That's awesome!"

I had tried to throw the gem away. To toss it and be rid of it forever. But I could not. "My flesh turns to stone, and you think 'that's awesome'?!"

"No no no, Alejandra!" The way he said my name hurt my ears. "I said that because it means you've already completed the Feat of Potentia!"

"I do not care about your Feats and your Potentias. How do I reclaim my body?"

"I can try to help—if you'll let me?"

I did not trust myself to make words, so I simply nodded yes.

"Put Blue in your hand. That's right. Now close it. Is it all right if I . . ." He reached for me.

I nodded again, and he laid his hand on mine.

"Okay." He produced his Stone from his pocket. It was round and mercury red. "Now you do the same."

I complied. What did I have to lose?

"When I need to power off, I try something like this." His ruby glowed hibiscus, and his presence—his soul—tentatively knocked on the door of mine, through his Stone.

A distant siren wailed. Police car or ambulance?

I let him in. Bienvenido, unlikely guest.

"Alejandra, I find that it helps to close my eyes."

I kept mine open. His Stone pulsed. Mine responded. Relief poured into me like agua de jamaica into a pitcher. I was transported far away from this city, from the traffic and the humidity and the tourists and the pollution and the noise, to the garden of mi abuela in Cuernavaca. The courtyard of the hacienda where I had spent every summer as a niña was still decorated in the classical style, with peacocks and flamingos roaming free. It was where I was most tranquil. This was before the clash of the grandmothers, before my parents accepted their first foreign posts, before we moved every few years.

The breeze in the garden.

The smell of the hibiscus boiled so tart my lips would pucker.

The lush pomegranates with seeds like jewels.

My turquoise earrings tingled.

I cannot remember when I had closed my eyes, but when I opened them, my limb had reverted to its natural state. It was mine again.

Mostly.

"All Potentias come with a Price." He tried to keep the concern out of his voice. "I'm sorry I couldn't . . ."

I pulled this Reed into a tight embrace. He squawked in surprise.

We spent the rest of the day walking through downtown Washington, DC. He told me everything he knew.

In front of the Vietnam Veterans Memorial, I learned about the Pentacle Portal. "So it will release a torrent of magic that will destroy us all?" I asked.

"Only if we fail to seal it."

As we walked through the Constitution Gardens, he explained the Feat of Locatio and how each Stone leads to the next.

"So there are five Stones?" I repeated back to him. "Red, Blue, Yellow, Green, and Purple." If my arm had not transformed to crystal a few hours ago, I would have never believed a word of his story. But the evidence was incontrovertible. "And once I activate the Feat of Locatio, I will not be able to use electricity, either?"

"Disjunctis is the Price for Locatio," he confirmed.

As we passed the National Museum of African American History and Culture, he told me about Señor Shaw.

"He's the Provost—our mentor, and a descendant of the family entrusted by the Pass One Bearers to guide the Bearers to seal the Pentacle Portal. Plus, he's like a gymnast/scholar/warrior/all-around badass Renaissance man extraordinaire."

"Someone has a crush on teacher." The rose blush on his pale skin was all the confirmation I needed.

By the time we made it to the Smithsonian Astrophysical Observatory, I did not just believe him. I trusted this Reed, with his crooked elbows and knees, entirely and completely. I've always been an excellent judge of character. That is why I did not have many friends.

"So I find Yellow, they find Green, and Green finds Purple. Señor Shaw teaches us Terminatio, then we Teleportare into the Pentagon Chamber, seal the Pentacle Portal, and save the world for the eleventh time?"

"Exactly!"

Also, he had healed me.

Mostly.

I traced the sliver of sapphire, just below the crook of my elbow. The part that had not changed back. It was kite-shaped, maybe five centimeters in length, angling down to my wrist. I would pass this off as a temporary tattoo if anybody asked. It still concerned me, deeply, that my body was changing. A reminder that things would always be different.

"And why isn't this Señor Shaw here now?"

"He is—I mean, he's back in the hotel. I wanted to make first contact. You know, as the Leader of the Bearers."

I arched an eyebrow.

"Red is traditionally the Leader," he backtracked.

"Why cannot I be Leader?" All these chicos were so fragile.

"Blue is the Warrior," he said, as if it were fact.

"Why can't I be Warrior *and* Leader?"

"Mr. Shaw says . . ."

"I do not care what Señor Shaw says. An arbitrary tradition means nothing to me. I will come tomorrow. And I will have a word with this Señor Shaw."

"But . . ."

I shifted my weight evenly between my feet, into a balanced combat pose. He understood that this was the end of the conversation.

Unlike Reed, I was not scared to confront this all-knowing Señor Shaw. Like the teacher last year who kept mispronouncing my name.

Ale. Simply the first two syllables of Alejandra. I still fail to see the challenge.

"So will you join me? Us?" He smiled big and open, like a puppy.

Mi zafira tingled in my pocket, warm for a change.

Was I really considering abandoning everything to go with this chico? It seemed so unlikely. So unlike me.

But the truth was, even with his misguided notions about leadership, I already felt like Reed and I had known each other for lifetimes. Like old souls who had been reincarnated. We enjoyed an ease, an understanding, an intimacy. I do not usually feel that with strangers. Especially gringos.

I nodded. He yelped with joy and almost embraced me but intelligently decided against it.

Logistics piled up high: school, parents, fencing. They may have daunted someone else, but I had already made up my mind. Besides, saving the world would be great for my social media presence.

"The Bearers must bond with each other, as the Stones bond to them."

Algernon de la Shaw
Provost, Pass Seven

CHAPTER 8

REED CRASHES

Something was definitely wrong.

It wasn't just the inky pool of melted plastic and shorted wires that had been his hotel alarm clock. It wasn't just his burnt fingertips, the Price he paid for forgetting about Disjunctis. In fact, he barely felt those.

It was something else. Something Reed couldn't quite place.

His tech-free life, in fact, had proved easier than he would've predicted—probably because he had so many other things to occupy him. But he did miss music. He had taken for granted how his life could be underscored with the touch of a button.

Mental note: ask Mr. Shaw to pick him up a secondhand acoustic guitar. Actually, make that a brand-new acoustic. If he could drop this kind of coin on barges and hotels, he could afford to get Reed a Collings. Or at least a midlevel Taylor.

Before its untimely demise, the alarm clock had told him he had one hour before the eight thirty training session with Mr. Shaw. Plenty of time before Alejandra's scheduled lunchtime visit.

What was it? What was wrong? What was different? He couldn't put his finger on it. Burned or not.

Nothing else hurt. His body was intact and unharmed. He either hadn't dreamed the night before or couldn't remember his dreams. He peeked under the sheets. He was dry. Nothing was amiss. Red was still safely ensconced under his pillow.

He sat up and got out of bed. He parted the outer shell of the blackout curtains, leaving the gauzy, translucent ones in place. The room awoke with him.

He stubbed his toe on the corner of the bed on the way to the bathroom. He braced himself for the two-second pain delay. But it never arrived, an Amazon package lost in transit. Was he becoming invulnerable?

Reed found the now lukewarm cup of coffee that Mr. Shaw had taken to leaving for him after he'd accidentally Disjunctis'ed the Keurig. Mr. Shaw must've brewed decaf, because Reed didn't feel any of the glorious side effects after sipping the thick, inky black. No sharpening of the senses, no quickening of his heartbeat, no sense of happiness and order to the universe.

During his shower, he could barely feel the heat of the steaming water blasting him from the fancy multifunction showerhead. He cranked the lever counterclockwise: twelve o'clock, eleven, ten, and finally, all the way to nine o'clock. Welts formed on his chest, and steam fogged over the glass shower door and the sink mirror. "A real pea-souper" was how Mr. Shaw would describe it. But Reed barely felt anything. Was his next power-up an elemental immunity to heat?

He experimented in the other direction, passing noon on the way to three o'clock. The steam dissipated, but he still felt nothing. What should've been an arctic blast barely registered. Except for some unfortunate shriveling.

Reed toweled off and applied moisturizer from the Lilliputian bottle. He brushed his teeth and ran some conditioner and product through his hair, paying extra attention to that damned cowlick. A sophomore year assignment on the environmental impact caused by hotels still haunted him. Sixty million tons of carbon dioxide emissions annually. He replaced the towel on the rack.

Saving the world from magical Armageddon was all well and good; if only there was a way to use the Stones to save the world from climate change. And gun violence. And economic disparity. And narcissistic dictators threatening nuclear annihilation and World War III.

He got dressed, then dug his Stone out from the mountain of pillows on his unmade bed.

For the first time since they'd found each other, his ruby lay dull. The thousands of facets on its spherical surface didn't so much as reflect or refract.

Reed picked up the Stone. It flashed to life. Like a flood breaking through a dam, emotions burst into him.

Exhaustion, barely finishing a race

His pinkie toe suddenly throbbed,

Guilt, of committing an unpardonable transgression

his chest stung raw,

Fear, wild, unpredictable, crippling

each movement against the suddenly itchy cotton of his T-shirt a lash from a whip.

Remorse for a penance he'd never get

The onslaught was relentless. He was a stag under attack by a pack of wolves,

Running-on-fumes emptiness

inflicting debilitating wound after debilitating wound in practiced coordination

Paralysis, incapable of any decision-making

until he collapsed and they could pounce in for the kill,

Psychic depletion that threatened permanence

devouring all that was left of him.

Who knows how long he lay there before Mr. Shaw found him, crumpled on the floor of his room in the fetal position, sobbing with a violence that scared them both. He held Reed, rocking him gently like a mother would an infant, using his body weight to anchor him, to stabilize the emotions that coursed through him like demons released after thousands of years in captivity, running amok and causing havoc with the fevered fury of freedom. Once Reed's violent heaving tapered into gentle sobs, Mr. Shaw picked him up, laid him in bed, and covered him in blankets. When Reed's own hands proved too shaky, Mr. Shaw held the cup of herbal tea to his lips.

"All right?" Mr. Shaw asked.

"Let Me Feel Low" by Cavetown featuring Miloe. D major^7–D, back and forth, for the first few lines.

He smiled weakly and took a soothing sip of chamomile.

"We'll have to be careful about overdrawing your Potentia, especially this early in your training." Mr. Shaw lowered the teacup back to its saucer. "But it could be worse."

"How?" Reed asked weakly.

"You could be in precalc."

Reed made a noise somewhere between a bark and a laugh. "I just realized—tomorrow is junior prom." Was Arno going? And if he was, what would he be wearing? And would he—just the thought pained Reed—be going with someone? Someone not Reed? He closed his eyes and forced himself to calm. He was still raw, with emotions breaking through him like leaks in a dam.

"The mission will be complete in a month and a half, Reed. And after we close the Pentacle Portal, you'll be able to resume your wanton, reckless teenage life. But until then—take it easy."

"It's so unfair—can you imagine if Superman suffered this way every time he used his powers?" Reed took another sip of tea. "Even in Final Fantasy, all you need is a tent or an inn to get your MPs back."

"This isn't a comic book, Reed. Or a video game. Each Price is as unique as each Potentia. Just as we're coming to understand yours, we'll have to help Blue understand hers." Mr. Shaw carefully moved an errant lock of hair off Reed's forehead. "Which is what I'm going to consult the Muraqqa about right now. Assuming you'll be okay without me?"

"Don't go disappearing on me, understand?" Reed was suddenly serious.

"Excuse me?"

"Don't front, Mr. Shaw. I've read the books. I've seen the movies. I know this genre. Obi-Wan sacrifices himself to save them from Darth Vader. 'You shall not pass,' and then Gandalf goes down with the Balrog. Moiraine tackles Lanfear through a ter'angreal, and they both go bye-bye into the Wheel of Time. And yes, the mentors eventually come back with a major level-up, but I don't think I could make it to Act Two without you, okay? So don't even think about some mysterious cliff-hanging, sacrificial mentor-disappearance act, got it?"

"I promise, Reed." Mr. Shaw matched Reed's sincerity. "I will stay by your side as long as you will have me."

Reed dozed off. After he awoke, he showered again and got dressed for the second time that day. By the time he was tugging on a clean Henley over his head, he almost felt like himself.

"Ms. Almada should be here in half an hour," Mr. Shaw called from the common room. "Are you still feeling up to our encounter?"

The urgent knock prevented Reed from replying.

Mr. Shaw and Reed tiptoed their way down the hallway to the front door of the hotel suite. Mr. Shaw peered through the fishbowl lens. "It's her!" he whispered. "Are you sure she said noon?"

"Poz," Reed whispered back. "What time is it now?"

Mr. Shaw held up his phone. 11:31 AM.

The knock came again.

"I suppose we should let her in, right?" Mr. Shaw asked in hushed tones.

"Why are we whispering?" Reed asked.

"I don't know," Mr. Shaw whispered back.

"For fuck's sake." Reed opened the door.

Alejandra stood on the other side of the door looking like she just stepped out of a fashion shoot. Large circular periwinkle sunglasses perched on her wide, flat nose shielded her almond eyes. She wore an off-the-shoulder print dress that came down to her midthigh. The three-inch boost she got from her violet glittery platform sneakers allowed her to look down on Reed literally as well as figuratively. "Hola."

"Come on in!" He didn't know whether to shake her hand or hug her, but she just walked past him.

"You must be Señor Shaw." She graced him with a curt head nod. "Mucho gusto."

"Encantado. Qué gentil que hayas venido," Mr. Shaw responded. "Can I see it?"

"You are worried—what? That I am an impostor?" Alejandra cocked her head and leaned forward, almost flirtatiously. "That I am not the real thing?"

"One cannot be too careful," Mr. Shaw admitted.

"I haven't told you yet, but our archvillain is an illusionist!" Reed blurted out.

"So you understand why we must be careful," Mr. Shaw concluded.

Alejandra nodded before unclasping the spaghetti strap purse hanging off an exposed, moisturized shoulder. The insides glowed azure, like underwater treasure. Even though his Stone wasn't responding to Blue, Blue was clearly reacting to Red.

When she produced the square-cut sapphire, Mr. Shaw's fists met at his core. He closed his eyes and bowed his head. "Hear me, all Chancellors and Provosts back to the first Pass. I vow to mentor the Five Stone Bearers and to teach them the Feat of Terminatio, which will seal the Pentacle Portal. Blue, the second Stone, the Stone of the Warrior, all this I say unto you." The American flag–blue glow from the Stone lit up the holy devotion on his face. "We welcome you to the quest."

"Where should we start?" Alejandra snapped the purse closed.

"What would you like to know, Blue Bearer?"

Alejandra interrogated Mr. Shaw about everything she and Reed had discussed yesterday.

Reed considered reading her. Would reading someone's emotional state without their consent count as a moral transgression? Her opaque sunglasses were making it even harder to tell what she was feeling. Was she relieved to be meeting Mr. Shaw? Excited to see Reed again? Was she actually going to drop out of school to join them? Or not? What would they do if she rejected the quest but refused to Relinquo the Stone?

Ultimately, Reed let his power hangover make the decision for him. In this state, he wasn't sure he could muster the Potentia to do anything. He dug his thumbs into his temples.

Maybe Alejandra was right. Maybe he needed to reconsider the whole Leader thing. It had always been easy with Arno, like in the GSA. They'd brainstorm ideas together, whittle them down to the achievable, and then Reed would delegate.

Alejandra didn't feel like the delegate-to type. That made him think—why hadn't he ever let Arno do the delegating? Or lead a meeting? On the other hand, it was hard to imagine a crueler punishment for Arno. During their humanities final, Reed had to force him to present some parts by himself. During those painfully awkward mumbles, Mr. Huff-Wells had to ask Arno to speak up four times.

Arno. Junior prom. Arno. Would it really jeopardize the mission if he just wrote him one letter? Just to let him know he was okay and not to forget about him?

"But Reed said the Portal would release a magic that would destroy us unchecked. How do we know this?" Alejandra queried.

"By evidence of the fact that we are still here." Mr. Shaw moved to afford her a view of the digital Muraqqa on his tablet. "Here are Princess Zeb-un-Nissa's records of Sarmad's True Dreams regarding the Pentacle Portal."

"What evidence do we have to support this theory? Is it possible that . . ."

A pounding on the door interrupted Alejandra and Mr. Shaw's conversation.

"Rupert Shaw! This is the police! Open the door and come out with your hands up!"

"Ironically, it is often more difficult to enlist the help of law enforcement. The challenges vary in different regions, but the most common factors include internal divisions, corruption, and white supremacy. Experience suggests avoiding local authorities at all costs."

Larkin Shaw
Provost, Pass Nine

CHAPTER 9

REED READS

"We know you're in there," a police officer barked.

"There must be some misunderstanding, right?" Reed whispered to Mr. Shaw.

The officers pounded on the door again.

"Do not let them in." Mr. Shaw ducked into his bedroom.

Alejandra leaped to her feet. "Quick, Reed!"

"What?"

"We gotta get out of here." She giggled nervously. "Because you won't believe what . . ."

She stopped abruptly when Mr. Shaw returned from his bedroom, fumbling with the contents of his patent leather briefcase. "Don't be naive, Reed. I am here with two minors, one of whom has been the subject of a missing person report since last week." He opened his case and began assembling battle gear. "Exits covered, windows sealed. Next time, we're staying on a ground-floor Airbnb. But now, I'm afraid we're going to have to duke our way out." He slipped on his newly assembled weapon: a high-tech gauntlet with a glowing orb pulsating in its palm. The battle armor powered up, vibrating like a deadly hummingbird. "This is clearly the work of JoAnne. I would guess she's fed these officers enough information to make it look like child trafficking, kidnapping—all sorts of goodies that will keep me wrapped up here for months."

"We're giving you to the count of three," the same officer hollered from the hallway. "One . . ."

"Should I . . ." The transformation began at Alejandra's shoulder, flesh turning blue, hardening, shaping into crystal.

"The less cause we give them for concern, the better," Mr. Shaw advised.

Her body morphed back.

"Two!" the officer yelled from the hallway.

"Do you think they're going to break down the door?" Reed asked.

"They probably have a search warrant or will fabricate an exception to the Fourth Amendment." Mr. Shaw kept his gauntleted hand trained on the entrance. "So they most likely have a key from the front desk, which means . . ."

"Three!" The electronic lock clicked open. Three police officers slowly entered the room single file.

The commanding officer, a white middle-aged woman, anchored herself in the doorway, cutting off any possible escape. The other two moved into the suite proper, blocking off the exits to the bedrooms. They kept their handguns aimed at Mr. Shaw.

"Drop your weapon, now!" the commanding officer in the doorway snapped.

Reed's imagination scrambled down all the possible paths in this choose-your-own-adventure nightmare. He quickly chose the only option that didn't involve physical violence. His Stone came to life, pulsing in anticipation.

He didn't need his Potentia to read the hierarchy among the officers: her superior status was as clear as the stripes on her sleeve and her handcuff case's extra wear. She would be his subject. "Officer, there must be some mistake."

What were the dynamics of her soul?

To an outside observer, the stout, middle-aged officer appeared calm, cool, almost bored. But Reed was no outside observer. He was an infiltrator, an emotional detective, an empathic Peeping Tom. He spied on her insides, and found

Concern, for the safety of minors

the syncopations of her inner musings

Caution, at an unknown enemy

talking her through protocol as bitten nails twitched against the trigger.

Unease, from a sublimated memory

"What was that, son?" Her gaze shifted to Reed, but her gun stayed aimed at Mr. Shaw.

"I said," Reed repeated with great deliberation, "there must be some mistake, officer."

Perhaps, if he'd been a math nerd, he would have experienced her inner workings as a geometric proof, full of axiomatic principles. But he was a musician, so she was a song. Bluegrass. Anticipating beats, alternating melody, mixing blues, jazz, and the sacred.

Underneath that taut melody, hidden behind those notes, Reed plucked her banjo strings: grace notes and dynamics that curled themselves under the main tune, getting faster and faster, exerting influence like a royal adviser cloaked in shadow, whispering into their regent's ear.

"There's no mistake, son. Kidnapping. Transporting a minor across state lines." The woman officer's Southern accent glided over the final consonant of "minor," letting the vowel drip. "The feds are gonna have a field day with this one."

This officer's hymn was in the key of morality. Her pedal was righteousness. That's why she'd joined the force, and even now, twenty years later, that was what kept her there.

But being in this hotel put her on edge. There was an image, blurry, seen through a rainy window. A childhood trauma?

"Now, Mr. Shaw, you'll never take all three of us out." She spoke with authority, a woman used to having her commands followed. "I'll give you to three to put down your weapon."

Reed worked even harder, even faster, fighting through his emotional hangover, using that officer's unknown unease to slice through the notes and dynamics between them.

"One . . ."

Something inside him protested, an exhausted muscle nearing permanent damage, like the time he'd finished a race on a pulled Achilles tendon. He'd come in second and paid for it with a month on crutches.

"Two . . ."

Alejandra shifted, moving her weight forward, poised to pounce on the nearest officer, a young Black man with tattoos peeking out of his sleeves and collar.

Reed peered into the infinity of the commanding officer's soul. He dived into that five-bar staff, learned its patterns, hopping from note to note, then chord to chord, finally arriving at the core, her center, the essence of her very being: a five-string banjo, tuned in classic bluegrass: G^4–D^3–G^3–B^3–D^4. All he needed was a few more moments to figure out how to clawhammer her frets.

"This is your last chance. Put. Down. The. Weapon." She spoke in polite, firm tones: mediation training, experience in high-pressure situations. Whole note legatos, supported but calm.

"Three." The officers took one step, in concert, forward.

Reed felt the moment transpire, that moment that threatened something horrible and irrevocable. He plucked what he prayed were the right chords on the instrument of her spirit.

"I said, there must be some mistake, officer. We aren't the kids you're looking for."

The silence hung thick, a precipitous moment with infinite possibilities.

"These aren't the kids we're looking for." She repeated the words with Reed's intonation.

Reed strummed again while she was still in the throes of his Orchestration. "It's okay that we're here."

"It's okay that they're here," she told the other two officers.

The dazed sergeant wordlessly turned around and left the room, with her confused subordinates following a beat later. They even mumbled apologies and replaced the DO NOT DISTURB sign before gently closing the door behind them.

Reed fell to his knees, arms crossed against his chest, rocking himself. The pain throbbed from his aching heart. His Stone fizzled out, cold and dark, like a broken streetlamp.

"*That's* my lad!" Mr. Shaw let out a *whoop* loud enough it could probably be heard by the departing officers. "You were positively nuclear!"

"How'd you do that?" Alejandra tossed her curtain of straight hair over a shoulder.

"Empathy powers up to Orchestration." Reed tried to keep the pride out of his voice.

"You see, Reed? How powerful you can be?" Mr. Shaw embraced him. "If you had a battle power, like you wanted, like Alejandra's—we'd be on the run now, warrants out for our arrest, bobbies on our trail. The rest of the mission would be compromised. But you fixed it! Take that, JoAnne!"

Reed wanted to respond, to celebrate, to bask in Mr. Shaw's praise, to answer Alejandra's questions. But he couldn't. He had nothing left. He was a tooth's nerve, raw and vulnerable and exposed. He was sure of only one thing.

"I"—he choked the word out—"I need to be alone." Reed began dragging himself to his bedroom. He didn't even let the knocking on their hotel suite door stop him. He didn't care. About that. About this. About anything. He just needed a barrier, something between him and the rest of the world.

But when Mr. Shaw opened the door and a second Alejandra entered, he knew he wouldn't get the solitude he so desperately desired.

"Now that I've ended my service as Provost and ascended to Chancellor, I am afforded time to research the elusive Trial of Potentia. A fragment from Pass Three leads to the tale of the Rabbi Akiva, a second-century CE scholar and sage."

Ignatius Shaw
Chancellor, Pass Nine

CHAPTER 10

LAS DOS ALEJANDRAS

Staring at myself was eerie for all the obvious reasons. But it also triggered something—a memory, a dream, a fantasia—that danced on the outskirts of my memory. Where had I seen myself before?

When I saw her, in that off-the-shoulder leopard print dress hovering on platforms, I forgave everyone who had ever made a pass at me. I looked good.

After a few seconds of astonishment, Señor Shaw sprang into action. He kept his eyes on the two of us, but spoke to Reed.

"Read them, Reed."

"Read, Reed! What's that called? A homophone. Or is it a homonym? Homo homo homos!" He sputtered and laughed at his own joke, like an ignoramus.

My impostor retreated when I advanced. That should have been proof enough that she was the fake.

"Señor Shaw, what's happening?" she said. "Who is she?"

The timbre was accurate, and so was the accent. All the more reason to establish myself immediately.

"I am the real Alejandra." I showed them the sliver of sapphire in the nook of my forearm as proof. Much to my surprise, she revealed an identical sliver. Had it been there a moment ago?

This was becoming a nightmare. But not as bad as the one I had last night, which made me scream so loud that I had awoken my suitemates. In that nightmare, I had been encased in a suit of sapphire armor. But unlike real armor, this suit did not move with my body. It did not move at all. My jeweled armor had become my coffin. It was the worst kind of nightmare, the kind that felt so real it never occurred to doubt.

"One of you must be JoAnne!" Señor Shaw said, as if that meant something.

"Who is this JoAnne?" I asked, as impostor me said, "The illusionist?"

"This should be simple enough to puzzle out." Señor Shaw lowered his weapon. "I'll simply touch each of you, and see if . . ."

"Do not dare," I snapped.

That apparently was the incorrect response, since Señor Shaw aimed his weapon at me. Many things happened next, very quickly.

I inhaled sharply, and my body, of its own volition, turned sapphire in the face of danger, just as

Reed's eyes flashed diablo red, and he lunged at Señor Shaw

just as

Señor Shaw's gauntlet powered up and discharged a burst of electricity.

Redirected by Reed, the attack zapped my double, the one who'd been in the room when I arrived. At the moment of impact, she disappeared in a shimmer. The transparent polycarbonate chair behind her paid the price, melting into a toxic puddle. The chemical stench burned my nostrils and stung my eyes.

"Alejandra Almada Navarro?" Señor Shaw extended a hand to me. I accepted it, and he pulled me close to him and poor Reed, babbling nonsense. "We have to leave, quickly. How soon can you . . . ?"

Another figure shimmered into the room. Someone my age, decked in sparkling denim and leather. One side of her head was shaved to the skull, and her mohawk spiked in wild shades of violets and pinks.

"Every one of my apparitions will just be replaced by another, Rupert." She had desperation in her eyes, as if she were crashing from an all-night ephedrine bender.

"Neat trick, impersonating Alejandra." Señor Shaw adjusted a dial on his weapon. "I'm guessing you must be Camouflaged in this room to employ a Glamour with such precision." He circled her now, like a shark. "Or next door? Lurking outside in the corridor?"

"Wouldn't you love to know, *Señor* Shaw? But just because I tricked you into divulging information doesn't mean I'll make the same mistake. Especially because I have no interest in you. It's the Bearers . . ."

She didn't get to finish, because Señor Shaw zapped her. The image flickered out, only to be replaced with a new one a few meters away. This one sported flowing locks of hair in all directions, like the leaves of an agave plant, atop an oval face and violet eyes.

"Reed, Alejandra, behind me. I'll handle this." Señor Shaw dispelled this incarnation of JoAnne before she had a chance to speak. "Which one of us is going to run out of power first?" he asked as the next JoAnne shimmered into being over the coffee table.

They continued this dance for a few minutes. Every time JoAnne appeared, Señor Shaw disrupted her with a blast from his gauntlet, destroying another part of the hotel room. Charred walls, melted chairs, burned sofas. A moment later, another variation of JoAnne would appear, each one different from the one before. Some were tall, imposing figures of occultists out of an epic poem. Others were lithe and androgynous, like the stars of glam rock. All were decked in materials fabulous—leather, denim, feathers, sequins.

After the sixth disruption, the figures became blurry, like photographs shot at the wrong shutter speed. By the tenth, they lost their opacity, becoming translucent and then finally transparent, like apparitions.

It was not until the twelfth or thirteenth version—a strong chin and nose, clothes that did not move when she did—that Señor Shaw's gauntlet stalled. This vision was so faint I could barely hear it.

"Reed, Alejandra, I can show you how to achieve true mastery of your powers."

"JoAnne, really, this is your master plan?" Señor Shaw popped his suitcase open and extracted a battery cell. "'Join me and the Dark Side, and you will know power you never dreamed of'?"

"He knows nothing about these precious Stones!" she cackled. Her voice came from every direction at once, as if she had hijacked the room's speakers. "Ask him who I am!"

The surge of electricity passed through the image, frying the gigantic television on the wall behind it. It sizzled and exploded like fireworks at a patron saint festival. Flames erupted, consuming the screen.

"Alejandra, Reed, we have to go." Señor Shaw spoke to Reed gently, like he was a child.

But Reed didn't move. "Who is JoAnne?"

Señor Shaw took a deep breath. "I said we must depart. Now." He pulled Reed up off the floor. "Señorita Navarro, if you please?"

I held Reed as Señor Shaw grabbed his suitcase and satchel.

I half-dragged, half-carried Reed to the door.

The hotel suite looked like the victim of a rock band's after-party. Scorch marks charred the formerly textured wallpaper. The furniture had been knocked over and, in the case of the unfortunate polycarbonate dining room chairs, eviscerated. The fire from the TV was spreading to the synthetic carpet as the fire alarm beeped incessantly. I used my arm to cover my nose.

"Who is JoAnne?" Reed repeated.

"We can talk about this—"

"Answer him," I insisted.

Señor Shaw took a deep breath. "JoAnne was the Pass Ten Purple Bearer."

Apparently, performing the Feat of Locatio on your first attempt is impressive. But what can I say? Things have always come easily to me. Mi zafira spun in my palm, my turquoise earrings tingled, and a ripple traveled up my arm and to my heart before my Stone emitted a beam of light that struck the map just outside Annapolis.

At the same time, something grand filled me. A sense of purpose. Of meaning. A new raison d'être. Everything else I had done or wanted in my life—fencing, grades, even the Olympics or the diplomatic corps—it all felt so silly. Tiny. Insignificante.

What Reed said made sense. I had been chosen to do something important with my life. It was mi destino.

When I finally agreed to join, Reed yelped with joy and hugged me. I let him.

I worried about my parents. I rejected Señor Shaw's idea to send them a ransom note, as if I had been kidnapped. I would not play into the international media's sensationalism.

Disjunctis made emailing impossible. If I doubted Señor Shaw's warning, the way my cellular sparked in my hand, burning me and shorting itself, was all the proof I needed. So I wrote an old-fashioned letter and left it for the concierge at our new hotel, with instructions to mail it to the Mexican Embassy in Spain. I told them not to worry. I told them I would be gone only six weeks. I told them I could not say more. I told them that I loved them and that they would be proud of me. I asked them not to tell my grandmothers.

Reed slowly emerged from his mind trap. His Price. When we are not careful with our powers, Señor Shaw told us, when we use them too much or without sufficient training, it is worse.

I understand this.

I traced the sapphire sliver in the crook of my elbow.

I have always understood that everything comes with a Price.

END OF BOOK II

INTERLUDE B

MUGHAL INDIA, 1653

ZEB-UN-NISSA RECORDS

“There are others like me, then?” A sapphire, as square as the ruby is round, floats out of a hidden pocket in Princess Zeb-un-Nissa’s robes. It hovers in front of her, protectively. “Others who were chosen to bear a Stone?”

“You will not believe what I have seen,” the boy whispers. “Or what we will accomplish together, you and I, Princess Zeb-un-Nissa, Jewel of Womankind.”

Zeb-un-Nissa’s sapphire bathes her side of the chamber in its indigo glow. As if responding to a challenge, the ruby also glows. The Stones meet in the center of the room and circle each other, two curs angling for position.

“I’ve traveled for days, without rest—I don’t even know how far.” His body sways with exhaustion. “Caravan. Horseback. On foot, until my soles blistered and bled.”

“But why?” Zeb-un-Nissa sheaths her dagger. She does not fear this scrawny boy.

“My Stone demanded it. As yours will.”

“When did you begin your journey?” Zeb-un-Nissa returns to her desk. Only a fool would lose the opportunity to record this information. She lays out a fresh sheet of paper and dips her quill. “When were you chosen?”

“One full paksha ago,” he answers dutifully.

“So the same day as I, exactly fourteen nights.” She speaks and writes at the same time. “And how did you know to find me here?”

“I told you, the Stone drew me to you. You will not believe the scale of the task before us, Princess Zeb-un-Nissa, as we endeavor to save the world.” The boy braves a step toward her. “Although I confess, I am surprised you do not remember me.”

She adjusts her dupatta and looks at him more closely.

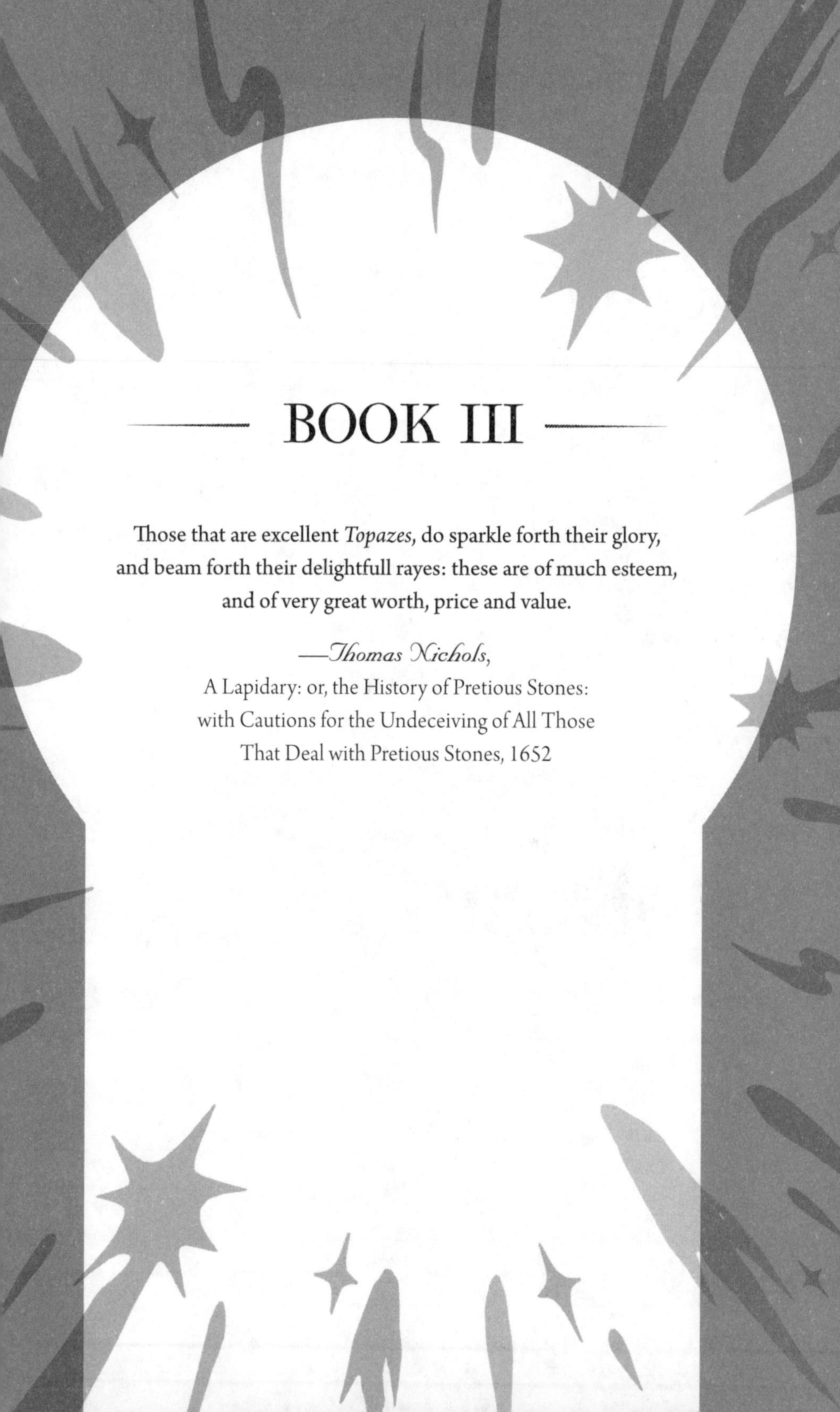

BOOK III

Those that are excellent *Topazes*, do sparkle forth their glory, and beam forth their delightfull rayes: these are of much esteem, and of very great worth, price and value.

—*Thomas Nichols,*
A Lapidary: or, the History of Pretious Stones: with Cautions for the Undeceiving of All Those That Deal with Pretious Stones, 1652

CHAPTER 1

REED AND CO MEET YELLOW

Reed battled a surge of class panic. The journey to find the Yellow Bearer culminated in a mansion on a sweeping cul-de-sac at the end of a long, rambling road. Underscored by the soft murmur of a creek that fed into the bay, it made for an effortlessly unaffordable, picturesque pastoral.

"Something about this place—it's familiar." Alejandra swung out of the saddle, her knee-high suede boots landing on the grass with an equestrian's grace. "As if I've been here before."

"Maybe you're developing another power, like déjà vu?" Reed eyed the grassy ground from his saddle with trepidation. Was it more embarrassing to fail another dismount or wait for Mr. Shaw's help?

"Or maybe I just partied here so hard that the rest is a blur." She stroked her horse's mane with more affection than Reed had ever witnessed her showing a human creature.

"Power-ups usually remain within the original domain, such as Reed's Empathy evolving into Orchestration." Mr. Shaw dismounted his steed. "It's difficult to imagine Alejandra would evolve a psychic ability when her Potentia originated in body modification." He extended Reed a hand.

Reed slowly extricated himself from his saddle with Mr. Shaw's help and without face-kissing the ground, as he had the last two times. He took it as a win.

A gentle wind rustled the crab apple trees where they tied the horses. Alejandra found sugar cubes in the saddle packs, and fed them to the whinnying creatures. They nuzzled their thanks.

How did she even know to look for them? Or that horses liked sugar cubes? Reed thought.

Just yesterday, in the new hotel where they'd taken refuge after fleeing JoAnne, Alejandra had performed Locatio on her first go. The next morning, Mr. Shaw had instructed a rickshaw to a stable on the outskirts of Washington, DC, where he procured three magnificent chestnut browns. Soon, they were riding east of Annapolis on the other side of Chesapeake Bay. Reed's running mental tab of the cost of the trip was reaching astronomical heights.

Mr. Shaw had spent the beginning of the journey telling Reed and Alejandra what little he knew about JoAnne. "She's originally from a suburb outside Boston but was on a trip with her parents to the Middle East during the Pass Ten manifestation."

"Was she like this then?" Alejandra asked.

"She always had a rebellious spirit, certainly, but not like this. Something happened to JoAnne after the Pass Ten Bearers sealed the Pentacle Portal. Something unprecedented. According to the other Bearers, she and her Stone simply . . . vanished. Of course, Father investigated but could not come up with a single credible theory. The investigation was limited, as well, since only Bearers can travel into the Pentagon Chamber. After she attacked us in Asbury Park, I asked Father to reopen the investigation. The Price of her Potentia was short-term psychosis, manifesting in hallucinations and paranoid fantasies. We believe she may be stuck in a permanent delusion, a Glamour of her own making. I'm sorry I don't have more information for you, but again, I'd rather not peddle more theories without substantial proof. The Pass Ten Bearers have been simply devastated by this turn, as you can imagine."

"And will we meet them?" Reed asked. "In a transgenerational, heartwarming holiday special?"

"Of course," Mr. Shaw said. "Traditionally, we wait for all five Bearers to be assembled before introducing them to the ones from the previous Pass. In some very rare instances, such as Passes Six and Nine, Bearers have been able to meet their predecessors from two Passes back as well!"

The trickiest part of the journey was navigating the traffic on the bridge that took them over Kent Island. Under Mr. Shaw's guidance, Reed employed a new variation of his Orchestration: crowd control. His ruby became a radio tower, broadcasting placating pulses of calm to everyone in range. The commuters on the William Preston Lane Jr. Memorial Bridge regarded the three horseback riders as everyday events, certainly not worthy of alerting the authorities, or even posting about on social media.

Blue had led them with absolute certainty the entire way. Reed didn't begrudge Ale picking up Locatio on her first go, only how blasé she had been about it. She was equally cool when presented with her horse, since she'd "learned to ride" when she was eight. Nobody "learned to ride" where Reed came from. And if they did, they'd have the decency to complete the phrase with its direct object. From the moment she first leaped onto her horse's saddle to now that the journey was over, Ale had conducted herself with a Mr. Shaw level of equestrian proficiency.

Once Mr. Shaw had secured all three horses to the crab apple trees, they approached the mansion. They passed the house's sweeping front lawn, bushes, and shrubbery, all perfectly manicured, like servants awaiting orders. Ground-to-ceiling windows ran the length of the mansion's first two floors, boasting rooms right out of an Ethan Allen catalog. An infinity pool that merged with the murmuring creek connected the main property to a guest cottage. Two boats bobbed lazily against the small whitewood pier. Even Reed knew this kind of waterside property had to cost some serious green. His stomach sank as he came to terms that the Yellow Bearer would be closer in class to Ale's than his own.

Maybe they'll be someone who works on this property, Reed hoped/prayed, *rather than someone who actually lives here.*

"So we approach together, yes?" Ale asked.

"I do think that's for the best," Mr. Shaw said. "Especially with only a little over a month until the Ikeda reaches closest approach."

Reed said nothing. His near failure to recruit Ale still stung. What if she hadn't accidentally sapphired herself and needed his help? What if he'd failed to persuade her to join the team?

Maybe this was exactly what great leadership was: getting your ego out of the way so that the job got done, regardless of who did it. Or how. Getting the Yellow Bearer to join up was the goal. The "how" was less important.

The three of them reviewed the plan as they walked the gravel path that snaked over the property's front lawn to its front door. Mr. Shaw would give the pitch. Alejandra would sapphire herself to prove they were for real. Reed would provide backup when necessary.

The house was quiet—so quiet that Reed would've assumed it was empty if not for the Jeep parked in front. He wrapped his fingers around the circular comfort of

Red. Was he receiving new sensations from his Stone because they were so close to Yellow? Or was Reed's mind playing tricks on him?

Mr. Shaw pressed the doorbell. F–A–G–C, the Westminster Chime Melody rang. C–G–A–F.

After a few unanswered moments, Mr. Shaw pressed the doorbell again. This time, Reed felt a distinct presence stir inside. They heard the unrushed strides of bare feet across the floor.

He answered the door wearing only a towel looped around his waist, beads of water still clinging to his lean, muscular body like jealous lovers. "Almada?"

"Dios mío." The edge in Alejandra's voice was sharper than a blade. "Hello, Hikaru."

"I know whereof I speak: Peregrination remains the greatest mystery among the forms after Benediction. But how shall we discover its many uses without more tragical accidents?"

James de la Shaw
Provost, Pass Two

CHAPTER 2
ALEJANDRA CONSIDERA

Reed and I watched, slack-jawed, in the game room of what turned out to be his family's second weekend house, as Hikaru's hummingbird of a topaz flew around his fingers. Unlike Reed's circular Stone or my perfect square, Hikaru's topaz was round on one side and tapered to a single point on the other, like a teardrop.

"Do you recall how you unlocked the Feat of Petrakinesis?" Señor Shaw asked for the second time.

"Dunno, dude." Hikaru's topaz landed on the tip of his outstretched tongue and spun like a top. "Just happened." His Stone had a more transparent quality than mine or Reed's, as if it were made of light.

"Check this out." He snapped and pointed his fingers, a magician performing a trick, and Yellow abruptly flew straight at my heart.

Someone else, like Reed, might have yelped. But I refused to give Hikaru the satisfaction. I simply stared the golden bullet down until it decelerated and hovered at my chest. "One more centimeter and I will demonstrate my power in all its impaling glory." I cracked my knuckles. "On you."

"Chill out, Almada."

I tried to swat his Stone. But it flitted like a fly, one step ahead of me.

"What else have you been able to do?" Señor Shaw typed on his tablet keyboard in what he thought was a discreet fashion. "Besides the Feat of Petrakinesis, that is?"

"That's it. So far."

Hikaru had let us in and thrown on a pair of pastel yellow Chubbies that landed halfway down his thighs. No shirt in sight. His muscles stretched taut over a lean frame from years of fencing and rugby. He looked like a Ralph Lauren model. Not that I would ever admit that to him.

Half-clothed, he had led us past the living room, with its overglossy white grand piano, and the dining room, which was set up to serve a dozen of his friends should they happen to stop by for dinner unannounced. We settled in the game room, complete with poker and billiards tables.

Hikaru sprawled himself on the pool table, legs dangling off the side. I sat in an overstuffed club chair next to Reed, who alternated between trying not to gawk over Hikaru's house and trying not to gawk over his physique. For someone who specialized in reading others' feelings, Reed had such little gift for concealing his own.

Señor Shaw launched into his rehearsed speech. "You found a topaz ten days ago." The zeal in Señor Shaw's eyes shone as bright as one of our Stones. "A valuable Stone that you told no one about, that you've kept on your body since."

Hikaru answered by silently willing his topaz to slip out of his pocket. It floated a few feet in front of his face, allowing itself to be admired.

"Hear me, all Chancellors and Provosts back to the first Pass." Señor Shaw's hands met at his forehead, in front of his third eye. "I vow to mentor the Five Stone Bearers and to teach them the Feat of Terminatio, which will seal the Pentacle Portal. Yellow, the third Stone, the Stone of the Illuminator, all this I say unto you."

When he finished, he told Hikaru about the Portal, the Stones, and how we were going to save the world. To his credit, Hikaru only interrupted with the occasional clarification question. For the most part, he simply listened. I had never witnessed him so silent.

As Señor Shaw spoke, I realized why this house looked familiar. I had seen it on the social media feed of my friends attending Hikaru's notorious weekend ragers. Images of Lucía and M. in various states of undress laughing in the pool and Jacuzzi scrolled through my mind. I had been invited, of course. But something about being a guest of Hikaru's felt like an invitation for my very own #MeToo moment.

I am not someone who takes unnecessary chances. In combat, I assess and calculate required risk versus potential reward. That is why I was still surprised, sometimes, that I had joined Reed on this fantastical adventure. But something about him outside the Lincoln Memorial, about his open eyes and heart and face, made me trust. I also believe it's what mi zafira wanted.

The truth is, my relationship to the Stone was fascinating, subtle, and mysterious. Since we had found each other, we had become inseparable. More than ten meters, and waves of nausea rippled through my body. I looked at mi zafira looking back at me, her square facets sparkling in the afternoon light. I usually preferred circular cuts, but I would not change a single thing about my square zafira. Her carved facade contained thousands of facets, each sparkle shifting with the slightest movement. She was mine and I was hers and we were each other's. Siempre.

How would Hikaru respond to being outed, as Reed had outed me on Sunday? Would I have responded differently if Señor Shaw and Reed had approached me together, as we had Hikaru? And how had Hikaru stumbled upon Petrakinesis? What would his Potentia be? Most important: if he joined, how soon before he did something that would make me want to kill him?

Maybe Hikaru would be different here, off the piste and out of school. I supposed we were going to have to find a way to get along. I wanted to find his silence hopeful, but my nature was to be en garde.

Señor Shaw finished by telling Hikaru about JoAnne. "She is crazed with a desire to stop us. To what end? Who knows. The motivation of villains is always a bit of a mystery to me. And to anybody who writes for the Marvel Cinematic Universe, apparently." Señor Shaw and Reed chuckled at what I imagined was a joke. "But that's what makes your joining us and leading us to Green all the more important."

"Don't worry, Shaw. I'm sure we can come up with a mutually beneficial sitch." Hikaru called Yellow to him and swung at it with an imaginary bat. Upon "impact," it arced up to the ceiling, in the center of the room.

Yellow refracted and reflected the sun in glorious ways, a chandelier sending sparkle into every corner.

It did dazzle.

"Of course, the simple words of Relinquo cannot solely be responsible for the transfer of the bond of the Stone from one Bearer to another (look at Appendix E for all relevant instances). Is it, perhaps then, another instance of the Stones' tapping into the Bearers' sentience?"

Hortense de la Shaw
Chancellor, Pass Six

CHAPTER 3

ALEJANDRA ACEPTA A HIKARU

What unnerved me most about the Feat of Petrakinesis is that it appeared as if Hikaru's topaz was its own sentient entity, with curiosity, desire, and intent. His Stone twirled and twinkled, our very own Tinker Bell.

"So what's your superpower?" Hikaru sat up, legs dangling off the billiards table.

"Empathy." Reed tried to melt into his club chair.

"I feel for people, too, brah."

"Reed can read people's emotions." Señor Shaw stepped in to aid Reed, squirming under Hikaru's gaze.

"Awesome. I'm gonna think of a number." Hikaru tapped his head. "Let's see if he can guess it."

"It's not a parlor trick, Hikaru." Señor Shaw pronounced the name with the correct Japanese inflection, emphasizing the first syllable sharply and rounding out the final vowel. "Even if it were, that's not the way it works. Reed can intuit what emotions individuals are really feeling, sometimes even unknown to them. And he's learning how to project and control emotions as well."

"I get it!" Hikaru tossed a billiard ball in the air. "That must be awesome with the ladies, am I right?"

"Oh—no, Hikaru." Reed was suddenly animated, shrugging off his discomfort like a cumbersome winter jacket. "That wouldn't work because a) it would totally violate consent and b) I've been out since middle school, so . . . you know?"

"That's cool, man." Hikaru continued tossing the billiard ball, unfazed. Did he consciously reach for the yellow number one, or was it just coincidence, like his wearing canary-yellow shorts now? "I mean, who hasn't sucked some D, am I right, Almada?"

Obviously, I did not respond.

"I just want you to know, I'm cool with it, bruh." Hikaru tossed the billiard ball at Reed, who caught it with surprising agility. "And when we're in battle and you need someone with real muscle, I got your back."

"Your Potentia has manifested?" Señor Shaw propped open his tablet, hands poised for more furious typing.

"Dude, not yet."

"Then . . ."

"We got an empath and Almada's bod mod. Next thing the team needs is some muscle." Hikaru rolled billiard balls against the banks, as unconcerned with the stakes of the conversation as if he were discussing his next vacation. "I'm thinking Hulk, or maybe swap over to a Deadpool track and splice some re-gen in there."

"How do you know my Potentia?" I asked him.

"Because the point of my Franchini broke when I flicked you, Almada. I'm sending you the bill, by the way." Hikaru pivoted to Señor Shaw. "Are the powers always so on the nose?"

"What do you mean?"

"Almada's always been cold and hard af."

Instead of responding verbally, I visualized my blood blue. It chilled through my veins as I extended, covering the meters between me and Hikaru like a retractable bridge spans a chasm. My sapphire fingers wrapped around his throat.

"Once I get my superstrength, I'll bust out of something like this ka-pow!" If Hikaru was scared, he did not show it. "But until then . . ." Hikaru blinked, and Yellow flew between my eyes. It emitted a blinding flash of light, shattering my concentration and allowing him to escape my clutches.

"And when did you learn to do that?" Señor Shaw asked Hikaru.

"Just now." Hikaru sounded only slightly surprised. "Pretty lit, huh?"

"Yes." Señor Shaw's fingers flew over his tablet keyboard. "Pretty lit, indeed."

As the red and black splotches clouding my vision faded, I looked for Reed. He was already by my side, Red in hand.

"Just like we practiced, okay?" He placed his Stone-clenched fist into my palm, and I wrapped my hand around it. His calmness flowed through me. Was it cheating?

Maybe. Did I hope to be able to do this myself one day? Of course. But for now, I would let myself rely on Red. And Reed.

Cuernavaca. Hibiscus. Peacocks. Pomegranates.

My turquoise earrings tingled in concert with my zafira.

Centimeter by centimeter, my sapphiric appendage retracted and reverted.

"I'm sure you have questions for me, Hikaru," Señor Shaw said, "about how to extricate yourself from your life and family so that you can join us, about what you're going to tell your parents, et cetera. But time is, as they say, of the essence. I've summoned our barge, which we'll use as an HQ until you've mastered the Feat of Locatio to lead us to Green. So I'd recommend—"

"—what're we called?" Hikaru interrupted.

"Excuse me?"

"We need an epic name that'll instill terror in JoAnne and whatever other foes dare to stand in our path." Hikaru sat up, abs rippling as they contracted. "Also for marketing and merch."

"You do remember"—Señor Shaw smiled—"that the key to my family's success has been staying in the shadows, right?"

"Your family can do whatever it wants, Shaw. But if I've got to drop out of junior year, schools are going to have questions." He ricocheted billiard balls against the banks of the table. "No reason not to make it into a résumé piece."

My arm slowly, achingly, had almost finished its restoration. Internal gears that should not be there turned and grinded against one another. I clenched my teeth so that Hikaru would not hear me groan against the pain.

"Really, when you think about it, there's no reason we should be doing any of this covertly." Hikaru got up from the pool table and walked over to the fully stocked oak bar. He poured himself a beer. He did not ask any of us if we wanted a beverage. "I'm sure Reed can tell us all about the joys and benefits of coming out, am I right?"

Reed opened his mouth, but I arched an eyebrow, and he shut it. I would have to teach Reed: most of the time, responding to Hikaru was a mistake.

"All of us should come out to build public support and a social media presence." Hikaru turned to me. "Almada, how many followers do you have?"

"Forty K," I managed to spit out over the lingering pain.

"See?" He took a sip from the heavy crystal beer mug. "Think about how much easier it would be to recruit Green if we've already got some cred. In fact, Green might even reach out to us! We'd skip Locatio altogether and—spoiler alert—

that way I could keep using tech. Why would I voluntarily give myself that major handicap?"

"I think the word you're looking for is 'obstacle,'" Reed muttered.

"Sure, bruh. Whatever."

Was Hikaru being facetious? It was so hard to tell.

"Son, the Muraqqa is very clear about protocol." Señor Shaw continued to smile, but his voice was tighter than my hand had just been on Hikaru's throat. "This strategy has proved successful for over three hundred years."

"That's exactly my point," Hikaru insisted. "The last time the Bearers were assembled, Reagan was in the White House, you still bought tunes on CDs—or was it cassettes?—laptops were a fantasy, and the idea of the internet would've been as ridiculous as the story you just told me. Why aren't we evolving with the times?"

"You raise many interesting points, I admit." Señor Shaw snapped shut his tablet and placed it in his leather satchel. "I look forward to discussing them back at the barge."

Hikaru took a swig of his beer, then squared off with Señor Shaw. They were the same height, but Señor Shaw had a few kilos of muscle on him. "Shaw, I'm used to being recruited. POC who doesn't need financial aid and could qualify for the Olympics in two different sports? Oxford, U of Tokyo, and Harvard have been knocking on my door since before high school. I know when I'm keeping it 100. And since I'm pretty sure you can't do this without me, I'm feeling pretty GOAT right now."

"You're feeling like a pretty goat right now?" Señor Shaw asked, perplexed.

"Greatest of All Time," Reed and I explained in unison.

Señor Shaw and Hikaru continued to face off the way only two machos could. I was reminded of how little our species has evolved.

"Reed," I broke the silence, "do you think they should just whip them out and see who is the bigger?"

"Straight guys." Reed shook his head.

"Straight-ish guys," Hikaru corrected him, still holding his ground.

"Reed," Señor Shaw addressed him without looking away from Hikaru. "How would you recommend we proceed?"

"Isn't that interesting?" Hikaru jumped in before Reed could respond. "Almost like he's trying to signal you to do something, Reed. I wonder what that could be?"

Red lay in Reed's palm, twinkling like a secret.

"I'm not going to front like I could stop you from Orchestrating me, Reed."

Hikaru and Señor Shaw were so close to each other now they could kiss. "And if you're any good, I probably won't even realize you're doing it. Who knows—maybe you already have? But how would you live with yourself if you did, when just a few minutes ago you said you'd never violate someone's consent? Hashtag MeToo, right, bruh?"

Reed didn't move. But his Stone went dull.

"You're right, Hikaru." Señor Shaw finally broke the standoff by extending a hand in peace. "My job as the Provost is to help the Bearers in whatever way I can. Join us, and we'll figure out the rest—social media, press, endorsements, whatever you want. The only thing that matters to me is that we seal the Pentacle Portal. I will make any sacrifice necessary to that end."

Hikaru clasped the extended hand and pumped it heartily. "I'm so glad we're on the same page, Mr. Shaw."

"An especially brief assemblage window, marked by geographic proximity, permitted the Bearers, especially Red and Purple, to play a pivotal role in the signing of the Treaty of Kyakhta. I will complete a more thorough analysis, after the Portal has been sealed, citing the factors that made this diplomatic feat possible. Having turned my thoughts for many years upon this important subject, however, one cannot help but wonder how much prodigious Good we could accomplish with the Bearers between Passes."

Bayard de la Shaw
Provost, Pass Three

CHAPTER 4

REED AND CO ON THE BARGE

Like a recalcitrant Hollywood star, Hikaru's topaz resisted all attempts to be photographed. As did all the Stones. But that didn't stop him from trying. Again. And again. And again. Reed couldn't help but admire his persistence.

"I still can't believe none of them show up!" Hikaru scrolled through the third set of pics he'd taken of the Bearers posing with the Stones.

"Like vampires?" It wasn't that Reed enjoyed Hikaru's frustration. Relished was more like it. Reed also couldn't help relishing the schadenfreude of Hikaru's frustration.

"The Muraqqa hypothesizes that precious metals are anathema to the Stones." To his credit, Mr. Shaw answered the question evenly, without any hint of the growing tension between them. "Perhaps their presence in the technology is the issue?"

"'Metals used in smartphone construction,'" Hikaru read from his screen, "'include copper, zinc, gold, platinum, and sometimes exotic alloys such as rare earth and germanium.'"

"I wish I had more information for you, son. I'd be happy to review that chapter in the Muraqqa with you after you complete Locatio." Mr. Shaw, at Hikaru's insistence, had emailed him the Muraqqa and provided a printed copy for Reed and Alejandra. But since most of it was written in Farsi, it did little to satisfy Reed's curiosity.

"It didn't occur to any of the Provosts to work out an English translation?" Reed flipped through the pages.

"Check your privilege, Reed," Mr. Shaw said. "Although the Stones surface within a few hundred kilometers of one another, they can appear anywhere in the world. The savannas of Africa. The Arctic ice cap. The archipelagos of Indonesia. We couldn't possibly translate it into every language."

"Spanish, Mandarin Chinese, and English would still be a pretty good place to start." Alejandra had barely flipped through her copy. "In that order."

"If the three of you are done with your glamour shots, perhaps Hikaru and I could focus on Locatio." Mr. Shaw bowed his head with faux deference. "But only if your schedule permits, of course."

It had been almost a full week since the party of four had boarded the barge. Much to everyone's surprise, Hikaru emailed his parents exactly what had happened. "I don't see why I'd lie about it," he'd responded after Mr. Shaw suggested several more clandestine approaches.

Later, Reed confessed to Alejandra that it made him wonder why he hadn't done the same. Sure, the story sounded far-fetched, but wasn't honesty the best policy? Ale nodded but didn't say anything. Typical.

The last six days had been the first leisurely part of the quest. They each had their own room on the barge, although Hikaru and Ale had been less impressed with their accommodations than Reed had been. They also resented having to do their own cooking and cleaning. The rotating crew of three who captained the tugboat ate, slept, and worked entirely on their vessel, and the Bearers had no interaction with them.

Mr. Shaw moved between tugboat and barge, but the Bearers were restricted to the barge itself, to protect the tugboat machinery from Disjunctis. The plumbing on the barge was rigged manually, and a twenty-pound propane gas tank powered their stovetop and oven, which they used actual wooden matches to light.

The day was divided into three sections. In the morning, Mr. Shaw trained them in combat using drones as teaching assistants. Ale and Hikaru easily outperformed Reed in this arena, as the bruises on his arms and legs testified.

In the afternoon, Mr. Shaw trained them individually: Hikaru on the Feat of Locatio, Ale and Reed in their Potentias.

After dinner, they worked as a group again on secondary Feats, such as Petrakinesis. "*Petra,* from the Greek word for stone, from which of course we also get petrification," Mr. Shaw lectured. "And *kinesis,* for movement. The Muraqqa dictates that we only teach secondary Feats after the primaries have been mastered. But since Hikaru has already stumbled upon this one . . ."

The trick, Hikaru explained, was not to overthink it. To use the least amount of mental energy possible. To assume the Stone would do your bidding. To take it for granted.

"No wonder it came so easily to you," Alejandra responded, earning a satisfying guffaw from Reed.

Mr. Shaw demonstrated the movements to unlock the Feat, which consisted entirely of hand, finger, and wrist gestures.

Reed and Ale both picked it up in a jiff. Hikaru was still the most adept, but by Day Five, Red and Blue were hang gliding curves like paper airplanes.

This week reminded Reed, in many ways, of the quarantined years of the pandemic. Of course, Tween Reed had had the company of his laptop, tablet, cell phone, gaming console, and TV. Surviving the lockdown without those companions seemed unfathomable. But to his surprise, he barely missed any of them. The training consumed him.

Before bed, they'd read something from the heavy, built-in oak bookcases in the barge's library. Without artificial lights or screens, they were usually asleep by 10 PM. Reed fell asleep exhausted and satisfied.

As they neared the end of that week, Hikaru still hadn't completed the Feat of Locatio. Nor did he show any anxiety about it.

"Sure, we can try searching for Green again," Hikaru responded, as if Mr. Shaw had suggested poached instead of scrambled eggs for breakfast. "But after lunch, we'll spend more time trying to pin those Stones down. I've scribbled up letters of sponsorship." Hikaru had a way of talking that made Reed feel like he worked for him. "My mom can get these to the CEOs of Nike and Adidas—I'm thinking bidding war, I'm thinking brand placement, and then I'm thinking we won't have to travel"—he gestured to their current surroundings—"like Palestinian refugees."

Reed tried not to choke on his blueberry muffin.

"However we can be of assistance, Yellow Bearer." Mr. Shaw's tone wasn't sarcastic, exactly. But it certainly wasn't genuine. In front of Reed and Alejandra, Mr. Shaw and Hikaru behaved civilly. But behind closed doors, their emotions flared like gasoline-drenched torches.

Reed and Ale didn't need to eavesdrop to know what the fights were about. Mr. Shaw accused Hikaru of intentionally failing the Feat of Locatio. Hikaru accused Mr. Shaw of withholding information that would let them go public with the Stones.

The week was, otherwise, productive. Reed learned some basic hand-to-hand and dodging techniques, and Ale learned to restore herself without Reed's help. Each transformation, however, left an additional sliver of sapphire on her body. Mr. Shaw offered many theories about how the length of transformation may relate to the size of the slivers, possible techniques for reversing the process, and its long-term cumulative effects. But until he had more data, he had instructed her to abstain from transformation unless a life-or-death situation presented itself. As much as Reed dreaded his mind trap hangovers, he knew he was lucky compared with Ale's Price.

Politely but firmly, Mr. Shaw denied Hikaru's repeated requests to attempt the Feat of Potentia before completing Locatio. Hikaru was so desperate he even asked Ale for help.

"No sé, Hikaru," she always replied. "I don't know how I discovered my Potentia. It just happened. Like you and Petrakinesis."

He also tried to enlist Reed, but Reed knew better than to take a side in this emerging power struggle. With Mr. Shaw's blessing, however, Reed did offer to help Hikaru unlock the Feat of Locatio.

"I don't want you inside my head," Hikaru responded. "And I don't think you could handle what you might find poking around in there. So no entry, brah, got it?"

Mr. Shaw used Reed's private training sessions to determine if his Potentia worked on animals—specifically, the birds flying overhead and the creatures living in the bay. So far, Reed hadn't had any luck with fish, crabs, or other shellfish. But he'd made some progress with the river otters. Mr. Shaw theorized that the more sophisticated the animal, the more success Reed would have. Dolphins, apparently, also inhabited the bay, although they'd yet to spot any.

Late in the afternoon of the sixth day on the barge, as the setting sun lit up the sky in pink and lavender sherbet swirls, Hikaru and Mr. Shaw got into their most heated argument. Reed and Ale gave up pretending they couldn't hear them yelling from the tugboat, where Hikaru had taken to following Mr. Shaw. The fight ended with Hikaru stomping back to the barge.

"That dude is just so full of himself," Hikaru growled in frustration. "So sure that his way is the best way."

"It must be muy difícil for you to imagine what that is like," Alejandra deadpanned as she worked her way through a series of fencing forms, the tip of her épée darting through the air like the Yaka Arrow.

"What were you two"—Reed searched for the most diplomatic word—"discussing?"

"I don't think he actually needs me to perform Locatio to discover Green." Hikaru considered before continuing. "I think he can do it with his technology. So I was like, 'Eff you and eff Locatio. Let's get to Potentia already!'"

"Your struggle bores me." Ale tapped her épée against the floor three times. "Marksman H," she called out to Reed.

Reed willed his Stone to her. She continued to practice, using Red as a target. Reed hadn't yet mastered Hikaru's grace, but he was able to Petrakinesis his Stone just quickly enough to avoid most of her jabs, slashes, and thrusts.

"Once I skip Locatio and unlock my Potentia"—Hikaru pumped a fist up in the classic Superman pose—"I'll be able to use technology, and then I can—you know—"

"Save the world?" Reed supplied.

"—be set."

"Hikaru, it doesn't seem like your family's exactly hurting in the financial department." Reed spoke slowly, struggling to split his focus between talking to Hikaru and Ale's target practice. "Why do you care so much about making a fortune?"

"Because I want to show my folks that I don't need them." Yellow slowly circled Hikaru's sculpted forearm. "Besides, we're giving up weeks of our life, school, friends, family—why not get something back?"

"Besides knowing we did the right thing?"

Hikaru scoffed as a flock of birds flew overhead in a V-shape formation.

"Ospreys, probably in their spring migration." Hikaru leaned against the rail of the barge, letting the wind rustle his hair. Reed found him most beautiful like this, slightly undone. "So, Ale—tell me again how you powered up."

"It just happened." Ale landed two consecutive hits on Red. "No sé, güey."

"Why does everything sound better in Spanish?" Reed asked.

"No lo sé." Ale smiled.

A boat glided by them, sails arched like a drawn bow. Reed returned the exuberant waving. Ale and Hikaru didn't bother.

"What's 'these precious Stones' in Japanese, Hikaru?" Reed asked.

"I don't fuckin' know. Ask someone who speaks Japanese."

"Sorry, I thought . . ."

"Yes, my folks are from Japan." Hikaru spoke with the practiced air of delivering a much-repeated speech. "But I was born in the good ol' US of A. I grew up in the US of A. I'm as American as apple pie, baseball, and colonialism. Don't let my eyes fool you. And don't even get me started on how the Asian guy just happened to get chosen by the Yellow Stone. It's like Power Rangers–level racism." The wind picked up. "I've never seen you work without your jacket and plate, Almada." Hikaru admired her form unapologetically. "Fetching."

Ale neither responded nor acknowledged him as she continued training.

"Okay, guys." Hikaru turned and walked away. "I'll catch you later."

"Are you going somewhere?" Ale actually stopped her training.

"I'm gonna take the motorboat into town."

"Um, does Mr. Shaw know?" Reed asked.

"'Um, does Mr. Shaw know?'" Hikaru imitated and exaggerated the anxiety of Reed's cadence by pitching his voice up. "When're you gonna start thinking for yourself, man?"

A few moments later, they heard the plunk of the motorboat dropping on the bay and its engine roar to life. Hikaru disappeared into the setting sun.

Reed and Ale ate a silent dinner of pasta and jarred red sauce that night without Mr. Shaw. Even though Hikaru's privilege grated on him like an out-of-tune piano, Reed keenly felt his absence that evening. Reed and Ale retired to their bedrooms even earlier than usual.

He woke up a few times, REM sleep eluding him like a complicated guitar riff. When he finally got up the next morning, Hikaru still hadn't returned.

"Aren't you worried?" Reed asked Mr. Shaw and Ale over cold cereal and fruit.

"He's probably booked himself into the Four Seasons to enjoy some proper room service." Ale poked with disdain at the breakfast Mr. Shaw had assembled. "And is working on a new marketing plan for The Five."

"The Five?" Reed shuddered. "Sounds like a Math Olympiad team."

"I'm sorry breakfast wasn't to your liking, Señorita Almada." Mr. Shaw cleared the dishes. "I'll pass your complaints along to the chef."

Ale arched an eyebrow but didn't respond.

They spent the day training. Ale was in an especially foul mood. Nothing was safe from her criticism: the sparsity of their accommodations, the humidity of the day, the sounds the birds made as they screeched overhead. Mr. Shaw interpreted each criticism as a personal attack. Reed tried to placate both but only succeeded in aggravating them further.

Even in the short time that Hikaru had been part of the party, its dynamics had adjusted to accommodate him. Now that he was gone, the group wobbled unevenly, like a lopsided stool.

Half an hour before sunset, in the midst of their first Synergia training session, a drone appeared in the distance, flying directly toward the barge.

Mr. Shaw slipped on his power gauntlet. "Behind me," he instructed Alejandra and Reed. They obeyed, but Ale's arm was already expanding and flattening into a tower shield.

The drone arced toward them lazily.

Mr. Shaw released a charge from the glowing orb in his palm, zapping the drone out of the sky. It plummeted into the water below.

"Makes you really understand 'Don't shoot the messenger.'" Reed leaned over the rail to spot the floating drone.

"Should I salvage it?" Ale asked.

"Have you seen the state of that water?" Mr. Shaw asked. "Dreadful."

Using the control panel in his gauntlet, Mr. Shaw maneuvered two of his drones to fish out the fallen one. An envelope in a sealed plastic bag was attached to its underbelly.

"McKeldin Square. Tuesday, 8 PM. Red and Blue Bearers alone. If you ever want to see the Yellow Bearer again."

"Is there any credence to the belief that cold iron repels or harms ghosts, fairies, witches, and other malevolent supernatural creatures? The following is my dissertation on the evolution of this superstition, and more specifically, my theorems for how precious metals interact with the Stones."

Bayard de la Shaw,
Chancellor, Pass Four

CHAPTER 5

LAS PREGUNTAS DE ALEJANDRA

I immediately performed the Feat of Locatio. "Is there any reason it would not work again?" Shoulder blades tensed. Rotate, angle, and extend, Blue cradled in my clenched fist, turquoise earrings tingling.

Señor Shaw scrambled to produce his tablet, and projected a map of our surroundings.

The azul beam of light, however, roamed over the image without stopping, an errant spotlight searching for its star. Mr. Shaw expanded the map. He shrank it. We even had Reed perform the Feat. When he finally got it right (third try, imagine), Red found me immediately. So why couldn't I find Yellow?

"JoAnne must be shielding the Stone." Señor Shaw scrolled through his tablet. "It's been theorized that calibrating a cage made of precious metals with electricity can cloak the Stones."

"Theorized?" I dropped my extended arms and abandoned the Feat. "Why do we have so many theories and so few facts?" I wanted to know what to do. Especially since the life of a teammate was at stake.

"JoAnne must've captured Hikaru last night, after he left the safety of the barge." Señor Shaw sat at the long wooden worktable that dominated the far side of his quarters. Tools and gadgets piled high around him. He dissected the messenger drone, looking for clues. Reed examined the letter. I moved through fencing forms. It helped me focus.

"I would chastise the two of you for not stopping him, but we all know that someone as full of beans as Hikaru does what he wants." Señor Shaw accidentally zapped himself and cursed in a language I did not recognize.

"How did she find him?" I slammed my fist against the wall of Señor Shaw's immaculately kept quarters. It would have been more satisfying if I had sapphired first.

"Perhaps Hikaru attempted to go public with the Stones? That would have made it easier for JoAnne to track him. But I accept responsibility for all this." Señor Shaw buried his face in his hands. "I should've never let him out of my sight, even if it meant keeping him prisoner here."

"Mr. Shaw, you can't blame yourself," Reed said gently.

I do not think Reed was using his Potentia, either to read Señor Shaw or to soothe him, but lately, he was playing the empath regardless. It was somewhere between annoying and very annoying.

"Thank you, Reed." Señor Shaw smiled, but the worry continued to crease his face. "What we must do now is devise a plan to rescue Hikaru as quickly as possible. I can't risk sending you two into what is clearly a trap."

"Why do you think she's waiting so long?" Reed held the note up to the light.

"Only five days." Lunge. Lunge. Feint.

"Sure." Reed closed his eyes, thinking. "But that gives us five days to prepare. To search. Why not tell us to meet tomorrow?"

"This is an excellent question, Reed." Señor Shaw connected the drone's central processing unit to his tablet. "Hypotheses?"

"Maybe the trap she's laying for us takes a few days to prepare?" Reed lit up like a prize pupil with something to prove.

"Strong theory. Another?" Señor Shaw replaced one of the cables, using the smallest of screwdrivers.

"She's doing something to Hikaru." Red slowly circled Reed's head, a moon orbiting a planet. "Turning him against us? Trying to steal his Stone? It's not possible to steal a Stone, is it, Mr. Shaw?"

"It is not." The eyepiece Señor Shaw was using to examine the drone's insides made him look like a cyberpunk jeweler. "During Pass Six, a hadjuk chieftain tried to steal Green, believing it simply an emerald of enormous value. The Stone neither transferred its power nor allowed itself to be taken."

"So if someone tried to take mi zafira . . . ?" I asked.

"It cannot physically be farther than 11.53 meters from you, give or take. That's almost thirty-eight feet," he added for Reed's benefit. "Watch."

Señor Shaw walked to the settee at the foot of his canopied bed and plucked my Stone out of the air. I squirmed, as if his hands were on my body. He left his quarters, getting as far as the deck. Blue refused to go any farther. Señor Shaw made a show of trying to move my Stone. He pulled. He pushed. He yanked. But mi zafira resisted, as if we were attached by an invisible, unbreakable chain. Señor Shaw could arc her around me. But she refused to increase the distance between us any farther.

"Okay—what if you put a Stone in the trunk of a car and tried to drive away?" Reed asked.

"Do you know how hard your Stones are?" Señor Shaw finally released Blue. "Sapphires, rubies, emeralds are close to a diamond's ten on the Mohs' scale. They would bore a hole through whatever tried to remove them."

I willed Blue back to me. This was the first time anyone else had laid hands on her. And, I vowed, the last. I yearned for a temazcal cleansing ritual. And not the kind they offer to gringos in Tulum. The real thing. The one mi citli would perform over the course of three days.

Señor Shaw returned to the dissected drone on his worktable. "The Stone can only be transferred when a Bearer enacts the Feat of Relinquo."

"So Hikaru could give me Yellow?" Reed asked.

"Not exactly, because you are already a Bearer, and nobody can bear two Stones. In that case, you would steward the Stone until you Relinquo'ed it to someone else."

"Maybe that's the plan: JoAnne is trying to get him to relinquish Yellow to her, or . . ." Reed trailed off.

". . . to someone she has groomed, loyal to her?" Señor Shaw finished, stroking his chin. "That's very interesting. And deeply nefarious."

"I hate to say this"—and I really did, but it needed to be asked, and it appeared as if the difficult task fell to me, again—"but what if JoAnne kills Hikaru?"

"Unfortunately, there is a precedent for this. Fortunately, I believe the precedent will protect Hikaru." Señor Shaw put down his tablet and turned to us. "In 1765, during Pass Four, First Purple was a concubine of Emperor Gaozong, the fourth Qing emperor to rule over China proper. A complex plot for her assassination had been planned months before she was chosen and enacted the day after the Bearers located her. When she was killed, Purple disappeared, only to manifest a few days later, bonded to Kiyohime, a Japanese peasant girl. The time it took for second selection seriously jeopardized the quest to seal the Pentacle Portal. Kiyohime, luckily, was preternaturally gifted and picked up Teleportare and Terminatio in record time.

"JoAnne learned all this during Pass Ten. So I suspect it's not in her best interest to kill Hikaru. If she did, she'd have no way of discovering the location of the new Yellow Bearer. Which supports Reed's theory that she is 'persuading' Hikaru to

Relinquo to someone of her choosing." Señor Shaw got up from the table, abandoning the drone altogether. "Which makes finding the Yellow Bearer all the more important. We have to act now, while his trail is still fresh. All rest, all training, all our work will be suspended until we save Hikaru!"

I was going to suggest that we go to Baltimore when Señor Shaw announced we were moving our headquarters there. "Don't bother packing," he told us. "Everything we need will be waiting for us."

Getting to the dock was our first challenge.

"The barge is too large to take us all the way into the Baltimore bay." Señor Shaw typed into his tablet as he spoke to us. "But fear not—arrangements are already being made."

We docked both the barge and the tugboat at an industrial park just outside Baltimore, where the Patapsco River opens up into the bay. A few rusty warehouses and cobalt sheds created an open bracket, enclosing the pier. It was quite well-maintained for being unpopulated. We had barely finished docking when a sailboat materialized on our port side, crewed by more of the androgynous, mute servants.

"It's so weird how they don't talk, isn't it?" Reed asked me.

I had not noticed.

I spent most of the trip protecting my hair, which was curly for the first time in years. Forget my phone, my tablet, my smartwatch. If I could choose any appliance to be excluded from Disjunctis, it would be a hair dryer. I had spent years blowing it straight to suppress my curls, an inheritance from mi abuela. I did not recognize myself in the mirror that first morning: a Medusa, frizzy tendrils framing my face like serpents. But after a few days, I stopped minding. Besides, I had to save the world. I did not have time to worry about how I looked.

The crew effortlessly and wordlessly worked the ropes and swinging sail, navigating us through the light of dusk. We disembarked at the docks of Baltimore thirty minutes later. Our Airbnb was a short walk from the pier: a first-floor industrial loft with concrete floors, porthole windows, and factory-height ceilings.

"Look." Señor Shaw handed us each a real, physical, three-dimensional key. "I chose an Airbnb instead of a hotel so you could come and go as you please. And we're on the first floor, so no elevator."

"See, Alejandra, I told you he cared," Reed sighed.

Señor Shaw took the master bedroom. Reed and I chose the next two largest, leaving the smallest for Hikaru. It was the only one without its own bathroom. "Serves him right for getting kidnapped," I said with a forced flippancy.

True to his word, Señor Shaw had taken care of everything. The loft was stocked with groceries, hygiene products, and more cargo pants and Henleys. Mental note: go shopping tomorrow. Despite Señor Shaw's instructions, I had brought my wallet, IDs, passport, and the few hundred I had stowed for emergencies. If I could get the salesperson to remove my credit card from my wallet, I should be able to avoid both Disjunctis and Señor Shaw's Communist ideas about what we should wear. The shade of blue was acceptable, but Henleys and cargo pants? No le creo.

A take-out dinner of fish and chips arrived a few minutes later. We ate as quickly as possible so we could begin searching for Hikaru.

The tall clock tower that loomed over the Baltimore docks showed a few minutes after 8 PM. Living without electricity had changed me. The first few days on the barge, I went through classic withdrawal. Just like when I tried to give up coffee last Lent. Anxiety, compulsions, even cold sweats. Was I losing social media followers? What trends had passed me by? I kept reaching for the phone in my pocket, forgetting it was not there. When I slept, I dreamed of screens. I had not realized it was an addiction.

But my mind and soul adjusted, and then a peace settled in. Could I choose to retain this serenity after we sealed the Portal? Would I consider joining the Luddite movement?

Irrelevant, now. Baltimore beckoned.

We passed restaurants, nightclubs, bars, discotheques. The city had built itself to the very edge of the water—even skyscrapers crowded up against the docks. Light, conversation, and music poured out of the establishments. They were nocturnal creatures, awakening now that the sun had set.

Was this the path Hikaru had taken the night before? Had any of these people seen him? Did they have clues about his whereabouts?

Being able to come and go from the Airbnb was a real luxury, apparently, after Reed's experience with the hotel in DC. But part of me wondered if Señor Shaw had chosen an Airbnb so that he would not have to explain to hotel staff what he was doing with the two of us. Or, really, me.

If we had looked like one another, I supposed someone might have assumed we were simply a motherless family, like so many of those Disney tales. Señor Shaw had the kind of ambiguous complexion that did not betray a specific country or region of origin, while still allowing him to benefit from white privilege. Reed was more cardamom—or maybe gingerroot, actually—with cotton candy swirls in his cheeks. His skin was so transparent you could see his blue veins, like an anatomical diagram. I pitied him how easily he must burn, but I imagine no one questioned the two of them when they checked into that hotel in DC.

But my dark brown skin made it impossible to imagine any mother that would make sense of this family portrait. Maybe one of my cousins, who looked white, at least in Mexico, would be able to pass. But even though I was only part indigenous, I was darker than my father, as chocolate brown as mi citli, so dark that my cousins referred to me as "la morenita" growing up. They did not mean it to be offensive, just descriptive.

In los Estados Unidos, I had been mistaken for everything from North African to South Asian. To most gringos, at least, brown was brown was brown was not white.

"We should split up," I offered. "Cover more ground."

"Never split the party!" Reed and Señor Shaw responded in unison. I pretended to listen when they explained the perils of that strategy but did pay attention when Señor Shaw talked us through how to detect JoAnne's Potentia. "Remember, despite JoAnne's artistry, her Glamours will never have substance. They are made entirely of light, so your hand will literally pass through them. Also, the three of us should create a password to help us verify one another's identities."

"Credenza," Reed blurted out.

"Nothing like a *Magicians* season five reference." Señor Shaw nodded.

Again, I nodded as if I understood their obscure allusions.

Did these precautions seem paranoid? Absolutely. Did I mind? Not at all. Medidas necesarias en tiempos desesperados.

The first two docks we visited were dead ends. But at the Baltimore Inner Harbor Marina, we found our first clue: the motorboat from our barge. The one Hikaru had used the night he was abducted.

"Interestingly, the Stones do not appear on Mr. Dickson's kinetoscopic, Messrs. Lumières' cinématographe, Mr. Korn's telephotography, or Kodak's panchromatic."

Ignatius Shaw
Provost, Pass Eight

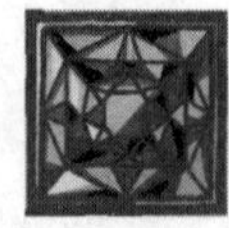

CHAPTER 6

LOS DIECIOCHO DÍAS DE ALEJANDRA

Everything on the boat appeared normal. The life jackets were tucked into the storage seating, the ropes neatly knotted, the bottles of water unopened in the cooler. Señor Shaw tested the engine. It roared to life on the first pull. We could not find anything wrong nor any clues that might lead us to Hikaru. Nada.

"You have to pay for these, right?" Reed asked.

"Pay for what?" I lifted one cushion for what must have been the hundredth time, trying to will a clue into existence.

"A parking spot for the boat."

"Excellent point, Reed." Señor Shaw leaped up. "I'll go speak with the rental office!" He walked away briskly, almost running.

"I got into a fight with Mr. Shaw, chatted with us for a few minutes, then took this motorboat into town." Reed stood at the wheel, walking through Hikaru's steps. "I parked here, and then what?" He stepped off the boat, onto the dock. "Did JoAnne's goons jump me? How did they know I was coming? Did they follow me into town and kidnap me there?"

The small hand on the face of the clock tower flirted with the ten. The nightlife was hopping. This is exactly the kind of Friday night that M., Lucía, and I would use to blow off steam after a long week. Reality changes so quickly.

Like when they renovated the main hall at Friends last summer. Every day for two years, I had walked through the same nineteenth-century brick facade. Then they made it handicapped-accessible and added a video wall, altering the entrance's appearance and layout. After three days, I had completely forgotten what it used to look like. It is frightening how easily we forget the way things used to be and adapt to the new.

Or maybe it is a comfort. Maybe it is the only way we survive.

Mi zafira and I found each other two and a half weeks ago. I met Reed five days later, on the second day of the fencing competition. Five days later, after the incident at the hotel, I joined this entourage. The landscape of my previous life, where fencing was my highest priority, had already faded. Now I was trying to save someone's life. And then, the world.

"How are we possibly going to find Hikaru?" I asked. "We do not even know if JoAnne is keeping him here. The whole thing could be a ruse to mislead us while the two of them flee somewhere else."

"The three of them," Reed said.

"Three?"

"JoAnne, Hikaru, and whoever was controlling the drone. She shouldn't be able to use tech any more than we can, right? So she must be working with someone. An accomplice? Maybe the person she wants to become the Bearer—someone our age?"

Señor Shaw returned, brandishing an e-receipt on his phone. "After I agreed to pay the bill, the manager forwarded this to me and said the boat was docked at approximately seven PM last night." Reed and I inspected the phone as much as we were able to. "The receipt and the story fit into our timeline."

"So another dead end?" Reed squinted into the distance. "There're too many possibilities and not enough facts."

"True," I agreed. "We could spend the next five days just searching the docks."

The letters on the neon sign to the Rusty Scupper restaurant, at the mouth of the dock, flashed on and off, reflecting on the inky water of the bay.

The mostly white and mostly hetero couples strolled the streets and docks, short-sleeve shirts and shorts with blouses and shorter skirts.

"Wait a second!" Reed held up an index finger. "There's a very simple fact that we've overlooked!"

"Really?" Señor Shaw asked.

"No," Reed admitted. "But I felt like that was the right thing to say."

"That's not funny, Reed," Señor Shaw said.

I simply glared him down.

"Do you two . . ." Señor Shaw looked away from us when he spoke, adjusting the straps of his leather satchel. "Do you two think you'd fare all right for a day or two without me?"

"Why, are you thinking of taking a vacation?" Reed affected his Anglophile idea of an upper-class accent. "I hear Tuscany is beautiful this time of year."

I tried not to cringe. Umbria, maybe. But Tuscany?

"Reed, please, I'm being serious," Señor Shaw said.

"What are you thinking, Señor Shaw?" I asked.

"I believe the most effective way to find Hikaru would be for me to descend into Baltimore's underworld."

"Like *The Wire*?" Reed asked.

"A little bit like *The Wire*," Señor Shaw conceded. "Minus the actual wire. It would require two days. Maybe three. With so few leads, I think it's our best bet. But I won't embark on it without your blessing."

"We're not children," I said. "Of course we can take care of ourselves."

"Absolutely not." Reed crossed his arms. "If this isn't the creepy, foreshadow-y scene before the mentor disappears, I don't know what is."

"I promise you, Reed, I'll be back before you know it." Señor Shaw squeezed Reed's shoulder.

"Promise?" Reed's lower lip quivered.

They engaged in a brief, fierce hug. "I told you I'll be by your side as long as you'll have me."

I couldn't tell who was closer to tears. Between them, of course. I found the scene a bit maudlin.

"It's settled then." Señor Shaw took a deep breath, held it for a moment, then exhaled. "We'll reconvene in two days at the Airbnb. If you don't hear from me after those forty-eight hours, use this phone." He produced a cellular from a side pocket in his leather satchel.

"Um, Disjunctis, anyone?" Reed asked.

"I want each of you to repeat the phrase, 'Desperate times call for desperate measures.'"

We did as we were told, while Señor Shaw fiddled with the phone.

"This cellular is now programmed to be activated by either of your voices, and only yours. I will leave it on the dining room table in our Airbnb. If you don't hear from me, either one of you can repeat that phrase and the phone will automatically dial. The voice that answers will say, 'What's the fastest way to the station?' Then you must respond, 'It depends on the traffic.' Then the voice will respond, 'Naturally.' That will be your confirmation. Then, and only then, reveal your location using GPS coordinates 39°17'27.2"N 76°36'41.8"W. You will hear the following response: 'We'll see you in the second compartment.'"

Señor Shaw made us repeat the sequence three times, making sure we were word-perfect. Remembering the numbers was challenging for Reed. Señor Shaw handed him a sheet of paper and pencil.

"And are you gonna tell us who'll be on the other end?" Reed scribbled the coordinates on the paper and folded it into his pocket.

"That, my dear mentees, will be the extraordinary Chancellor." Señor Shaw shuddered. "And, to be honest, at times like this, I wish he were still Provost. He would know what to do. Father always does."

"It appears as if Second Red has taken to her Stone like Major Bloodnok to curried eggs."

Larkin Shaw
Provost, Pass Nine

CHAPTER 7

REED IN PARADISE

Reed spent all night handing out photocopied "Have You Seen" flyers that Mr. Shaw had made. He knew this couldn't possibly be the most efficient use of his and Ale's time, but he didn't have any better ideas about how to find Hikaru. They visited bars, restaurants, cafés, clubs, convenience stores, pharmacies—any establishment that was still open. They even approached strangers on the street.

No one recognized the picture. At 2 AM, they stumbled back to their loft Airbnb, exhausted, with nothing to show for their efforts. Reed fell asleep without brushing his teeth and woke up with the taste of roadkill in his mouth.

They spent the entirety of the next day canvassing.

"If you were Hikaru, where would you have gone first?" Reed asked.

Ale obtained a paper map at the Chamber of Commerce and plotted out the nearby five-stars hotels.

"You have any idea how long it'll take us to walk to all these?" Reed asked.

"Who said anything about walking?" Ale spied a public bike station, neatly tucked away next to a 7-Eleven. "In fencing, everything can be used to your advantage. So we think that Disjunctis is an impediment, but actually . . ." She ran her fingers over a docking station, and a few sparks later, a bicycle popped free. "Voilà!"

"I like the way you move." D#–D#–Cm–G#–A#. "I like the way you move, Almada."

"That's what Hikaru called me." Her voice betrayed no emotion.

Sometimes Reed wanted to grab her by her shapely shoulders and shake her until she showed something resembling vulnerability. Obviously, he didn't. He didn't even use Red to read her, as tempted as he was to find out what was happening under her neutral mask.

Soon, they were biking to the Four Seasons.

Then the Sagamore Pendry. Then the BlancNoir. Then The Ivy. Ale told Reed that hotel receptionists weren't actually allowed to tell them if Hikaru had checked in. But Reed didn't need verbal confirmation. Using his Potentia, even a flicker of recognition when they scanned the flyer would register on Reed's emotional radar. Much to their disappointment, he didn't get a single blip.

"Is there any point in looking at the four-star hotels?" Reed asked.

Alejandra arched an eyebrow instead of wasting words saying no.

The next day was equally quixotic. They spent another fruitless morning and afternoon together. When Reed suggested they hire a plane to skywrite "Desperately Seeking Hikaru," Alejandra told him it was time to split up.

"This isn't just about efficiency." She flipped her curls back. "This is about me not killing you."

"Okay." Reed swallowed his automatic "Don't split the party!" response. "Meet back here at midnight?"

"And if Señor Shaw isn't back, we can . . ." She let the sentence trail off before departing.

Reed would've bet that the possibility terrified him far more than it did her.

The strobing disco lights, the pulsing music, the bustle of the docks: they all served to remind Reed how isolated he'd been, stuck on the barge with only Ale, Hikaru, and Mr. Shaw.

Or maybe the isolation he felt had more to do with being the only queer person on the quest?

But he checked himself. He couldn't recall Ale talking about any boy, let alone anyone, romantically. And even though Hikaru carried himself with a straight bro's privilege, his crude sexual comments ran the gamut of the gender/orientation spectrum. In fact, Mr. Shaw was the only one of the three of them who had come out as openly straight. Reed tucked these musings away. All that mattered now was finding Hikaru.

"Excuse me, have you seen . . . ?" Reed held up a flyer with Hikaru's photo on it. Just like every other patron, waiter, restaurant manager, and worker before, the people standing under the green awning to Club Paradise regarded Reed with a combination of curiosity and amusement before shaking their heads no.

His one-on-one sessions with Mr. Shaw practicing the Feat of Sweet Sweet Relief had strengthened him against the emotions of strangers. Protected in his meta-tower of meta-bricks, Reed detached from the hopes/desires/fears of the Sunday night crowd.

Emotions reverberated more powerfully at night. Was it that people felt more keenly then? Or did it have something to do with lunar and solar energy? Especially where there was music. Especially where there was alcohol. Each club was a jewelry box, emotions sparkling an invitation to try them on.

Reed joined the line. It slowly snaked forward, past a poster of a Black drag queen's face, lips puckered in simulated shock, somewhere between scandalized and flirtatious. The line moved so slowly Reed was able to commit the entire poster to memory: A halo tiara spiked out in peaks, framing her. Pink letters on the top: VERSA MILITUDE: ONE WEEK ONLY.

The slow-snaking line outside Club Paradise also allowed Reed to reestablish his defenses. He still needed to dedicate most of his attention to fighting the onslaught of strangers' feelings, *beat beat beating* against him, like peasants armed with pitchforks and torches, demanding entry. He pounded his fist into his open palm and stomped left and right, moving through the Feat of Sweet Sweet Relief, until he fortified his inner tower brick by brick. He finally reached the front of the line.

"Excuse me, have you seen . . . ?" He handed a flyer to the Club Paradise bouncer, a lithe figure of basketball proportions, sporting a three-quarters-length leather trench coat that would've been floor-length on anyone else. Their nails were long and sharp.

The next two people in line bounded past Reed and up to the bouncer. "You remember us, Riḍwan, don't you?"

"IDs," Riḍwan demanded, before nodding their head the barest fraction and granting the eager duo entry. The bouncer turned their attention back to Reed. "That kid had one of the best fake IDs I've ever seen." They spoke with a low rumble that, somehow, could be heard perfectly above the din of EDM pumping out of the club.

"You've seen Hikaru!" Reed exclaimed.

"A few nights ago." The next set of IDs, apparently, weren't as impressive. With a speed that surprised Reed almost as much as the three punks seeking admission, Riḍwan produced a pair of scissors from their leather trench coat and sliced the forgeries in clean halves. "Now get outta here." The punks scrambled away, blushing and huffing under their eyeliner.

"What else do you remember?" Reed practically begged.

"Sorry, kid. I only pay attention when they're coming in." Riḍwan nodded in a group of androgynous alts and some suspiciously dressed preps.

Reed felt for Red. His Stone was there, calling to him like an instrument begging to be played.

Hunger to dance your ass off

But the moment he employed his Potentia,

Tedium of being here all night

the bricks in his tower began disappearing,

Thirst for that alcohol numb

and emotions flooded him, invaded him, threatening to level him flat.

Red barely allowed him to pull out.

"You might have better luck inside." Riḍwan either didn't notice Reed's brief episode or pretended not to.

"Thanks!" Reed ducked under the velvet rope, breathing deep to slow down his pulse.

"Yeah, only." Riḍwan held out their hand. "ID, please?"

"You let Hikaru in, right?" Reed asked with all the flirtation and charisma he could muster.

"You gonna make it worth my while?" Riḍwan just barely rubbed their thumb against the next two fingers. "Like he did?"

Reed wasn't morally averse to bribing. He just didn't have any cash. "Thanks for your help," he mumbled, doing his best to sound sincere.

The backstage of Paradise was crammed with things, entirely unlit, and infinitely less glamorous than Reed had imagined. He navigated his way through the dark obstacle course, opting for discretion instead of using Red's glow to light his way. Even moving as slowly and carefully as he could, he injured himself twice. The first time, he smashed the same knee he'd bruised when scrambling through the basement window he'd coaxed open in the alley behind the building. The second time, he smacked his head against something hanging lower than it should be.

There must be an office back here somewhere, Reed reasoned. A manager who might remember Hikaru, or could be persuaded to look at Thursday's security footage. Failing that, he'd brave the dance floor and the bar to see if any of the bartenders could tell him something, anything, that might be of value. It was a long shot, but it was his only shot.

Beyoncé's "America Has a Problem" blasted over the club's speakers, and the bass rumbled in his bones.

Stand-alone version, featuring Kendrick Lamar.

Chorus: C# minor–C# minor–D–Bm–C# minor–C# minor–D–Bm–C# minor

Reed tried the knob that he hoped would lead him to the offices, only to discover it was a fake stage door standing on a frame. He walked through, and straight into a wall he didn't see, cursing under his breath as his forehead and nose paid the price.

After a few more minutes of groping in the darkness, a sudden barrage of emotions was the only thing that stopped him from stumbling directly onstage. He fumbled for a slit in the curtains to spy on the club proper. Sweaty bodies moved as one to the *thump thump thump* of the techno beat. He continued groping the curtain until he was safely on the other wing. Hopefully, Ale was having better luck.

He didn't realize the slice of light on the floor led to a dressing room until he'd opened the door and stepped inside. The room—closet really—was packed with a garage's worth of stuff: wigs, costumes on hangers, makeup cases with their contents spilling out, hatboxes, hatbox lids, hats, chairs of all shapes, cleaning supplies, paper towels, bottles of disinfectants, mops, brooms, towels, laundry baskets, shoe racks, shoes, and buckets.

"What took you so long, honey?" She sat with her back to Reed, making eye contact through the wall of mirrors on the far side of the room. "We're on in ten, and you certainly can't go onstage dressed like that. You can't really go anywhere dressed like that." She rose and began pulling costume pieces off racks. "Let's see—with those pasty tones and positively skeletal frame, you're not really giving me much to work with. Luckily for you, I'm a magician!" She handed him a burgundy sequined jacket with rhinestone lapels. It wasn't nearly as dazzling as the entirely white sequined dress she herself was wearing, bodice flaring out in chiffon curls at the waist. "And here are your charts." She tossed a three-ring binder, which Reed barely caught with his free hand. "I insist we review the tempos before we go on, especially after what happened in Rehoboth. Don't worry about those animals out there. From what I understand, the drinks here are stronger than Kamala Harris on the debate stage." She adjusted the perfectly coiffed platinum blond curls that framed her flawless Black face. "What are you waiting for, Danny?"

"I'm sorry." Reed put down the three-ring binder and searched for space on the rack to hang up the sequined jacket. "I think there's been some mistake."

"The only mistake here is your tardiness. And your outfit." She donned a halo tiara with spiked peaks and turned to face him. "Now hop to—our audience awaits."

"You're the drag queen on the poster outside! Versi, Verse . . . ?"

"Honey, if I'm verse, you're a Marine." She cackled at her own joke. "I am Versa

Militude. And I am not a drag queen. I am a drag godd-ess!" She flipped a light switch and drew herself up to full height. The bulbs framing the dressing room mirror sprang to life, framing all six foot plus of her sparkling, dazzling, sequined glory. "And you're Danny, my replacement accompanist because Rodrigo got another gig and how much notice did he give me two hours that's how much and that's the last time he's pulling a stunt like that!"

"Ms. Militude, I wish I could help you." Reed finally found space to hang up the burgundy sequined jacket between a bear costume and a latex singlet. "But I've barely touched a keyboard since I dropped piano two years ago. And more important, I have to find my friend. Have you seen him?" Reed held up one of the Hikaru flyers. "It's important. Like life-or-death important."

Using his Empathy on Versa would've been a quick fix. But it took all of Reed's concentration to protect himself from the throbbing, dancing, alcoholic mass on the dance floor. He was a ship on their tempest-tossed sea, and diverting even a fraction of his concentration would result in shipwreck and destruction, leaving him a blubbering mess on her dressing room floor.

"Okay, kid." Versa took the paper in one of her perfectly French manicured hands. "We're both in a bind. I don't do a cappella, and your friend has gone missing, in what you claim to be a life-threatening situation. I think we can agree that my predicament is the more dire. You play for me, and I'll help you find your boyfriend." She gestured vaguely at the flyer.

"How do I know you even know him?"

"Hikaru, that entitled prick?"

"You've got yourself a deal!" Reed's face lit up. He held out his hand to shake on it.

Ladylike, Versa placed her exquisitely manicured fingers in his. "So what're you waiting for? Change already. Don't you dare make this Magical Negro late."

Reed picked up the hanger with the glittering burgundy jacket. "What exactly do you wear with sequins?"

★

"Please find an updated recommendation for the reclassification of primary, secondary, and tertiary Feats."

Larkin Shaw
Provost, Pass Nine

CHAPTER 8

REED PERFORMS

Clad in the burgundy sequined jacket that Versa Militude insisted he wear shirtless, Reed sat at the piano onstage, plunking out the chords to "It's Raining Men."

C–D–B–Em

He offered an apology to The Weather Girls for every mistake he made in the surprisingly complicated verse, fingers twisting around themselves from D♭ major^7 to E♭, with a few F minors thrown in for good measure.

But accompanying Versa wasn't the challenge. It was splitting his concentration between the performance and his defenses. The emotions in the club, enhanced by alcohol and music, bounced around like a multiball bonus round, ricocheting into his tower of protection from all directions.

His fingers stretched for the piano chords.

B^7–Em–Am–B–B^7

Almost there!

The sequined jacket refused absorption. Pools of sweat accumulated in the nooks of Reed's armpits and lower back. His fingers slicked over the ivory and ebony keys of the surprisingly in-tune upright.

The chorus, blessedly, had the simplest progression. All he needed was to land the final C–D–B–Em and he would be . . .

Done! Thank God!

One song down. One song closer to Hikaru.

"We'll be back in a sec, so don't you cretins go anywhere. Not that you have anywhere to go, now do you?" Versa surprised Reed by ending the first set after one song and dragging him offstage with her.

“Would you hold these for me?” Versa handed Reed the rings she slid off her fingers.

“Sure.”

“You know what? Never mind.” Versa took the rings back. “I simply cannot abide this angry Black woman trope. So instead of slapping some sense into you . . .” She cradled his face in her hands. “What you’re doing out there, Danny, it doesn’t have a lick of truth in it.”

Humiliation

“That’s not music,” Versa continued.

Disbelief

“It’s rigor mortis.”

Rage

“I told you I hadn’t touched a piano in years!” Reed’s anger flared. “So tell me if you wanna do the rest of the set by yourself!”

“You’re not going to be like that, honey, are you? Because I’m not talking about your skill. I’m talking about your truth. You have to be present out there. To listen to me.” Versa’s makeup glistened. “And to them.” Her silver eye shadow, fading up. “And yourself.” Her perfect lips. “But most of all, me.”

“I thought I was,” Reed responded sheepishly.

“You’re fuller of shit than the Porta Potties at the Fyre Festival. Now help me out of this.” Versa turned so Reed could unzip her dress. She stepped out of the white chiffon into a floor-length gown of metallic squares, each one reflecting a fraction of Reed’s face back to him.

“I have to be”—Reed searched for how to talk about his Stone—“careful. Not to lose control.”

“Why?” Versa gestured to the zipper on the back of her gown. “Tug.”

“Because I’m not sure what will happen if I do.” He yanked the zipper up and hooked the clasp at the top.

“Are you telling me you’ve never let yourself go?” When he didn’t respond, she continued. “I’m not Socrates, honey. That wasn’t a rhetorical question.”

“Not really,” Reed admitted.

“When you’re on your own, you do whatever you want, kid. But we’re a team out there. A team that consists of one of God's most fabulous creatures on this green earth, and you. And everything we do affects each other." She grabbed the lapels of his jacket and tugged him close. "I see you, okay? I. See. You. And I see you performing the safest version of yourself. We get so good at it we forget we're even doing it. We sacrifice our authenticity every day for someone else's comfort." Versa released him and switched her jewelry, replacing the white luminescent accessories of a goddess with the polished metal of a warrior. "But in here, in Paradise, you get to be your truest self. So unleash." She adjusted her bra and plumped up her cleavage. "Besides, if you don't loosen up, I'll never be asked back to Club Paradise, and Mama needs to pay off her student loans. Now—" Versa produced a flask from somewhere on her body and took a healthy swig. "Drink."

"Booze?" Reed took an equally healthy swig, his eyes tearing as the concoction stung its way down his throat.

"While performing? Surely you jest." Versa finished the flask with a final gulp. "It's ginseng, ginger, horseradish, habanero, lemon, turmeric, and raw apple cider. It will keep you real. Now get that skinny white ass of yours on that stage and terrify us all with your authenticity."

The opening G–F–C–G chords of "Born This Way" poured out of Reed's fingers, into the piano, through the microphone he made sure not to touch, and out of the speakers into Paradise. Each chord progression dismantled his tower of defense, brick by brick. Removing it seemed counterintuitive at best, suicidal at worst. Its cold protection and stark security were his armor, and he was undressing in the middle of combat.

The spice of Versa's tonic stung his throat almost as much as her reprimand had stung his ego. He pushed the hurt aside and forced himself to do as she had instructed. To be authentic. To be present. To listen.

Versa pouted her platinum lips and blew him a kiss across their tiny stage the moment before those opening notes came tumbling out in her throaty alto. The last and only other time he'd been unprotected in a crowd like this was before the fencing tournament when he first spotted Alejandra. The trauma of losing himself in everyone else's desires haunted him. Confusing the wants of other people for his own, their fears for his: it threatened his already tenuous sense of identity.

But he didn't have the music then. Or Versa.

The music was his solace, the tempo his anchor, the chord progressions his guide. His fingers slid across the keyboard in a glissando that launched them into the first chorus.

The entire song evolved from that G–F–C–G progression, building on itself, insisting on itself, until it could not be denied.

He had to coax, threaten, push, negotiate, even beg some of those defensive bricks away. This was no simple demolition job—it was a game of Jenga with his soul at stake. With every chord his fingers plunked on this plane, his metaphysical self willed a brick to disappear. The piano keys were smooth, but the bricks were rough.

If it had been a real tower, he would've started at the top and worked his way down. Or maybe he would've just smashed it, wrecking ball–style. But he was undoing a metaphor, working his way out of a construct of his own making. There was a process, a code to crack, an order of deconstruction, lest he send himself spiraling into madness.

Reed wouldn't have been able to contemplate, let alone attempt, what he was doing without Versa. Her absolute, uncompromising insistence on being in the excruciating moment of now served as a living, breathing Platonic ideal. She whispered the spoken interlude, a sacred rite between her and the transfixed audience, then launched into the mostly a cappella second verse of "Born This Way" with a religious fervor that demanded devotion.

G–F–C

G–F–C

G–F–C

The music was a wave and the surf he needed to ride it. It was their divinity, a holy ritual performed for their midnight congregation. Versa was the High Priestess and Reed her acolyte, granting communion to their zealous disciples.

Was it his imagination, or were the ivory keys turning scarlet under his calloused fingertips?

By the time they hit the first of the final back-to-back choruses, Reed welcomed the barrage of sensations, like gamma radiation flooding him with superpowers. Instead of fleeing, he bathed in them, accepting whatever mutations would follow. If everyone was beautiful in their own way, he could be, too.

He connected to all sixty-four people in Paradise, then connected them to one another, and then, finally, to Versa. They all became one, a fabulous dancing hive collective.

Then, in a communal decision that felt rehearsed but couldn't possibly have been, everybody spontaneously joined in the final chorus. Like Lady Gaga, they coaxed an extra syllable, turning "way" into "wa-ay," jumping the fourth step as if there were no other way to sing the word.

They immediately rolled into the opening E^7–B^9 of Gloria Gaynor's "I Will Survive," obliterating the rubble that was left of Reed's protection, (Am) leaving him vulnerable, (Dm) naked, (G) raw.

C major^7

Red escaped from his pocket. Reed grabbed at the Stone, doing his best to play the chords one-handed.

F major^7

But then he decided

Bm^7–B^5

Fuck it.

$Esus^4$

Fuck it all.

E major.

He, too, would survive. He may not know how to live quite yet, but he would stay alive.

In Paradise, anything that sparkled belonged.

Red, released, unabashed, flew high. His Stone became a fixture of the landscape, above Versa's armor dress, the glitter, the mirrors, the nylon, the spandex, the chiffon. Reed's ruby soared high, a disco ball revolving without a care in the world, sending thousands of cherry fireflies into every corner. For once, Red and Reed could just fucking be.

And they were. Connecting. Amplifying. Broadcasting. Receiving. Supporting. Performing. Free. They were an ecosystem—he, Versa, the music, the audience, creating moisture and sustenance and recycling it back into the environment so all the organisms could feed and be fed, live and let live.

For once, everything made sense.

His heart *thump-thump-thump*ed against his rib cage, and the sweat poured down his back, and something inside him blossomed opened released escaped, and just as they reached the final chorus . . .

Am

. . . he saw Hikaru.

Dm

His goldenrod silhouette.

G major

Dancing in Paradise.

C major^7

Shirtless, of course.

F major^7

Here.

Bm^7–B^5

As vivid as a signature cologne.

Esus^4

But not now.

E major

Then.

A minor.

And the vision of Hikaru faded.

They encored once with the Scissor Sisters' "Let's Have a Kiki," until Versa pulled him offstage.

He was drenched, down to the underwear clinging to him under the resilient sequined jacket. "We could've gone all night, Versa. They were eating us up!"

"Yes, darling, they were eating *me* up. But you have to leave them wanting more. They would never forgive us if we satiated them." She spoke over her shoulder as she made her way to the dressing room.

"Next time—just hear me out, okay?" Would Reed ever know a more powerful rush than the audience cheering? "I'm wondering if we want to start with 'Born This Way' and then take that into . . ."

"A taste of the spotlight and she already has ideas!" Versa stepped out of her platform heels.

"It's your call, of course, I just thought . . ."

"You thought what, honey?" She turned to look at him. "You're going to drop out of college and I would show you the world, shining, shimmering, splendid? I would be your magic carpet ride, and the world would be your oyster?"

For a moment, Reed allowed himself the fantasy. Of quitting the mission. Of starting a new life. Where illusionists didn't abduct his friends. Where mentors didn't disappear. Where he didn't have to save the world. Where he could turn his back on it all and follow Versa from gig to gig, learning everything she had to teach him about music and life.

"You're not giving up your life to tickle the ivories with me." She yanked her wig off unceremoniously and ripped off her eyelash extensions, dismantling her illusion without a shred of sentimentality. "That makes no sense."

"You're right, Versa, of course." Reed couldn't abandon his friends. Let alone the mission.

"If only more people shared that belief."

"Besides, I have to find Hikaru."

"Oh, that's right." She stepped out of her gown. "Your boyfriend came to Paradise Thursday night, stayed after the show, and bought everyone rounds. Then he said something about having to get back to a barge. I mean, a barge, for God's sake!" Versa slipped on a sensible silk robe with a floral motif. "He's not in trouble, is he?"

"I don't know." Reed's mind scrambled to accommodate the information and how his new power-up could help him solve the mystery. "But this really helps."

"You did well out there, Danny. Now, I can't send you back out in the world dressed like that." She gestured to the sparkly burgundy sequined jacket Reed was about to take off. "Keep it. Now skedaddle. My boyfriend's coming back to congratulate me, and three's a crowd. Except when it's not, of course."

Reed gathered himself, searching for the words to tell Versa how much this night meant to him. "Versa, I . . ."

"I know, Danny. I know." She spritzed some dizzying perfume on her wrists and neck. "But don't get sentimental. Some things are best left unsaid."

Reed changed into his cargo pants and Henley. Had he really spent his life wearing clothes that didn't sparkle?

He was almost an hour late to his rendezvous with Ale at the clock tower.

"Tell me you had more luck than I did, güey." During their time apart, she had changed into a lapis-blue single-shoulder-strapped dress that ended in a miniskirt just above the knee. "Do we return to the Airbnb and wait for Señor Shaw?"

"Not yet, Ale." Reed was barely able to contain his excitement. "I think I know how to find Hikaru!"

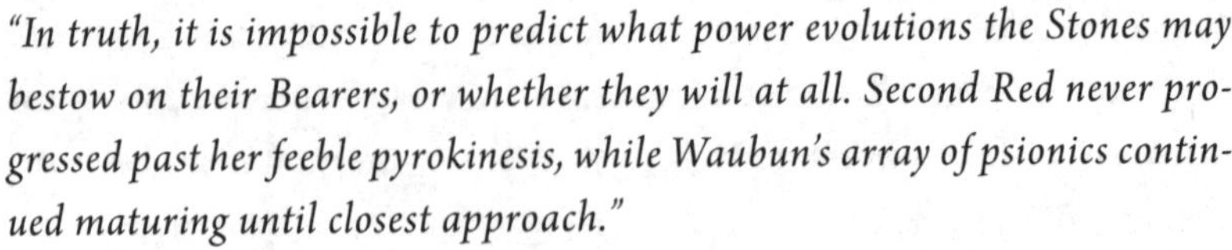

"In truth, it is impossible to predict what power evolutions the Stones may bestow on their Bearers, or whether they will at all. Second Red never progressed past her feeble pyrokinesis, while Waubun's array of psionics continued maturing until closest approach."

Ignatius Shaw
Provost, Pass Eight

CHAPTER 9

ALEJANDRA REALIZA LA LLAMADA

Reed closed his azul-as-my-Stone eyes and concentrated on his rojo-as-his-hair ruby. Somehow, Red looked both darker and more transparent, as if the cosmos lay between its carved facades. Did the Stones change appearance, or was it just our perception of them that changed? It floated in front of Reed, at his chest, like a second heart. His Stone pulsed light in ever-growing spheres, until the entire motorboat was housed inside its crimson dome. When Reed opened his eyes, they were scarlet slits: pupil, iris, sclera, all pigeon's bloodred, as if he were possessed by el diablo.

He didn't just look at the motorboat. He looked into it. *Through* it.

"Hikaru was here," Reed intoned like a priest at Sunday Mass.

"Didn't we already know that?" What good was his new power if it only gave us information we already had? We should be en route to the Airbnb to see if Señor Shaw had returned. But Reed insisted on trying this first. The irony was not lost on me: for once, I wanted to follow the instructions, and Reed was breaking them.

"So you discovered a new Potentia while playing piano for a drag queen in a gay club?" I knew Reed would never lie to me, never deceive me in any way, but this sounded far-fetched at best.

"I wish you had been there! Versa was—God, how do I even convey a fraction of her fabulousness?" His description did not make much sense, but I did not question it any further. With most things, it was simply easier to accept. "Ale, how far are we from the Ikeda's closest approach? Thirty days?"

"Thirty-five," I corrected him.

"You think we'll power up around the same time, based on the Ikeda's proximity?"

"Yo no sé. We can ask Señor Shaw when he comes back."

Reed had walked so quickly to the docks that I almost had to struggle to keep up. I had never seen him so excited.

"Empathy, Orchestration, Post Cognition! I wonder what other powers I'll get!"

"Post Cognition?" I speak three languages, but I swear I need a translator when Reed pontificates in geek.

"Post Cog is when you can look into the past. It comes in very handy for paranormal detectives. You pick up the murder weapon, and bam!—see who committed the crime. Maggie had it on *Charmed*, but they called it psychometry. Longshot and Blindfold are the two big Marvel postcogs, and of course, Cordelia from *Angel*—"

"You're a walking wikinerdia," I cut him off. "So you think you will sense Hikaru's presence on the boat?"

"I'm not sure if it's Hikaru or Yellow that I picked up on. Like, would my Post Cog work on non-Bearers? Lots and lots of questions. Few answers. I can't wait to show Mr. Shaw. I'm sure he'll know . . ." He broke into a full run when we finally arrived at the docks.

Reed jumped onto the motorboat. It took him half an hour of strolling its length and experimenting with movements, humming different songs, before he could re-create the Feat and enter the trance.

"It's Thursday night." Those bloodred eyes remained fixated on what only they could see. "Hikaru docks. He's relieved. He's excited." Reed's head snapped to the other side of the boat. "He takes out his cell phone and sends a few texts." He followed a trail only he could see onto the dock. "He jumps off the boat, onto the dock, and . . ." His eyes flickered, and they returned to their original color. "Aaaaand, I'm back. It's gone. Sorry, all."

"What do you see when you are in this 'Post Cog'?" I asked.

"I can spy the past. It looks like security footage—grainy black and white. But Hikaru's presence pops out vivid, in yellow. And it was weird, but—I think there were two of him?"

"Maybe he finally unlocked his Potentia!" I gasped.

"He can double himself?" Reed shuddered. "Can you imagine two Hikarus? Or even more, like Multiple Man?"

"One is already enough." I tried to wipe my mind clean of the suggestion.

"Versa made it sound like Hikaru intended to return to the barge immediately after Paradise. That means JoAnne must've abducted him after he left Versa and before he returned here." Reed stepped back onto the boat. "His presence is strongest at the wheel. I guess that makes sense, since this is where he would've spent the most time. But"—his eyes flashed red again—"hold on . . ." Red floated just above his head, shining light on the wheel. "One presence is more vivid than the other."

"More vivid how?"

"More vibrant, almost opaque, like an egg yolk. The other one is weaker. Transparent, like a butterscotch wrapper."

"Do you think the egg yolk is on its way to becoming a butterscotch wrapper?" I asked excitedly.

"What do you mean?"

"Are they traveling along the same color wheel path?" Why was it taking Reed so long to understand where I was going with this?

"Why does that matter?"

"Maybe"—I did not need to see what Reed saw to theorize—"he was on the boat on two separate occasions, which is why one presence is stronger than the other. If we can record the rate at which the vividity of the images diminish, we may be able to determine how much time elapsed between his two appearances. Like the half-life of isotopes." It all came to me rushing, dizzying, edifying.

"Should we do that now or go back to the Airbnb and see if—you know . . ." Reed shrugged. "It's been over forty-eight hours."

A moment of silent dread deflated the rush of my epiphany. It hovered between us, like the ghost of an unavenged ancestor. "You stay and 'Post Cog.' I'll go and see if Señor Shaw is back."

"And if he's not?"

"Then I will make the call."

We rehearsed the instructions Señor Shaw had left us. I was, of course, word-perfect.

It took me ten minutes to jog back to our Airbnb. I played in my mind how I would bring Señor Shaw to the motorboat and show him our progress. Unless, of course, he had already freed Hikaru and they were both in the loft. Then all three of us would return to surprise Reed before returning to the barge. I would force Hikaru to perform Locatio. We would recruit Green, then Purple, and save the world already.

I let myself into the building of our loft, noticing the arabesque red and blue tiles on the floor for the first time. I took a deep breath at our front door before unlocking it and stepping inside.

"Señor Shaw?"

The apartment was dark.

I repeated his name, louder this time.

No one responded.

But I was sure I was not alone.

Another presence was there, quiet, lurking.

A glass shattered in the kitchen.

This darkness invited an ambush.

My hand extended into a wicked blade as I charged.

Two aquamarine eyes met me in the darkness. I hurled Blue at them. She lit up as she flew through the air, revealing . . .

The fluffy face of a white cat staring at me, whiskers splayed like spider legs. A broken glass on the floor. The cat hissed, as if I were the intruder, then slipped out a slightly ajar window.

The apartment was empty, otherwise.

I poured myself a glass of wine and caught my breath before doing what needed to be done. I approached the cell phone, lying on the dining room table.

"Desperate times call for desperate measures."

"What's the fastest way to the station?" Father had picked up on the first ring, as if he'd been waiting by the phone. His accent was even crisper and more British than Señor Shaw's.

"It depends on the traffic, señor." I held my breath, scolding myself for adding that "señor." I never made such amateur mistakes.

The cellular phone on the dining room table stared at me, unfeeling. Three interminable seconds passed before the voice responded. "Naturally." Father's voice creaked like finely aged leather.

I gave him the coordinates, number-perfect.

"We'll see you in the second compartment," he responded.

This is the moment, in an old movie, when I would hear the ominous dial tone of a landline. But cell phones are far less dramatic.

I grabbed some food and a change of clothes for Reed, thought about sweeping up the broken glass but decided it was not worth it, and made my way back to the motorboat.

Reed was waiting for me in a pile of what looked like garbage. I shook my head at the question in his eyes so that he would know Señor Shaw had not resurfaced. "I made the call."

"And so what now?" he asked.

"Help comes? But that doesn't mean we stop what we're doing and wait for it." I stifled my 2 AM yawn. "What have you learned?"

Reed showed me a gamut of yellow objects he had placed in chromatic sequence from vivid to faded: a bouquet of marigolds, a squeezed half of a lemon, a banana peel, a SpongeBob SquarePants sticker, the stub of a number two pencil, an old tennis ball, and two mustard bottles. "I created a color wheel to measure the atrophy. So far, the stronger aura started at marigolds and traveled over to SpongeBob sticker. The weaker aura, on the other hand, started at number two pencil, passed through tennis ball, and faded into mustard bottle. All we need to do is measure how long it takes the stronger aura to get from sticker to pencil and we'll not only have an idea of how much time transpired between his two stays but how long he was on the boat the second time!"

"You know what, Reed?"

"What?"

"Bien hecho. That means 'well done.'"

He accepted my compliment with a blush and a nod.

Every fifteen minutes, he would enter his trance state and report on the movement of the colors. I would notate them on the side of the boat using the stub of the number two pencil. By three thirty in the morning, we had our answer.

"That doesn't make any sense." Reed scrunched his forehead up.

"What doesn't?"

"If your theories and my observations are right, it looks like Hikaru spent almost exactly twenty-five minutes on the boat both times." Reed tapped his head with an open palm.

"If there is no such thing as a coincidence . . ." A theory formed in my mind.

"And it took Hikaru twenty-five minutes to travel from the barge to the dock on this motorboat." Reed picked up on my thread.

". . . and he spent twenty-five minutes on the motorboat again at the end of the night . . ." Our thoughts were tumbling on top of each other, building momentum.

". . . then maybe . . ." Reed flapped his hands in excitement.

". . . just maybe . . ." I wanted to be the one to say it!

"Hikaru returned to the barge!" we said in unison.

"Even before his first Evolution, it was difficult to imagine Chibundu's Potentia being used for anything other than destruction. One sees why in many of the ancient languages, the word for 'blessing' and 'curse' was the same."

Algernon de la Shaw
Provost, Pass Seven

CHAPTER 10

LOS DRAGONES DE ALEJANDRA

"But then how did the boat get back here, to the Baltimore docks?" Reed asked me. "And how did Hikaru leave the barge again? And how . . ."

"No sé, Reed." I settled back against the padding of the seat. "I do not have all the answers. But this is our only lead, ¿sí? So let us return to the barge, retrace Hikaru's steps, and see what we can learn."

"You can do whatever you want. I'm going back to our Airbnb to wait for Father." Reed tossed all the yellow items into a bag and climbed out of the boat.

"Is it that you are scared or that you resist this plan because you are not the one who devised it?"

That stopped him in his tracks. "You really think I'm that petty?"

"I think you have fanciful ideas about yourself and leadership." Did I really need to explain fragile masculinity to him?

"Fine. We'll do whatever you want." All the intonation left Reed's voice.

"What is going on with you?"

"Nothing."

"Nothing?" I spat the word at him.

"Is it happening again?" he monotoned.

"¿Qué?"

"I must've overdrawn my Potentia using all that Post Cog. It means I won't have access to it for a while. Or my emotions. It also means I'll probably have a breakdown sometime soon." He might as well have been reciting equations from a calculus exam.

"Bueno. Cannot wait."

Robo-Reed contemplated this. "That's a joke, right?"

"I hope that breakdown arrives soon, because humorless you is even more unbearable."

With somebody else, perhaps I would have felt relief. Relief at knowing that at least now, for a period of time, they could not use their power on me. That is what would make a Potentia like Orchestration so dangerous with a different Bearer. But Reed would never. And of course, I would know if he tried. Then I would use my Potentia to break him like a birthday piñata.

Our first challenge: how to return to the barge. My suspicion that the fuse for the gas engine used electricity proved correct when I almost set the motorboat on fire.

Neither of us had the skill to woman a sailboat, even if we could procure one. But Reed surprised me, once again. "Don't you remember, yesterday afternoon, we passed . . ." He led me around a shopping gallery to the Chesapeake Bay Boat Rental. "Now all we have to do is wait a few hours until the store opens and my power comes back and I can Orchestrate someone into letting us borrow one."

"Or I can get my Adelita on." I had not had many opportunities to transform in the last week. I missed it. All of it. Even my blood chilling as I turned zafira.

I had no moral qualms about using my machete hand to snip the padlock chain and liberate a boat.

Thank goodness Señor Shaw and I had spent all week working on my restorations. With Reed powerless now, how long would I have remained in this state? How much more of my body would fail to revert to flesh?

Deep breath.

Cuernavaca.

Peacocks.

Hibiscus.

Turquoise earrings tingle.

The gears turned. I gritted my teeth.

It still hurt like the devil, but at least I could do it solo.

Perhaps I should have chosen a less conspicuous ride. But I do not always do the things that I should. I ran my hand affectionately down the silver dragon-shaped paddleboat. We climbed into the first row of her flat body. The front and back arched up almost a full meter in an open-jawed head and a spiky tail. Black painted scales jutted out of both sides.

Just as Reed and I finished experimenting with the pedal mechanism at our feet, he tried and failed to suppress his first sob.

"Breakdown?" I asked.

He nodded yes, and his eyes released waterfalls. It is different when someone with blue eyes like Reed cries—their corneas almost become transparent, like a portal opening to their soul. Brown eyes like mine do not do that. Not that I cry.

I normally would not have let him put his head on my shoulders, let alone stain my dress with his mucus and tears. But I remembered how he held me outside the Lincoln Memorial. How he had been present for me when I needed him. Like Masuda, when I found out that my father had been reassigned and that we would be leaving Egypt. Or Timothée, when I found out my father had been reassigned again and we would be leaving France. I wish I had WhatsApped them one last time before Disjunctis. If being indebted to Hikaru did not gall me, I would have asked him to do it before he got himself kidnapped. After we free him, I will insist he do it, as payback.

I wrapped my arm around Reed. The intensity of his sobbing doubled. I held him even tighter.

He was all right, this Reed. We would take care of each other. We would solve this mystery. We would save the world. Then I would reclaim my life and all my social media followers. Maybe Hikaru was right—maybe going public was a good idea. Maybe, after we saved him, I would even tell him that. Maybe.

Reed wept for ten uninterrupted minutes. His tearstained face blotched pink and red under his milky skin. Slowly, he pulled himself back together.

"¿Bueno?" I asked him.

"Sure." Reed wiped his nose on his sleeve. "Bueno."

Paddleboats were not made for this kind of trip, but as my mother always said, do the best with what you have. It is all you have.

The sun was beginning her journey across the sky as we began ours back to the barge, pedaling down the Patapsco River in our silver dragon boat with black scales. I had been awake so long I was past exhaustion.

"We're like a janky Medea." Reed buried his post-breakdown embarrassment with furious pedaling.

"The child killer?"

"After she killed her children, she transformed into a god and flew away in a dragon chariot."

"That must be why she is so reviled. Not just because she killed her children. But because she got away."

On the way to the barge, we passed many other vessels—early-morning sailboats and motorboats, who courteously cut a path for us in our small paddleboat. Most honked or whistled or waved as they passed. Reed waved back to everyone. I did not.

"They're not waving to you, Reed."

"Oh really?"

"Of course not. They're waving to Xiuhcoatl." I stroked the dragon boat affectionately.

We pedaled and we pedaled and we pedaled.

"This would go faster if I transformed my hands into oars," I offered. Why had I only considered using my Potentia for weapons?

"No."

"¿Por qué no?"

"The sapphire patches on your skin—they're multiplying, aren't they?"

I did not respond. My body was not his business.

"Like Mr. Shaw said, essential transformations only. Otherwise, who knows? You might reach the point where your whole body is stone. Like one of Medusa's victims." Reed froze in an exaggerated pose, aiming for shocked statue but arriving closer to horrified silent-movie star.

"Do you know any other lore?"

"Besides Medusa?"

"Besides the Greco-Roman. The world is full of other stories."

"Like?"

The sun rippled in the glossy water below. A breeze skittered across the wide river, rustling the trees guarding the coast.

"Xiuhcoatl, the turquoise serpent form of Xiuhtecuhtli, the fire god of the Aztecs."

"I dare you to say that three times fast," Reed responded, aiming for comedy.

"The indigenous words may be challenging for you, but so is English to many people."

"I hope the Green Bearer is nicer than you."

"I hope the Green Bearer isn't some stupid American who can only speak one language and has never left their country. Maybe they'll be Brazilian and can tell us about their iconic dragon, Boitatá."

"And then you two can talk in Spanish about the stupid American and I won't even know!"

"Portuguese is the primary language in Brazil, not Spanish." I did not even try to keep the disdain out of my voice. "Or maybe she'll be from China and can tell us about their rich tradition of dragons, which predates the Europeans."

"Okay." Reed, to his credit, didn't get defensive. "I may not have had the privilege of having lived all over the world, but I'm sure I could outgeek you. For example, did you know that the inspiration for the Mandalorian warrior culture comes from a combination of Spartan, Celtic, and Norse civilizations?"

"So you must know that Yoda and his teachings are stolen from Carlos Castañeda's book on shamanism."

Reed's silence was its own admission of ignorance.

I know I should have stopped. But putting him in his place was as satisfying as a winning lunge.

"And you undoubtedly know that Princess Leia's hairstyle was modeled after the soldaderas, the women who fought alongside Pancho Villa."

"Of course I know *that*." Reed clearly had no idea who Pancho Villa was or what role he played in the Mexican Revolution.

I said nothing, to let him salvage some shreds of pride.

We pedaled in blessed silence.

"Thanks, Ale."

"For explaining your ethnocentric ways?"

"Sure, but also, really, back there, when . . ."

"When we boarded Xiuhcoatl, you mean?" I patted our boat affectionately again.

"I'm not sure we should be naming or showing affection to inanimate objects, but yes. After I fall into those mind traps, it's like I'm being ripped open from the inside."

"No hay problema, Rojo." Sharing an iota of vulnerability would make him feel better. "Outside the Lincoln Memorial, after my first transformation, when I could not change back, I had never been so scared in my life."

"About that time . . ."

"¿Si?"

"I just wanted to tell you . . ." Reed took a pause, gathering courage. "Thanks for signing up. I couldn't imagine doing this with anyone else."

I did not know how to respond to his sentimentality, so I did not.

"All right then." Reed let the moment settle. "You think we can really do this?"

"Do what?"

"Outwit JoAnne, find Hikaru, locate the Green and Purple Bearers, and seal the Pentacle Portal?"

"When you put it like that . . ."

Reed slumped back. ". . . it feels pretty impossible, doesn't it?"

"I was going to say"—I gathered myself up—"no hay problema."

"All right then, amigo." Reed stumbled over the Spanish, but his face lit up. "Or would it be *amiga*?"

"Better than either: amigue."

"Amigue?"

"Friendship has no gender."

"Amigue." Reed smiled his guileless, open smile. "Hey, look—I think I see the barge!"

★

"'If you have cotton in your ink, look well that there be no hairs at the nib of your pen.'"

Bayard de la Shaw
Provost, Pass Three

CHAPTER 11

REED AND ALEJANDRA'S RETURN

It took Reed and Alejandra almost two hours of paddling to reach the industrial park where the barge and tugboat had been docked a few days earlier. Their working theory, concocted during the paddling, was that JoAnne and her accomplice must've sneaked onto the barge, laid in wait for Hikaru, and abducted him the moment he returned without waking them or Mr. Shaw, then used the motorboat to return to Baltimore.

A swarm of clouds canvassed the sky, making it feel like the gray day never really started. They docked the paddleboat right next to the barge, tying it to the pier with a scratchy, weatherworn rope. The U-shaped industrial dock was too well-maintained to be abandoned, but everything—the yellow cranes, gray warehouses, and cobalt-blue sheds—appeared untouched since they left a few days ago. There was nary a soul to be seen.

They boarded their barge, full of hope. After a half hour of fruitless searching, those hopes quickly evaporated like the morning dew.

"Even if I could Post Cog, I'm not sure it would help." Reed considered and rejected trying to access his Potentia. "Hikaru's presence would be everywhere."

"Looks like we're going to have to do this the old-fashioned way." The breeze ruffled Ale's curls.

Reed and Ale searched every inch of the ship, looking for signs of Hikaru or JoAnne or her accomplice. They started with the kitchen and dining room, painstakingly working through every nook and cranny of the wood-paneled rooms.

"What exactly are we looking for?" Reed asked.

"Something out of place? Signs of combat? Hikaru must've put up a fight, right? Or maybe Hikaru was able to leave us a clue?"

They spent the next hour on the deck of the barge, where, weather permitting, they had enjoyed meals outside.

"Remember those pandemia months when we could only eat with other people al fresco?" Alejandra emptied the contents of a storage bin: rope, life jackets, more rope.

"Who's Al Fresco? A mobster?"

"It means dining outdoors, Reed." She looked down at him. "It's Italian."

"Sorry, your multilingual highness," Reed snapped back.

They continued searching in strained silence. When they found nothing on the deck, they searched the interior spaces, starting with the library. They removed each book from the built-in bookcases. The most exciting outcome was a particularly vicious string of sneezes after Reed opened a dusty tome of *Paradise Lost*.

Next, they inspected Hikaru's bedroom. They emptied the contents of his desk, making sure to avoid the tablet, Oculus headset, and laptop that he'd brought despite Mr. Shaw's instructions.

"I still don't feel great about being in here." Reed paused just before opening the bureau. "It feels like a kind of violation, don't you think?"

"No."

All they found in Hikaru's room was an impressive stash of edibles and the expected gray cargo pants, yellow Henleys, snacks, and hygiene products.

Ale sat at Hikaru's desk, careful to avoid the laptop cycling a slideshow of shirtless, thirst-trap-worthy Hikaru shots: Hikaru hanging off the barge, Hikaru standing proud at the steering wheel, Hikaru doing a handstand on the tugboat deck, Hikaru lounging on the motorboat. "Why didn't we ask Mr. Shaw to access his computer? I bet it has a clue."

"You know he's got that passworded." Reed unwrapped a chocolate chip granola bar and took a satisfying bite. "What next?"

They moved on to Mr. Shaw's room, which yielded the same amount of leads as the rest of the barge had: zero. They even inspected the empty rooms, where the Green and Purple Bearers would reside.

"Cargo pants and Henleys." Ale shuddered. "I hope the next Provost is not as cruel to his Bearers."

"I won't be," Reed responded over his shoulder.

"You?" Ale asked.

“When Mr. Shaw—I mean, this was before we even found you,” Reed backpedaled immediately, “he said he didn’t have a son, and if I showed him that I had the stuff, he’d . . .”

Ale’s face was as opaque as a statue.

“It’s always a guy, I think.” Reed knew he was just digging himself in deeper, but he was powerless to stop himself, like a plane tailspinning. “At least, that’s what—”

“Silencio, Reed.”

Reed gratefully shut up.

The silence created all the space for Reed to ask the questions he would bet she was asking now. Why did the Provost always have to be a guy? Why hadn’t Mr. Shaw considered Ale? Or was it possible that he had, and she just chose not to say anything to Reed?

After an hour, they found nothing that either corroborated or refuted the theory that Hikaru had returned here the night of his disappearance.

“I give up, Ale.” Reed poked at a bowl of granola bars. “We’ve searched every inch of this stupid barge. Wouldn’t there be a single clue or lead or whatever if Hikaru did actually come back here?”

“Of course!” Ale punched Reed in the shoulder.

“Ow?” Reed scrambled to keep up with Ale, who was suddenly running back to the Bearers’ quarters.

“We’re thinking about where we would be if *we* came back here,” she called back over her shoulder.

“As opposed to?” Reed held his probably bruised shoulder.

“As opposed to Hikaru!” Ale barged into Hikaru’s room and beelined straight for the laptop. The Hikaru thirst-trap slideshow continued its dutiful loop. “Watch!”

Hikaru dodging a drone.

Hikaru flexing in what looked like a TikTok push-up challenge.

Hikaru hanging off the barge.

Hikaru standing proud at the steering wheel.

“There!” Ale pointed from a healthy distance. “And the next one!”

Hikaru doing a handstand on the tugboat deck.

“There’s no captain’s wheel on the barge!” Reed finally caught up to Alejandra.

“And we did not handstand on the tugboat deck because . . .”

“. . . because I can’t do a handstand, for one,” Reed scrambled, “but also, because . . .”

“You and I were confined to the barge”—Ale was already tugging Reed out of Hikaru’s room—“because of Disjunctis.”

"Unlike Hikaru"—Reed followed Ale down the ladder, to the pier—"who could've gone, and often did go, on the tugboat!"

"¡Exactamente!" Ale broke out into a run, reached the tug, and climbed up, skipping every other rung on the ladder. "Maybe he learned something about JoAnne and needed to tell the captain to change direction?"

"Then why didn't he wake up Mr. Shaw?" Reed followed Ale at a slightly more careful pace. "And how did the motorboat get back to Baltimore?"

"Yo. No. Sé. But I do know that if you continue asking those questions, I will lance you right here," Ale snapped. "It costs us nothing to inspect the tugboat, so why not just do it?"

Reed nodded a bit more enthusiastically than he needed to.

The deck and winch area of the tugboat was as clue-free as the barge had been. Ale transformed two fingers into sapphire scissors and snipped through the lock on the door leading to the engine room and quarters below.

"Cute," Reed commented.

"Right?" She snipped the air twice more before reverting.

WATERTIGHT DOOR: KEEP CLOSED WHILE AT SEA. White sans serif letters popped against a distressed red background on the inside of the cut-out door.

"I'll lead."

Reed didn't argue.

They closed the door behind them and pulled the latch tight. Reed and Ale used their Stones as lanterns to guide them through the windowless engine room.

They inspected the washing room.

Nothing.

The quarters.

Also nothing.

They stood outside the door, listening.

Gulls screeched outside.

"Shall we descend?" Ale asked.

"The only way this could feel more like the last scene in a slasher flick is if we split up."

They took one slow, creaky step at a time, Ale leading again, down the narrow, exposed staircase to the engine room. The cold steel banisters steadied them.

"When is a staircase so steep it becomes a ladder?" Reed whispered in Ale's ear.

"Silencio, Reed," Ale whispered back.

When Ale reached the bottom step, she held up her hand for Reed to stop.

"Did you hear something?"

Reed shook his head.

The tide shored up against the tugboat, a caregiver rocking a baby's cradle back and forth. Back. And forth.

Then they both heard the distinct sound of a moan.

Blue changed its hazy orb into a directional cone of light. Ale sent her Stone in a slow sweep of their surroundings, like a searchlight over a military encampment. It illuminated the white pipes running from the floor up into machinery and through walls, a metal workbench, a red fire extinguisher hanging from a blue piece of machinery that looked like a suspended furnace, and a cluster of mustard-orange John Deere generators, power units, and engines.

Reed closed his eyes and opened his heart, using his replenished Potentia to search the room. "There's someone down here! And it's . . ."

"Hikaru!" Ale exclaimed.

Strapped to the metal workbench, arms handcuffed up to the pipes above, Blue revealed Hikaru's shadowed form.

He moaned again, his voice muffled by the ball gag lodged in his mouth.

Ale upped Blue's light. They both gasped when they saw Hikaru. His face was bruised, left eye so swollen it looked like a slit drowning in a dark, puffy purple-black sea. A scar stretched halfway up from his lip to his good eye, disfiguring his face with an asymmetrical smirk.

"Jesucristo," Ale cursed.

Incisions sliced his shirtless torso and chest. Some of the cuts had been crudely sewn shut, disturbingly Frankensteinian. Other wounds had been left open to fester, oozing pus. Hikaru's torture had been performed with strategic, cruel, and malicious precision.

Reed heaved. That chocolate chip granola bar didn't taste nearly as good the second time around.

"We have to get him out of here." Reed covered his mouth until a second bout of heaving passed.

Ale was already moving, arm elongating into a sword. First, she sliced the straps suspending Hikaru's arms above. Then she moved to his handcuffs, using finger blades carefully inserted between skin and steel to slice him free. Hikaru collapsed into her arms. She steadied him, unstrapping the ball gag with her flesh hand.

"Almada?" The exertion of speaking sent him into a blood-speckled coughing fit. "My knight in shining armor."

"Can you stand?" Ale tried to help Hikaru to his feet.

"Stone." He jerked his head toward an inlaid metal jewelry box perched on a pedestal. Its Art Deco angles reflected in gold, silver, and bronze. Two thick, tentacle-like cables connected it to a horse-size orange engine.

"No hay problema." Ale sapphired her other hand into a second blade. The sharp edges glinted as Ale x-sliced the cables.

The Disjunctis recoil sent her flying into a pipe as if she had been launched from a catapult. The box fell to the floor with a metallic clank.

"Ale!" Reed ran over to her fallen body. "Are you okay?" He waved his index finger in front of her face. "How many fingers am I holding up?"

She extended a solitary, long sapphire middle finger in response.

"So you're fine." Reed nodded.

"Fine enough." She accepted Reed's extended hand to get up and inspected the depression in the steam pipe behind her. "If I had not transformed before impact, my head would be the dented thing."

"We have to get him out of here," Reed said. "You take point; I'll get Hikaru."

"Great plan," Ale snapped. "It would have never occurred to me."

"Are you seriously snarking me now?"

"Are you seriously ordering me now?"

"I'm just trying to do my job!"

"And what is that, exactly?"

"To lead!"

"Get this into your gringo cabeza," she hissed. "I do not care what Señor Shaw told you, and I do not care what you think you are going to become. No one tells me what to do. ¿Comprendes?"

Reed swallowed his retort as nasty as the regurgitated chocolate chip granola bar a moment ago. Time was of the essence, and they didn't have any to waste on conflict.

"Since we're not actually fighting about what to do," Reed offered, "can we agree to just do it?"

"Good idea, 'Leader.'"

Reed made his way through the pipes and machinery to Hikaru, huddled on the floor, cradling the jewelry box to his chest.

"Yellow's inside?" Reed asked gently.

"Help." Hikaru put Reed's hand on his exposed, lacerated chest. "Please."

Reed understood the request and the invitation that accompanied it. He leaned his forehead against Hikaru's. They both gasped when Reed entered him. He probed his being, gently parting the barriers around Hikaru's psyche, locating their hidden spots of entry and gliding through them. He saw everything about him, his entire life, mosaic impressions in images and sounds and excerpts and fragments. The flashes from childhood moved Reed with their innocence. The more adult, intimate ones made Reed blush, but he didn't pull out. Reed took it all in, saw everything that made Hikaru Hikaru, until they found what they were looking for: a thing trapped in amber, like a prehistoric creature.

The casing was thick and hard. That didn't stop Reed. He pounded into it, over and over, unrelenting, until it shattered. The two Bearers exhaled in unison. Only then did Reed withdraw. The scarlet conduits connecting them retracted into Red. Reed convulsed, and his body spasmed, spent.

His work was done. But Hikaru's wasn't, even if he'd have no memory of the next few moments. Such were the rules of the Feat of Potentia.

Worlds flashed through Hikaru's nonswollen eye before he erupted in a smile, his new scar curving up across the side of his face.

"Level up." His eyes glimmered gold.

Level up, level up, level up, level up, level up. Thank you, Ciara.

Am–Bm–Em–D–C

A hissing emanated from inside the jewelry box prison a moment before a molten golf-ball indentation appeared in its side. Yellow melted its way through captivity and emerged, reborn and defiant, to return to Hikaru's side.

Hikaru moaned when Bearer and Stone were reunited.

"Okay, lovers." Ale hovered at the base of the staircase, with sword and shield. "Vamos."

Reed helped Hikaru up. He half-propped, half-dragged, half-carried him to the foot of the metal ladder-stairs.

They all froze when the latch above turned and the door swung open.

A figure appeared at the top of the stairs, blindingly backlit by four drones hovering at its side.

Reed and Ale exchanged a bewildered gaze.

At the same time, they said, "Mr. Shaw?"

★

"On Synergias: First, they are as unpredictable as the Potentias themselves. Second, they encourage a bonding between Bearers that is perhaps more intimate than advisable. Finally, and perhaps most relevantly, there is no reason to believe that Synergias other than Terminatio serve our needs, making them a distraction at best, and, at worst, calamitous."

Algernon de la Shaw
Provost, Pass Seven

CHAPTER 12

REED REALIZES

"Mr. Shaw! Thank goodness you're okay!" Reed exclaimed. "We found Hikaru! He was here the whole time!"

"¡Estúpido!" Ale smacked Reed's head with the flat side of her sword.

"What?"

"Him! Him!" Hikaru scrambled behind Reed.

A terrifying notion popped into Reed's mind. "Is that JoAnne Glamoured as Mr. Shaw?"

"Of course not!" Ale smacked Reed a second time.

"Then what's the problem?" Reed rubbed the spot on his head where a bump threatened to rise. "Do we have a second villain who's also an illusionist? Or a shape-shifter?"

Ale smacked his head a third time.

"Oh, Reed," the figure at the top of the staircase sighed. "As Occam's razor states, the simplest explanation is often the truest. I am Mr. Shaw. And I can prove it. Credenza!"

Hikaru's whimpers turned into full-out wails of distress.

"I am so very sorry," Mr. Shaw continued, "that you stumbled upon this."

"Him!" Hikaru repeated.

"What?" Reed's mind wrestled with the incomprehensible, just like . . .

. . . two years ago, when his mom sat him down and told him he'd been adopted. All the evidence had been there, lying on the table, staring at him, clear as day: different hair and eye color than his mother and sister, different body type, different tastes, no pictures of his mom pregnant with him, like she had been with Rose.

But because the truth was outside the borders of his imagination, it had simply never occurred to him. Just like . . .

. . . now.

The arguments. Disappearance. The arrival of the drone. The letter. Mr. Shaw's absence. Their wild-goose chase through the docks of Baltimore over the last few days, conveniently removing them from the barge.

"I Won't Go Out Today" by molly ofgeography.

Performed almost entirely a cappella, so no chords.

Just a melody that becomes a harmony searching for understanding in unadorned confusion and pain.

"Mr. Shaw did this?" Reed asked Hikaru, forcing himself to look at the grotesque cuts lacerating his face and body.

Hikaru nodded vigorously.

"I can't tell you how much I regret that it came to this." Mr. Shaw took a step down the staircase. "But it was truly unavoidable."

"Unavoidable?" Ale spat at him. "You are worse than the Sinaloa! Who does this to another person?"

"Did you know Hikaru was intentionally failing the Feat of Locatio?" Mr. Shaw sat on the metal staircase, his face in his hands. "That he was jeopardizing the mission because of his arrogance, his selfishness? That I offered him countless opportunities to relinquish Yellow, all of which he rejected?"

"Chose. Me." As if to emphasize Hikaru's point, Yellow flared especially bright, a will-o'-the-wisp with a vendetta.

"We have yet to locate the final two Bearers!" Grief and worry creased Mr. Shaw's features. The meager light from the Stones threw shadows across his face. "You have no concept how challenging the Feat of Teleportare can be. Or the Synergia necessary to perform Terminatio. The Muraqqa protocol is exceedingly clear about how to handle a saboteur." For the first time, Reed thought to himself, Mr. Shaw looked old. "I even consulted Father. He agreed that this was the only path forward."

"And that's your rationale for torture?" Ale took a step forward.

"Señorita Almada, my only concern is sealing the Pentacle Portal. I would gladly sacrifice my life to achieve that goal. I didn't want to hurt Hikaru, and I'll never be able to tell you what this cost me. I know there is no return from something like this. But as Father taught me, we cannot fear the difficult path when it is the only means to accomplish our goals." Mr. Shaw used the steel banister to steady himself as he rose. "My hope was to protect you two from all this. If Hikaru had performed Locatio. If he had relinquished his Stone. If he had bothered to think about anyone other than himself. I gave him many alternatives. But there is no reason we cannot continue working together once he performs Relinquo."

"Are you freakin' kidding me?" Reed's scrambling brain was finally able to produce words. "We're not working with you after this! You lied to us. You betrayed us!"

"You feel it, don't you?" Mr. Shaw spoke deliberately, like a mediator in a hostage situation. "We are at an intersection, and the choices we make in the next few moments will determine our futures. Please choose wisely. Especially with the fate of the world in the balance. All the two of you need to do is leave. We will never speak of this again. I will take care of the rest, and your hands and souls will remain clean."

Was there any universe, Reed surprised himself in considering, *in which he could take that path and live with himself?*

Life would be so much easier if there were.

But he couldn't "Sit Still, Look Pretty" any more than Daya did.

D–G–G/E–D–G–G/E

Ale didn't have even the briefest moment of hesitation.

"I disagree with your assessment, Señor Shaw." Ale spat the words out as Blue embedded itself in her navel. "We are not at an intersection." Her torso transformed to match her already sapphire arms. "You have already lost your way. And it falls to us to right it." Her legs completed the ensemble. Ale stepped forward, angled planes of turquoise, cerulean, and violet clanking against the metal floor.

"Full plate!" Reed gushed, admiring her living suit of armor.

"Looks like you're not the only one powering up, Rojo."

The first blast of electricity was aimed at Blue, embedded in Ale's torso. The surge from Mr. Shaw's gauntlet would have scored a direct hit had Yellow not interceded. Hikaru's topaz darted forward, absorbing the attack.

"That was a warning shot, Bearers," Mr. Shaw said. "As well as your last chance for a peaceful resolution."

"This is *your* last chance, Señor Shaw." Ale's legs elongated until they were positively arachnid. She bound over the remaining three steps between them in a single stride. "Depart and never contact us again. Or else . . ."

"Reed." Mr. Shaw used his teacher-authority voice. "Call her off."

"Even if I wanted to, which I very much do not, I'm certainly not in a position to give any of my teammates orders." Reed used his Potentia to gently probe Mr. Shaw. The emotional defense tower he encountered was impenetrable.

"We both know that won't work, lad. It's over, you two." Mr. Shaw held his hands out and pressed a button on his gauntlet. "I have the higher ground."

"Y eso, ¿qué importa?" Ale tilted her head in puzzlement.

"It doesn't have any actual significance, child." Four drones appeared behind him. "I just needed to buy a moment for my reinforcements."

"Reed—look out!" Ale yelled.

Two of the drones whizzed past her, firing pulses that Reed barely dodged by hurling himself off the staircase and scampering behind a mustard-orange horse-size generator. The pulses ricocheted around the room. One ripped a hole in a floor-to-ceiling pipe. Steam hissed out, filling their close quarters.

Meanwhile, Ale engaged the two remaining drones. Her buckler expanded into a tower shield that deflected their blasts but hampered her ability to land a solid attack. Hikaru, meanwhile, hid under the staircase, Yellow circling him protectively.

Reed scrambled over, under, and in between pipes and machinery to evade the drones. He almost slipped twice, the sweat of his palms making it increasingly difficult to stay ahead of them. Their pulse attacks shredded pipes, machinery, walls, and anything else unlucky enough to be in their way. The more steam filled the room, the harder it got for Reed to avoid the potential traps and pitfalls. He jerked his body back and down in the most awkward limbo a moment before the jagged teeth of an obliterated pipe would've sliced his face.

Between breaths, he tried to access Mr. Shaw. But his mentor's defenses proved too formidable. The doorless, seamless, perfectly formed tower loomed over him, impenetrable.

"Duck!" Hikaru yelled.

He dropped under the drone's pulse just before a burst of electricity singed his hated cowlick. Momentum sent him stumbling forward, and he smashed his shin against a circular handwheel valve. He crumpled, howling in pain.

The two drones that had pursued Reed backed him into a corner, predators closing in on their prey. Their helicopter blades twirled so fast Reed could only see the steam they dispersed.

"Take him down, Ale!" Two small guns, attached to the drone's underbelly, turned and locked on Reed. "Don't worry about . . ."

Reed didn't need to finish the sentence because Yellow darted straight through one of the drones, a lava bullet ripping through its enemy.

The other drone fired at Reed. But his week of combat training kicked in. Reed tumbled toward the flying robot instead of away and grabbed it by its protruding guns. Knowing that Disjunctis was coming didn't make his blistering palms hurt any less. But the same charge shocked the drone long enough for Reed to bash it against the wall. He was rewarded with the satisfying crunch of plastic and metal against solid steel. Two more bashes reduced the drone to rubble.

"Surrender, Alejandra," Mr. Shaw almost begged as he fidgeted with his forearm remote control. "The last thing I want is to hurt either one of you."

Ale had retreated a few steps down the staircase in exchange for reducing her original attackers into scrap metal. She faced off against another three drones that had arrived to take their fallen comrades' places.

"I have many more drones, Señorita Almada." Mr. Shaw stayed at the top of the staircase, out of her reach. "But have you considered the Price you will pay for a transformation of this duration? I worry that your organs will be affected. Maybe even your ability to bear children."

"I would worry more about your organs than mine, Señor Shaw. And about your assumptions. Like thinking you understand the rules of this engagement." Ale's sword transformed into a Death-worthy scythe and sliced clean through the stairs above her, like a paper cutter. "Hikaru, the supports!"

Yellow resumed its molten state. It flew straight through the staircase's thin metal support poles.

The staircase wobbled once.

Twice.

Then the top half of the edifice collapsed, toppling down with Mr. Shaw in a heap of rubble.

Ale turned back to Reed and Hikaru. "To me." Fully suited, she looked as invulnerable and incontrovertible as a knight from legend.

They needed no further encouragement.

"Hold on tight." She swept Reed and Hikaru in one jeweled limb, then extended the other diagonally into the open space where the upper portion of the staircase had been. A grappling hook locked on to the handle of the door above. She retracted her arm, carrying all three of them through the few feet of empty space like a cable car.

"Xiuhcoatl?" Reed asked.

"Xiuhcoatl," Ale confirmed.

"Xiuhcoatl," Hikaru repeated without any clue what they were talking about.

"Now that the secondary coterie of Bearers has successfully performed the Feat of Terminatio and sealed the Pentacle Portal, I can devote time to my account of the insurrection most foul led by Green of the first coterie. The first sign of something amiss was . . ."

Hortense de la Shaw
Provost, Pass Five

CHAPTER 13
REED'S BETRAYAL

Reed and Ale shouldered Hikaru's weight as they fled the tugboat. When they hit the pier, Ale reverted to her original form.

"Um, maybe wait a few?" Reed panted. "Until we're clear?"

"Tapped." She barely caught her Stone as it fell from her navel. "Out."

They ran past the barge, finally arriving at their silver dragon paddleboat. The sun had seared a hole through the gray cloud tapestry, burning off the rolling fog. Reed's fingers trembled with adrenaline, fear, and exhaustion as he fumbled with the knot tying the boat to the pier.

"¡Dios mío! How long to recharge?" She tapped her Stone as if it were an unresponsive screen while Reed continued fumbling with the rope. "Move." She slapped Reed's hands off and tugged the knot free.

Reed and Ale lowered Hikaru into the back row of the paddleboat, then took their places in the front.

"Where to, Ale?"

"Just paddle." They kicked their feet with all their might, shoving off the pier along the coast, back to Baltimore. "We just have to get far enough away so that if Mr. Shaw . . ."

As if the utterance of his name summoned him, Mr. Shaw appeared in the air over the water, suspended by two drones, each affixed to one of his shoulders.

"Please think this through." Six more drones swarmed around him. "What can you accomplish by yourselves? Hikaru shan't complete the Feat of Locatio for you. You shan't locate Green. And without my tutelage or the real Muraqqa, you won't even know how to determine the location of the Pentacle Portal, let alone seal it." He wiped some blood from an open cut on his forehead. "Reconsider, please, so we can work together."

"Your idea of working together is manipulating us to do what you want," Reed snarled.

"Reed, I expected better from you." Mr. Shaw continued moving through the air, closing the distance between them.

"That's just because I'm the only one stupid enough to do everything you told me to. I thought"—he choked on the words, fighting back tears—"I thought you were training me to be the next Provost."

"Reed, you are a sixteen-year-old from the suburbs of New Jersey. I am a grown man who has spent his entire life preparing for this threat. In the same way that you submit to your teachers, or a coach, you must trust me to determine what's best."

"Being older does not alone confer you with wisdom," Ale snarled. "Or decency. Look at all the coaches and teachers and priests who have betrayed their covenants."

"And all the other coaches and teachers and priests who covered for them," Reed added.

"Do not let him inside your head." Ale put a hand as sturdy as stone on Reed's shoulder. "It's a cheap tactic every losing opponent tries."

Hikaru grunted agreement from the back.

"All you're proving, Reed, is that you'll never pass muster." Despite torn clothes and bruises, Mr. Shaw still spoke with unwavering authority and conviction. "Lads like you never do."

"Shut up!" Red flashed in Reed's eyes.

"It's time to put an end to this tomfoolery." Mr. Shaw and his drones had covered most of the distance between them. "You will return to the barge, and I will decide how we will proceed." He punched into his forearm control, and four of the drones broke formation and swarmed to the silver dragon boat.

"I have nada, Reed." Ale glared at the unresponsive Stone in her hand.

"I can't Orchestrate him. I can't even access him." Reed reached out for Mr. Shaw's psyche and was rebuffed, again, by the formidable stone tower. "He's trained his whole life to shield himself against my Potentia."

"So what would you recommend, Leader? We just admit defeat and let him have his way with Hikaru?" Ale scoffed. "You are all we have now, Reed."

"Battle Cry" by Angel Haze, featuring Sia, with one of the greatest beat drops after the first verse.

"Here goes nothing."

Verse: Am–F–C–Em^7. Reed didn't have the luxury of waiting to be stronger one day. He would have to be stronger now.

He wound up and hurled Red at Mr. Shaw, like an outfielder throwing a runner out at home plate. The Stone settled midair, between them, and two scarlet conduits extended from it, connecting him to his mentor. Inside his psyche, Reed encountered the perfectly formed tower of Mr. Shaw's defense, dwarfing him in its enormousness.

Reed eyed the structure, looming ten stories above him. Goliath to his David. Its sheer size and formidability were almost reason enough to give up.

Almost.

He had no control over the tower. But he could control himself. Reed became a vessel for Red. He allowed himself to be filled by it, to let it expand his boundaries. He was a waterskin growing to accommodate a seemingly endless volume. He relinquished control and let it rip.

"Come now, Reed." Mr. Shaw's voice broadcasted, surround sound. "Just surrender. We both know you're not a fighter."

When Reed reached a quarter of the tower's size, he willed red ruby gauntlets around his fists. He punched into Mr. Shaw's defense.

The tower immediately regenerated itself, new rocks appearing to fill the holes.

"That's enough of that." Back in reality, Mr. Shaw pressed a few buttons on his gauntlet. The drones hovering in front of their silver dragon boat targeted Red. Reed flinched and twitched as bursts of electricity blasted his Stone.

"Do something, Yoshida!" Ale's eyes flashed blue for a moment before reverting to their natural terra-cotta. "Or are you just going to lie there like a puta and take it?"

Hikaru closed his eyes, and Yellow launched out of its protective orbit. It darted around Red, absorbing the drones' attacks, buying Reed the time he needed.

"All right, then." In the spiritual plane, Reed let his fury fill him, growing larger, until he reached half the tower's size. "It's clobbering time." He pummeled into Mr. Shaw's tower again with glowing fists of rage.

Again.

And again.

And again.

"Sick of U" by BoyWithUke, with Oliver Tree. Chorus: F–F–C–Dm. Reed would show Mr. Shaw what it really meant to fuck with someone's head.

This was the opposite of when he dissembled his own tower of defense in Paradise with Versa. That was glorious, self-inflicted surrender. This was crude brutality. Even clad in the ruby gauntlets, his bones crunched with each impact, knuckles in the real world bruising as fists in the spiritual plane punched. Pummeled. Smashed.

Mr. Shaw's tower grew to match Reed's growth. Scale lost meaning as both enlarged, scrambling to outdo the other.

"Your hands!" Ale sputtered.

In the real world, Reed refused to look down at the blood slicking the crevices between his knuckles. But in the psychic plane, he was hell-bent. "I'm going to teach you about 'lads' like me, Mr. Shaw."

Punch. Crunch. Punch.

"You think we're just some nice, happy-go-lucky faggots?"

Kick.

"That's just a show."

Knee.

"A show we put on for people like you."

Jab. Jab. Uppercut.

"But push 'lads like me' far enough, and we'll show you what we're made of."

Was it just his imagination, or was Mr. Shaw's tower regenerating more slowly? The possibility gave Reed the hope he needed. Even though his ruby gauntlets lay at his feet in shattered shards, he didn't stop. He pummeled, punched, and pounded with his bare hands until they were bloody, fractured, swollen lumps of meat.

"You'll never survive this!" Mr. Shaw yelled at him.

Reed was too angry to make words. Instead, he willed himself even larger until he matched, then surpassed the tower.

"Came To Rage" by Riot Ten, featuring Bok Nero, only uses chords in the verse. The rest of the song doesn't need them because of the

He arched his head back and slammed it down,

thumping dubstep and hardtrap production in the chorus and drop

screaming in pain as he demolished the tower,

Riot Ten and Bok Nero weren't the only ones who came to rage then reached in and plucked Mr. Shaw's spiritual self out of the ruins.

"Stop this instant!" Mr. Shaw yelled on both planes.

Reed came to rage Reed came to rage REED CAME TO RAGE.

"I gave up everything for you," Reed hollered, "and you betrayed us! Who knows what else you've been lying to us about?" King Kong Reed yelled at the miniature Mr. Shaw in his grasp. "But I know how to find out. Let's see what you're made of, Mr. Shaw."

Now that the protective tower had been demolished, Reed was able to plunge into his mentor's psyche. Former mentor.

"Get!" Mr. Shaw yelled. "Out!"

But Reed was already inside, surfing through rivers of memories and emotions and history and soul, pillaging his past, looting through the stuff that made him him.

Indecipherable flashes: the Muraqqa. The Stones. Mr. Shaw as a child. JoAnne and the other Pass Ten Bearers. An absent mother. A terrifying Father. Training. Boarding school. More training. Still more training. University and graduate school. More training. Candlelit meetings. Animal masks. Experiments with buckets of diamonds and onyxes. They whizzed by so quickly Reed didn't know where they started, ended, or how to make sense of them.

Mr. Shaw screamed, full throttle, a soul-shattering, primal, ravaged howl as Reed breached his inner defenses. The defenses Mr. Shaw had spent a lifetime developing collapsed. The defenses, Reed now understood, designed to prevent Reed from doing exactly what he was about to.

In reality, Mr. Shaw fell out of the sky and into the water like a wounded bird.

"What are you doing, Reed?" Terror and awe tinged Ale's voice.

Reed knew Mr. Shaw better than the police sergeant in the DC hotel room and Hikaru. He was already familiar with Mr. Shaw's cadences and his dynamics, his melodies and the chords that supported them. Without that intimacy, he wouldn't have been able to bypass the lifetime of training Mr. Shaw had invested to defend himself against this very scenario. Reed flew through the sheet music of Mr. Shaw's soul, surfing whole notes through staffs and tempos and dynamics, until he found the secret chord that was his very essence. He only had a few beats to pluck this Orchestration.

"Fly, you fool," Reed whispered.

He flung Mr. Shaw aside in the spiritual plane like a soiled rag. The psychic plane dissipated around them.

"I thought we were friends, Reed. I simply cannot believe that you would violate me like that." Compelled by Reed, Mr. Shaw was forced to turn and swim away. "But I suppose I shouldn't be surprised, given what you did to Alejandra."

The red flashed out of Reed's eyes, and Red returned to him in the silver dragon paddleboat.

"Vamos, Reed," Ale said. "We're done here."

Ale had to do most of the pedaling because Reed had so little of anything left inside him.

"You still haven't told her, have you?" Mr. Shaw yelled to be heard as the Orchestration forced him to swim away. "About what happened that day at the Lincoln Memorial?"

The words hung, like one of their Stones, suspended in the air. Reed stopped pedaling.

"Rojo, what are you doing?" Ale gave him a shove. "We have to—"

"Ale, I have to tell you . . ." He wiped his bloody, swollen hands, staining his pants. "That day, when I found you, after you first changed, at the Lincoln Memorial . . ."

". . . you used your Potentia to help me transform back." Ale abandoned her pedaling. "So?"

Reed took a deep breath and swallowed his shame. "And . . ."

"And . . . ?"

"Sorry" by Halsey. Chorus: C–Em–G–Am–C–Em–G.

"I used an Orchestration to make you trust me and join the team." Reed blurted the words out quickly, before Mr. Shaw could.

"You what?" Ale stared him down, face as inscrutable as a mask.

"Sorry" by Justin Bieber. Prechorus: F–Am–G. Just like the chorus.

"It was the only time I did it, I swear! And you have to understand . . ." Reed's lower lip trembled with fear and self-loathing. "Mr. Shaw told me it was my task to assemble everyone. As Leader. And you were so suspicious you would've never come otherwise. It was the only way."

"Sorry" by Nothing But Thieves. Chorus: B–C# minor–G# minor–F#–E.

"Just like torturing Hikaru was the only way?" Ale shook with rage. "What is it with you men and your pathetic justifications?"

"Ale, please, I never . . ."

"You fucked with me! You made me think those were my thoughts. My feelings!"

"Swallow My Pride" by The Ramones.

"All Apologies" by Nirvana. No, the Sinéad O'Connor cover.

"Not Strong Enough" by boygenius.

The list went on and on.

Reed looked away, at the river, at the barge, at Mr. Shaw. Anywhere but Ale. He couldn't bear the hurt in her face, the betrayal in her eyes. "Yes. I did."

Even flesh, her punch was strong enough to dislocate his jaw. "You're just as bad as Mr. Shaw. What he did to Hikaru's body, you did to my soul. You violated me, Reed, and I will never forgive you."

Ale stood and stepped onto the ridged shoulder of the paddleboat.

"Please—Ale—wait!" Reed tried to rise but couldn't find the leverage. He slipped and howled as his bloody, raw hands broke his fall. He stared helplessly from the paddleboat as Ale dived into the bay and disappeared.

The white foam of the parting water was the only warning before the nose of a submarine emerged, sharklike, in the opposite direction. The rest of the glass-domed vessel emerged above the waterline.

The glass cockpit cover hinged open like a jaw. A distinguished, silver-haired figure rose from within.

"Father!" Mr. Shaw grabbed a handhold on the submarine's diving plane and slowly crawled toward the cockpit on all fours.

"Rupert." Father tinkered with the control pad in front of him. "As always, a disappointment."

Mr. Shaw hung his dripping head in shame as he climbed into the empty seat.

"And you are the upstart displaying such insolence?" Father barely moved his mouth when he spoke. His regal, serpentine wrinkles folded into his skin like scales. "The Muraqqa presents a Reset as a last resort. But then again, sometimes the last resort is the only resort. Our charge is too important for us to fear the difficult path." He pressed a button on the submarine's control panel. The glass dome hinged shut, and a projectile sped through the water, straight at the silver dragon boat.

There was no doubt in Reed's mind that the torpedo would've blown him and Hikaru into a million pieces if Yellow had not interceded. It darted forward and pierced the projectile before it reached them. The detonation sent both vehicles spinning.

Hikaru screamed, as if the blast had hit him directly. His body jerked, limbs and neck flailing.

The resulting geyser and explosion thrust the silver dragon boat onto the coast and spun the submarine away from them.

"Hikaru, I'll get you to a hospital, okay?" Reed climbed into the back of the dragon boat, taking Hikaru in his bloody hands.

The Yellow Stone barely limped back to its Bearer. It stared up like a distressed pet.

"Not gonna make it, bro." Hikaru's voice was as pained and thin as his breathing.

"What do you mean 'not gonna make it, bro'? I'll tell you something, 'bro,' okay?" Reed wiped his tears with a bloody sleeve. "You are going to make it. You're going to make that Constitution saving throw or I'm going to spontaneously power up into some healing and . . ."

"I, Hikaru Yoshida, bequeath to you, Reed de Vries," Hikaru's voice rasped, ". . . topaz, this precious Stone." Hikaru wheezed his last two ragged breaths.

Yellow fell. Reed fumbled to catch it in his bloody fists. He failed.

The Stone clunked against the floor of the boat, as lifeless as Hikaru's body.

There were many places Reed knew he shouldn't be. Here was at the top of that list. Hidden in shadow, on the boardwalk of Asbury Park, Reed waited for Arno.

— END OF BOOK III —

INTERLUDE C

MUGHAL INDIA, 1653

ZEB-UN-NISSA REMEMBERS

"And how did you know to find me here?"

"I told you, the Stone drew me to you. You will not believe the scale of the task before us, Princess Zeb-un-Nissa, as we endeavor to save the world." The boy braves a step toward her. "Although I confess, I am surprised you do not remember me."

She adjusts her dupatta and looks at him more closely. He is not unfamiliar.

"I suppose," he continues, "we both have changed in the time since the dedication of—"

"—the Taj Mahal! Almost five years ago! You were in Uncle Dara's entourage!" Zeb-un-Nissa's quill smudges across the parchment. She will have to send this page to be recopied by a scribe. *What am I thinking? I must recopy it myself, of course. Too dangerous to have anyone else lay eyes on this information.* "Are the rumors about you true?"

"Which ones?" he asks wickedly.

"You were talked about much in the court of Deccan, Sarmad." She remembers his name, thank Allah. "Just as you were in the court of Akbar."

"And what do they say," Sarmad relishes the question, "when they talk about me?"

"That you are responsible for Uncle Dara's liberalism." Zeb-un-Nissa chooses her words deliberately. "His decadence. His hedonism."

"Are those the words they use?"

"Why do you ask questions to which you know the answers?"

"Because you handle me with a diplomat's gloved fingers." He recalls his ruby to him. "The word they use is 'heresy.'"

She rises from her desk and regards him, weighing her options.

"Nobody knows what you truly believe." The direct approach would be best here.

"I was born a Jew. And an Armenian. Then, I became a Hindu pujari and a Muslim who follows the Quran."

"It is not possible to claim all those faiths."

"Just because you cannot imagine it doesn't mean it is impossible. Much like what I have to tell you now." He dares to approach her desk, almost close enough to touch her. "I have only braved this journey because I have seen the extraordinary task before us. You and I must assemble the Five Stone Bearers. Together, we will use our Blessings to travel to the Pentagon Chamber, where we will harness the awesome power of the Pentacle Portal."

BOOK IV

Whenever you touch topaz, it touches you.

—*Pablo Neruda (1904–1973)*

CHAPTER 1

REED RETURNS

The sight of Arno was a balm to Reed's aching soul. He looked exactly the way Reed remembered him: gentle, wise eyes hiding behind unruly curls; enveloped by a short-sleeve button-down two sizes too big. Even the beat-up dull gray New Balance rip-offs triggered nostalgia.

Reed fought the impulse to run to him. Arno was why Reed had made the trip back to Asbury Park. But now that he was within reach, Reed couldn't find the courage to abandon the safety of his hiding place. Better to stay obscured and observe from a distance on the boardwalk.

Arno settled on their bench and took out a pair of knitting needles from a brightly colored woven bag. He scrunched his face, examining the rows of red and blue wool, as if the stitches held a secret message. Satisfied, he introduced a strand of canary-yellow yarn into the knit.

This was one of those days—one of those glorious early June, early summer days—where the sun popped, a lemon gumball surrounded by puffs of cotton candy clouds against a raspberry slushy sky.

Unlike the day he and Arno kissed for the first time (could it really have been) almost four weeks ago, the boardwalk was in full post–Memorial Day swing today. The volleyball nets were up, the stores were open, and the beachgoers sporting beach tags dotted the boardwalk like poppy seeds in a slice of thick, buttery pound cake.

Soon, beach tags would be required on the weekdays as well. After July Fourth, every good-weather weekday would be as packed as the boardwalk this second Sunday in June. Families and couples and individuals and groups bustled on the boardwalk of weathered wooden floorboards and the parallel sandy stretch of beach.

Why had he chosen their favorite hot dog vendor as his hiding place? Every time she opened her vat, the scent of savory, salty sausages taunted, teased, and tortured him. The fantasy of a dog with the works—squiggly lines of bright yellow mustard intersecting fire engine–red ketchup and dollops of jeweled green relish—made him drool. Just a few weeks ago, it would've been the easiest fantasy to fulfill. Now, his grumbling stomach reminded him how far he'd fallen.

When was the last time he'd had a proper meal? He couldn't remember. Most of the weeklong bicycle trip home from the Chesapeake Bay was a blur. He preferred it that way. If only he could forget the look on Alejandra's face that had seared itself into his memory: confusion turning into comprehension, then rage, just before she socked him. It came to him, nightly, in his dreams.

Ale starred in those full-length horror flicks, as a demon version of her pursued him through sulfur-drenched, lava-scorched planes. Recently, the nightmares changed, and he was dueling Ale, or rather, trying to duel her as she sliced and hacked him down. Even when he managed to get the recommended eight hours in a night, he awoke exhausted, as if he'd barely slept at all.

Reed rubbed his still-aching jaw. He should've gone straight to an ER or urgent care. But he decided to tough it out. He couldn't risk anything that would put him on the grid, anything that would make it easier for Mr. Shaw and Father or JoAnne to find him. After that week, the swelling had mostly gone away, and the creaky pain mostly subsided. Maybe, in another week, his jaw wouldn't pop out of its socket and swerve to the left on full extension.

He considered a different vantage point for spying on Arno, far from the olfactory torture of the hot dog vendor. But no other spot afforded him the perfect cover.

The promise of getting to see Arno was the only thing that had kept Reed going. It was the ribbon at the end of a race, the divine reward for completing a herculean task. But now that he'd arrived and Arno was a mere few feet away, he didn't know what to do.

Reed had been in Asbury Park two and a half days. He'd spent every waking minute waiting. He had survived by panhandling for change and scraps, with meals consisting of the discards of others. Familiar faces had sent him back into hiding until he realized that no one recognized him: not classmates from school; not Rose's friends' parents; not even the members of his mom's book club, who had congregated monthly in his living room over bottles of white wine last year.

He'd spent nights under the boardwalk. At least it wasn't winter. Dips in the still-cold water had been as close as he'd come to showering. The salt of the ocean clung to him, like an exoskeleton, nestling in the grooves between his toes and still-swollen knuckles, caking his limbs and hair.

Looking for Arno at school was off-limits: he'd bet that Father and Mr. Shaw had Asbury Park High under surveillance. Going home was out of the question for the same reason. He'd hurt enough people that he cared about. He couldn't let anyone else pay for his mistakes.

Despite having no guarantee that Arno would arrive today, or ever, he was not in the least bit surprised when he showed up, sat down, and took out his knitting. Bamboo needles continued bobbing at a steady pace, working the mustard strand into the red and blue scarf. Coincidence?

Any wool would've been wrong for the season, but the thick tonnarelli-like strands Arno was using were especially out of place. And yet, like everything about Arno, it made its own sense.

A breeze, cool and delicious, blew across the boardwalk. Arno put down the needles and looked up.

Reed wanted, more than anything else, for Arno to see him. For them to skip the awkward transition of explanation and apology and more explanation and just be themselves again. As much as he'd thought about this exact moment, he still hadn't figured out how to bridge the gap from now to then. The few feet that separated them may as well have been the two hundred miles he'd biked up here over the last week, one eye over his shoulder all the while to make sure he wasn't being followed.

Reed closed his eyes and conjured his last image of Arno: sitting in precalc, with a saintlike halo. As if they had been telepathically linked, Arno had looked up and caught Reed staring at him. Why couldn't he do that now? Reed opened his eyes.

I'm right here! he wanted to scream at Arno's oblivious form. *SEE ME!*

"See Me, Feel Me" by The Who, on the *Tommy* album. E♭–F–F–G. A guitar solo that Reed dreamed he could one day do justice to. If he ever played again.

Where had his bluster gone? His confidence? Why didn't he just saunter on up next to Arno on their bench? If only he had some great opener. But "Sorry I disappeared in a mysterious-as-fuck way, but I had to save the world, which I'm pretty sure I bombed worse than last year's geometry final" didn't really play.

"Nobody" by Mitski. Opening chords: G–G^7–Dm/F–Em^7. Don't let the upbeat tempo fool you. Or the chorus, which just repeated the title over and over again, changing chords and emphasis each time.

Arno turned in Reed's direction. For an agonizing few seconds, he stared directly at him. Reed ducked behind the hot dog cart, ignoring the vendor's shade-throwing glare.

Would Arno even recognize Reed now, unshowered, unkept, unwanted?

In the cart's stainless steel siding, Reed caught a glimpse of his reflection. Sunburned, discolored patches breaking up his otherwise pale pink skin after a week of solar punishment. The memory of the one truck stop shower he'd begged outside Wilmington drowned in the stench of his own BO. His face was longer than he remembered, uneven patches of facial hair sprouting like weeds in a desert.

The cotton cargo pants and the burgundy Henley were creased and soiled and stained and ripped. Yet somehow, through the stringy strands of his clumpy hair, his singed cowlick still popped up, defiant. The only thing with any spirit left.

"You gonna buy something?" The stout hot dog vendor finally asked in classic Jersey Shore. "Or you just lurkin'?"

Orchestrating this vendor would've been a cinch. He'd sent three police officers from the scene of a crime. He'd conquered Mr. Shaw, who'd spent a lifetime establishing defenses against Reed's power. He'd already bested level-end bosses. This hot dog vendor wasn't even a sidekick. She was, at best, a henchwoman.

If only he could access his Potentia.

If he were able to tap into his Stone, he might've been able to figure out a better way to travel back up here. If he were able to access his Stone, he certainly wouldn't have slept outdoors the last week. And he absolutely wouldn't have had to scavenge for every scrap of food.

But like a ghosting ex-boyfriend, Red hadn't responded to Reed since Chesapeake Bay. Since Ale. Since Hikaru. His Stone lay lifeless in his pocket, next to the equally lifeless Yellow.

Reed turned away from the hot dog vendor and Arno. He'd traveled so far, and all for nothing. He couldn't let Arno see him like this. He scratched at one of the many mosquito bites on his ankles with unclipped nails. Anything was better, actually, than letting Arno see him like this. He rose and bolted, almost crashing into a lesbian couple who appeared out of nowhere. He wove between patches of pastels and neons as fast as his blistered feet would take him. The burst of activity left him panting, the air pushing through his dry, cracked lips. A particularly nefarious baby stroller materialized, womaned by yet another lesbian couple. Reed stumbled, tripping over his own feet and going down. He didn't bother getting up.

Maybe, just maybe, he could approach Arno after cleaning himself up.

Or maybe it wasn't even worth it. He should just Relinquo both Stones and let their new Bearers deal with them; let them and their tremendous burden float far, far away. Mr. Shaw was right: Reed wasn't a fighter. He tried to get up and settled for rolling into a Gollum-like squat.

"Reed?" Arno's face slid into his field of vision.

The only way to make sure he wasn't an illusion was to make contact. Arno caught Reed as he fell forward.

The scalding water ran over Reed's body, washing away the filth and dirt and salt and sweat and grime. He shampooed his hair a third time, digging his fingers into his scalp, wondering if he'd ever be free of the feeling of grease clinging to his follicles. If he hadn't depleted the Lilliputian shampoo bottle, he would've given his hair a fourth lather.

He wanted to cry, to wallow in the painfully joyous release. But the tears wouldn't come. They hadn't come since Chesapeake Bay. He wrote it off, at first, as an extension of the mind trap, the Price he paid for Orchestrating Mr. Shaw. But by the third day, sleeping at a bus station outside Philadelphia, he started wondering if he'd permanently lost the ability to release in that way. Every time he felt the urge, the welling of emotion faltered, like an electric kettle that turned itself off just before boil. Maybe he'd never cry again. Maybe he had no tears left in him. Maybe he'd lost that ability permanently, sacrificed like so many other things on this "adventure."

Arno had pulled him off the boardwalk and led him down Ocean Avenue to the Empress Hotel. They had passed the same brick buildings that Reed had seen his entire life: the arcade, the casino, the hollowed-out carousel. He hadn't even been gone a month, and yet everything looked different. Fake. A two-dimensional Hollywood facade fabricated to capture every minute detail, hiding the unpainted flats of wood where the cameras didn't shoot.

The round, young Southeast Asian woman behind the front desk in the lobby of the Empress Hotel smiled when she saw Arno, an asymmetrical dimple dinging her left cheek.

"Sunny, can I use a room for a few hours?" Arno asked. "Maybe more?"

A furrowed brow replaced her smile when she looked at Reed.

"No junkies, Arno." She tapped her multiringed fingers against the counter. "You know the rule."

"Please?"

An infinity of communication transpired in that moment. The simplicity of the transparent plea. Sunny's faith in Arno. The hovering moment, a spinning coin, of Sunny's decision-making. The coin slowing down and finally landing on the side that said yes. She didn't need more information to trust Arno.

"Four forty-eight." She popped a key card into a slot and punched some numbers into a keypad. "And don't forget to fill out your time sheet, okay? Including Manny's shift you picked up on Tuesday." She extracted the key card and slid it to Arno.

"Thanks, Sunny." Arno pocketed the key. "And if I don't see you tomorrow, happy birthday, okay?" He produced a pair of thick, hand-knit woolen knee socks, in alternating stripes of pink and yellow, matching the streaks in Sunny's hair.

"Aw, shucks, Arno." Her smile returned, along with the asymmetrical dimple. "I can't believe you remembered."

They passed modular, square furniture on the way to the staircase. It wasn't lux like the boutique hotel of DC. Which was probably for the best. In his current state, Reed would've felt more at home in a flophouse than any place where the sheets were regularly laundered.

Arno flipped on the lights when they entered the room. Both queen beds were made up with crisp striped linens, a patterned red throw pillow perkily centered on a sea of white and off-white. A brass lamp on a small round table separated the two beds. A desk on the far wall was the only other piece of furniture in the room.

"I'll find you a change of clothes. I think we'll want to burn those. Are you hungry?" Arno lingered at the door of the hotel room, fidgeting with his brightly woven knitting bag.

Reed nodded. He didn't trust himself to make sound yet.

"Just take your time—we're not in a rush." Arno crossed to the windows and parted the curtains. Light flooded the room.

Reed flinched.

Arno didn't ask questions. He drew both the transparent and blackout curtains shut, then turned on the nightstand lamps. "I'll be back soon, okay?"

Reed nodded again, slowly.

"And Reed?" Arno lingered by the door. "It'll be okay. Whatever it is. I promise." He closed the door gently behind him.

Reed stripped, tossing his clothes directly into the garbage. He was still taking the longest shower of his life when the door clicked open and Arno (he hoped it was Arno) let himself in. He continued scrubbing well after his calloused fingertips wrinkled into prunes.

When his body was squeaky clean, Reed stepped out of the shower. With his forearm, he wiped a clear swath in the foggy mirror. Freckles, like dandelions in a field, dotted his face. Working slowly, he applied moisturizer, paying special care to the peeling patches around his neck and face. Then he wrapped a neatly folded towel around his waist.

He tried, and failed, to make order of his hair. But for once, he found an odd comfort in his cowlick and its indefatigability. He surrendered to the aroma of food.

"Remember MOGO Taco?" Arno was holding a take-out bag in one hand and fidgeting with the temperature control with the other. "The Korean fusion place on Cookman? We went there after finals sophomore year and got the Angry Shrimp . . ."

Arno turned and ingested the sight of Reed in a towel.

He dropped the take-out bag. It landed on the floor.

"Sorry. Sorry! I'll just leave this here." Arno picked up the bag of mouthwatering tacos and put it on the desk. "And this is what I found at Rescue Mission . . ." He laid a pair of denim shorts and a T-shirt on one of the beds. "I picked up some underwear at the pharmacy. I didn't know what size you were—underwear size, I mean!—I hope they're okay." Arno put a pack of boxer briefs and a bundle of socks next to the clothes. "Why don't I just come back in a few minutes, after you've had a chance to change and eat?"

"Arno?"

"Yeah?"

"Don't go." Reed sat down, not bothering to dress, and ripped open the bag of tacos. "And Arno?" He stopped right before his first tantalizing bite. "I hope you never know how good it is to see you."

★

"Yellow, dead. Blue, in absentia. Red, on the run. It is finally time to consider The Cyclops Stratagem."

Broughton Shaw
Chancellor, Pass Eleven

CHAPTER 2

REED RECALLS

Reed sat at the desk, his own table for one, and wolfed down the shrimp tacos, the tortilla chips, and the kimchi pico de gallo. His hunger finally retreated, an army admitting defeat after an unsuccessful siege.

Arno sat on the farther of the two beds, barefoot and cross-legged. He let Reed eat in blessed silence, occasionally putting down his knitting needles to consult a scrap of paper. The mustard yarn worked itself into the red and blue rows at a snail's pace.

Reed licked the salt off his fingers. "You haven't asked me what happened yet."

"You'll tell me when you're ready." Arno switched to blue, his needles bobbing like rabbits' ears.

Reed ripped open the Fruit of the Loom boxer briefs and slipped on a pair underneath his towel before letting it drop.

Arno remained focused on his knitting.

Reed tugged on the denim shorts and yanked the T-shirt over his head, messing up his already tousled hair. It hung loose on his skeletal form. He almost hopped onto Arno's bed but decided against it. Too close. Too tempting. He settled on the other. "You didn't seem surprised to see me."

"Why would I be? You left me a clue in your note."

"I worked so hard to find the right way to reference Juan Pujol García without being too obvious!" Reed remembered that night, waiting for Rose and his mom to go to sleep, writing then rewriting the note until he had it just right. How excited he'd been. How naive. How stupid.

"'I see now that life would be so wonderful if we only knew what to do with it!'" Arno recited from memory. "Even if your mom had let the note be circulated publicly, I don't think anyone else would've gotten it. I mean, first you'd need to know it was a Greta Garbo quote."

"Then you'd need to know that Garbo was the code name the British gave to double agent Juan Pujol García in World War II." Reed nodded.

"I mean, it was in our humanities final presentation, and I still had to jostle my memory."

"But I knew you'd get it, Arno." The corners of Reed's lips cheated up in a smile—those dormant muscles' first activity since Chesapeake Bay. "You always do."

"The last time I saw you was outside precalc, talking to Mr. Shaw, the morning after . . ." Arno went for the knitting, realized he had put it down, almost started again, then decided against it.

. . . *the morning after we kissed!* The words hovered between them, thick and heavy as the clouds that day. But no, Reed couldn't go there. That's not why he came back.

"Arno, I'm going to tell you what I've been doing. And I know it'll sound bonkers. And no, I don't even have any real proof. But you've got to believe me, okay?"

"Scale it, with one being 'you won't believe what happened at GSA yesterday' and ten being 'aliens are real.'"

Reed considered. "Twelve?"

"Wow." Arno gathered his knitting into his woven cinched bag and yanked it shut. His dark brown eyes settled, pools so deep that Reed could spend eternity staring into them. "I'm ready. And I promise, Reed, I'll believe you."

Reed started by extracting the Stones from the tattered, ragged khakis he'd tossed into the garbage. *Sparkle a little, just to make this story easier to believe,* he begged. But they remained obstinately dull. "The next morning, I was outside precalc about to ask you to prom when . . ."

"It would've been so much more fun with you!"

"What?" Reed blurted. "You went?"

"Yeah?" Arno admitted.

"Oh." Reed had far too much pride to ask Arno whom he'd gone with. "Who with?"

"Xanny dumped Amineh a few days before, but Ami still really wanted to go and Linsay didn't have anyone to go with, either, so the three of us went together."

"You must have been the hottest thruple there." The growling envy monster rumbling inside Reed disappeared as quickly as it had been conjured, leaving only a faint whiff of foolishness.

"I'm pretty sure I'm the only person whose date *ran away from home* to get out of having to go."

Arno was kidding, of course. But the joke opened a window, giving Reed the chance to let Arno know how he felt, how much he cared, how the possibility of seeing him was the only thing that kept him going this last week. There was so much Reed wanted to—needed to—say.

"Arno, I . . ." His fingers pressed "The Night Is Still Young" against his palm.

A–B–Cm

The song they should've danced to.

"Yes?" Arno's eyes opened wide, like seashells.

"I . . ." But Reed couldn't get there. Wouldn't let himself. "I'm glad you got to go."

Was Arno disappointed? Or relieved? Without his Empathy, Reed couldn't be sure. He'd become so accustomed to using his power, he had stopped relying on his intuition. Now that he was on his own, he was dead reckoning: flying blind without map, chart, or radar.

Nothing left to do but tell his batshit story. Mr. Shaw's approach. The tricked-out car. The Stark Tower–Bat Cave extravaganza. JoAnne Glamoured as Reed's mom. The elevator fight. Locatio. Horseback. Barge. Potentia. DC. The fencing tournament. Alejandra.

Whenever the story got really genre, Reed could sense Arno's unspoken questions. Even for Reed, who had lived it, certain details coming out of his mouth sounded especially fantastical.

Reed reached the point in the story when he—even thinking about it made him taste bile—Orchestrated Ale at the Lincoln Memorial.

"You used your power on her?" Incredulity lifted Arno's bushy eyebrows. "To get her to do what you wanted?"

"We had to save the world, Arno! And you know how Mr. Shaw is," Reed offered half-heartedly. "I didn't want to disappoint him."

Arno held Reed's gaze. He didn't need to say anything.

"But of course, that's on me." Reed forced himself to swallow his transgression and all its horrid moral ramifications. "No one *made* me do it."

"It's better to own it, isn't it?" Arno said simply.

"At least it's the beginning." Reed nodded. "And I want you to know, I'd never do it again, Arno. Ever." *Especially to you,* Reed hoped Arno understood.

Arno accepted his confession without judgment.

Reed continued. The first mind trap in the hotel room. JoAnne disguised as Alejandra. Orchestrating the police. Alejandra completing Locatio on her first try.

"That's the Feat that lets you discover the next Stone?"

"Yup—so we went to—" Reed stumbled on the name as a lump formed in his throat.

Hikaru had died saving him. Maybe if Reed had been smarter, faster, a better Leader, Hikaru would still be alive and Reed wouldn't be here now, endangering the life of the person who least deserved it.

"—to Hikaru's house. I mean, we didn't know it was his house at the time. You should've seen it. Like the mansions in Sea Girt. But fancier. And Hikaru looked like he stepped straight out of a thirst trap."

Arno bristled at the description, so Reed pivoted. "I mean, if you're into that kind of tall, lean, muscular jock thing. Which I most certainly am not." Reed was pretty sure that trying to make things better was only making them worse. "So Hikaru joined up. But he didn't do whatever Mr. Shaw said, like I did."

Reed finished the story. The barge. Mr. Shaw and Hikaru fighting. The drone with the note. The search. Club Paradise. Versa and the Post Cog power-up. The silver dragon paddleboat with black scales.

"Then we found Hikaru on the tugboat! But he hadn't been kidnapped by JoAnne, it was—"

"—Mr. Shaw, obviously," Arno finished for him.

"How did you know?" Reed asked.

"Come on! The signs were so obvious."

"Really?"

"I never trusted him, to be honest. I mean, who wears that much linen? If that doesn't code villain, I don't know what does."

The rest of the story came out in fragments. It was the most recent and should've been the freshest in Reed's mind. But it was still too close. Too painful. His deep dive into Mr. Shaw. The confession to Ale. The punch. Her disappearance. The arrival of Father. Hikaru saving Reed's life and bequeathing him Yellow, just before he . . .

Reed wrapped up the story with a sentence about the trip back to Asbury Park. He didn't need to bore Arno with the minutiae of what he'd endured to make it back home, or the nightmares. He'd already exceeded his crazy quota for the day?—week?—month?—lifetime?

Finally, he picked up the topaz. He placed it next to the equally lifeless ruby, making the top two-thirds of a traffic light, on the striped bedspread.

"Red hasn't done anything since Chesapeake Bay. So I don't know what to tell you, Arno. I wish I could just make this Stone float up and break the rules of gravity and science as we understand them and prove to you that my story is true. But I can't anymore. Maybe ever."

It was the first time Reed had said the words out loud.

He tried to perform the Feat of Petrakinesis. The one that required the least concentration.

Nothing.

No glimmer, no sparkle, no whisper of their bond, as if it had never been. As if he'd gaslighted himself and hallucinated the entire thing.

"That wouldn't exactly work," Arno interrupted Reed's musing.

"What do you mean?"

"Showing me magic right now would only actually prove that magic is real, not necessarily that your story was true. And if magic were real, there could be hundreds of other explanations. So making that ruby fly through the air wouldn't prove the truth of your story any more than Mr. Shaw telling you about the Stones in the first place makes his version right. It's a fallacy of logic."

"Arno, have you always been this smart?"

The corners of Arno's lips curled up in the smallest of smiles as he blushed from Reed's compliment.

"Or have I always been this gullible?" Reed fell back against the embankment of pillows.

"We usually believe what we want to believe," Arno said simply.

Reed regarded the Stones on the striped bedspread of the hotel bed. Red, round, like the stolen eye of a Cyclops statue. Yellow, tapering to a single point, like a teardrop. In the dark hotel room, lit only by two lamps, the Stones looked more like cheap costume jewelry than magical artifacts tasked with the fate of the world.

Had Reed hallucinated the entire thing, like a drug trip? Or maybe the magic had scrambled his memory? Could he be stuck in one of JoAnne's Glamours? Or had his relationship with reality become so severed that he had no idea what was real and what wasn't? Was questioning his sanity proof that he wasn't crazy? Or the opposite? Or . . .

"So what can I do, Reed?" Arno leaned forward. "How can I help?"

"First ask is easy—tell my mom and Rose that I'm okay."

"Are you scared to see them?"

"Yeah, because of Mr. Shaw and Father and JoAnne." The truth, which Reed could barely face, was that even if seeing them didn't endanger them, he was not sure he'd be able to see his family. Not like this. "But here's the second ask. And, spoiler: it's something I have no right to ask, something dangerous at best, and at worst . . ." Could he really bring himself to do this?

"I don't know if I'm superhero material, Reed, but of course I'll join you if that's what you want. You know you can count on me."

For the first time since that horrible day on the Chesapeake Bay, something shifted inside Reed. Tectonic plates realigned and allowed him the briefest moment of hope. "But what about school? And your family? And . . ."

"My parents won't miss me. I don't mean to sound, whatever, but it's true. Nothing's been the same since I came out. It's not like they beat me or anything. But I'm tired of having to apologize for who I am. You're the only one who's never made me feel that way. As for the rest of it—school, work—we'll be gone, what, a few weeks?"

"Four weeks."

"That's not so bad." Arno hopped from his bed to Reed's. "So what now?"

"I don't know, actually."

"One way to find out, I guess."

Arno quickly grasped Yellow.

They waited.

The wheels of a cleaning cart squeaking E♭ to F outside the hotel room.

A particularly pissed-off seagull screeching outside in quarter tones.

"Well"—Arno regarded the dull jewel in his hand—"that was anticlimactic."

"There's one other thing." Reed didn't want to say it. Didn't want to admit it, let alone risk Arno changing his mind about joining. But it would be wrong not to. "Before you become a Bearer, you should know . . ."

"Yes?" Arno's face lit up.

"I Want the One I Can't Have" by The Smiths was a funny song. No bridge, just verses and choruses, and those choruses (Am–Bm–C–D) were almost twice the length of the verses. But somehow it all works with Johnny Marr, the god of clean guitar sounds and whole note strums.

"I can't—" Reed stood up and looked away. This was almost as hard as asking Arno to risk his life. "I can't . . . be with you."

"Why?" Arno's sinking face made it almost impossible for Reed to continue. "Is it something I did?"

"Of course not!" Reed exclaimed.

"Is there someone else?" Arno's pale olive skin got even paler.

"Never."

"Then what?

"I don't trust myself anymore." Reed swallowed, hard. "What I did to Mr. Shaw. I ripped him up from the inside. I didn't think I was capable of something like that."

"That was self-defense."

"And what about"—he could barely choke the words out—"what I did to Ale?"

Even Arno couldn't muster a defense for that.

"Until I know what I'm capable of, I can't be with anyone, Arno. Especially someone like you."

"I see." Arno placed Yellow back on the bedspread.

"If that's a deal-breaker, I get it." Reed gathered the Stones up. "Or if you changed your mind regardless. It's an unfair ask."

"You may have joined because you wanted to save the world. And Ale may have joined because you Orchestrated her. But you're my reason, Reed. What you said doesn't change that. Besides"—Arno stood up, facing Reed, square on—"anything worth having is worth waiting for."

Reed nodded in agreement, not trusting himself to make words.

"Okay. Hikaru bequeathed the Stone to you, right?" Arno held out his hand, palm open. "So maybe you have to do the same to me?"

When Reed embarked on this adventure, it was the coolest thing ever, like the comic books, graphic novels, TV shows, movies, and books he'd grown up on.

Now, he understood more. About cost. About sacrifice. About how Potentias weren't the only thing that came with a Price.

How could he possibly wish even a fraction of that on Arno, whose purity and innocence were among the few incontestably good things left in the world?

He didn't wish it on Arno. Nor could he guarantee that Arno would survive it. The only thing he could guarantee, if he did survive, was that Arno would be changed. As Reed had. But he didn't know what else to do or who else to turn to. He needed Arno. He needed to make things right.

Reed placed the topaz in Arno's open palm and covered it with his hand. They stayed like that for a moment or forever, the Stone ensconced like a pearl inside an oyster. "I, Reed de Vries, bequeath to you, Arno Sarkisian, topaz, this precious Stone."

The Stone blinked to life, a resurrected firefly, before emitting a single, blinding flash of golden light.

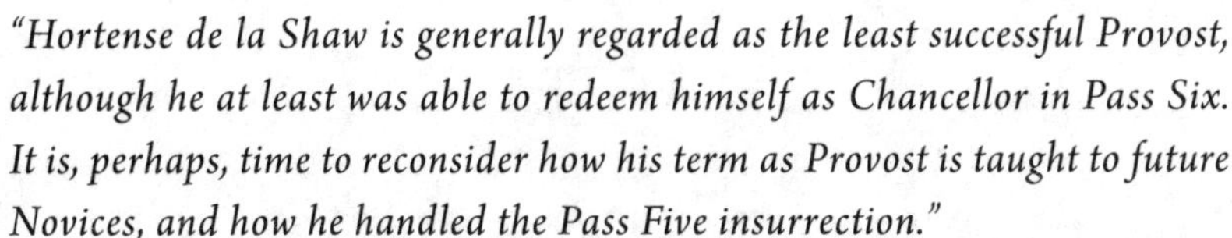

"Hortense de la Shaw is generally regarded as the least successful Provost, although he at least was able to redeem himself as Chancellor in Pass Six. It is, perhaps, time to reconsider how his term as Provost is taught to future Novices, and how he handled the Pass Five insurrection."

Rupert Shaw
Provost, Pass Eleven

CHAPTER 3

ARNO REFLECTS

"I can't be with anyone, Arno. Especially someone like you."

Those words cut into Arno more than anything the people at church had said after he'd come out. What did they even mean? "Especially someone like you." What was Arno like that made him be someone Reed *especially* couldn't be with?

But he couldn't show his pain, couldn't show any weakness around Reed right now. Reed, who'd always moved through the world like he was blessed. Reed, who barely resembled himself anymore.

Waiting for him hadn't been hard. The clue in the letter was all the proof Arno needed. It gave him a secret to protect. Something special. Something that was only his. He carried the secret close to his body, the way people carried hot potatoes in ye olde days to stay warm. It was the opposite of being in the closet. It's funny how some secrets can weigh you down and others can send you soaring like an angel.

Arno didn't remember exactly what Reed said next. He hadn't read those Dungeons & Dragons books, the ones that might've given him some context. It wasn't that Arno didn't believe Reed's story. But the Stones and the Feats and the Pentacle Portal and the Ikeda comet and the Provosts and the Chancellors and the Bearers—it was a lot to take in. And how could magic possibly exist in God's universe, where only saints could perform miracles?

It was impossible. And yet he believed Reed. When he was younger, it would've been difficult for Arno to reconcile those two things. But now, it wasn't. Two totally different truths could coexist. He'd understood that since freshman year, when he turned his back on the Armenian Church and the religion that had defined his entire life. At the same time, he considered his devotion to God now more profound than it ever had been. Arno believed that He created the universe and humankind in His image. He believed that Satan existed as the embodiment of Evil. He believed that Christ came to earth and died for our sins. He believed that the day of reckoning would come. And that Jesus Christ loved him exactly as he was. He lived his life by those precepts and the desire to be worthy of them.

He would use his evening prayers to reflect. For now, he just closed his eyes. It helped him concentrate.

"Hikaru bequeathed the Stone to you, right?" Arno considered the teardrop jewel. Yellow had always been his favorite color. The color of God's light. "So maybe you have to do the same to me?"

He held out his hand, palm up. It would be so easy to extend a few inches and touch Reed again. To make contact with the person he'd thought and dreamed and fantasized about.

The Yellow Stone was heavier than Arno anticipated.

"I, Reed de Vries, bequeath to you, Arno Sarkisian, topaz, this precious Stone," Reed pronounced, like a Reverend Father.

It felt so right, to touch and be touched by him again.

They stayed like that for a moment—an eternity—before the Stone emitted a single, blinding flash of heavenly light.

Finding himself in a golden crystal world didn't necessarily make every other part of Reed's story true. But it did go a long way. As did his perfect replica, staring at him intently. Reed told him he wouldn't remember any of the Feat of Potentia. All the more reason to cherish it while he was here.

Arno had never looked at himself much. At home, he shared a bedroom with his older brother Tigran, the sibling closest to him in age. Their room wasn't large—certainly not intended for two teenagers, two beds, two dressers, and a secondhand desk. The layout made it impossible for Arno to see his whole self in the slim mirror hanging on the back of the door.

He had hoped that his bear of an older brother would go away to college after graduating high school last year. Like his parents, Tigran had barely spoken to him since he'd come out. Tigran had taken to dressing and undressing in the bathroom.

Every time Arno got dressed or undressed with his brother in the room was its own trial of awkwardness. Arno had never had his own room, and he thought maybe, just maybe, Tigran's going away to school would give him some blessed privacy. But their mom had lost her job two years ago, and with Davit and Emin still in college and Nazani starting med school that fall, "it was decided" that Tigran would commute to Brookdale Community College for two years.

"It was decided" was something that often happened in the Sarkisian household. It meant their parents would hand down a decision to them, like Moses handing the stone tablets of the Ten Commandments to the children of Israel.

There was nobody in this crystal plane to decide anything, other than him and his double. His double looked at Arno with the same curiosity Arno was sure was on his own face.

Arno had never spent so much time looking at himself.

His height, or lack thereof, surprised him. He never thought of himself as short, even though he was still wearing Davit's and Emin's clothes from middle school. One of the many nonperks of being the youngest of five was that your entire wardrobe consisted of hand-me-downs. Even underwear.

Arno had been able to tell himself that his clothes fit him okay. Seeing himself forced him to acknowledge that lie: shorts hanging low and loose, sagging below his knees; a striped, short-sleeve button-down billowing around his torso; sneakers so faded you'd never know they were the one thing he'd purchased new.

His double's curly hair didn't have the glossy bounce that models' did in billboards. It frizzed instead, pointing in all directions like a crown drawn by an unhappy child. An unhappy, untalented child. His heart-shaped face rounded out at his chin. His slouch made him look like the "before" in a scoliosis poster.

He'd always known his family wasn't rich: classmates at school talked about the Christmas gifts they'd received, the sleepaway camps they went to, the vacations they took. In his household, each child received one gift for Christmas. They didn't go to camps: they spent summers completing household projects and reading lists. His family's idea of vacation was hiking in the Poconos for the day. Five kids meant five mouths to feed, five sets of gifts for friends' birthday parties/bar and bat mitzvahs/confirmations/sweet sixteens, five college tuitions to save for. A family of seven couldn't fit in a normal-size car, and his parents couldn't afford two vehicles, so every choir practice, piano lesson, soccer, hockey, or rugby game had to be coordinated with the gray Kia Rondo older than Arno. Sometimes that meant an hour or two of waiting at school, enduring the ire of whatever teacher was unlucky enough to have to wait with him. Theirs was most certainly not an Uber household.

"It was decided" that Arno wouldn't go to church when he came out rather publicly and spectacularly during Christmas services his freshman year, trying to impress the boy he liked, the boy who broke his heart. Arno thought he'd never like anyone else ever again.

Until Reed.

The sigh that escaped from Arno's body surprised him, and not just because his double sighed as well. Even after all this time, he sighed whenever he thought about Reed. Reed, whom he'd met brokenhearted freshman year. Reed, whom he'd been crushing on since sophomore year. Reed, who had disappeared the day after they'd finally kissed. Any doubts Arno had that he'd fallen for Reed evaporated like morning mist when he saw him again, crouching on the boardwalk, dirty and damaged and broken.

His double sighed again. Arno was surprised to see how much baby fat he still had in his face. Was it ever going to melt away?

Besides its unlikely sunlight hue, the crystal world was far less remarkable than its population of two. It was as flat as plains, vast and wide and open, stretching out in all directions without a single discerning feature. The pineapple sky glowed far above, a firmament that darkened to honey in its second ring and finally flaxen where it met the horizon and the somber buckwheat and mustards of the ground. It was the opposite of a labyrinth. It was a place without boundaries, without anything to distinguish any part of it from another, whose infinite homogeny could disorient you more than any maze.

He didn't think it was Heaven. He was pretty sure it wasn't Hell. Armenians didn't believe in purgatory or limbo, so Arno didn't really know where he was. Where this was. What this was.

It was impossible to figure out where the light was coming from. There didn't appear to be a sun, or moon, or stars. But the whole world glowed saffron, the kind of diffused cloudy light that his sister, Nazani, who put herself through college by shooting weddings, claimed was best for photography. Even the ground glowed, like the yellow brick road. But without grass or pavement or cobblestone, there was no path to follow.

There was nowhere to go. You are here.

Arno liked it. It was calm. There was nothing to distract or upset him. He wouldn't describe himself as a misanthrope, but in a house of seven, being alone was a luxury he was rarely afforded.

He slipped his sneakers off his feet and, using them as a pillow, lay down to take a nap. Napping was one of his greatest joys in life. Arno could fall asleep anywhere—in the back of a car, sitting at a desk, lying outside on a blanket on a warm spring or summer day. Especially after being with people, a nap was how he restored his sense of self.

When he did it right, he didn't even need to set an alarm. His body would wake up of its own accord in twenty or thirty minutes. When he did it right, it was just a quick dip into sleep. Just enough to recalibrate his insides and restore his equilibrium.

Sleep came easily. He felt his double, around ten feet away, dozing off. If he'd been totally alone in this crystal world, it might be scary. But having another presence there, especially one that demanded nothing, lulled him into an easy slumber.

There was no way to measure how long Arno slept, but it didn't matter. He woke up feeling refreshed.

He didn't need to go to the bathroom. He wasn't hungry or thirsty.

He was learning the rules of the crystal world. He liked them.

It occurred to him that this was some kind of test. It occurred to him that he should find a way out.

"Are you going to show me the way out?" he asked his double and was asked by him.

They both waited.

He couldn't touch the other him—a thin, invisible barrier on a perpetually shifting axis separated them.

But why try to leave when it was so lovely here? He knew Reed was waiting for him, but he also knew that regardless of how much time he spent here, in this plane, he would return to that one with no time having passed. He didn't know how he knew this. He just did. There was no rush.

The first goal Arno articulated for himself was to stand up straight. He tried imagining a string running from the base of his head up to the sky, as his choir teacher had instructed during warm-ups. Arno rounded his shoulders back and stuck out his chest. He tucked his lower back in, then out.

After years of slouching, he didn't have an internal sense of what good posture was. Tracking the movements in his double, Arno saw how unnatural true upright felt. Instead of going by his feelings, he used the resource of his double to work it out.

The first few bouts left his body sore. He couldn't walk with good posture for more than ten or fifteen minutes at a time. His stamina increased over the course of his self-imposed curriculum. He also found that rotating his knees and his ankles out supported his feet and improved his stance.

He worked slowly and methodically, praising himself for his progress, criticizing his setbacks. After working without the visual cues of his double, he saw that he'd been overcorrecting, sending his shoulders too far back, like a strongman at a circus.

After days, or weeks, or months, Arno fixed his posture.

What a gift, Arno thought, *the privilege of this time and solitude.*

Someone else, perhaps, might've become frantic without more to do, people to be with, a book to read, music to listen to. But not Arno. When he was lonely, he sang Armenian Church hymns. They echoed in this world. Echoed against what, Arno had no idea—everything was flat and endless and open, the way he imagined the plains of Kansas, with fields of wheat and corn. But echo, they did.

He and his double couldn't harmonize, unfortunately. But the duets they sang together rang through their honeyed world, filling his soul with peace.

If the Church were a building, its foundation would be so rotten, so eroded, the entire edifice would need to be demolished. Yet it had produced so many beautiful things. Like this music. Another paradox.

Arno and his double didn't embark on a second project until he was satisfied with how they walked, owning all five feet and four inches of his body with an upright confidence that Arno wouldn't have recognized in himself. Even his ill-fitting clothes didn't look quite so ill-fitting anymore.

He considered their options for a second project. Exploring the crystal world was the natural possibility, but he wasn't sure he wanted to leave his double. After considering it during prayer, he compromised: a single experimental journey.

One, two, three . . . four hundred fifty-five, four hundred fifty-six.

He decided to walk in a straight line, in what he imagined was "east," until he discovered something noteworthy or reached ten thousand steps. Whichever came first.

Three thousand seventy-five, three thousand seventy-six.

The only variance in the world were the mosaic patches of mustards and buckwheats in the ground.

Six thousand two hundred twenty-five? Or had he skipped one? Six thousand two hundred twenty-five, six thousand two hundred twenty-six.

If only he'd had some lavash or pita, he'd leave himself a Hansel and Gretelesque breadcrumb trail.

Nine thousand nine hundred ninety-eight, nine thousand nine hundred ninety-nine. TEN THOUSAND!

This part of the world was no different from where he'd started. Indistinguishable. Minus his double.

It was possible that if he looked farther and wider and longer, he would find something different. But he'd been happy where he was. Why look for more when he had been content?

He decided to turn back.

One, two, three, four.

When would he be able to make out his double, walking back to him?

Two thousand three hundred fifty-nine, two thousand three hundred sixty . . .

Without a landmark or way to mark his path, disorientation was his most dangerous foe.

Seven thousand! Seven thousand one, seven thousand two . . .

He started getting worried around eight thousand. Shouldn't he be able to see his double approaching from the other side by now? By eighty-five hundred, he was genuinely anxious.

Eight thousand five hundred sixty-one. Eight thousand five hundred sixty-two.

What looked like a straight line could easily, subtly, and invisibly curve.

By the time he reached his twenty thousandth step that day, he knew he was lost. His double was nowhere to be seen. Either his initial journey hadn't been as straight as he thought, or his return path had swerved. Or both.

He circled back and forth, trying to find his way back to center. Nothing helped. His feet ached, blisters throbbing against sock and shoe.

He sat.

He despaired.

He considered his options.

There weren't many.

He breathed.

Then he did what he always did to restore his faith.

He sang.

Ձեր ճանապարհները ուղիղ են։ Միայն ես եմ մոլորվել։ Օգնիր
ինձ, Տե՛ր, իմ նեղության մեջ, ինչպես մի ժամանակ օգնեցիր
Հովնանին, և ողորմիր ինձ։ Տպրտվելով, ես ցատկում եմ։ Եղիր
իմ նավապետը և ձեռքդ մեկնիր ինձ։ Փրկիր ինձ վտանգից,
ծովերի ալիքների մեջ կոտրվող նավից։

Your paths are straight. Only I have gone astray. Help me, Lord, in my trouble as once You helped Jonah, and have mercy on me. Tossed about, I am floundering. Be my Captain and stretch out Your hand to me. Save me from danger, from the ship breaking up in the waves of the seas.

He wandered as he sang louder and louder, until he was raspy and hoarse, vocal cords like sandpaper, barely croaking out sound. Just as he was about to give up, his solo became a duet. He followed the sound until they found each other again. If they could've embraced, they would've.

He decided against exploring the world again. Not enough to gain. Too much to lose.

Besides, something else was happening. At first, Arno thought he was imagining it. But as he contemplated his third project in this world, he found it communicating with him. The world. Guiding him. Drawing him in.

When his skin was in physical contact with the ground, the communication was stronger. More vibrant. Although it changed his posture and challenged much of the work he'd done, he took to walking barefoot. The flat of his feet grew accustomed to the cool, smooth ground. When he squatted down, hands in contact with the ground as well as feet, the discourse was most powerful.

The world didn't communicate in words. It spoke in memories and fragments and sentiments and images. An all-women's market with spices and fabrics as colorful as the Stones. Snippets of Australian-accented English interspersed with a language he shouldn't be able to recognize but absolutely knew to be Aboriginal Warlpiri. A raven's feather. A chamber of five colors. It hummed in melodies of irreproducible notes in crystal vibrations. Arno listened.

He crouched on one of the darker patches of his good earth, a patch so perfectly toffee-colored it looked sweet to his tongue. Arno lost himself in the world's cadence for hours, maybe days. Something inside Arno opened, and the world poured into him. The patch of ground turned butterscotch, then butter. At the same time, his hands dazzled, like fireworks.

He held on to the light for a few ecstatic moments. It burned through his blood like a religious epiphany. He could see and hear and smell things that he never could before. It was so beautiful it hurt, like an achingly sweet confection. He had to release it.

The light poured out of his hands, and for a few glorious seconds, they flashed like sparklers, leaving traces as he etched patterns in the air. That patch of ground darkened to its original toffee as he released the light.

This Blessing became his next project. He calibrated how much light he could absorb. How long he could hold on to it before needing to release it. How long he could live with the humming, thrilling, dizzying rush racing through his body.

The first uses of this miracle left him so exhausted he needed to sleep, not just nap. Gradually, he built stamina and endurance and fortitude. His Blessing strengthened.

He experimented with what he could do—sparkle, flash, burn, dazzle. The power was pure liquid joy rushing through his veins. If he held it too long, he risked combustion, like a piece of TNT from the old Saturday morning cartoons.

Sometimes, in the window between absorbing and releasing the light, Arno saw faces staring back at him from the ground, expressions scratched into the surface, like prehistoric cave drawings. When he released the energy, the opacity returned, obscuring the faces once again.

He observed his double during the light-absorption process. How far they could project light. How it dazzled under their olive skin.

He collaborated with his double, creating symmetrical firework spectaculars. They "ooh"ed and "aah"ed together, performer and audience, spectator and spectated.

During one training session, he accidentally discovered lasers by sending a searing beam at his double. An identical laser seared past him, a line of energy so pure and lethal that it singed his hair and clipped his ear, barely missing more vital parts.

They bled. Drops of red marred the otherwise sunny world. The ground didn't absorb their blood. The drops just lay there, like raspberries dropped from a basket. They each ripped a patch from their T-shirt and used it as a makeshift bandage until they stopped bleeding. It took much longer than it should've.

He closed his eyes to gather his thoughts. It was easier that way.

For the first time since he'd arrived, Arno understood that he couldn't stay here forever. If the laws of nature that stopped him from having to eat or use the bathroom also slowed down his own healing, what would've happened if he'd caused more serious damage to himself? What would happen if he bled out in this world? He and his double could do a lot together, but there were certain ways they would never be able to take care of each other.

The drops of his blood sparkled like little rubies.

Rubies.

Red.

Reed.

Reed needed him. It seemed impossible. When Arno spied Reed hiding behind their favorite hot dog cart, he was sure Reed would eventually approach him. But he didn't. By the time Arno had reached him, Reed had been hunched on the boardwalk, panting, crying, wild, more animal than human. Then Arno understood. It hadn't occurred to Arno, who had always relied on Reed, that Reed could ever need him.

But Reed did need him now. Arno knew how to take care of people. Like his grandmother, whom he'd quarantined with. Whom he'd visited daily afterward until she joined God's angels in Heaven last year.

He approached his double. They nodded to each other, understanding and resolution reinforced in their eyes. They held out their hands overhead in a V, absorbing light from the citron firmament above, amber ground below, and everything in between. His soul buzzed with the power, blazing like a torch that threatened to flare into a conflagration.

When he thought he couldn't take any more, he and his double reached out to each other. He let his other self lead.

They turned themselves into pure, beautiful, incandescent light. In a flash that would've been blinding if there were anyone there left to blind, Arno left his golden Eden.

"My investigation of what actually occurs during the Trial of Potentia comes up frustratingly short. The Diwan of Zeb-un-Nissa references Makhfi—the Hidden One—repeatedly. Was this perhaps more than just a pseudonym? A fragment from Pass One of the Muraqqa heretofore considered unreadable also references ٱلْمَسِيحُ ٱلدَّجَّال*—the Dajjal. A false messiah, liar, the deceiver. Is this another clue? Is it possible the Bearers have conspired, across generations and Passes, to withhold this information? This final piece of the puzzle is all that stands between us and Cyclops."*

Broughton Shaw
Provost, Pass Ten

CHAPTER 4

REED RECRUITS

Yellow emitted a blinding flash after Reed completed the Feat of Relinquo. He waited for the sunspots to fade from his field of vision.

"So you'll do it?" Reed's hand still covered Arno's, ensconcing the topaz between them. "You'll become the Bearer of the Yellow Stone?"

Instead of answering, Arno lowered his palm, taking the still-glowing Stone with him. Was Reed's imagination playing tricks on him, or was the luster of the teardrop Stone changing? The Stone shimmered closer to tangerine than gold, losing some of its transparency along the way. At least it looked like itself again, rather than the dull piece of costume jewelry it had been in Reed's possession.

Arno held the topaz up to his eyes, tilting his head to one side, as if the gem were a tool or artifact from a forgotten civilization whose original purpose was unclear.

Then Yellow floated out of his palm, and Arno's eyes twinkled like two fireflies.

Reed pulled Arno into a deep embrace. His relief wrapped itself around them like a warm towel after a shower. Reed needed someone who knew him, who would remind him who he was when he forgot himself. But it wasn't just relief, of course.

Suddenly, their intimacy was palpable. Wouldn't this have been his dream before he got sucked up into this wretched adventure—to be with the boy he liked, *alone,* in a hotel room? He had to fight the desire to kiss him, to take solace in the comfort of his mortal, physical presence. He had been so wretched this past week—so painfully, miserably alone. And now . . .

As quickly as he had embraced Arno, Reed pulled away. He couldn't risk it. He couldn't trust himself with anyone, let alone someone as pure and good as Arno.

Someone like Arno deserved much better than Reed, who ruined everything he touched.

His family, abandoned.

Alejandra, betrayed.

Hikaru, dead.

He couldn't be with Arno. But he could protect him. Without a Provost or the Muraqqa, Reed would step up. He wouldn't lead the way Mr. Shaw did, with lies and truths intertwined like vines. He wouldn't lead the way he'd tried with Ale, assuming superiority. He would do it however Arno wanted. On Arno's terms.

The firefly glow faded from Arno's eyes.

"Okay—are you feeling up to trying Locatio?" Reed sat them down on the bed. "That's the one that locates the next Stone. Mr. Shaw said that's supposed to be the first Feat. But like you said, who actually knows? Hikaru was Petrakinesising when we met him, and Ale unlocked her Potentia immediately. Potentia's tricky, because your memory is immediately wiped after you pass it, and . . ."

"I know, Reed."

"How could you . . . Oh!" Another Bearer who unlocked their Potentia immediately. As if Reed needed a reminder of how remedial he was.

Now that he was looking for it, Reed sensed the change in Arno. Deep currents of sadness passed through him. Something horrible must've happened during his Feat of Potentia. Maybe the forgetting was a good thing?

Arno continued to consider the glowing Stone, floating in front of him. Then he reorganized his body—there was no other way for Reed to describe it. Shoulders shifted back and down. Chest forward. Everything stacked around itself until a new Arno emerged, one who belonged to his body.

"In that case, you're definitely ready for Locatio." Reed moved his feet hip-width apart and squeezed his shoulder blades together. "It took me a few tries to get this right, so don't feel bad if . . ."

"What else can we do," Arno asked, "rather than just follow Mr. Shaw's plan and locate Green next?"

"Nothing," Reed insisted. "The Ikeda is a little less than a month away!"

"Reed, you have to un-brainwash yourself. You have no idea if the Ikeda even exists."

"Of course it does! Didn't you listen to me? The Stones were assembled to close the Pentacle Portal—"

"—that threatens to destroy the world every thirty-seven years, give or take."

Arno sat on the desk, using the chair for his feet. "That's just what Mr. Shaw told you. We have no reason to believe that's true. I'm not saying it's not. I'm just saying, here are the things we know: the Stones give you power. Mr. Shaw tortured Hikaru. The Price for Locatio is Disjunctis, which stops magic and electricity from working together. And then there are things we suspect, but we have to distinguish between those things now. We don't even know if there really are five Stones. There could be just Red, Blue, and Yellow. Or hundreds!"

"Fair 'nuff," Reed conceded. "So what should we do now? I thought about performing Locatio again, to find"—Reed stumbled—"to find Alejandra, but I can't get my Stone to do anything. Besides, I'm not even sure it's my place to look for her."

"It's not," Arno stated. "She'll find you when she's ready."

"If."

"When," Arno repeated with a certainty Reed envied.

"So?" Reed asked. "What's our next move?"

"Do you remember when we were working on our World War II project, studying the treaty the US and England made with Russia?"

"Sure—Roosevelt and Churchill allied with Stalin against Hitler." Reed scratched his head. "So?"

"'The enemy of my enemy is my friend.'"

"I thought that was an old Klingon expression."

"Sanskrit treatise from the fourth century BC," Arno corrected him.

"I still don't get where you're going with this."

"Shnery, voronk' krrvum yen mimyants' dem, kmiavoren uzhery gayli dem. It's an old Armenian saying. 'Dogs that fight each other will join forces against the wolf.'"

"Am I a dog in this scenario? Or the wolf?"

"Are you going to make me spell it out?" Arno scratched the back of his head. "I think we need to find JoAnne."

"What?!"

They spent the better part of the next hour debating the JoAnne Approach.

"You weren't there, Arno," Reed repeated for what must've been the thousandth time. "She tried to kill us!"

"Did she, though?" Arno showed no signs of impatience.

"She impersonated *my mom*! She told me Rose was in the hospital! Then she infiltrated the hotel room as Alejandra!"

"That doesn't sound like trying to kill you. I think if JoAnne wanted to kill you, you'd probably be dead," Arno protested. "And have you considered JoAnne might have some actually valuable information about the Pentacle Portal since she was the last Purple?"

It was night now. Not that the hotel room at the Empress looked any different, shielded by the impenetrable blackout curtains.

"It sounds to me," Arno continued in his slow, deliberative way, "like all she's been trying to do is stop the Provost and Chancellor."

"So what? We should invite her over to Disney+ and chill? Even if we decided to pursue this cockamamie idea, how would we find her? Fire up the Bat-Signal?"

"We'll figure out the logistics if we decide that's the right course of action. But for tonight, get some rest, okay?" Arno rose, took his woven knitting bag, and slipped on his sneakers. "I'll take care of everything."

True to his word, Arno did. The way he always did what he said he would. He arranged to have the hotel room for another few nights so Reed could stay, protected from the world. He stocked the room up with Lilliputian bottles of shampoo, conditioner, and moisturizer.

Reed stripped to his underwear and crawled into bed. He dreaded this part of the night. It wasn't that he couldn't fall asleep. He was just terrified of what awaited him there once he did.

Reed drew his Stone-clenched fist into his heart, shifted his feet, and bent his knees. It had been weeks since he'd last performed the Feat of Locatio. Did he even remember the sequence of movements, let alone the minutiae necessary? "Squeeze shoulders. Slide those lats down, lad." He banished the memory of Mr. Shaw and his British accent. It was time for him to stop being such a coward. It was time for him to make things right. He concluded the Feat by rotating his arm and shooting his hand out sharply, straight ahead.

He must've done something wrong. Because according to Locatio, Ale and Blue were so close they had to be right there, in Room 448 of the Empress Hotel.

"Hola, Reed."

He turned out of the Feat so quickly that he tripped over his own feet, stumbling and barely catching himself on the small desk, where he'd wolfed down those shrimp tacos just a few hours ago.

Could it really be? Dare he dream?

"Ale, is that you?" Reed squinted against her cerulean glare.

"You look like shit, güey." Alejandra sported a blueberry jumper that stopped just above her knees, the kind of thing Reed might see on TikTok but not that anyone he knew would actually wear.

"Where did you go? How did you get here?" Reed fumbled over all the questions. "Is everything all right?"

"So many questions, but not the one that actually needs to be asked."

Trust Ale to get to the heart of it so quickly. He knew exactly what she meant. He always did.

"What can I do to make it better, Ale?" He would beg. "Please." He would do anything to earn her forgiveness.

"Nada, güey. Nothing you can do." Ale's voice held no remorse. "Certain sins are unforgivable."

"I don't accept that." The room was so dark, but with the blackout curtains drawn, Reed couldn't tell if it was night or day. "There must be some way."

"Always insisting. Always insistent." She transformed her hand as she stepped toward him, as if she'd slipped on a sapphire glove. "But first you must suffer, as you made me suffer."

"Okay." He swallowed, hard. "Name it."

"You used your Potentia against me. So you will know what it is like to be on the receiving end of mine."

He nodded his consent.

She took his hand in hers. The sensation started there, crawled up his arm and shoulder before spreading over the rest of his body. The grinding of bone to stone made him whimper. How could she possibly endure this every time she changed?

"For how long?" he managed through clenched teeth.

"Forever, güey."

His torso, abdomen, and legs stiffened as the grinding pain invaded every bone and joint in his body.

Reed awoke screaming from the nightmare about Ale. He spent the rest of the day in bed. He thought he'd grown accustomed to the nightmares, but this last one—this was new. He didn't have the energy to do anything today, but he certainly couldn't risk slipping back into unconsciousness. So there he stayed. Maybe—since his Potentia wasn't working—he could at least click the TV on. But a shorted remote control that Arno would probably have to pay for told him that Disjunctis was still alive and well.

Arno had put the PLEASE DO NOT DISTURB sign on the outside doorknob. Reed left the talisman there to protect him. If only he had a DO NOT DISTURB for his dreams. Nightmares.

As promised, Arno returned that afternoon. He brought a stack of snap-lid plastic containers, each holding its own deliciousness. Arno knit while Reed devoured the cracked wheat, meat-and-cheese pastries, stuffed peppers, and gooey pistachio desserts.

"What did you tell your family?" Reed asked between mouthfuls.

"There're seven of us. You think anyone's going to miss this?" Arno gestured with his bamboo knitting needles to the pyramid of containers.

By sunset, Reed let himself be coaxed outside the room on one condition: "No JoAnne talk."

Monday night was quiet on the boardwalk. By July, even this saddest of weeknights would be bustling. But now, only a handful of people passed them on this evening of gentle breezes.

Reed and Arno talked about high school, about television, and of course, about Reed's family.

"I actually made dinner for your mom and Rose last week."

"Really?" Reed felt the pang in his heart, the empty space reserved for the missing of his family. "Are they okay?"

Arno considered. "They're okay enough."

A world lay beneath those words. Reed decided he could brave the details he didn't realize he'd been avoiding. "Tell me."

His mom freaking out after his disappearance. The trips to the police station. The offered rewards for clues. The false clues, the dead ends. Each detail stabbed Reed with guilt.

"And Rose?"

"She's like, 'Mom, he said he'll be back in a few weeks. Chill.'"

"So Rose."

"So Rose. And yet . . ." Arno trailed off before deciding to continue. "I also think she's putting on a brave face for your mom."

For once, Arno did most of the talking. Reed relaxed in the role of listener.

“You won’t believe it, but”—Arno put his hands in his pockets and shrugged—“I’m running for Student Council president.”

“Oh!”

“You’re not mad, are you?” Arno looked away. “I only did it because you couldn’t.”

“And because Raul is a fascist-in-training and Jane is high seventy-five percent of the time.”

“That, too.” Arno smiled.

“Of course I’m not mad,” Reed said. “Arno, you’re going to be the best Student Council president Asbury Park High has ever seen. Leagues better than I would’ve been. Galaxies better!”

How would Reed return to his life after all this? No wonder Odysseus had such a hard time reacclimating to Ithaca after ten years of fighting in the Trojan War and another ten spent making his way back.

After walking their stretch of the boardwalk, past their bench, their mini golf place, and the french fry place with the special sauce, they strolled down to the beach. They slipped their shoes off, tucking their socks inside.

Reed had no idea how hard it would be to not hold Arno’s hand on this boardwalk stroll. He could barely focus on the words coming out Arno’s mouth. They drowned in the vacuum where the sensation of their contact should have been.

Arno didn’t seem at all concerned or upset. He didn’t even seem bothered when Reed told him that they couldn’t be together the night before. As if, during their time apart, Arno had gotten over him. Or maybe Arno was never into him. He had no proof that Arno would’ve said yes if Reed had asked him to the prom. Maybe it was presumptuous to have assumed that that’s what Arno wanted. What made Reed such a catch, anyway? Maybe he should be grateful to the Stones for saving him from that embarrassment. Some Empath.

The Feat of Potentia had changed Arno. Reed couldn’t exactly articulate how. His body was physically the same—if Arno had taken a physical before and after, Reed was sure the results would have been identical. But something about his essence had been altered. It was fundamental and profound, a subtle molecular of alchemy.

Reed wanted to dive into Arno, to quantify and qualify the change. But he swore he’d never do that again without consent. Besides, Red lay dull in his pocket. Cold. Lifeless. Much like the way Reed felt, most of the time, ever since . . .

“Reed?” Arno waited for him to respond to an unheard question.

"Sorry, what?"

"We must be close to where you found Red, right?"

Reed nodded. Which meant, also, this was close to the spot where they first kissed. Once. In a galaxy so very far away.

The ocean waves crashed gently against the shore. A calming *whoosh*, broken by a furious seagull squawking at a real or imagined offense.

"And what happened after?"

"I told you—Mr. Shaw stopped me right before precalc."

"No, I mean immediately afterward. What did you tell me yesterday happened right afterward?"

"Oh, that's right. That creepy little girl appeared."

"And what made her creepy?"

"She had—purple eyes?"

Arno suddenly grabbed Reed's hand and tugged him in close for an embrace.

No! Everything in Reed's mind screamed out: *We shouldn't do this. You can't trust me! I can't trust me*! But his body screamed out something else entirely.

Being this close to Arno, inhaling the scent of his squeaky soap; feeling the cotton of their T-shirts rub up against each other; the solid, warm weight of his hands around Reed's body: it was too much for him. He dropped his shoes and surrendered, letting his body rest against Arno's.

"Just play along," Arno whispered into Reed's ear. "I think someone is following us."

Reed's brain reset, from the terrifying and thrilling scenario, recalibrating parameters and recovering in what he hoped was an acceptable amount of time. "Really?" Reed rested his forehead against Arno's, looking into those bottomless brown eyes. "Who? Where?" Reed whispered as seductively as he could.

"Around ten feet behind me."

Reed cheated a peek over Arno's shoulder. "That straight couple walking away?"

"No—there's a curtain of light, a shimmering—I don't know how else to describe it. Hiding somebody. Or something. Can you use your Empathy to tell if someone is hiding there?"

"Normally, yes. Right now, no." Even if his Stone were working, it was hard enough to focus on what they were supposed to be talking about when he was this close to Arno. Perspiration sprouted in the thin crevice between their hands. Reed's knee rested against Arno's thigh. How was Arno so clearheaded when Reed could barely form a thought?

"I'm going to try something." Arno pulled away from Reed. "Get ready to move." He turned around, took a deep breath, closed his eyes, and brought his hands up to his chest. He interlaced his fingers and extended his hands out, cracking a few knuckles along the way.

At first, it looked like Arno was casting strands of light, rainbow spaghetti noodles weaving and warping in the air. But soon, Reed saw they were actually traveling into, not out of, Arno's fingers.

Their source was a figure, slowly shimmering into visibility. Reed crouched, moving forward carefully, making sure to avoid the weaves of light. On a bright sunny day, Reed wasn't sure how vivid the image would be. But in the darkness of dusk, it was bonfire bright. Could anyone else see it? The straight couple was fifty feet away, backs to them, clueless. The luxury of holding hands without vigilance.

The shimmering curtain undulated slowly, a tapestry unweaving itself and then, abruptly, disappeared altogether, revealing a figure their age, average height, with spiky purple hair and a sinister smirk.

She looked at Arno, at Reed, then Arno again, befuddled. Finally, JoAnne held her hands up, took herself in, and realized she was no longer invisible. "Fuck a duck."

★

"In a truly unprecedented event, Pass Ten Purple has returned to Pass Eleven. The list of queries about how this is possible is as long as it is unlikely. She appears not to have aged during the interim years, but of course, she may just be disguised behind her formidable Glamour Potentia. Although the situation continues to grow more and more dire, we are hopeful that her survival hints at the possibility of Ignatius's Pass Eight revelation."

Rupert Shaw
Provost, Pass Eleven

CHAPTER 5

REED AND ARNO VERSUS JOANNE

"Arno, run!" Reed searched for something—anything—he could use as a weapon. He settled for kicking sand into JoAnne's eyes.

"What the . . . ?" JoAnne swatted at the tiny projectiles. "Stop that!"

"Reed, where are you?" Arno turned and twisted, like an inflatable air dancer balloon, hands sparkling all the while. "I can't see a thing!"

"Hold it!" JoAnne blinked the sand out of her eyes and turned to Arno.

"Stay away from him!" Reed launched himself at JoAnne.

She barely threw herself out of the way in time to dodge him. They both ended up prone on the beach: Reed tasting sand, JoAnne in a crumpled pile of denim, camo, Lycra, and safety pins.

"What did you do to him?" Reed crawled toward JoAnne. "If you hurt him, I swear . . ."

"Bite me, narbo!" JoAnne scrambled away.

This was the opportunity, Reed knew, to connect to her. To use his Potentia before she could gather herself and counterattack. To see what made her tick and how to stop her. Maybe even conduct an Orchestration that would permanently remove JoAnne as an obstacle.

He lobbed Red into the space between them. It dropped to the sand, dull, unresponsive.

The precious window of opportunity slammed itself shut in his face.

JoAnne blurred into an army of fifty JoAnnes, encircling him.

"Listen to me," they hollered in a deafening chorus.

"Mirror Image, like level twenty-five?" Reed pivoted, the balls of his feet digging into the dense, wet sand below. "Very Doctor Strange. But since even the slightest physical contact disrupts your Glamours . . ." Reed barreled forward, dispelling apparitions. "Don't worry, Arno. I'm gonna get us out of here."

Reed didn't know he was capable of such a guttural scream until he burned himself on Arno's glowing hands. It was worse than last Thanksgiving, when he forgot to use an oven mitt and tried to pick up the cast-iron skillet straight from the oven.

He dropped to his knees, still screaming, tasting more sand when he stuck his already blistering fingers into his mouth.

"Finally, I have you where I want you." The remaining JoAnne apparitions tightened their circle over Reed.

A hidden sand bubble thwarted his attempt to flee and sent him sprawling back down on a twisted ankle. He barely felt the abrasions on his knees through the curtain of accumulated pain.

The JoAnnes blinked back into one. She drew her arms back into a fatal, finishing blow, and a disc of silver light surrounded her. It rotated slowly,

menacingly,

and turned into . . .

an old-school boom box.

"Arno, turn until you're facing the source of the sound," JoAnne's amplified voice commanded. "More. More. There you go. Aim higher. Now release."

Silent fireworks surged out of Arno's sparkling hands over the Atlantic Ocean, lighting up the night sky, an early Independence Day celebration. Stars made of stars within stars exploded out of his fingers in solar, cosmic, and golden bursts against the black night sky above, reflecting in the water below.

"You wanna step off, or throw down some more?" JoAnne popped the collar on her safety-pinned camo jacket in Reed's direction. "'Cause I can totally go all night."

Of all the unlikely scenarios Reed had imagined, the least likely was sitting across from JoAnne at the oldest gay bar in Asbury Park eating buffalo wings.

"Are you sure you don't want any?" Arno asked, gesturing to the plate of wings in front of them.

JoAnne shook her head. "Scarf away."

Reed grabbed the last Tangy BBQ wing with his unbandaged hand, ripped its meat off with his teeth, and threw the bones onto the pile in front of him. He still couldn't believe Arno had talked him into this after the scuffle with JoAnne on the beach. But so much had already changed in the forty-five minutes since Arno's vision returned.

"Can you see anything yet?" Reed had asked Arno when they sat down at their bench.

"Nothing." Arno's amber-glazed eyes didn't respond when Reed's hands passed his field of vision.

"Like, just black?"

"No—it's a blinding yellow-white." Arno didn't sound terrified, the way Reed would've been. Just curious, like a child.

"He'll be able to see again in a jiff." JoAnne hovered a respectful few feet away.

"Keep your distance, okay?" Reed warned her.

JoAnne feigned indignation.

"This must be the Price of your Potentia, like my mind traps." Reed glanced at JoAnne. "Now, what're we going to do about her?"

"Where is she now?" Arno didn't need his sight to know who Reed was talking about.

"Having a superintense conversation in a language I don't recognize with a pigeon."

"You think she can talk to animals, too?" Arno asked.

"No," Reed responded. "Her Price makes her bananas. It's a major liability."

"You think?" Arno tilted his head. "Don't you sometimes see or hear things that no one else does?"

Reed knew that Arno couldn't see the smile that crept on his face as all the songs that underscored his world played in simultaneous cacophony. "How come you always know what to say, Arno?"

"Because I remember that old Sanskrit-Klingon saying." Arno smiled back.

Reed fought the impulse to give Arno a quick kiss and settled for a shoulder squeeze that aimed for affectionate but landed closer to awkward weird bizarre. *At least he can't see how uncomfortable I am.* "You better be right about this." He took a deep inhale and exhale before resigning himself to the inevitable.

"Where to, JoAnne?" Reed dared to interrupt what had become a heated exchange with now three pigeons over a pile of seeds.

Eventually, she withdrew from the pigeon drama and Glamoured them fake IDs with appropriate birth dates to get them past the bouncer and into Georgie's.

Even on a Monday night, Georgie's was full of regulars: sitting at the bar, watching basketball on the flat-screens, drinking beer, and shooting pool.

They ordered a platter of wings and three beers from the waiter, who plopped it all down on a wobbly booth in the wood-paneled, pressed tin–ceiling room. "Just wave me down if you need anything else." His contralto scratched with whiskey and cigarettes.

Reed was halfway through his beer. Arno had taken a few respectful sips of his. JoAnne hadn't touched anything.

"Isn't this where you deliver some big monologue"—Reed finally broke what he considered to be the interminable and inexcusable silence—"that challenges everything we thought we knew? And then we have a moving, sentimental reconciliation?"

"Let's not and say we did." JoAnne traced patterns in the dew of her untouched pint glass. "'Cause it would be so much easier for us just to talk. You know. Like in a conversation?"

"Okay—then," Reed began casually. "Let's start with, 'Did it ever occur to you to JUST COME OUT AND TELL ME THAT MY MENTOR WAS EVIL?'"

"I tried, you dip, but you wouldn't listen!" JoAnne insisted. "And then I tried again. And then I tried one more time at the hotel, but I still couldn't get through to you or the Blue Bearer. Have you tried asking yourself why you fell for him so hard?"

"He has an awesome car?" Reed offered weakly.

"And his clothes were really nicely tailored," Arno piped in.

"I guess I can't really blame you," JoAnne admitted. "We all fell for Father in Pass Ten, and he's around a gazillion times eviler than Rupert. They've had hundreds of years to figure out how to present themselves."

"As someone you want to believe." Arno used a fork and knife to eat a Parmesan wing with substantially more delicacy than Reed.

"And as a total DILF," Reed added.

"If only I'd gotten to you before him." JoAnne shook her fists in frustration. "But by the time I figured out how to Locatio, you were already in his clutches."

"You didn't remember how from Pass Ten?" Arno asked.

"Purples usually don't have to Locatio," JoAnne responded. "One of the many things that set us apart."

"So your solution was to impersonate my mom?" Reed didn't quite mean for it to sound like an accusation.

"Gnarly, right?" JoAnne most pointedly did not apologize. "But I didn't have a lot of time to come up with something, so sue me."

"If you wanted to deliver me into Mr. Shaw's clutches, you did great," Reed snapped.

"Look, you two," Arno cut them both off. "Rather than arguing, wouldn't it be better to figure out what to do next?"

Reed and JoAnne mumbled apologies in semiashamed unison.

"So, JoAnne." Arno took a sip of his beer. "Where have you been the last thirty-seven years?"

"I don't totally know." JoAnne shook her head. "I remember being in the Pentagon Chamber with the other Bearers. I remember Terminatio and sealing the Portal. After that, and I know this is going to sound far-fetched, all I remember is being inside my Stone."

"Inside Purple?" Reed asked.

"I don't know how else to say it." JoAnne shrugged. "But you can't take my word for anything, since my Price is seeing, hearing, and sometimes even smelling things that other people don't. By this point, I'm pretty much cuckoo for Cocoa Puffs."

"Great," Reed said. "You have no memories of Pass Ten that can help us, no memory of how you spent the last thirty-seven years, and no idea what we should do next."

"Who said I didn't know what we should do next?" JoAnne asked indignantly.

"This should be good," Reed drolled.

"Reed," Arno reprimanded him.

"After the hotel, when I realized you and the Blue Bearer were already brainwashed, I decided to hunt down the Muraqqa. That's why I wasn't around when Mr. Shaw . . ." JoAnne trailed off. ". . . did what he did to the Yellow Bearer."

"And did you find it?" Arno leaned in.

"The good news is yes, I did."

"And let me guess," Reed jumped in. "The bad news is that it's in Farsi."

"Affirmative." JoAnne spread her hands, and a shimmering grimoire appeared before her.

"But it's not a total dead end. When I infiltrated Father's HQ, I eavesdropped on one of his conversations with Rupert, and that gave me another idea. I want to go back to Pass Ten and see what happened right after we sealed the Portal."

"And how do you propose we do that?" Reed asked.

"Just a little Synergia I've been cooking up," she said. "Between you and me."

"Is there even a precedent for how a Synergia would work with Bearers from different Passes?" Reed asked.

"I thought you would've figured that out by now. I wasn't just the Purple Bearer last time, you space cadets." JoAnne casually held out her hand. Inside, twinkling plum in the low light of the bar, sparkled a perfectly oval amethyst. "I'm also the Pass Eleven Purple Bearer."

New Jersey rock icon Bruce Springsteen used to dream about songs and wake up in the middle of the night to scribble down the fragments of lyrics and melodies. The only one of these fragmented melodies that actually became a full recorded song was . . .

"Surprise, Surprise."

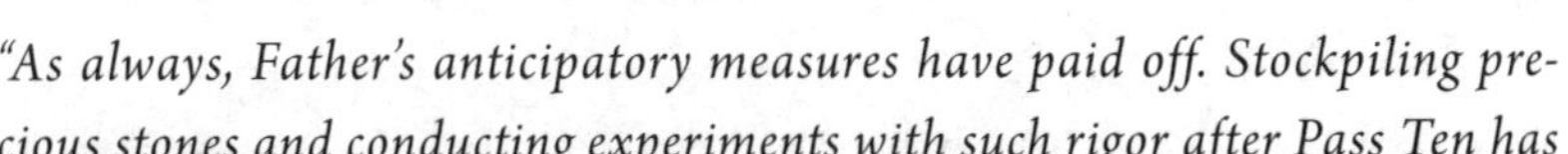

"As always, Father's anticipatory measures have paid off. Stockpiling precious stones and conducting experiments with such rigor after Pass Ten has paved the way for The Cyclops Stratagem."

Rupert Shaw
Provost, Pass Eleven

CHAPTER 6

REED'S FIRST SYNERGIA

Arno put his squeezed fists on either side of his head and splayed his fingers open. "Boom!"

"I thought the Stone Bearers couldn't be old!" Reed said.

"Bite me," JoAnne snapped. "Besides, time functions differently in the Stones. So I don't have an actual age. I'm still sort of a badass fifteen-year-old from Pass Ten, and also the survivor of a bizarre chrono-experiment that puts me somewhere in my fifties."

"I wish you could see the artistry of her Glamours." Arno turned to Reed. "They're part magic, part mystery, part light, and totally mind-blowing."

"Your power is light-based, right?" JoAnne asked Arno.

"I absorb light in one form"—he nodded—"and then release it in another."

"Light alchemist?" JoAnne offered.

"Photo-alchemist!" Reed dropped his voice to James Bond movie trailer pitch. "Arno Sarkisian, photo-alchemist."

"Ooh, I like that!" Arno clapped his hands together.

"So that's how you unraveled my Camouflage back at the beach?" JoAnne wiggled her fingers, and an instant replay of the event unfolded in her palm.

"Your illusions are just light, aren't they?" Arno asked.

"That's like saying dinosaurs are just reptiles," JoAnne scoffed.

"Actually, we know now that dinosaurs were birds," Reed retorted. "One of the many things we've discovered in the last thirty-seven years."

"The good news is that we have only one Bearer left to find," Arno jumped in before JoAnne and Reed could antagonize each other anymore.

"Assuming Ale . . ." Reed trailed off. "But we still have no idea how we're going to seal the Portal after we find Green."

"Why do we have to seal the Portal?" Arno asked.

"Because—" Reed began.

"The Yellow Bearer is right," JoAnne cut him off. "All we know is the propaganda that we've been fed by the Shaw dynasty. So let's check out what actually happened in Pass Ten. We gotta jet." JoAnne waved her hand over the small black faux leather folder holding the check, and a pile of cash appeared.

"We're not leaving fake money, are we?" Arno asked.

"Either of you have moola on you?" JoAnne arched an eyebrow.

Reed shook his head. "Mr. Shaw told me to leave my credit card at home."

"You have your own credit card!" JoAnne exclaimed. "Cool beans!"

"I've only got ten bucks." Arno displayed his wallet's meager contents.

"Dine and dash." Reed shook his head, getting up to go. "Has it really come to this?"

"But when the register is short, our waiter is going to have to cover it," Arno responded.

"So Reed can Orchestrate the manager," JoAnne suggested.

"No Reed cannot because Reed is not using his power that way." *Even if Reed did have access to his Potentia, which he does not currently.*

"Is Reed going to continue referring to himself in the third person?" JoAnne asked. "'Cause that's annoying as hell."

"I'll deal with this." Arno picked up the check. "Will you two be okay together by yourselves?"

"As long as he doesn't start with me." JoAnne burped.

"What she said." Reed leaned back against the banquette of the booth.

"You're both hopeless." Arno disappeared into the back, toward the offices.

"Seriously, dude." JoAnne looked Reed up and down. "What's your damage?"

"Ran away from home, betrayed by my mentor, betrayed my teammate, held my other teammate as he died in my arms, convinced my only real friend I still had to join this stupid adventure, and then found out my antagonist was actually an ally," Reed rattled off. "How about you?"

"Grew up in a world that had no idea what to do with me, got sucked into a Purple crystal world with no temporal reality, had my memory of that time and my previous life distorted, bombarded by historical visions in languages I shouldn't be able to understand every time I make a Glamour, and worst of all have to team up with some dweebs I wouldn't have been caught dead with in high school," JoAnne listed, equally unsentimentally.

They nodded at each other in appreciative silence.

Arno reappeared. "I told the manager that we were unexpectedly short and that I'd drop off the money as soon as possible."

"And they were okay with that?" Reed was already getting up.

"Yup." Arno nodded.

The Bearers grabbed their things and left.

"We need a nice big open space for this Synergia," JoAnne instructed.

"How about the carousel?" Arno suggested.

"Great idea!" Reed exclaimed.

Reed let Arno lead them down Fifth Avenue, past a block of large houses that had been split up into apartments.

"You're going to take us back there, Reed." Subtle lavender swirls surrounded JoAnne as they walked.

"Back where?"

"Pass Ten. December 17, 1986." JoAnne closed her eyes. "To when Rahalleh, Vlad, Nalja, Efrat, and I sealed the Pentacle Portal."

They turned right just before they hit the boardwalk, down Ocean Avenue, walking parallel to Reed and Arno's most-traversed stretch.

"JoAnne, I'm going to need to throw a saddle on the Ikeda itself and ride it like a bronco to power up to time travel," Reed responded.

"Red and Purple can do it, you dip," JoAnne snapped.

"It? What is 'it'?"

"Rupert didn't teach you about Synergias? Power combos?"

"Too busy betraying us, I guess," Reed snapped back.

"Okay—Potentias can be used together to radical effect, like Vlad and Nalja's prismatic rainbow thing." JoAnne gave a few more examples of Synergias from Pass Ten. "If you use me as an anchor, you should be able to Post Cog Pass Ten. And I'll cast it as a Glamour so that we can all look for clues."

"A Phantasmagoria!" Reed exclaimed.

"Call it whatever you like," JoAnne scoffed.

"What do you think we'll find?" Arno asked.

"Something about the Portal's true nature that'll help us come up with another plan." Her voice dipped softly. "In the moment before we completed Terminatio,

I think I saw something in the Portal's heart. Something that I think is clutch to figure out what we need to do."

"I've only used space as the anchor," Reed stalled. "The club, the motorboat." Why was he so hesitant to tell JoAnne that he didn't have access to Red's powers? "I'm not sure how I'd Post Cog using a person."

They arrived at the carousel. Reed couldn't count how many times he and Arno had hung out in this huge, copper, empty shell of a building, with its fancy, swirly glass arches. Sometimes a band would hold a concert here, but most of the time, the rotunda lay empty, a reminder of Asbury Park's former glory.

"Why don't I show you how it's done?" JoAnne closed her eyes, and Red floated up and out of Reed's pocket, landing in her palm.

How is she Petrakinesising my Stone?!

It was wrong. A violation. A transgression.

"Leave it alone!" Reed snapped. "Red's my Stone!" Fury seized him, irrational, wild, uncontrollable, as he unsuccessfully tried to Petrakinesis his Stone back from JoAnne's grasp.

"Reed . . ." Arno reached out and tapped the sparkling round red jewel hovering between them, dispelling it in wisps of light. "It's just a Glamour."

"I told you, never say 'just,' Arno," JoAnne said. "Everything has its own worth." She turned her gaze to Reed. "You ready to try now? Or still scared you're never going to be able to tap into Red again?"

Reed ran his hand over his pocket, feeling real Red's reassuring bulge as the last glimmers of the Glamoured ruby faded into nothing.

He walked through the forms he'd strung together in the motorboat to unlock this evolution of his Potentia. Stand, feet shoulder-width apart. Stomp. Step. Rotate foot. Extend elbow.

Nothing.

"I'd forgotten about those heinous Feats." JoAnne paced around him. "Is that how you first Post Cogged?"

"Yeah," Reed mumbled.

"You know those movements are garbage, right? The Provosts have no idea what they're talking about. What were you feeling when you first discovered it?"

Reed smiled as the memory of sound and sweat of performance washed over him, in the glory of accompanying Versa in Paradise.

Lady Gaga's "Born This Way." G–F–C–G. Piano, not guitar. Not that he'd ever need sheet music for that one ever again.

Elation.

Euphoria.

Surrender.

Freedom.

Red floated out of Reed's pocket, into the middle of the room.

"Hella dope." JoAnne sent Purple to meet Red.

"If this is a trick, JoAnne, or if anything you told us wasn't true . . ." Reed spoke evenly.

"Then what?" JoAnne challenged him.

"You have no idea what I'm capable of." Reed stripped all the emotion out of his voice.

"Ooooooo, I'm so scared!" JoAnne smirked. "You wanna lob some more flaccid threats my way, or can we get to work already?"

Red and Purple met each other in midair. They began to circle each other, slowly and suspiciously at first, inching closer on each rotation. They spun faster and faster, strobing a silent magenta siren that transformed the empty carousel into the Pentagon Chamber.

The communication that Reed had experienced between the Stones amplified exponentially within the Synergia. He connected to Purple through Red, the way he felt when he was performing with the other musicians in Ragna Rock. Everything Red did affected and was affected by Purple. He almost felt like he could Petrakinesis Purple through the transitive link.

"Phantasmagoria!" Reed yelled.

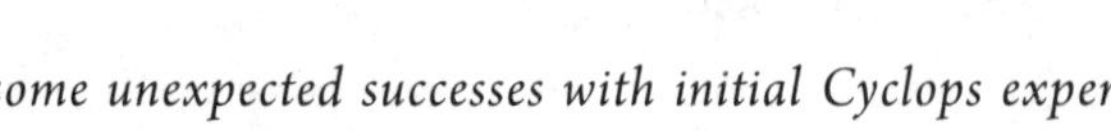

"We have achieved some unexpected successes with initial Cyclops experimentation. One must remember, however, that everything comes with a Price."

Broughton Shaw
Chancellor, Pass Eleven

CHAPTER 7

ARNO WATCHES AND LEARNS

The magenta strobe transformed the empty carousel into the Pentagon Chamber before Arno's unbelieving eyes. The arch windows on the circular perimeter shimmered into five impossibly tall, jeweled walls. Each one was approximately the length of a tennis court and corresponded to one of their Stones. The Pass Ten Red, Blue, and Yellow Bearers stood in front of their respective walls. Arno squinted up, trying to make out the top of the Chamber, but the walls disappeared into the darkness above.

1986 JoAnne emerged from an undulating gateway in the amethyst wall, her tight black leather blazer hanging open over a lacy lavender bra. Her high-heeled, fish-netted feet landed on the smooth floor of the Chamber as the gateway behind her shrank down to her oval amethyst.

"Jo, did you really Teleportare before Efrat?" Pass Ten Red spoke with the same musical lilt as Arno's Iranian cousins.

"Take a chill pill, Rahalleh," 1986 JoAnne responded.

"Maybe you should go back, make sure she makes it?" Blue was built like a linebacker, his frame thicker than his Russian accent.

"She'll be fine," 1986 JoAnne insisted. "I don't care what Father says, you all underestimate Efrat."

As if on cue, the emerald wall rippled and a strawberry blonde stumbled through, barely catching her Stone in time. "Whew! Glad I only have to do that one more time!"

The Phantasmagoria shimmered as Reed dropped to a knee. "I'm not sure"—

the strain in Reed's voice made it difficult for Arno to understand what he was saying—"how much longer I can . . ."

Concern flashed over Present JoAnne's face. "Fast-forward, then. We need to get to the end!"

Reed furrowed his brow and scrunched his face. Everything sped up.

The Portal opened.

It grew from a star small enough to fit in Arno's palm to one large enough for him to walk through.

The Bearers sent their Stones into the pentacle's arms.

The Stones formed a circle, which spun into a sphere.

The sphere contained, then shrank the Portal.

"WATCH! LISTEN!" Present JoAnne screamed at them. "This is the moment we've been waiting for."

Time slowed back to normal as the heart of the Portal opened, revealing the depth of the cosmos inside of it.

Magic poured out.

It was . . . Arno tried to wrap his imagination around the most awesome phenomenon he'd ever witnessed.

Powerful.

Pure energy, without form.

Inspiring.

Somehow, both colorless and all colors at the same time.

Alien.

And most certainly not evil unto itself.

Like the sun, or any force of nature, the magic erupting out of the Portal's heart, battering into the sphere containing it, had no intention.

It could destroy, like all power.

But channeled, it could also create, heal.

As the Sphere of Terminatio shrank the Portal down, it tugged the Bearers closer and closer to its center, to its very heart.

"What's happening?" The fear in Efrat's voice made it crack. "Do you guys feel it, too?"

"We're performing Terminatio exactly as Father taught us," Rahalleh assured the Pass Ten Bearers. "All we have to do is—"

Red disappeared into the Portal first, taking the Pass Ten Red Bearer with it.

"Rahalleh!" both JoAnnes screamed.

The Blue and Yellow Stones disappeared into the Portal next in quick succession, pulling their Bearers in with them.

"JoAnne?" Efrat reached out for her. "I don't think . . ." but the words turned into a wail as the Portal consumed her and Green.

In the moment before Purple disappeared into the Portal, a chorus of voices erupted in the Chamber, speaking languages Arno couldn't recognize, let alone understand. The cacophony awakened something in 1986 JoAnne. She looked up, up into the impenetrable dark of the Chamber, and then—Arno wanted an instant replay to make sure his eyes weren't playing tricks on him—she disappeared into Purple, like a djinni into a lamp.

A second later, the amethyst followed the rest of the Stones into the heart of the Portal.

The Sphere of Terminatio imploded, sealing the Pentacle Portal in Pass Ten, as the modern-day Synergia unraveled in wisps of plum and mauve.

"It is humbling to consider how many pearls, diamonds, onyxes, quartzes, jets, obsidians, tourmalines, howlites, agates, and moonstones we have expended during our experiments."

Rupert Shaw
Provost, Pass Eleven

CHAPTER 8

ARNO STUDIES

"We all die at the end!" JoAnne stomped around the now-empty carousel. "This sucks the big one!"

"Does that mean"—Arno struggled to comprehend the horror—"that to seal the Portal, Provosts and Chancellors have been sacrificing Bearers every Pass for hundreds of years?"

"Explains why Mr. Shaw was so sketchy whenever I asked about meeting the Pass Ten Bearers." Reed sat down on the floor, against a pillar.

"Sorry, love, I would put you in touch with them"—JoAnne transformed into Mr. Shaw, British accent and all—"but they're all bloody dead!"

"Except for you, JoAnne," Arno said. "You may be the only Bearer who's ever survived a Pass."

"It's like Arno said." Reed spoke without intonation, as if he were reading an instruction manual. "We can't trust anything that Mr. Shaw told any of us."

"Like the Portal being evil?" JoAnne asked.

"And also . . ." Reed massaged his temples.

If only he'd let me do that for him. Arno stopped his thoughts before they could wander further. "What?"

"That whole thing about training me to be the next Provost." Reed wrapped his hands around his knees. "Just another lie."

He looked so drained. So sad. So broken. Arno fought the urge to hug him.

"At least we found a clue to the mystery to my survival. Purple took me in!" She stroked her Stone affectionately. "I wish we could go back to Pass One and see Zeb-un-Nissa and Sarmad." JoAnne kicked a stray rock. "See what they did before the Provosts and Chancellors took control of everything."

"Are you going to tell her," Arno asked Reed, "or do you want me to?"

"You." Reed's voice came out thin and reedy, almost cruel. "I can't do much. My Price. Mind trap."

"It's not impossible . . . ," Arno began.

"Say what?" JoAnne demanded.

"If Reed's first Post Cogs were anchored in space, and this one was anchored by a person"—Arno preferred to have whatever he was going to say worked out before, rather than speak on thought, but desperate times—"it stands to reason that he could use an object that was physically present at Pass One as an anchor for the Phantasmagoria."

"So we're going to Teleportare to India and steal something of Zeb-un-Nissa's from a museum?"

"We could." Reed shrugged. "Or we could just use Red."

"Reed, you're brilliant!" An eruption of lilac and lavender exclamation points exploded around JoAnne.

"Why don't we head back to the Empress, rest tonight, and then we can see how we feel tomorrow?" Arno feared that JoAnne was going to try to talk Reed into trying another Synergia right there and then.

Arno took JoAnne's silence as agreement.

Reed spent the entire next day in bed, recovering.

"How come it's hitting Reed so hard but you're ready to run a marathon?" Arno asked JoAnne as they walked on the shore the next morning.

"Maybe I'm just stronger with the Stones? Or maybe it's that I've had all that time since Pass Ten to practice with Purple. And I know this is going to sound out of this world, but when I'm in Purple"—she paused for dramatic effect—"there's a perfect double—someone who looks and acts exactly like me. That helps."

"But if they do everything you do," Arno asked, "how can they teach you anything?"

"It's something about having eyes outside of me and at the same time being able to watch myself. I can see what I'm really doing, and that helps me figure out what I want to do." JoAnne walked so lightly on the sand she barely left footprints. "Like using a mirror to knot a tie."

They walked through the Asbury Park Convention Hall, passing coffee stands and boutique stores.

"You'd think things would've changed so much in the last thirty-seven years that I'd be like, 'Wow! The future!' you know?" JoAnne stopped to pluck something out of her fishnet stockings. "I have no idea what oat milk is, those handphones look like a miracle, and everything's way more expensive, but otherwise, it looks pretty much the same."

Arno scanned their surroundings, trying to imagine what it would be like to see them through JoAnne's eyes. "So what've you learned in your crystal world?"

"The forms that supposedly unlock the Feats are heinous. I actually think the Provosts made them up and all this bullshit mythology around them to limit what we can do. I had to unlearn all that garbage for us to be able to work together."

"Us?"

"Us, as in me and Purple. Together. You've felt it, right? Our Stones—they're not just things. They have thoughts. Feelings? Will. And the more we work *with* them, the more outrageous our moves."

They emerged from the convention hall. It was just warm enough that Arno welcomed the breeze skidding over the water, through his frizzy curls.

"So can you show me how to work with Yellow the way you work with Purple?"

"You want *me* to play mentor?" JoAnne gestured to today's especially alt getup—ripped fishnet stockings, a shiny vinyl ultraviolet jacket, and jagged miniskirt. "You have any idea what I was like when I was in high school?"

"Please, JoAnne. We're all going to have to step into shoes we haven't worn before."

"But I wouldn't even know where to start." They had reached the carousel. Infinitely less spooky during the day. JoAnne leaned against the sprawling mural of fantastic sea creatures on the side of the building. "What I figured out only makes sense to me."

"Why don't you just show me how you get back to your crystal world." Arno didn't want to cause JoAnne any more unease, but he knew she was the only hope he had. Someone was going to have to protect them from Mr. Shaw and Father. And with Reed in his current state . . .

"If you call me Ms. Akalaitis, even once, we're through."

"Deal." Arno smiled.

She led him down the wooden stairs to the beach proper.

"Better that I'm starting with you." JoAnne settled on the sand. "It's going to be so much harder to teach Reed Teleportare and the rest of the stuff."

"Why?" Arno sat down next to her.

"He'll have to unlearn all that bogus Feat nonsense. But you haven't learned the wrong way of doing something yet."

"I just wish I had more time."

"There is no time in the crystal world, Arno, at least not in the way you've been thinking about." JoAnne shook her head. "Make yourself comfortable."

Arno took off his sneakers. The warm sand dug into crevices between his toes. "Now what?"

"Okay—let's try it like this. Close your eyes. Breathe. And listen."

Arno closed his eyes. Arno breathed. Arno listened.

"You have to—I don't know how else to put it—reach out to your Stone." JoAnne's voice sounded like it was encompassing him, coming from all sides. "To its rhythms. Its pulses. You have to open yourself up to it. Let it fill you. I know this sounds corny, but sometimes I imagine I'm a flower, opening up to the Stone's morning light. Or a pitcher, and the Stone is the liquid that fills me."

The sound of the waves, the seagulls screeching overhead, the toddlers screeching just a few feet away from him: it all faded into the background, into a dull lull as Yellow's radiant energy washed over him. Through him.

"You feel how we are so much more than just this body, right?" JoAnne's voice whispered. "How we are connected to everything?"

He didn't know if it was working, because he had no idea what it was supposed to be like, or how to know when things were right. That was okay. It was nice, sitting on the sand, feeling the sun on his face, the breeze caressing his ears.

"Feel how even right now, when it feels like you're not doing anything, you're doing the most important thing. You are being. Being is doing."

Yellow tingled in his pocket, warm and playful as a golden retriever.

Is this what meditating is? Arno asked himself. He'd never meditated before—it felt like something far too mystical, far too sophisticated, far too exotic for a boy like him from New Jersey to be doing. But he prayed every night, and the feeling wasn't dissimilar. Like those moments of absolute serenity, as a kid in church, when the ancient Armenian hymns washed over him, the sounds carrying their own meaning.

His mind released and let it all go: Reed, school, Bearers, Reed, Mr. Shaw and Father, Green, Reed, until only the teardrop of his topaz remained.

Arno hummed Diramayrn, the Mother of the Lord, composed by Saint Gregory of Narek in the tenth century. One of his favorites. Like angels, soaring.

A particularly ambitious wave scooped in below him. He opened his eyes in surprise.

But instead of sand, Arno saw a crystal world of canary light.

"A relief to be writing with good news, for once. I have persuaded Father to experiment with Ignatius's Pass Eight revelation, the Terminatio alternative that does not necessitate the sacrifice of the Bearers' lives."

Rupert Shaw
Provost, Pass Eleven

CHAPTER 9

REED DREAMS, AGAIN

Reed drew his Stone-clenched fist into his heart, shifted his feet, and bent his knees. It had been weeks since he'd last performed the Feat of Locatio. Did he even remember the sequence of movements, let alone the minutiae necessary? "Squeeze shoulders. Slide those lats down, lad." He banished the memory of Mr. Shaw and his British accent. It was time for him to stop being such a coward. It was time for him to make things right. He concluded the Feat by rotating his arm and shooting his hand out sharply, straight ahead.

Stone spinning. A tingle, traveling up his arm, just like before.

But he must've done something wrong. Because according to Locatio, Ale and Blue were so close they had to be right there, in Room 448 of the Empress Hotel. But that couldn't . . .

"Hola, güey." Alejandra's ruffled dress swooped down over a shoulder, asymmetrical, and wrapped itself around her rib cage. It clung to her all the rest of the way, even the slit that lanced down her thigh. "You look like shit."

"Tell me what I can do to make it better, Ale. Please." Reed squinted against the damask glare engulfing her.

"There is nada, güey. Nothing you can do." Ale's voice held no remorse.

Familiar. He had done this before, hadn't he? Which meant . . .

"We both know this is a dream." That would show her.

"So?" His imagination of Ale captured her perfect blasé. "It does not change the truth that certain sins are unforgivable."

"I don't accept that, here, or there, in the real world." Knowing it was a dream should allow him to affect its outcome. Right? "There must be some way to earn your forgiveness."

"There might be."

"Anything." He put his hand to her face, something he would've never dared in real life. "Anything. Just tell me what."

"That is your work to do, güey." Her eyes softened for a moment. "Because we both know . . ."

". . . that since you're just a figment of my imagination . . ."

". . . I do not actually know anything . . ."

". . . that I already don't," Reed finished.

"So smart." She delivered it with the real Ale's exact mocking sarcasm. "No wonder you make such a good Leader."

He let her take his hand. The sensation started there, crawled up his arm, his shoulder, over the rest of his body.

If this is just a dream, I should be able to stop it. Wake up, Reed! Wake up!

"Not yet, güey."

The grinding of bone made him whimper. How could she possibly endure this every time she changed? His torso, abdomen, and legs stiffened as the sapphire petrification spread and enveloped every bone and joint in his body. Telling himself it was just a dream didn't make it hurt any less.

"You still must suffer," she whispered into his ear. "Suffer every night if you want to discover how you may right your sin."

Reed's scream woke him in Room 448 of the Empress Hotel in Asbury Park. Sweat stained his twisted sheets.

The memory of the dream—nightmare—lingered, grinding through his body.

"The ophthalmologist has questions."

Broughton Shaw
Chancellor, Pass Eleven

CHAPTER 10

ARNO RETURNS

Arno and his double sat cross-legged across from each other, knees almost touching, in their crystal world of canary light.

They smiled, sharing the intimacy of an inside joke, before launching into Yekeghetsin Haikakan, "Hymn of the Great Entrance." Appropriate, if slightly blasphemous. During their a cappella duet, Arno went deeper and deeper inside himself, luxuriating in the power that their stillness afforded.

Then they got to work. And it was work. Maddening. Frustrating. Like the first session in his German immersion last summer, not knowing what was being said, how to respond, and feeling that you were already weeks behind.

They started by reviewing what little they knew. They experimented with gestures and movements and words and thoughts.

As JoAnne said, the actual physical movements that Mr. Shaw had taught Reed to perform the Feats had absolutely no value unto themselves. Sometimes they helped Arno focus, but whether this toe was pointing in that direction or that wrist had rotated x degrees was as irrelevant as whether you cast on your knitting needles long-tail or backward loop.

The only way to reliably learn the Feats was through excruciatingly slow, old-fashioned, trial-and-error repetition. You had to try and fail. Then try and fail again. Over and over and over. Each failure might close a door, but it gave you permission to open another. Sometimes, learning what not to do was the only way to discover what could be done. Other times, something that felt brilliant in theory proved ridiculous in practice. It was the process of elimination, charting geometry without a Cartesian coordinate plane, fumbling through the dark, knowing that the stumbling and bumping was inevitable, hoping you'd emerge without too many bruises. And somehow, staying hopeful through it all.

When he was finally able to surrender to the inevitability of failure, to truly accept that the process was not just a means to an end but an end unto itself, then and only then did the possibility of success emerge, as unpredictable and welcomed as a sunny day in winter.

First, he learned he could emit light from any part of his body—his head, his eyes, his butt, even. His outstretched fingers made it easier for him to control color, formation, and duration. It became a convenient default.

Also, inside Yellow, there was no Price. That was the real blessing of being there. The opportunity to fail without repercussions. So different from the real world.

He and his double shared a smile as a jubilation of pyrotechnics exploded around them.

Potentia, done.

He switched his focus to the Feat of Locatio.

He imagined Yellow as a compass, and Green as magnetic north.

Nothing.

He tried again.

The cardinal directions. A needle flickering.

Again, nothing.

Arno understood, now, why JoAnne couldn't explain how she did it. The path she had found made sense only to her, and so Arno would have to find his own way. There was no easy transfer here, no copying each other's notes. He'd have to discover his route, entirely on his own terms, through the abstract labyrinth. Then he could start having fun.

He closed his eyes and shaped his thoughts around the sparking emerald. He crafted the image with the kind of loving care he imagined Michelangelo devoted to *David*. He took time to etch every excruciating detail until it appeared in his mind's eye as vividly as he had seen it in the Pass Ten Phantasmagoria. Rectangular, but with angled corners, like a formal tray.

And the verdant green of a forest after rainfall. Lush. Prosperous.

Still nothing.

He kept the compass and the emerald vivid in his mind's eye and prayed to Gregory the Illuminator, the patron saint and first official head of the Armenian Apostolic Church. Gregory, who left his wife to pursue a monastic tradition.

Gregory, who survived twelve years imprisoned in a pit to save King Tiridates III from lycanthropy through faith, converting him to Christianity, making the Armenians the first Christian nation in the world in AD 301. The last time they had been ahead of their time, Arno chuckled to himself.

His breathing slowed.

The first tugs were so gentle Arno didn't recognize them, didn't even understand they'd been there all along. Acknowledgment was their nourishment, feeding them, letting them grow in intensity and insistence to maturity. Yellow wanted to do the finding. Green wanted to be found. Gradually, Yellow showed Arno how to locate its sibling. There was no "aha!" moment; no epiphany. Just a slow resolution as blurry focused into clarity. Arno bid adieu to his double and returned to Asbury Park Beach, where the sun had begun its descent.

JoAnne was in the same position that Arno had left her in.

"JoAnne?"

She stared ahead, in a trance, pupils dilated. Applying what he'd just learned, Arno opened himself to a ray of the setting sun. He held its intoxicating warmth in his soul, converted it, and then released it as the tiniest sparkle between JoAnne's eyes.

"Who? What? Where?" JoAnne blinked wildly. "What happened?"

Arno shared his crystal-world experience.

"Wicked." JoAnne smiled shyly. "Can I show you what my double and I played around with today?"

Arno nodded, his vision returning.

JoAnne began morphing. Her shoulders broadened, hips narrowed, breasts melted into pecs. The whole process took less than five seconds, and the essence of JoAnne didn't change at all. Arno was sure he would've been able to identify him?—her?—them?—in a lineup.

"Even before Purple chose me, as long as I can remember, like, I'm talking five years old in kindergarten, when the teacher would split us up into boys and girls, I didn't know which group I should go with." This incarnation of JoAnne spoke in a resonant baritone. "And the locker room was the worst. When we were changing for phys ed, I sometimes felt like I didn't belong there, but not like I necessarily wanted to be with the boys, either, you know?"

"Locker rooms are hell." Arno nodded.

"And it's been like that since. I mean, sometimes I felt like a girl. But other times, the idea of having to put on makeup or a dress sent me into these panic attacks." A barrage of squiggly lines popped up around JoAnne to illustrate her point. "And other times when I felt like a boy, and got mistaken for one, I'd feel this rush. But most of the time, I feel like neither, or both. When I discovered my Potentia and could change my outsides to match what I was feeling inside, I finally felt like myself. Like the world made sense. Nothing makes the illusion of gender more obvious than—well—being an illusionist!"

"So I think you're saying you're nonbinary?" Arno asked.

"Say what now?" This masculine JoAnne leaned forward.

"I have so much to catch you up on!" To the best of his ability, Arno gave JoAnne a history of trans and nonbinary people. Since he couldn't speak from lived experience, he didn't totally feel comfortable presenting some of the more nuanced details around gender fluidity and queerness. But he let the years he spent with marginalized gender folx at the GSA, as well as some of the reading he'd done on his own, guide him. He was surprised how, in some ways, it was easier than having to explain his own identity to yet another family member. For this, he didn't need to draw on his own trauma. "Most forms you fill out now even offer a third or fourth option for gender."

"But isn't it confusing," JoAnne mused, "to use 'them' for one person?"

"It can be," Arno admitted, "but so was using 'he' as a default, which everyone did for forever. Maybe, after we've sealed the Portal, you can come to our GSA, and someone there can explain zie/hir, xe/xem, and other options. To be honest, I'm not totally sure how they're different."

"You're not pulling my leg?" JoAnne asked. "This is really a thing now?"

"Just like cell phones, streaming, and gay marriage!"

"Gay marriage? Really? Okay, okay, lemme think!" JoAnne exclaimed. "Even though I sometimes still feel like a girl, and sometimes a boy, most of the time I feel like both. Or neither. Does that make sense?"

"It makes total sense to me. Like your age, JoAnne. You defy category. But since experience is unique, all that matters is that it makes sense to you. Do you want me to use they/them and see how you feel about it?"

"How would that sound?" JoAnne asked shyly.

"'Green Bearer, it is my pleasure to introduce you to the Purple Bearer, JoAnne.'" Arno spoke to an imaginary person. "'They're a superpowered illusionist who was also the Purple Bearer in Pass Ten, and their experience is going to help us save the world. I think you're really going to get along with them.'"

"Why"—a lilac heart surrounded JoAnne—"does that feel so nice?"

"It's about being seen, I think, as your authentic self." Arno spoke slowly, on thought, processing feelings he'd never said out loud. "I thought about this when I came out. Why cause this drama for everyone? Why was it so important that they know, or that anybody knew, for that matter? Why couldn't I just keep it to myself?"

"And?"

"There's something in us—I can't speak for everybody, obviously—but there's some special rush we get when people see us the way we see ourselves. Like wearing clothes that fit."

"No wonder Yellow chose you to be the Illuminator!" JoAnne smiled.

"Yellow didn't choose me." Arno dug a heel into the sand. "Reed did."

"Listen to me, Arno." JoAnne moved closer to Arno. "You're as much of a Bearer as I am, as any of the Bearers, you understand?"

"So why don't we go with they/them," Arno redirected, which was how he handled every situation that made him uncomfortable. "And if you wake up and feel like you want to have a she/her or he/him day, just tell me, okay?" He leaned back on the beach and began the process of rewiring his thought process. Before evening prayers for the next few nights, he'd practice JoAnne's new pronouns out loud. He'd probably mess it up a few times and use the wrong ones by accident. But he'd do his best, correcting himself whenever he slipped so she wouldn't have to. They. *So they wouldn't have to.* "Do you want me to tell Reed, or do you want to, or . . ."

"I'll tell him when I'm ready, okay?"

"Of course." Arno nodded.

During a lull in foot traffic, JoAnne transformed back to their previous form, and the two of them headed back to the Empress to check in on Reed. They took the snoring they heard through the hotel room door as a good sign. Arno made sure the DO NOT DISTURB sign was secure.

Arno and JoAnne hit the local library next. JoAnne's shriek was the only thing that stopped Arno from accidentally Disjunctising the search computers. The librarians offered to help, but JoAnne treated them all like possible spies for Mr. Shaw and Father and decided the two of them should work in privacy. A newspaper clipping with a picture of the recent mayor was all JoAnne needed to Glamour into a reasonable enough facsimile of Mayor Saxena, who signed out the Bradley Room for the rest of the day.

"Now show me what you learned." JoAnne-as-Mayor-Saxena rolled out a map of the tristate area on the large wooden table that dominated the room.

In the mental landscape of his psyche, Arno conjured the crystal world. An image of his double smiled back at him as his topaz spun, sending sensation up his arm as a golden laser beam shone on the southern tip of Cayuga Lake, in the Finger Lakes region of New York.

"Bitchin'!" Mayor JoAnne twirled in lavender swirls. "It's nice to know where you're going, isn't it?"

Arno nodded. It was nice.

After swinging by Georgie's to settle up their bill ("I can't believe you actually came back," the waiter rasped), Arno and JoAnne spent the rest of the day researching their next destination: Ithaca, New York.

"I consider how this all would've played out differently if Larkin had been my Chancellor, rather than Father. I don't have many memories of Gramps, and of course his professional persona may have differed wildly from his personal one. But, I suspect, we would all be on a very different path."

Rupert Shaw
Provost, Pass Eleven

CHAPTER 11

ARNO LEARNS

The next morning, sitting on an Empress towel on the Asbury Park Beach next to JoAnne, Arno returned to the crystal world. Time lost all meaning, and he spent days, maybe even weeks, in his golden paradise. He hopped back to "reality" every now and then to apply what he and his double had discovered.

He learned that he could absorb only natural light: light from the sun or from a fire. His attempt to draw the light from a nearby store lamp resulted in a shorted socket, exploded light bulb, and Arno without vision for almost an hour.

"And at some point—what—do you think I just go blind forever?" he asked JoAnne, sitting on a bench, as his vision slowly returned.

"Stop bitchin'," JoAnne snapped. "At least you have a power that can do something real."

"JoAnne, come on." The whiteout in Arno's field of vision receded into golden bursts. "If Reed or I achieve, like, one tenth of your aptitude, it'll be a water-to-wine-level miracle."

"But still, they're just illusions, just like you said. And meanwhile, my Price makes me . . ." JoAnne trailed off. "Just so you know, I'm twirling my fingers on either side of my head."

"It's getting worse?" Arno asked gently. "Like Reed?"

"Yesterday, I thought that I was a member of the Choctaw tribe at the time of the Louisiana Purchase. This morning, I thought that I belonged to the hadjuk infantry in the Ottoman Empire." Was that the sound of JoAnne manically scratching their forearm? It's not that his other senses heightened when he lost his sight. But he did find that without the distraction of the visual world, it was easier to concentrate on the rest.

Once his sight returned, JoAnne cataloged the permutations of his Potentia. "Fireworks and blinding blasts are all good, but we need some actual firepower."

In the crystal world, Arno worked up the courage to experiment with lasers. His upper ear tingled with phantom pain each time he folded the light unto itself, over and over and over again, like puff pastry dough, until he produced a single, hair-thin laser beam. Back in reality, he used it to fuse a patch of sand into glass.

"This is fantabulous!" JoAnne yelped.

"I'll take your word for it." The white spread through Arno's vision like heavy rain on a windshield. Was it weird that he sometimes found himself looking forward to the blindness, to the calm of not having to deal with the visual barrage of the world?

After Arno's sight returned, they went back to the Empress to check in on Reed.

"How are we going to get to Green and Ithaca without public transport?" Reed had been feeling well enough to join them that afternoon, but a heaviness weighed him down, like chains. "Bikes? Horses?"

"It's about time you two dweebs learned how to Teleportare anyway." JoAnne cracked their knuckles. "Especially since it's the only way to get into the Pentagon Chamber." They led them downstairs to the basement of the Empress Hotel, where a few cans of paint awaited. Arno chose not to question how they had been procured.

"When you Teleportare, you meld two surfaces of the same color across space, so you can walk through one and come out the other. So I can meld a purple wall in New Jersey with one in Timbuktu or Brazil."

JoAnne dipped their brush into a can of heliotrope paint, so brilliant it was almost pink, and painted two door-size rectangles next to each other on the cinder block wall. "Watch and learn, bozos."

Arno knew better than to focus on JoAnne's physical movements. Instead, he opened himself to the intention behind the Feat. Purple floated up and lodged itself in the center of the first purple patch, like a medieval knocker. It radiated ovals until it melted into an elliptical doorway. An identical doorway flashed open on the second patch of painted purple wall.

The rest happened so quickly Arno needed to see it three more times to follow the sequence of events: JoAnne stepped through the first gateway, then out the second. The moment they cleared, both portals shrank down. The first blipped out entirely; the second became Purple.

"Voilà!" JoAnne twirled.

"Wow," Arno whispered.

"I want to do *that*!" Reed exclaimed.

JoAnne had them sit on the floor cross-legged and told them to focus. "The easiest way to do it," they instructed, "is to get you back to your crystal world, where you and your double will figure it out."

But unlike Arno, Reed could barely sit still for a few seconds before breaking the silence. "It's just—my mind's hopping around all over the place, like a kangaroo. I remember some school assignment I didn't finish, then wonder about Rose and Mom, then hop back to Mr. Shaw and Father. And of course, I'm always thinking about . . ."

Reed didn't need to say her name.

"Why don't you try again?" Arno said. "Instead of trying to force the distractions away, observe them, and see if you learn anything."

After a few restless moments, Reed interrupted them again. "Are we supposed to detect a pattern?"

JoAnne just shook their head and told them to try again.

Arno was about to reenter his crystal world when Reed interrupted a third time.

"Why don't you just show me the forms to perform the Feat of Teleportare?" Reed got up and stretched out his legs. "It worked for the last ten generations of Bearers, right?"

"Reed, I abandoned all that after Pass Ten!" JoAnne snapped. "So, at least by some measure, it's been almost forty years since I used those heinous forms. Even if I wanted to teach them to you, I don't remember how."

"I am getting really tired of you flipping back and forth between a hapless fifteen-year-old and our wise mentor whenever it suits you," Reed snapped back.

"Not as tired as I'm getting of you trying to make me into something simple that your limited imagination can comprehend."

Perhaps Arno should've stayed and mediated. But the solace of the crystal world was a welcomed haven from JoAnne and Reed's bickering, as was his ever-calm double. Time bent elastic there, like a rubber band with five dimensions that stretched in the most unpredictable of ways.

There were no vertical surfaces, so he practiced using two identical sunflower patches a few feet apart on the ground of the crystal world. This time, he would pray to Princess Khosrovidukht, sister to Tiridates III of Armenia, whose vision of how to save her brother from madness led to the salvation of the entire Armenian nation. Khosrovidukht, who was accused of insanity and demonic possession, but whose faith never wavered. Whose jewels funded the building of the first churches in Armenia. Soon, Arno and his double showed each other how to conjure the image of the two planes, and then, how to meld them into one.

Once he felt confident, he returned to the "real" world. Hours had passed, and the sun was setting.

Both he and JoAnne squealed with delight when he stuck his hand through one patch of marigold wall and it emerged from another, three feet away. JoAnne even Glamoured an applauding audience for him.

But Reed was still struggling.

"I don't feel like I'm any closer to doing it," Reed admitted when JoAnne had gone to the bathroom. "I just sit there and try not to get bored while you two breathe and chant and shit."

After two days of meditating, chanting, and practicing, Arno could Teleportare with an almost 50 percent success rate. Reed, however, had yet to do it once. JoAnne wanted to leave him kicking and cursing at the brick-red painted patches, but he insisted on joining them while they researched destination possibilities in Ithaca. After raiding Asbury Park High's college pamphlets, they identified multiple crimson walls at Cornell University.

"Apparently, Cornell's mascot is something called a Big Red." Arno flipped through the glossy trifold of students frolicking in autumnal splendor.

"Their mascot is a stick of gum?" JoAnne tilted their head.

"Forget that." Reed pointed to a brochure. "There's a theater called The Cherry Arts. They must have a red wall or something."

Arno had already packed everything he wanted to take. It all fit in his book bag: knitting supplies, neatly packed into their own woven satchel; two changes of clothes and basic hygiene products; a few books, including his Armenian Bible; the few hundred dollars that was his life's savings. Besides the gold Armenian cross around his neck that his grandmother had given him for confirmation, Arno didn't own anything else of value.

He was looking forward to leaving this life behind. A few days of Disjunctis had put Arno in awkward positions over and over again. He was running out of excuses for why he couldn't get into the ancient Kia Rondo or participate in any family activities. For once, not having a cell phone proved to be a blessing. The gas oven at home meant he could still help with the cooking, but he had to make excuses for why he couldn't vacuum or do other household chores. A shorted traffic light he accidentally leaned on and Tigran's tablet that he may have intentionally shorted as revenge for years of bullying were both explosive reminders that this world was no longer for him. Sunny had raised an eyebrow but didn't ask questions when she approved Arno's request for a leave from work.

He questioned his decision not to write his parents and siblings a note. But he didn't want to lie, and they wouldn't believe the truth. Though they'd miss him, he suspected they'd mostly feel relief. It wasn't a pretty thought, but sometimes not-pretty thoughts were the truth, and there wasn't any point in pretending otherwise.

They returned to the Empress Hotel basement, and Reed swore he wasn't leaving until he successfully opened a Teleportare gateway. It took him hours of experimenting with forms to open a circular, cherry-red patch in the wall.

"Look!" Both of Reed's hands were stretched forward, palms facing out. "I'm doing it!"

"Quick!" JoAnne held up the pamphlet of The Cherry Arts. "Meld with this!"

Reed swung his arms and hands this way and that and peered into his shimmering gateway. "Ale, is that you? I'm coming, Ale! Wait up!" Reed stepped into and disappeared through the gateway. A moment later, it shrank shut behind him.

"He's gonna be in for a rude awakening." JoAnne sauntered into the middle of the basement.

"What do you mean?" A sinking feeling dropped in Arno's stomach.

"I Glamoured an image of Alejandra so that he'd step through."

"You did what?" Arno almost raised his voice at JoAnne.

"Let's be honest—it was a miracle he was able to Teleportare at all. Who knows when he'd be able to open another gateway?" JoAnne responded, unfazed. "You head to that Buddhist monastery with the yellow shrine, I'll get to that jewelry shop with the mauve accent wall, pick up Reed, and we'll meet downtown at the bronze statue. Got it?"

Arno tightened the straps of his book bag around his shoulders.

Goodbye, Asbury Park.

His topaz flew into the painted dandelion patch of wall. It rippled and expanded into a teardrop gateway just large enough for him to walk through.

Hello, Ithaca!

END OF BOOK IV

INTERLUDE D

MUGHAL INDIA, 1653

ZEB-UN-NISSA RECKONS

"Just because you cannot imagine it doesn't mean it is impossible. Much like what I have to tell you now." Sarmad dares to approach Zeb-un-Nissa's desk, almost close enough to touch her. "I have only braved this journey because I have seen the extraordinary task before us. You and I must assemble the Five Stone Bearers. Together, we will use our Blessings to travel to the Pentagon Chamber, where we will harness the awesome power of the Pentacle Portal."

Her first instinct, of course, is to laugh. What he is saying is outlandish, at best. At worst, it is punishable by death. But his sincerity is compelling. He believes what he is saying to be true. And this is the first clue she has encountered that may help solve the mystery of her own Stone.

"How," Zeb-un-Nissa asks, "have you seen this?"

"In my True Dreams."

She tilts her head. An invitation, or a command, to speak more.

"Since I was a child, I have dreamed of what may be." His Stone flares as he speaks, accentuating certain words. "But in the last paksha, the True Dreams come every night. In a deluge, unrelenting, like a monsoon. The night I was chosen by the Stone, I dreamed my youngest nephew fell into an abandoned well. When he was lost the next day, I knew where to find him. The next night, I was bestowed another True Dream. Of you and me."

His Stone flares.

"Of five Stones, of crystal worlds, of pentacles in the heavens. Of us, leading the Bearers of the Stones."

Flare.

"Of hope."

Flare.

"Of possibility."

Flare.

"Of salvation."

She hears the footsteps just in time.

"Hide! Quickly!" Zeb-un-Nissa shoves Sarmad underneath her desk just before two guards enter her chambers.

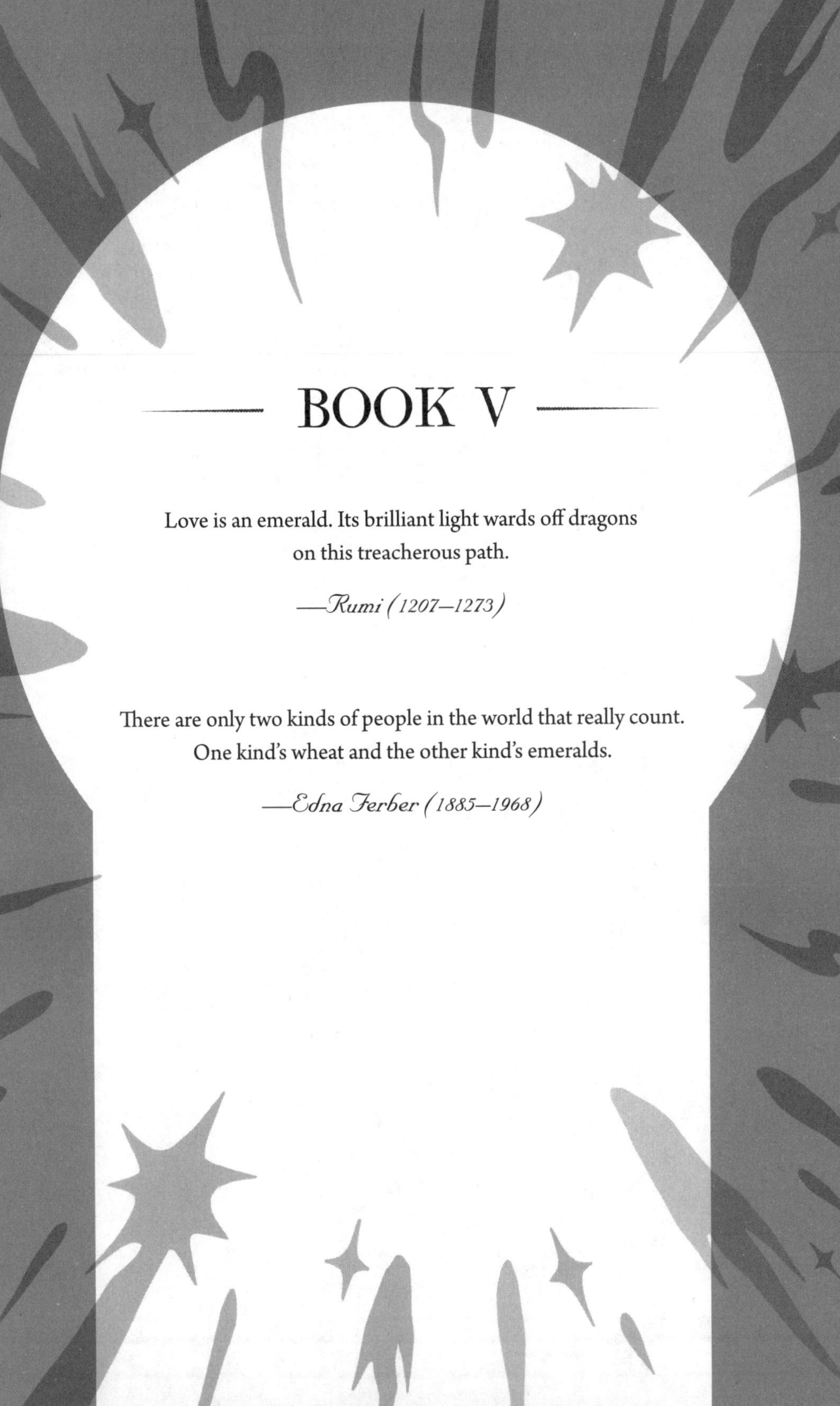

BOOK V

Love is an emerald. Its brilliant light wards off dragons
on this treacherous path.

—*Rumi (1207–1273)*

There are only two kinds of people in the world that really count.
One kind's wheat and the other kind's emeralds.

—*Edna Ferber (1885–1968)*

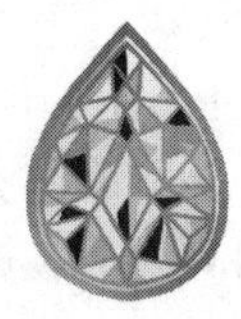

CHAPTER 1

ARNO IN ITHACA

The most interesting moment for Arno was the in-between, that infinite second after he stepped through but before he emerged from the Teleportare gateway, a limbo so brief it would fly by unless you knew to look for it. What was that space? What could he learn from it? What would happen if he tried to stay there?

As he emerged in Ithaca from the teardrop-shaped gateway, it shrank back down to Yellow. Arno swayed while the world tilted haphazardly, first to one side, then to the other, like an indecisive seesaw. The nausea hit him stronger than the times he'd hopped around the Empress basement, stronger than the motion sickness after a five-hour ride in the very back of that old gray Kia Rondo.

There was so much he still didn't know about Teleportare: did the distance traveled affect the severity of the side effects? What would happen if he tried to bring someone else with him? Or if he tried to walk through another Bearer's gateway? There were only three weeks left before the Ikeda arrived—so little time. They still needed to find Green, persuade them to join, and get them up to speed. And more important, come up with a plan. No one actually knew what they were going to do now that they were Provost-less, Chancellor-less, Muraqqa-less. Not to mention the constant threat of Mr. Shaw and Father and whatever evil plans they were cooking up, on top of . . .

Arno centered himself by closing his eyes and taking a few deep breaths. Stressing wasn't going to make it any easier. It never did.

Five buildings made up the Namgyal Buddhist Monastery. Four were identical two-story yellow structures, forming a square that functioned as the campus perimeter. The fifth and tallest building, the shrine, towered in the center: a round, floor-to-ceiling glass edifice intricately bordered with red, blue, and white. Each part of the shrine represented a different element: the windowed room, water; the triangular pagoda perched on top, fire; the final architectural geometric flourish, air.

He was in no way prepared for how peaceful it was here. As if even the grass grew more calmly. If only he could stay.

Arno continued to lean against the now-solid dandelion wall of the administrative building, grateful no one had seen him appear, grateful his stomach was settling, grateful his spaghetti legs were reverting back to muscle and bones. There wasn't much to be grateful for these days. It made it all the more important to cherish what he could. He took a tentative step and then another, still leaning against the building for support, waiting for the world to right itself.

The monk approached so quietly that Arno didn't hear him until he spoke. "Hello, son." He was Southeast Asian, Arno guessed, and wore a burnt-orange robe, folded over itself, leaving one shoulder exposed. His shaved head reflected the sun.

The world was tilting less, so Arno braved the possibility of standing up straight before responding.

"Hello, Reverend Father?" Arno knew the Armenian honorific wasn't right, but it felt more respectful than nothing.

"Just 'hello' is fine here." The monk smiled. "Although, if you are feeling formal, you may refer to me as Venerable One." The monk placed both palms together and bowed his head slightly. "Did you just arrive? I don't remember seeing you at the morning puja."

"Yes." Arno kept his answer simple to avoid an untruth.

The monk and Arno regarded each other for a quiet moment.

"You have a lot to do," the monk finally said.

"Yes," Arno agreed solemnly. "And I don't have a lot of time."

"I would suggest"—the monk gestured in the direction of the monastery's exit—"that time isn't something that can be had. That is why impermanence makes everything possible."

They stood together in another silent moment while Arno digested this. Then he thanked the monk and excused himself. He followed the winding path out of the monastery, onto a gravel driveway that snaked under an embossed archway with twenty-foot bloodred columns adorned with tassels of gold, pink, mauve, purple, marigold, and navy.

It was a three-mile walk on a two-lane highway to Ithaca's Downtown Commons.

He passed Ithaca College on the right and an office complex on the left before the road sloped downhill and things got residential. An obscenely large apartment building and a slightly less obscenely large Marriott squatted, like sentinels, on either side of the entrance to the Commons.

By the time he arrived at the bronze statue of a young woman sitting at an equally bronze café table, JoAnne and Reed were already there. Fighting, predictably.

"I *still* don't understand why you told Arno you were using they/them pronouns, but not me, JoAnne." Reed's frustration made it clear this wasn't the first time he'd made this point.

"Because I totally knew you would find a way to make it be about you, and lo and behold . . . ," they responded. "Also, from now on, I'd prefer Jo."

Arno clocked this. JoAnne to Jo should be easy enough to remember.

"I'll call you whatever you want as long as the three of us approach the Green Bearer together," Reed insisted.

"Too overwhelming." Jo (*Jo, Jo, Jo,* Arno repeated to himself) had styled themself punk today, spiky mauve hair and one feather earring dangling down, just another member of the Ithaca Commons alt crowd. Their black midriff cut featured a lilac star, almost as tight as their ripped black leggings. "We don't want to scare them away."

"Then I'll go solo," Reed said.

"Um, negative," Jo responded. "I'm the most experienced. I should go."

"This is exactly what Mr. Shaw was training me for!"

"That's mental."

"*That's* mental? What if you have one of your episodes while recruiting Green?" Reed turned to Arno. "They were dancing around the pigeons when I got here. They may as well have emailed our coordinates to Mr. Shaw and Father."

"We can't shame each other for our Prices." Arno hated disagreeing with Reed, especially in front of anyone. "I don't do that to you with your hangovers, and you help me when I can't see. Besides, I've started thinking . . ."

"Yes?" Reed and Jo asked at the same time.

"Maybe our Prices aren't just curses," Arno mused. "Maybe there's more to them."

"He's just still sore about my Alejandra Glamour." Jo flicked their dangly feather earring. "I've already said I'm sorry—you want me to get down on my hands and knees?"

Arno sat on a brass chair across from the bronze metal girl at the bronze table and let them hash it out. He was tempted to mediate, as he sometimes did with his parents. But he knew Jo and Reed would have to figure things out on their own. He ran his fingers over the words CHILD OF ITHACA etched into the side lip of the table.

"Why do you think this statue is here?" Maybe a diversion would deflate Reed and Jo's escalating argument.

"It's commemorating a much-loved member of the community." Reed's eyes flashed scarlet, Post Cogging. "College student. Car accident."

Arno traced the sculpted bronze journal on the café table. On the other side of the table, directly opposite CHILD OF ITHACA, were etched the words CITIZEN OF THE WORLD.

Who had this young woman been? Who had loved her so much to commemorate her with a statue? Would anyone remember him after he was gone?

"Maybe you should use your powers less?" Reed's suggestion interrupted Arno's rumination. "I mean, do you really need to change outfits multiple times every day?"

"You're the one who just Post Cogged a statue!" Jo changed themself into a scarlet-eyed Reed to illustrate their point. "How long before Arno and I are gonna have to pay for your mind traps?"

"The way Arno and I cover for you all the time?"

"Do all men feel entitled to try to control other people?" Jo's eyes flashed indigo. "Or just fascists?"

"Okay, 'most experienced one.' Let's see how much forethought you gave to tricking me through the gateway. Do you know, say, where we're going to sleep tonight?" Reed barreled on when Jo didn't respond. "That's what I figured."

"I've had enough from you." Jo's Purple Stone floated up between them, glinting like a blade.

"Bring it, JoAnne." Red met Purple.

"Okay, you two, that's enough." Arno swiped both gems out of the air.

Reed and Jo both squealed in protest.

"Jo—" Arno stopped himself just to be sure. "It's Jo now, right?" Even through the squirming discomfort of having someone else touch their Stone, they smiled at hearing their right name. "You *are* the most experienced among us, at least by some measure. So I hope you'll lead by example and be the most mature as well." Arno released Purple, and it bobbed back to them. "Reed, remember how you reconciled the poly and ace factions during the GSA drag show debacle? That's the kind of generous leadership we need now, okay?"

Reed looked down at the ground and mumbled something that sounded close enough to an apology that Arno released Red.

"I'm going to locate Green. Maybe then we'll learn something about the best way to approach them." Arno closed his eyes and prayed to Gregory the Illuminator.

Calm and warmth flooded into him. His heart and soul opened to the universe, to its possibilities, to its joys. Time slowed down and sped up.

Now that he knew how to look for it, Arno could identify the tug immediately. Especially because it was close. And getting stronger. And since Arno wasn't moving . . . "Green is coming to us!"

They heard the chants just before the crowd turned the corner.

"We are unstoppable/Another world is possible!"

"They can't stop the climate revolution/We are the climate solution!"

"Coal, gas, oil, don't dig it/Keep it in the ground/It's time to get with it!"

A dozen posters (ONE EARTH, ONE CHANCE; SAVE OUR PLANET; CLIMATE JUSTICE NOW) floated by as the climate change rally of fifty passed the three Bearers.

"Was it too much to hope that the world would've figured this out in the thirty-some years I was gone?" Jo asked.

"Way too much," Reed responded.

"At least they're one of the protesters." Arno shuddered. "Can you imagine if Green was a climate change denier? Or an alt right extremist?"

The three of them joined the march just as it arrived at its destination: a small outdoor stage built into the slope of the sidewalk. A few protesters took their place by a lectern on the raised area, framed by steel beams that supported a trapezoidal glass roof. Others ducked into the local Starbucks. Many of the rest were already on line at the street vendors set up in front of the local banks and stores, advertising organic snacks and beverages.

"'Organic' pretzels?" Jo asked. "As opposed to what? Synthetic?"

"It means they're additive-free," Arno explained.

"I guess they really like that here." Jo scanned the rest of the food vendor signage.

"You okay?" Arno put his hand on Reed's shoulder.

"Crowds are a real treat for empaths." Reed scrunched his eyes and forehead as he shifted through the Feat of Sweet Sweet Relief. "Can you sense the Green Bearer?"

"Hold on, hold on." Arno pivoted his head sharply, like a hawk spotting prey. "There. On the stage. Second chair from the microphone." He focused on a white, pear-shaped girl with seafoam-green eyes, cat eye glasses, and frizzy brown hair that fell down to her shoulders. She adjusted her note cards on the lap of her flowered sundress as she waited for her turn to speak.

"If we're going to have to wait for this to be over before we approach, I'm gonna need some major snackage," Jo called over their departing shoulder.

"Why didn't you tell me?" Reed asked Arno once they were alone.

"Tell you what?"

"About Jo using they/them, back in Asbury Park?" Reed spoke casually, as if it didn't matter to him, but Arno could hear the hurt underneath.

"They asked me not to."

Reed didn't respond.

Arno decided not to push it, nor ask Jo a moment later how they procured the organic pretzels and cider, which all three of them dug into as the event started. The first speaker was a middle-aged white woman decked in beaded jewelry who called for the end of fossil fuels. She was followed by an even whiter, even older man in an ivory tweed jacket who spoke with great passion about the exact same topic, but for twice as long. As he was winding down, Green slipped her note cards into a hidden pocket in the dress, wiped her cat eye glasses clean, and scrunched her face in vocal warm-up exercises before her turn at the lectern.

"Friends, nobles, countrymen, lend me your ears. I'm Noa Rosenstein, a senior at Cascadilla High and president of our Drama Club. I'm not going to lie: we have some hard work ahead of us." Green spoke into the microphone with remarkable articulation and vocal strength. "And I'm here to talk about how my generation is going to address environmental problems."

The audience cheered and chanted: "No more coal, no more oil/Keep your carbon in the soil!"

"How long do you think this is going to take?" Jo asked.

Reed and Arno looked at each other, the long line of speakers seated on the stage, and back to each other.

"I'd say"—Reed dabbed a morsel of pretzel into a small paper cup of brown mustard and popped it into his mouth—"make yourself comfortable."

"I have named Ignatius's revelation in Pass Eight the Feat of Stabilitas. Early experiments are promising, but what I would give, of course, to be able to work with the actual Bearers and actual Stones to truly evaluate the feasibility of the Feat itself."

Rupert Shaw
Provost, Pass Eleven

CHAPTER 2

ZEB-UN-NISSA REALIZES

"Hide quickly!" Zeb-un-Nissa shoves Sarmad underneath her desk just before two guards enter her chambers.

As she convinces the guards that hers was the only voice they heard ("I often speak aloud when preparing for a mushaira, using different voices to anticipate what my opponents may say. Yes, just me preparing for a contest of wits. You have nothing to worry about.") she also wonders: why does she not simply reveal the infiltrator to the two eunuchs as they question her? He could be a spy sent from a dueling house. Or from another empire.

Similarly, she wonders why she has told no one about the sapphire she found exactly fourteen days ago. She has not even mentioned it to her mother.

This infiltrator, he bears a Stone, like hers. They share that. She will trust him, at least for now.

After the guards are gone, she beckons him forth.

"Why should I believe your tales?" she whispers.

"How else could I know about your Stone?" Sarmad is entirely unfrazzled both by almost being caught and by her question. "Or about the ambassador from the deposed king of Great Britain who arrived unexpectedly yesterday?" He grins slyly.

"You could've"—the princess searches for possibilities—"passed his royal train on the road."

"And how would I know that a feast will be thrown for him outside"—Sarmad relishes delivering this information—"in the garden?"

"You eavesdropped?" Zeb-un-Nissa considers. "As Sireli, you could've spied on Miyabai."

"Even eavesdropping would not make me privy to your clandestine meeting with him tomorrow evening."

"I was sworn to secrecy by the emperor and my father on pain of death." Her mind scrambles for other possibilities. "How could you . . ."

"Our Stones grant us a Blessing. Mine is to see what will happen." Sarmad gestures to her sapphire. "Will you let me help you discover yours?"

"At what cost?" Zeb-un-Nissa sits down slowly on a cushioned seat. She has seen her mother at work enough to know: ask questions. Keep him talking. Gather as much information as possible.

"Why do you assume everything comes with a price?" he asks innocently.

"Nothing is truly free, in my experience," Zeb-un-Nissa responds as uncynically as possible. "What else have you dreamed about?"

"That we must save the planet from the Europeans."

"The pale pink merchants who wear wools when they visit?" She stifles a laugh. "Their naval engineering is impressive, surely. But how will they endanger our entire planet?"

"They may not arrive here with guns, as they did in the Americas. But they will conquer us nonetheless, with the equally insidious weapon of trade. Then they will use fire and metal to conquer nature itself." He cheats toward the arches leading to the balcony. "At great cost. The air we breathe, the earth on which we tread, the very water we drink will pay the price." Sarmad's eyes glaze over, recalling his True Dream. "Covered chariots will crawl over the world's surface, like insects, spewing fumes and filth. Factoriums will create an arsenal of destruction that make their cannons look like the toys of children. Plagues. War. Famine. Pestilence. And then, the end."

"Of what?"

"Everything."

Zeb-un-Nissa has never contemplated the possibility that humanity is capable of destroying itself, let alone the entire planet. It terrifies her.

"And you and I are tasked with preventing this?" Zeb-un-Nissa adjusts her dupatta.

"You and I must assemble the rest of the Stone Bearers. We number five in total. Ruby, sapphire, topaz, emerald, amethyst."

"Like the precious stones that grace the peacocks of the Jeweled Throne." She returns to her desk. The compulsion to take notes is too great.

"The world's salvation lies in our unity!" He reaches a hand out to her. "Will you join me, Zeb-un-Nissa?"

She knows she will. The scale of what they must prevent is formidable, surely. There is much she does not know. But learning, as her great-grandfather once said, is a plant that grows in all climes.

"Sleep continues to elude me. I resist pharmaceuticals. Too much experimenting as is. Instead, I retrace my actions, using the Provosts' precedents, wondering what I could've done differently. Is it possible, as in all tragedies, that the outcome was inevitable?"

Rupert Shaw
Provost, Pass Eleven

CHAPTER 3

ARNO AND THE GREEN BEARER

Arno watched the Phantasmagoria unravel, luscious jewel tones and vaulted ceilings disappearing to reveal the chocolate brown and robin's-egg blue of the Ithaca Airbnb. Reed winced when Red dropped onto the hardwood floor with a dull clunk.

"You okay?" Arno asked him.

Reed simply nodded. Even that looked hard.

Arno helped a swaying Reed around the upscale coffee table to the unfortunately named ottoman in the living room of the carriage house that belonged to Noa's parents. The Airbnb was decorated with a hotel room's anonymity: just enough chachkes or chatchkes or tchotchkes to make it feel cozy without actually feeling like anyone lived there.

They had approached Noa at the end of the two-and-a-half-hour environment rally. When they asked her about Green, she'd ushered them here to talk in private. She challenged them to "show, not tell" the Stones' power and backstory, so Jo had suggested a Phantasmagoria.

"Two birds, one Stone!" Noa had exclaimed, delighted with her own cleverness.

"More like two Stones, one Synergy," Reed had responded.

That was an hour ago, when Reed still had the energy for quips. Now that the Phantasmagoria was over, he could barely stand.

Arno lowered him onto the ottoman. To hold him longer, to let their touch be more than just platonic . . . he removed his hands from Reed's shoulders. God, give him strength to support Reed while respecting his boundaries.

"'Art and baleful sorcery!'" Noa swept over the area rug in the middle of the room, where Zeb-un-Nissa and Sarmad had appeared just moments before. "You told me the Phantasmagorias would feel like VR, but virtual reality has nothing on them! I could *smell* the jasmine. And those mangoes!"

"It's truly, truly outrageous," Jo said. "Truly, truly, truly outrageous."

"Think about all the potential applications!" Noa plopped down on the sectional next to Reed, propping her feet up on the coffee table. "We could find a thousand uses for it at Thank You, Places!"

"Thank you, what?" Arno asked.

"Thank You, Places! My high school theater troupe, for which I humbly serve as president." Noa stifled a yawn. "Sorry—between starring in our Spring Shakespeare, running the company, studying for finals, and prepping for my summer internship, I'm beat." She covered another yawn. "We open *Hamlet* in two weeks. You think you can use those Phantasmagorias for our sets?"

"Are you listening to us?" Jo's fury seemed comical in their masculine preppy eighties visage: pink Izod, khakis, single diamond-stud earring. "We are trying to show you why Green picked you to save the world. With us. In three weeks!"

"'Mend your speech a little, lest you may mar your fortunes.'" Noa took Green out of the pocket of her sunflower sundress and put it on the low, block coffee table. The rectangular Stone with diagonal corners stared back at Arno, unblinking. "That's *King Lear*—last year's Spring Shakespeare."

"Were you in that, too?" Arno asked innocently.

"In the titular role, duh," Noa said. "I wish you could've seen our blinding scene!"

"We're all about to witness a blinding scene," Jo muttered in what Arno was sure was a hyperbolic threat.

"There aren't many perks to being my size"—Noa ignored Jo and gathered herself in her most regal pose—"but one of them is that it makes it easier to get cast as kings."

Noa certainly was the largest of the four assembled Bearers. Arno shifted, trying to figure out why her frankness about her weight made him uncomfortable. Was it because he was so unused to anyone, let alone a girl, speaking so candidly about their body? Or was it because in this size lineup, he would be next? He hadn't quite understood that he was chubby until he'd seen himself in the crystal world. His round face and pudgy middle contrasted with Reed's lean, runner's form. And Jo—well, it was impossible to know what they truly looked like, although Arno couldn't help but note that all their personas, regardless of gender identity or style, manifested as lithe.

"Okay . . ." Noa shuddered. "If everything you say is true, where's Blue?"

"She's gone," Reed said, tight-lipped.

"When's she coming back?" Noa persisted.

Reed shrugged.

"So why don't you just"—Noa searched for the Latin—"Locatio?"

"She will find us." Reed, still on the ottoman, shifted away from Noa. "If she's ready."

"*When*, not if," Arno amended.

"But she doesn't know how to Teleportare, right?" Noa either didn't pick up on Reed's discomfort or chose to ignore it. "So even if she decided to look for us, she couldn't actually—"

"It'll happen when it's meant to, Noa," Arno gently but firmly cut her off.

"Well, excuuuuuuuse me," Noa said. "Everyone says that I'm too honest. But it's not my problem some people can't handle the truth."

"This is the truth, Noa." Jo plopped themself down on the sofa. "We need you to learn the Feats and help us figure out what we're going to do on Pentacle Portal day."

"Not to scare you, but right now is when you're most vulnerable." Reed massaged his temples. "After you've been chosen, but before the Stone manifests any of its powers."

"Besides, we have no idea what Mr. Shaw or Father are up to," Arno added.

"Do you think they know you're here?" Noa asked.

Arno, Reed, and Jo exchanged glances.

"I'm going to go with no," Reed said.

"They must've lost the trail after Baltimore," Arno guessed. "Otherwise, they would've tried something in Asbury Park, right?"

"I don't think you're giving them nearly enough props." Jo tapped their fingers against the sofa armrest, thinking.

"'Time is out of joint: O curséd spite/That ever I was born to set it right!'" Noa held her Stone up in her palm and stared at it in the classic Hamlet skull pose. "I wish Green had never chosen me."

"Why?" Reed asked.

"I don't want to be the Green Bearer. No offense, but I'm not like the rest of you. I like my life. I would never run away from home. It would kill my parents.

And my brother, Ezra." Listing everything she loved made Noa tear up. "I'm graduating from high school this month. I missed eighth-grade graduation because of COVID-19, and I don't want to miss this one, too. And I'm playing Hamlet!" The tears accumulating in Noa's eyes threatened to spill, like a little waterfall. "There must be a way to get rid of the Stone, right?"

"Of course." Reed described the Feat of Relinquo. "And I don't blame you, Noa. What these Stones ask of us . . . you have no idea what your Potentia will be, or what Price it'll come with and how it might damage you. I wouldn't wish this on anyone."

The words stung Arno. Why had Reed invited him if he wouldn't wish this on anyone?

"It's not as bad as he makes it sound, Noa," Jo said. "Besides, I don't think you have much choice."

"If she doesn't want to do it, we shouldn't force her," Reed mumbled.

"Thank you!" Noa smiled at Reed. "Can you show me the Feat of Relinquo?"

"This is how Hikaru did it, right before he . . ." Reed choked up. "You hold it up to your heart"—he demonstrated as he spoke—"say 'I, Noa Rosenstein, bequeath to you, the name of whomever you've picked, emerald, this precious Stone.'"

"That's it?"

"Yup."

"Okay." Noa stepped up from the sectional. "I'm an observational learner, so can you show me again, exactly, how you would Relinquo your Stone to me?"

Reed held Red up to his heart, with the thumb and index finger of each hand. "I, Reed de Vries, bequeath to you, Noa Rosenstein, ruby, this precious . . ."

"Stop!" Jo and Arno screamed in unison.

"Are you actually going to bequeath Red to Noa?" Arno asked.

"Oh my God—no!" Noa fell over herself with apologies. "I don't want one Stone, let alone two!"

"We don't need to spend time practicing how to Relinquo, because we don't have anyone to bequeath *to*." Arno cleared his mind. "Noa, it might feel like we're asking a lot, but it'll only take three weeks of your life. Then you can go back to *Hamlet* and graduation."

"How about this?" Noa twirled a strand of her frizzy hair. "You need a place to convene, right? An HQ? Especially if Blue decides to find you."

"*When* . . . ," Arno amended.

"And I don't want to miss graduation—"

"—or have to drop out of your play." Jo didn't even try to keep the disdain out of their voice.

"You see where I'm going with this?" Noa asked.

"Stay in Ithaca." Arno considered the words as he heard them leave his mouth.

"In this carriage house!" Noa exclaimed. "I can block the dates on Airbnb for a week. It's a two-bedroom, so Jo'll get their own room and Arno and Reed can share the other one. That's okay, right?"

Luckily Noa didn't stop for either of them to actually answer which was for the best because Arno's tongue was somewhere between stuck and turning loops over itself trying to come up with a response that didn't betray how excited and terrified but mostly excited he'd be to share a room with Reed.

"Summer's the best time to be in Ithaca anyway!" Noa barreled on. "All the students are gone, and the waterfalls are just gorgeous. I'll even have Ezra put the interior lights on a motion sensor for you folx, so who cares about Disjunctis! I'll practice with you, and if you can't teach me how to perform the Feats in one week, I'll just Relinquo. That'll give you plenty of time to find a different Green Bearer!"

The other three Bearers looked at one another.

"Anyone have a better plan?" Arno asked.

"I refuse to let a few setbacks dissuade me from the viability of the Feat of Stabilitas. Ignatius's drawings and research, especially from his time as Chancellor, are proving to be invaluable resources."

Rupert Shaw
Provost, Pass Eleven

CHAPTER 4

REED'S NIGHTMARE

"Ale, is that you?"

"Hola, güey." Alejandra twirled to show off the slate-blue cocktail dress that sloped in a sharp V down her back. The skirt swooped around her, shredded strips of silk spinning like the blades of a fan. "You look like shit."

"I think . . . ," Reed struggled to bring himself to say. "I think I know what I can do. To make it better."

"Tell me." Ale's voice held no emotion. "Tell yourself."

"To promise never to use my power that way on anyone else, ever again."

"Close." Ale considered before continuing. "But not enough."

"No?" he asked. Begged.

"No." She stared him down. "You must ensure you will never do it again."

"But the only way to do that is to Relinquo."

"So smart. No wonder you make such a good Leader," she delivered with the same flat sarcasm that the real Ale would've.

"Isn't that giving up?"

"We all have difficult decisions to make."

"But how can I abandon the mission? And Arno?"

"You must prioritize your obligations."

"So I have to choose between your forgiveness and success?"

Ale said nothing.

"That's bullshit." Reed marveled at how much the dream version of their Airbnb bedroom looked like the real one. Minus Arno, of course. He was probably happily asleep in his oh-so-close twin bed. "Besides, this is just a dream, anyway."

"So?" This Dream Ale captured her perfect blasé. "Does that make it any less painful?"

They both knew it didn't.

"All right then, can we just get this over with then?" He held out his hand to her.

The sensation started there, crawled up his arm, his shoulder, over the rest of his body. The grinding of bone made him whimper. Wherever the real Ale was, he hoped that she didn't have to use her Potentia. Or, if she did, that she had figured out a way to make it hurt less. Because this was something nobody should have to endure once, let alone repeatedly. His torso, abdomen, and legs stiffened as the grinding pain conquered every bone and joint in his body.

"You will suffer, like this, every night," she whispered into his ear, "until you've made your choice."

Reed woke from the nightmare panting, sweating, clawing at his body.

He fell out of bed and landed in the carpeted stretch between the twin beds in the chocolate and robin's-egg blue bedroom of the Airbnb. The pain was a relief. Proof that he could still feel. He tried to get up, but a net of sheets and blankets entangled him. He toppled to the floor in slow motion, a giant felled by a trap, an AT-AT whose legs had been cable-tied by Luke's T-47 airspeeder. He didn't realize he was screaming until Arno appeared at his side.

"It's okay." Arno gently shushed him like a baby. "It's okay. I'm here."

Reed leaned his head against Arno's chest and let himself be held.

The two of them barely fit in the carpeted alley between the beds. Arno's body, his presence, his beating heart and pulsing blood flooded into Reed. Was this Red? Or was this just them?

"Another nightmare?" Arno asked.

Reed whimpered "yes."

"Ale again?"

Reed nodded this time.

"I'm worried about the Phantasmagorias." Arno gently ran his hand through Reed's hair. "The Price—it's damaging you."

"It's the only way, Arno."

"Maybe I can find another?"

"Then find it. But until then . . ." Reed unwound from Arno and the sheets and blankets and pulled himself back into bed.

"Reed?" Arno stayed on the floor a little longer.

He didn't respond. Too raw. Too dangerous.

Slowly, Arno returned to bed.

Come here! Hold me! Why couldn't Arno hear Reed's heart screaming?

Was Arno fixated on Reed's breathing the way Reed was fixated on Arno's? Was he obsessing over every detail, looking for clues, for anything, that he could construe as an invitation?

Eventually, Arno's inhales and exhales regulated to the gentle sounds of slumber.

The alarm clock glowed a neon 4:12 from the other side of the room. Reed watched the numbers climb slowly as Arno's breathing slowed into snoring, as the skies turned from black to navy blue to cerulean, as the sun peeked its giant eye above the horizon, as the bustle of the morning made itself known. It's not that Reed couldn't go back to sleep.

He was just too scared about what would be waiting for him there if he did.

★

"Unlike Father, I believe we would have been able to puzzle out the Feat of Stabilitas, even without the actual Bearers and the actual Stones. Had we the luxury of actual collaboration, I cannot help but wonder what other Feats and Synergias we may have been able to unearth."

Rupert Shaw
Provost, Pass Eleven

CHAPTER 5
REED AND THE WATERFALL

The suburban grid of houses they followed Noa through looked surprisingly like Reed's neighborhood back home in Asbury Park.

Was Asbury Park still home? Did he still have a home?

"Someone remind me why we don't just Phantasma-whatever-we-call-it in the Airbnb again?" Jo asked.

"You have to check this place out. Trust me." Noa picked up an errant candy wrapper and threw it into a public trash can. "Besides, it'll be healthier for your work/life balance."

"Jo, did Father say anything about Zeb-un-Nissa or Sarmad in Pass Ten?" Arno asked.

"Heck if I know. You know what a hard time I have distinguishing between what actually happened and my delusions." Jo resumed humming an aggressive guitar riff. "Although I wish you could've seen the sunset I imagined last night. Or the Edwardian tea I think I attended this morning!"

"Zeb-un-Nissa was a princess of Hindustan, who ruled India and much of southern Asia from the sixteenth to eighteenth centuries. She was part of the Mughal dynasty." Noa rattled off the facts like a waiter giving the daily specials. "She was an accomplished poet and legal mind and is considered one of the most remarkable women in history, despite fabricated stories by European writers designed to eroticize and Orientalize her. In 1657, her grandfather, the emperor Shah Jahan, fell ill and her father, Aurangzeb, seized the throne in an especially bloody war of succession, beheading his older brother Dara and killing a few others along the way. Even though Zeb-un-Nissa was his favorite child, he imprisoned her for the rest of her life after assuming the throne."

"Which means she might have survived the first Pass?" Arno's face lit up. "Maybe all the Bearers did?"

"It's possible!" Noa said.

"I wouldn't count on it," Jo scoffed.

"Noa—" Reed stifled a yawn. "Did you Google Sarmad, too?"

"There's a lot less on him—the stuff about being an Armenian Jew who converted to Islam checks out. As does being in Prince Dara's entourage. Some people think they were lovers."

"Are we close to this cave or whatever?" Jo asked. "'Cause I hate to be a bad-news bear, but we still have no idea what the hell we're gonna do come Ikeda day and only six days before Noa check outs."

Noa gestured for them to stop at a T-intersection. Across the street, a verdant park stretched wide.

"Up this way?" Jo gestured to the right, where the road inclined.

"Just follow me, okay?" Noa turned to Reed. "Are they always this bossy?"

"Nail. Head." Reed smiled, miming a hammer. He predicted then ignored Jo's scowl.

A car slowed as it passed Reed, Arno, and Noa. The front passenger lowered their window.

"Your dad is a perv!" A college student screamed at Noa from his white BMW with a Cornell bumper sticker before he sped away.

"Um . . ." Reed looked to Noa, but she just stared straight ahead, as if the incident hadn't happened. "Everything okay, Noa?"

"It's fine." She adjusted a flyer for a reggae festival on a power pole while waiting for the light to turn.

"You wanna talk about it?" Arno asked gently.

"Just a little mix-up at Cornell." She twirled her frizzy hair nervously. "I'm sure it'll get figured out soon. But you know—small towns like this, everybody knows everything. Or at least they think they do. My dream is to live somewhere big enough that when you make out with someone at a cast party, it's not on social media by the time you get home."

Reed didn't need his Stone to tell him there was more to this story, but he didn't push. Besides, he didn't have the bandwidth to deal with any more drama.

When the light finally changed, Noa led them across, turning left to enter the park. After a block, the sidewalk cut right and turned into a trail, running parallel to a creek, where water rambled lazily around the rocks a foot or two below.

**ITHACA FALLS NATURAL AREA
WARNING
NO SWIMMING
PROCEED WITH CAUTION
STAY ON MAIN TRAILS
KEEP AWAY FROM CLIFF EDGE
BEWARE OF FALLING ROCKS AND LOOSE STONES
DO NOT THROW OR KICK STONES INTO GORGE
PEOPLE ON TRAIL BELOW**

"Check this one out." Arno pointed to another nearby sign.

**GORGE REGULATIONS
SWIMMING PROHIBITED
PLEASE REMAIN ON TRAIL
VIOLATORS ARE SUBJECT TO ARREST
PEOPLE HAVE DIED SWIMMING HERE**

"People have died swimming here?" Arno gestured to the black-and-white graphic of a swimmer being sucked into a whirlpool. "That's reassuring."

They couldn't have been walking for more than a few minutes when the creek turned a corner. All four of them stopped to take in the towering waterfall, cascading, thundering sheets of foaming water.

"Whoa." Jo balanced on a rock, taking in the force and velocity and sheer magnificence.

"It's . . ." Reed searched for the words.

"Totally," Jo agreed.

"I forget how lucky I am to have one of these in my backyard." Noa gave her cat eye glasses a quick wipe before popping them back on. She led them to the base of the waterfall, where a ridge of rocks buffed smooth was just wide enough for one person to crab-walk across. Noa easily climbed up the two feet, using natural protrusions as hand- and footholds. "Follow me." In a few seconds, she disappeared behind the curtain of water.

Reed, Jo, and Arno moved slowly. The rocks were slippery with slime, moss, and moisture. Reed risked a backward glance every few feet to make sure Arno was keeping up. The fall was only ten feet into the water below, but Reed couldn't tell how deep the water was, or if rocks just below its surface would cause some real damage.

They followed Noa's footprints, which were especially helpful when the ledge became so shallow that just figuring out where to put your feet was treacherous.

Without Noa's trail, Reed would've never found the entrance to this secret cave. He ducked down to enter, then let his senses adjust to the darkness. The cave wasn't much larger than his living room back home. Every surface—ceiling, wall, sittable boulders—was textured with ripples, streaks, folds, and protrusions. It felt ancient. Holy. Untouched.

"Will this do, m'lords and ladies?" Noa asked with a bow and flourish.

Arno coughed gently and subtly tilted his head in Jo's direction.

"Will this do, m'lieges?" Noa corrected herself and bowed deeper.

"It'll do." Jo was already sending Purple into the middle of the dark limestone cavern.

"Why don't we practice Teleportare today?" Arno ran his hand along a side of the cave, wallpapered with moss. "Or help Noa discover her Potentia?"

"I thought the whole point was to Phantasmagoria Pass One again to get a clue about what we should be doing." Noa reclined familiarly on a chair-shaped boulder.

The muffled sound of the waterfall rumbled in the background.

"If Jo can have another go, so can I," Reed said with more enthusiasm than he felt. If only he weren't so damn tired all the time. If only Ale didn't haunt his dreams every night. If only, if only, if only . . .

"I'm not sure the reasoning follows there," Arno said with intentional nonchalance.

"It's cute," Noa sighed, "you trying to protect your boyfriend—"

"He's not my boyfriend," Reed and Arno squawked in unison.

"The ladies doth protest too much, methinks," Noa responded.

"None of what we're doing matters"—Jo ignored them both—"without an actual plan. And Phantasmagorias are the only way to come up with one."

"I just—" Arno tried again.

"It's fine, Arno." Reed cut him off. "I'll say when enough is enough." Reed immediately regretted snapping at Arno, especially in that snippy tone. As if he didn't feel bad enough, the way Arno shut up and sat down made him feel even worse.

He should just reach out and apologize right now. He knew that. But if he didn't get into this Phantasmagoria soon, he wasn't sure he'd be able to at all. And then the whole day would be a wash. And with only six days left until Noa made up her mind . . .

Reed turned to Jo. "Ready?"

They nodded.

"Places, everybody." Noa ushered Arno to the far wall of the cave.

"Thank you, places," Arno responded.

Red and Purple hovered into the center of the chamber. The Stones twirled and flashed like the lights on a police car, illuminating the rich textures of the cave in waves that merged magenta.

Reed braced himself for the sensation of connection to Purple. To have another consciousness so close to his own . . . even at his best, it would be an intrusion. But now, after those nightmares had worn down his psyche, it was almost assault.

Rocks changed to luscious pillows; lanterns and candles twinkled into existence, their dancing flames illuminating the jeweled tones of silk throws and cushions as dankness and moisture changed to the jasmine and ambrosia of Zeb-un-Nissa's quarters.

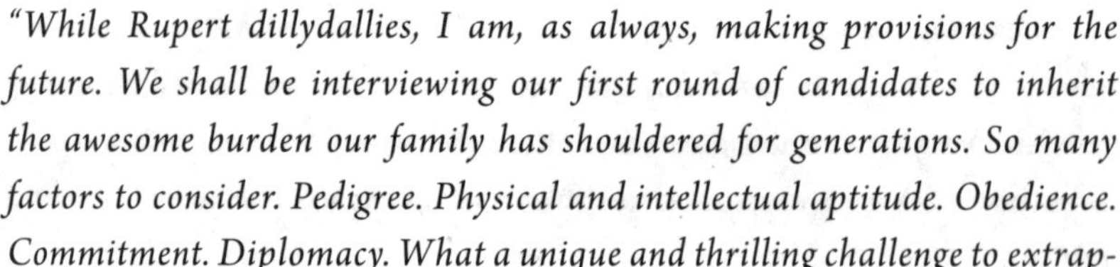

"While Rupert dillydallies, I am, as always, making provisions for the future. We shall be interviewing our first round of candidates to inherit the awesome burden our family has shouldered for generations. So many factors to consider. Pedigree. Physical and intellectual aptitude. Obedience. Commitment. Diplomacy. What a unique and thrilling challenge to extrapolate who somebody is versus who they may become."

Broughton Shaw
Chancellor, Pass Eleven

CHAPTER 6

ZEB-UN-NISSA AND SARMAD CONSPIRE

Zeb-un-Nissa regards Sarmad, sitting across her desk, as he regards the dice on the onyx-and-ivory-inlaid backgammon board. It is night. The fireplace roars with a small inferno, casting their shadows through the balcony arches.

She has come to cherish their time together. It is a welcome tonic, after days like today, spent in court, listening behind screens, so that she may best advise her father. She is grateful, flattered even, that he trusts her so. But after hours of standing and listening, it is a relief to sit and talk and laugh. When Sarmad leaves her, she is aglow with the same joy of companionship she feels after spending time with sisters or ladies-in-waiting. But with him, there is no competition.

She has insisted that he remain dressed as a servant girl, even when they are alone. The risk is too great, otherwise. His face is surprisingly smooth, especially for an Armenian. That and his slight demeanor make this disguise plausible.

The small diamonds on the faces of the dice twinkle in the firelight. With great deliberation, he moves two of his ivory backgammon pieces.

They reach for the dice at the same moment. A spark erupts between their fingers.

"Please, forgive me—" he starts.

"No, I . . . ," she overlaps.

They erupt with laughter, dispelling the awkwardness that otherwise would have settled like a dust cloud.

"Why is it so easy to be with you?" she asks him with uncharacteristic openness.

"Because I am not drawn to you the way other men are," he says shyly.

"So the rumors about you from Uncle Dara's entourage are true?"

He simply nods this time, testing the waters of her response.

"Do not worry, Sarmad. I am not one of those extremists who consider it a sacrilege. My great-grandfather even wrote about falling in love with a boy when he was your age."

"Truly?"

"It must be why you see me as other men cannot." She nods. "But it does not mean that I will take it easy on you." She picks up the dice from the backgammon board. "Allah, please listen to your humble petitioner," Zeb-un-Nissa prays, "and grant me a five!" She continues to chant "five five five" as she winds up and releases the dice with a flourish. They pirouette, elongating the suspense, spinning and spinning, until they slow down, wobble, settle, to reveal . . . ten sparkling diamond flecks. "Aha! So not only are both of my pieces permitted to reenter, but I also capture your piece! And safely escape!"

"Normally you would," Sarmad tells her with a world-wise weariness.

"So why not now?" she demands.

"In this phase of the game"—he adjusts the red robes of his servant girl's uniform—"when you roll doubles, you forfeit your turn altogether."

"You know what I think, Sarmad?" she asks with a sweetness as syrupy as gulab jamun.

"Tell me."

"I think you have fabricated this falsehood."

"And why do you say that?" he asks innocently.

"Because it stinks more mightily than elephant dung. Besides, I can tell every time you take liberties with the truth."

"The sapphire has finally granted you its Blessing?" He is suddenly alert. "To always discern the truth?"

"As if I need a divine gift to discern your falsehoods!"

"So enlighten me, Princess." Sarmad stops scratching his nose. "What betrays me?"

"Why would I reveal to my opponent his tell?"

"I am your opponent, now? Then I forfeit the game immediately." He swipes all the pieces off the backgammon board into Dalmatian disarray. "Anything to be your ally, again, Princess."

"And anything to avoid losing a game to someone who has never played before." She smiles a tiger's smile.

"You are insufferable. You know this, yes?" Sarmad shakes his head. "Discovering the topaz Bearer so easily has only made you worse."

"Am I to blame that you had to travel weeks, while I located Belawadi on a day trip to the women's markets in Deccan?"

"I did not know such a thing existed."

"We should visit Nupi Keithel in Imphal. Its women's market dwarfs ours as the elephant does the pangolin!"

"It was not just Belawadi's proximity that made it easier for you to find her," he pouts. "You had aid."

"Is it not beautiful?" Zeb-un-Nissa produces a heavy brass compass from a secret drawer in her desk. "A gift from Lady Borjigit, the Empress Dowager in China." She holds it up to the light. Two rings of Chinese characters adorn the brass perimeter: the outer, etched in black; the inner, in red. A long, tapered needle flickers along its face.

"When will you teach Belawadi to use the compass to find the emerald Bearer?" he asks.

"Tomorrow," Zeb-un-Nissa replies. "By then, she will have grown comfortable enough with her Stone and the power it affords her."

"The emerald Bearer will teach us how to travel to the chamber." Sarmad's gaze moves from the compass to the horizon of the night sky. Then, someplace farther. "There, all our Stones will sing with power."

"You True Dreamed this?" Zeb-un-Nissa asks.

"Last night!"

"Next time, dearest Sarmad, start with the revelations"—she shakes her head—"and save the playing of games for after."

"In my dream, I saw the chamber." He still stares off to what only he can see. "Five towering walls, one for each of our jewels!"

"Five jeweled walls?" Zeb-un-Nissa blinks, not believing. "The amethyst wall alone would fund our kingdom for perpetuity."

"You are still thinking of the mundane, of expenses and empires." His voice risks rising above the whispers they have confined themselves to. "I am contemplating the divine power of gods!"

"You blaspheme to even say it. Need I remind you of the Tower of Babel? Arrogance is the greatest obstacle to tawhid." She listens to make sure the mahaldar is not listening at her door. Again. "If my father or any of his men heard you speak those words, you would be exiled. Or worse." Zeb-un-Nissa returns the compass to its secret compartment in her writing desk. "Now let me share my discovery."

"Why not lead with that next time"—Sarmad smiles—"and leave the playing of games for later."

"Are you challenging me to a mushaira?"

"I, a simple Armenian peasant boy, know better than to engage a princess in a contest of wits. Especially one who memorized the Quran at age seven and became a Hafiza." He kneels and bows so low that his lips can kiss the floor. "I would never dare so high above my station, Princess."

"Now you mock me." She waves her hand, dismissively. "Remove the backgammon set."

"I am not to be ordered like a servant!" Sarmad clenches his teeth. "After we have harnessed the power of the Pentacle Portal, all this hierarchy, of master and servant, of castes, of royalty and peasant—all will fall away."

"Forgive me." Zeb-un-Nissa packs up the backgammon board herself, without ceremony. "I simply . . ."

"I would've done it, of course." Sarmad backpedals and helps her. "I just didn't want to be *ordered* to do it."

"Naturally." This is when she is most grateful for the dupatta, and how it conceals both her face and exactly how much irony she intends. Once the desk is clear, she unrolls a parchment of astrological charts. "Even before you found me, I had asked Ustad Bayaz to focus my instruction on astronomy."

"The study of celestial objects in the heavens?" Sarmad asks.

"Yes, as well as astrology, the study of how those objects affect us here on this planet." She points to a chart of the skies. "This dotted path is our planet's journey around the sun, as the famed astronomer Jabir ibn Aflah discovered. But here"—she traces an elliptical orbit with a painted nail—"is the path of the Ikeda comet. For reasons unbeknownst, its trajectory has changed. We believe it will pass closer to our planet than any celestial object in recorded history."

"And you believe," Sarmad puzzles it together, "that the appearances of our Stones are related to the new path of the comet?"

"And that the Portal will open when the comet is closest to the earth. According to my calculations, in just ten days!"

"The same day we must travel to this Pentagon Chamber!"

"We have ten days"—she dips a quill into the inkwell and makes a list—"to find the emerald and amethyst Bearers . . ."

"... learn how to travel to the Chamber..."

"... and discover how to master the Portal's power." She finishes the list with a calligrapher's flourish. "It is not much time."

"But what could we not accomplish together?" He jumps onto her desk, his scrawny form assuming a hero's pose, fist raised to the sky. "You and I, together?"

"You and I!" She joins him on the desk, feeling as free as she has ever felt in the confines of her quarters. "Together!"

"Even I can no longer continue to hold out that the Feat of Stabilitas will be the deus ex machina we have been searching for. Or, at least, that I have. We must cut our losses and commit to The Cyclops Strategem, as Father has insisted all along. Is it ridiculous to be studying the myths of King Odin?"

Rupert Shaw
Provost, Pass Eleven

CHAPTER 7

ARNO MEDIATES

Even though Noa insisted they all take Sunday off for mental health, the Bearers' next practice session was even more of a debacle than Arno's last family camping trip. In fact, given the choice, he would've picked the off-grid cabin in Raccoon Creek State Park with his father praying, his mother cursing, Nazani swearing this was her last family trip ever, and Davit and Tigran wrestling like the bears who'd stolen their food packs earlier that day. At least the fate of the world didn't depend on his family's ability to get along.

It began during the walk to the cave that Monday afternoon.

"Can you help me discover my Potentia today?" Noa asked after Cornell students heckled her about her father again.

"But we're finally figuring out what happened in Pass One!" Exclamation points popped up around Jo. "Like, who knew the original plan wasn't to seal the Portal but to harness its power?"

"So?" The dark circles under Noa's eyes were giving Reed's a run for his sleep-deprived money. "If I can't Potentia, I can't Teleportare or Terminatio."

"There's not actual proof that we can only learn the Feats in a certain order," Jo pointed out. "In fact, based on Hikaru's Petrakinesising and Alejandra and Arno discovering their Potentia before Locatio, it's pretty clear that's just another lie."

"Please?" Noa took a swig from her glass water bottle. "We've only got four days before I make up my mind about whether or not to join this troupe."

"I think it's a good idea." Arno looked to Reed.

Reed kept his head down and said nothing.

Once they arrived at the cavern, Reed took the lead.

"Don't tell me you think you're the one who should be in charge now," Jo scoffed. "You can barely perform the few Feats you do know."

Reed ignored Jo and talked Noa through the Feat of Potentia, as Mr. Shaw had taught it to him. After an hour of coaching her through the forms without result, Jo stepped in.

"You've got to chill, Jo. It can take days to discover your Potentia," Reed said.

"We don't have days, Reed." Jo took over the lesson. They sat on the floor cross-legged and told the rest of the Bearers to do the same.

The next snag came during the meditation, when Noa tried to help Arno breathe through his diaphragm. He didn't necessarily mind her putting her hands on the fleshy cul-de-sac where his ribs met. But when Jo told Noa to focus on herself, Noa countered with an extended and detailed history of her thespian breath training. Reed's reminder that they had already wasted half of their precious four remaining days just stressed everyone out more, leading Noa to insist they take a lengthy mental health break.

Even with Arno doing his best to mediate, the session devolved into chaos. Reed still struggled with the new Feats and got more and more frustrated every time he failed. When the Bearers ignored Noa's suggestions to use improv and role-play to work through their conflict, she pouted until Jo told her to get her shit together. Instead of fighting back, Noa just crumpled.

"Maybe, I don't know—maybe there's something wrong with me?" Noa lamented on her throne-like rock formation. "Maybe I should just Relinquo now, and you can find someone who isn't such a grande déception!"

"A grand deception?" Arno asked.

"It's French for 'great disappointment,'" Noa explained. "My French came in très handy last fall when I played Olga in our site-specific *The Three Sisters*."

Even Arno, by this point, had learned that asking Noa any questions about her production history was an invitation for a half-hour recitation/re-creation.

The only tangible result of meditative breathing was Reed and Noa falling asleep. After Arno needed to gently wake them a third time, Reed left their circle to review the Feats he knew, earning Jo's protests that repeating the old ways would only make it harder to learn the new ones.

"You see how yesterday's Phantasmagoria broke you?" Jo towered over Reed, Glamoured as a nine-foot version of themself. "I might be from the eighties, but you're the one stuck in the past, buster."

"Have you considered that maybe the reason I'm using a PS4 while you're next-genning it," Reed spoke slowly and deliberately, "is because you are such a bad teacher?"

"Arno picked it up in a jiff," Jo countered. "You're just brainwashed by the patriarchy and your limited imagination of mentorship." Jo Glamoured themself into Mr. Shaw. "Would you take me more seriously if I looked like this, lad?" The resemblance was frighteningly accurate, as was the accent.

"That's not funny." Reed poked at the Glamour, and it shimmered away, revealing Jo. "Don't do that again."

"Stop. Telling. Me." Jo got up in Reed's face. "What. To. Do."

"Then stop pushing me," Reed snapped.

"Just because you fail yourself," Jo snapped back, "doesn't mean you get to take it out on us."

Instead of responding, Reed turned around and stomped out of the cave.

The rest of the Bearers sat awkwardly, looking at one another, waiting for someone to do something.

"'An angel of silence has passed over us,'" Noa intoned.

"Maybe he needs some time alone?" Arno ventured.

"You understand so little about boys." Noa was already on her feet, going after him.

"What's his damage?" Jo asked the cave.

"He's not sleeping well." Should Arno talk to Jo about Reed? On the one hand, it felt like a betrayal of sorts. On the other hand, they might have insight that could help. "Hasn't been, I think, since the whole thing with Hikaru. And Ale, of course."

"He's losing more and more of himself every day."

"Do you think so?" Arno had hoped it was only his hyperconcern that had led him to the same conclusion.

"Definitely, and that's coming from the team member who knows more about Prices than anyone." Jo perched on a boulder by the cavern's entrance, gargoyle-like. "Maybe Noa isn't the only one who should consider Relinquo."

"That's not very kind, Jo," Arno said.

"I'm just being realistic."

"It's the Price of the Phantasmagorias," Arno countered. "Is there some way for me to take his place in them?"

"You know Synergias don't work like that," Jo said wearily. "Just like you know the Phantasmagorias are *literally* the only way we have of figuring out what we're supposed to do right now. Just think—if Reed could keep up with me, we could Phantasmagoria every single Pass. And then we'd really know what we needed to do. If only we knew!"

"If only we knew." Noa appeared at the heart of the cave. "Do you know Olga's speech from Act IV in Chekhov's *Three Sisters*?"

Arno and Jo shook their heads no, although they both suspected they were about to.

"OMG, you're in for a real treat." Noa vibrated her lips, screeched like a siren, then launched into some tongue twisters. "Whatta to-do to die today at a minute or two 'til two. A thing distinctly hard to say and harder still to do," she chanted. "Red leather, yellow leather. Unique New York, unique New York."

"Is this Chekhov?" Jo asked Arno under their breath.

"I think she's still warming up," he whispered back.

Once her vocal warm-up was complete, Noa turned around to face them.

"Okay—imagine me in a corset made from recycled plastic." She ran her hands over her rib cage. "And we used a tin steel drum as the samovar. It was very repurposeful." Noa cleared her throat before launching into the performance.

"'The music is so happy, cheerful. Oh yes, I want to live! Oh my God! The day will come when we're gone forever, too—and they'll have forgotten us—our faces, our voices—all forgotten—and they won't even remember there were three of us—but what we suffered will become joy for them—for all those who live after us. Happiness and peace will at last come to the earth, and they'll speak well of us and bless those of us who are living now. Oh, sweet sisters, our life is not finished yet. We'll live! The music is so happy, so joyous, and I can imagine that in just a moment more, we'll know why we're living, why we're suffering. If we only knew.'" Noa looked at them directly for the first time. "If we only knew!"

Arno trained with Jo the next day in the basement of their Airbnb, while Reed spent the day in bed upstairs. Noa joined them after school that Tuesday.

"Reed's so lucky he gets to play hooky." She yawned. "Is he always so . . ."

"He's really going through it." Arno immediately leaped to Reed's defense.

Jo cocked their head to one side: their assessment differed from Arno's.

"I guess we should cut him some slack. Sleep deprivation is real." Noa covered another yawn. "Even though—not that it's a competition—I'm playing the greatest role in the Western canon, keeping up my grades, running a Drama Club, and helping this merry band. And I'm fit as a fiddler on the roof."

Although Noa was more focused than she'd ever been, she still had no success in her Potentia or any other Feats. Green lay, dull as a weed, in her open palm. "No Petrakinesis, no Potentia, nothing. Do we even have to wait another three days?" She dropped her Stone in frustration. "You should just give up on me now."

"Don't say that," Arno said as supportively as he could authentically muster.

"Why not?" Jo asked. "It's a legit idea. Suggesting it doesn't make her a traitor. Consider this: Reed Relinquos to you, Noa to me, and we find some wicked Betties to do this with us instead of these wannabes."

Arno didn't respond. He'd never abandon Reed, even if Reed wanted to abandon him.

Shortly after, Noa received a text message and had to excuse herself. Jo tried to persuade her to stay, but Noa insisted she had to go. "I totally forgot we had a Thank You, Places! meeting to vote about whether to remove the comma in our name. I *have* to be there."

"Which way are you going to vote?" Arno asked.

"If you even have to ask . . ." Noa huffed as she climbed up the stairs and out of the basement.

The next day, Arno and Jo decided to take a break from practicing Feats to research everything Zeb-un-Nissa.

"Look." Arno pointed to a passage in a particularly dusty tome in a sparkling new public library. "Her name means 'Jewel of Womankind.'"

"And her father, Aurangzeb, his name means 'Honor of the Throne.'"

Nothing, however, gave them any further information about the Ikeda, the Stones, the Portal, or the Chamber. After two hours of book finding, researching, and reading, Arno excused himself to check in on Reed.

He took an especially circuitous path to their Airbnb. He wasn't avoiding Reed, exactly. But the last few times they were alone, Arno felt like—how could he put it—that Reed wasn't Reed anymore. That whatever was happening to him was so profound, so elemental, it was changing the essence of who he was, crossing that threshold where his erratic behavior was just becoming the new normal. It hurt Arno to see it, and it hurt Arno even more that he was powerless to stop it.

Gourmet olive oil and vinegar stores, jewelry shops, yoga boutiques, art galleries: they all beckoned to Arno during his downtown stroll. He politely declined their invitations. He had never had money to spend at those places and didn't want to waste the salespeople's time.

Why were so many of the downtown storefronts empty? Were they victims of the massive COVID-19 lockdown? Or from before?

He spent a few of his precious dollars on a delicious, bitter, aromatic coffee from the Press Café, and then a few more on what was truly the best doughnut he'd ever had in his life from One Ring. He returned to the brass chair across from the bronze Ithaca Girl statue and ate the still-warm lemon-lavender deliciousness that could've gone head-to-head with the flakiest nazook from his church's winter bazaar.

An hour later, he finally returned to their Airbnb. An ear to the door confirmed Reed snoring heavily, a sound that gave Arno more joy than chiming church bells. He went down to the living room and fished out the half-mitten from his knitting bag. He offered a small prayer in gratitude for his electricity-free hobby.

He worked in stockinette on the size eight bamboo needles, knitting an entire row of the main hand part, then purling his way back. He loved the way the Vs lined up in this stitch, neat and tidy, like well-folded clothes.

Was Noa right? Was it possible they didn't have a chance? That a broken Leader, missing Warrior, insecure Illuminator, inept Traveler, and delusional Mystic were never going to come together?

The knit rows came faster, and Arno whipped through them on his bamboo needles. The purl rows required more attention. Purling was one of the reasons he'd gone back to bamboo—the slippery metal needles made it easier to drop a stitch, and even one dropped stitch could undo weeks of work.

If Noa really did Relinquo, did he know anyone from Asbury Park who could step up and take her place? Or maybe all of them should Relinquo and wash their hands of all this.

His needles bobbed up and down as he lost himself in the glorious calm of knitting. He had made a few mistakes in the first mitten and was still trying to convince himself that the final product was richer for those idiosyncrasies. But he promised himself that this second mitten would be perfect, even if it meant penelopizing. If only life could be unraveled and reknit as easily as yarn.

Everyone Relinquoing didn't sit right with Arno. Like so much of what had happened since they got to Ithaca. He wished he could articulate it or make more sense of what was scratching at him, as if he were allergic to the detergent used to launder his clothes. Something wasn't right. But what?

Arno was especially proud of this mitten's thumb. It was easy enough, in theory, to loosely cast on three additional stitches, stockinette your way up, and then decrease rows by knitting two stitches together to create the tip. But working on something so small, so finite, required an entirely different set of skills than a beginner's scarf. This pattern called to break the yarn and sew up the side of the thumb—the first time Arno had to do so. Many firsts for him, lately. The first mitten's thumb had been stitched too tight. But Arno was getting this one just right.

He had just finished the first decreased row when he heard the screaming from upstairs.

"Now that we have committed to The Cyclops Stratagem, I begin to consider more technical concerns, such as depth perception."

Rupert Shaw
Provost, Pass Eleven

CHAPTER 8

ANOTHER NIGHTMARE, REED

"Hola, güey." Alejandra wore a pair of powder-blue trousers that flared out, landing just above her open-toe, chunky-heel platform sandals. Her ruffled vest top was unzipped halfway, lined with metal spikes. "You look like shit."

"We're getting closer, Ale. We're figuring it out!" Would that persuade her? "Something about harnessing the power of the Portal."

Dream Ale said nothing.

"It doesn't matter, does it?"

She shook her head.

"There's only one way to make things right with you, isn't there?"

This time, she nodded.

"If I Relinquo here, does that mean I relinquish in the real world as well?"

"There is only one way to find out." She smiled her enigmatic, Cheshire cat smile.

If this were the real Ale, he might've pretended. But it wasn't. So he didn't need to front. This was exactly what he actually wanted. All he'd been looking for all along was an excuse to give up. To be free of this nightmare. Once and for all.

He knew it was wrong.

Flash.

He knew that it was cowardly. But to be free . . .

Flash even brighter, like a supernova.

"How does it go?" he asked Ale.

"Have you already forgotten," she challenged him, "the words Hikaru said when he died in your arms?"

The third *flash* was so bright his retinas screamed in protest and everything washed in a sea of yellow-white.

He awoke in the chocolate and robin's-egg blue Airbnb bedroom.

"Reed, it's me!" Inexplicably, Arno was pinned beneath him, shielding his face with his hands.

"What did you do?" Reed couldn't remember the dream-nightmare entirely, but he knew he was close—oh so very close—to being free, to leaving this all behind. And that Arno had stopped him. But why was he on top of Arno, fists raised, as if about to strike? "I was so close . . ."

"Close to what, Reed?" Arno's eyes glazed over as his Price claimed his sight.

"To giving up my Stone!" Reed snarled. "And freedom!"

"I'm not going to fight with you." Arno stopped resisting. He even dropped his hands, leaving himself totally exposed. Vulnerable. "If you can't tell that something's going on, then I don't know what to say. But you're not going to push me away. I'm not Alejandra or Jo. I'm Arno. Your Arno. And I know this isn't really you right now. So go ahead. Say or do your worst. But we are going to figure out what they're doing to you. Because I can't see you like this."

Reed's fists squeezed, as if of their own volition, but he forced himself off Arno before he could do anything else he would regret. He'd hurt enough friends.

"I have no idea what's . . ." Sobs broke Reed's words, and he curled his heaving body into the fetal position. "I can't do this anymore."

Arno sat up and gently took Reed's head on his lap.

"I can't tell the difference between what's actually happening and my dreams and my nightmares," Reed confessed. "And each world has different rules, and they blur into each other, and sometimes I'm sure I'm in one but I'm really in the other but I don't know until after because . . ."

"Something's going on with Noa's sleep, too." Arno gently ran his fingers through Reed's hair. "Do you think Mr. Shaw and Father have figured out a way to attack you in your subconscious?"

"Who cares anymore?" Suddenly, a ray of hope. "What if—what if we didn't wait two days for Noa? What if we both, right now, performed the stupid Feat of Relinquo? We could be home tomorrow!"

"Pro/con it," Arno told him evenly.

"Pro, we can go back to how things were before." *And be together,* Reed wanted to say but couldn't find the courage to.

"Pretty big pro," Arno conceded.

Contemplating an escape—just knowing it was possible—gave Reed hope. Hope that the crushing weight bearing down on him could go away.

"But con," Arno countered, "the world ends."

"We don't know that!" Reed responded. "You're the one who's always saying we can't believe the things Mr. Shaw told us without proof."

"True," Arno conceded again. "But we'd be abandoning our friends. And giving up. We don't do those things." Arno continued to stroke Reed's hair. "Give me two more days to find out what's really going on, okay? I'll do whatever you want after, as long as we stay together, okay?"

"Promise?"

"Promise. Just don't leave us, Reed." Arno allowed his hand to rest on Reed's cheek. "Don't leave me."

★

"Rupert has volunteered to go first. I accepted his offer, given how he is responsible for so much of this disaster. I am confident that The Cyclops Stratagem is the correct path to right the errors that have been committed and ensure the sealing of the Pentacle Portal."

Broughton Shaw
Chancellor, Pass Eleven

CHAPTER 9

ZEB-UN-NISSA, THE HIDDEN ONE

A curtain of damask muslin billows on the wall opposite the fireplace in Zeb-un-Nissa's chambers. She sits at her desk, writing so furiously that she does not see the circular shimmer in the middle of the curtain grow until it is large enough for someone to step through. Only when Sarmad stumbles out of the curtain and into her chambers does she put her quill down and quickly wrap her dupatta around herself.

"Why don't you join us . . . ," he gushes as the circular shimmer shrinks down into his ruby Stone. "The mangrove trees, extending their skeletal roots and branches into the winding river. The ruins of a stone temple. The clear sky. And the birds! Chirping like our own orchestra!"

"If only . . ." Zeb-un-Nissa trails off, wistfully. "But we have already agreed that I will not leave the zenana. Do you not remember?"

Instead of responding, Sarmad unhooks and folds the damask muslin curtain. "This Color Walking that Henry has shown us truly is a miracle, is it not? But not as miraculous as his Blessing, to travel wherever he desires, without needing to create these doorways through space!"

"Every day, we discover new Blessings, new powers." She chooses her words carefully. "The Stones truly are a wonder."

"You work hard to reconcile what we are learning with your faith, Hidden One." Sarmad places the damask fabric at the bottom of an inlaid ivory chest, next to its cobalt, copper-green, saffron, and violet siblings.

"Do you not wonder, Sarmad, whether we mere mortals are meant to perform such miracles?" The heat and humidity make everything she is wearing cling to her.

"The only miracle is that Henry has only wet himself twice," Sarmad scoffs. "I have never met someone so easily frightened."

"It is difficult to believe that people like him, from London-town, will rule the world."

"First, they will restore their own monarchy. Then they will enslave us all before conquering the world itself. That is why it is so important for us to act." Sarmad closes the chest. "Although I am sure that is not what the exiled king's emissary tells you."

"Of course not. But the way his eyes light up whenever we pass the gemmed peacocks of the Jeweled Throne—his greed betrays him."

"They are all the same. The lying British with their fake democracy, all the while claiming colony after colony. The Portuguese. The Dutch." He spits out these words, like curses. "All crucifixes and ships and artillery." Sarmad weighs his following words carefully. "What if Henry is not meant to be among us?"

"What do you mean?" Zeb-un-Nissa asks.

"I worry he will betray us, despite the oath we all took as Bearers. Do you truly believe he will help us undermine his own people? What if the emerald made a mistake?"

"Henry is as much a Bearer as you or I," Zeb-un-Nissa says evenly. "We must trust the Stones."

"Then you must guide him." Sarmad sits across from Zeb-un-Nissa, at her desk. "He will never summon the courage to locate amethyst on his own."

"I will teach him the movements that help me focus." She has spent her life advising men. But not one has listened to her the way Sarmad does. "From the Muraqqa I have been compiling."

"Why do you bother?" The sun peeks out from behind a cloud, and Sarmad squints in the new light. "The time you spend on writing and calligraphy should be spent discovering your Blessing."

"Our journey must be chronicled." Zeb-un-Nissa leans into the light like a cat. "And besides, should we fail, I want future Bearers to benefit from our knowledge."

"How is it that I can see into the future but you are the one always preparing for it?"

"That is why we work so well together!"

“Of course, Makhfi.” Sarmad grins his sly grin. “My dearest Hidden One.”

“I only write under a takhallus because I must.” She adjusts her dupatta.

“I reveal all of myself to you, but a part of you always remains hidden from me.” Sarmad’s eyes search hers, trying to find something only he can sense. “A part of you that I will never see. And I do not mean your face. Even in my True Dreams, you are obscured.”

“You know me better than any man, even my betrothed, Sarmad. You see me.”

“And you, me,” he tells her. “That is why we will triumph in three days. I have seen, in my True Dreams, how we will harness the power of the Pentacle Portal into the Stones themselves.”

“Three days,” she repeats.

It is so little time.

“The Bearers continue to suspect nothing.”

Rupert Shaw
Provost, Pass Eleven

CHAPTER 10

REED STUMBLES

Red dropped to the ground with a clunk like a dead bird. If there were anything left inside of Reed, the Phantasmagoria would've taken it. But there wasn't. He was depleted, running on fumes, running on empty. Barren. Broken. Bare.

"Sarmad was about to tell us his plan!" Jo yelled. "We gotta go back." Purple hovered in the middle of the cavern, directly over Red.

"That's enough." Arno stepped between Jo and Reed.

"He's a big boy," Jo snapped. "He can speak for himself."

"Yeah, Arno." Reed tried and failed to Petrakinesis Red back to him. "I don't need you sticking up for me."

The thick humidity made the already miserable day even worse. Every exertion made Reed's damp clothes stick to his skin.

"And we don't need to break one of our teammates to find a solution." This was the closest Reed had ever heard Arno to raising his voice. "If we do, we're no better than Mr. Shaw and Father."

"This reminds me of a dispute we had during a rehearsal last week," Noa began. "We had just started on Ophelia's madness scene, and . . ."

"Noa, shut up," Jo barked.

"I just thought," Noa continued, unfazed, "it might help you all to hear how we—"

"Noa, this isn't the time," Arno cut her off.

"Why?" She held her hands up. "You're the one who said Reed's losing it."

"You said that?" Reed turned to Arno.

"Of course not," Arno scrambled. "I'd never . . ."

"'I'd never! I'd never!'" Reed imitated Arno before turning his wrath on Noa.

"And the last thing I want is to hear about how you and your merry players trust-exercised your way to harmony in rehearsals." Reed was too raw for barriers, too spent for inhibitions, too broken to stop the words he'd been keeping at bay. "Or a jaunty quote from Shakespeare or Chekhov," he added quickly, cutting her off before another pontification. "In fact, the only thing I can imagine you doing that would be helpful is shutting up, sitting down, and trying something with that emerald of yours because you have *literally* made zero progress this week." He wasn't done. "And you, Jo—are you sure you're not the supervillain? Because ever since you joined up, this entire adventure has gone straight to hell."

"LOOK AT YOURSELF." Jo conjured a mirror so that Reed could see exactly how miserable he'd become in the last few days. But they must've been exaggerating the Glamour, because he couldn't possibly look that gaunt, eyes sunken, like a zombie.

"Okay, you two," Arno began gently, "maybe we should . . ."

"Maybe you should step up and do something, Arno, instead of just being our freakin' Pollyanna all the time." Reed knew he shouldn't be saying this, knew he didn't actually feel it, knew there was no universe in which it was okay to speak to Arno like this. But he couldn't stop himself. It didn't even feel like he was doing it—just watching someone else who sort of resembled him finally unleash. "I'm done. With this. With you." *In for a penny,* as Mr. Shaw once said at an assembly . . . "Screw this. Screw the Stones. Screw the Portal. Screw the Ikeda." . . . *in for a pound.* "Screw you all." Reed tried to Petrakinesis his Stone back to him again. And failed.

It lay on the ground like a rock. Reed grabbed his Stone on his way out of the cave, forcing himself deaf to Arno's entreaties. He scrambled out of the cave so quickly he almost slipped on a wet, mossy rock during his descent.

Maybe I should just let myself fall. Let myself get hurt. At least that way I'll have an out.

Reed stumbled through Ithaca as if he were drunk, making his way through the maze of houses back to their Airbnb. He needed the desperate surrender of sleep but was terrified of what he'd find there.

He collapsed onto his bed without changing his clothes, too tired to even get under the covers. His circadian rhythms could not be convinced that it wasn't afternoon, that the sun wasn't up, that this was an absolutely normal and perfect time for him to be under.

"Go to Sleep" by Radiohead.

In that deeply disjointed 10/4 time signature

First Verse: Gm–Gm–Gm–Gm–B♭–C–B♭–Am–G

Then the folky grooves out

Second Verse: Gm–Gm–B♭–C–B♭–Am–G–B♭–C–B♭–Am–G

No chorus

No bridge

Just a little outro riff

Jonny Greenwood in all his sampling, looping, programming glory.

Over and over and over again until Reed could finally do what the song's title told him to.

Blessedly, there were no dreams this time. No nightmares. No torture. No Ale. It was dark when he awoke, almost refreshed. As close to as centered as he'd been for weeks. Or was it months? The alarm clock blinked a neon 12:00. A power outage? Doesn't matter. No clue what the actual time was, and no way of finding it out. Midnight? 4 AM? 10 PM? It didn't matter. But why wasn't Arno in his bed? And what was that noise coming from Jo's room?

He tiptoed down the hallway, Scooby-Doo style, Red matching his ups and downs. A patch of light sliced its way out of Jo's slightly ajar door. *All the better to spy on you with, my dear.*

His eyes couldn't believe, couldn't accept, couldn't process, what they saw.

Jo.

Arno.

Kissing.

Illogical.

Impossible.

Inexcusable.

How could Arno do this to him?

"Tonight?" This Jo, masculine and pierced and tattooed in all the coolest ways, kissed Arno again, long and deep and hard. "We'll run away tonight?"

"And finally be free of it all." Arno nodded. "And especially him."

Fight or flee? Grief, anger, fury, and betrayal coursed through Reed, ripping itself through his insides, shredding everything it found. Better to flee. He didn't trust what he'd do if he fought.

He bolted down the stairs. At least now, he had nothing to keep him here. Finally, he would be free of the Stone, leave the stupid thing behind forever and ever and never think about it or this again.

He plucked Red out of the air and hurled it as far and as hard as he could. It shattered a living room window before boomeranging back to him. Again and again and again, he tried to snap that invisible leash that kept them bound to each other. He broke more windows, some lamps. An appliance or two. But curséd Red kept returning, like a cold sore.

The bond between him and the Stone proved unbreakable. Unlike whatever he and Arno had. Had had.

Suddenly, another presence. In the living room. Near.

Would it be Jo or Arno who dared approach him? Both, he hoped. So that he could finally tell them what he really thought of them. But . . .

"Ale, is that you?"

"Hola, güey." Alejandra wore a pair of skinny jeans that hugged her in all the right places. The two inches of the cyan suede ankle boots made her tower over Reed. He didn't know a single person who could afford those boots, let alone pull them off. "You look like shit."

"What have you been doing?"

"Learning." Ale looked straight at Reed.

"And what have you learned?"

"It's so much better without the Stone, Reed. So much easier." She was next to him suddenly. It would've been alarming had she not opened her arms to him. Reed let himself surrender to her embrace.

"What?" Reed asked hopefully. "You Relinquo'ed?"

"Sí."

"I can't do it anymore, Ale." Reed's body deflated against hers. "Just getting out of bed every morning is . . . I can't tell what's real, and now . . ." He broke down. "First I lost you, and now him."

"Be free," Ale whispered.

Reed knew what he had to do.

"I, Reed de Vries . . ."

He didn't even feel guilty.

". . . bequeath to you, Alejandra Almada Navarro . . ."

Just the anticipation of relief.

". . . ruby . . ."

Like leaving a band you know you're too good for.

". . . this precious St—"

The sapphire blade emerged from Ale's rib cage like a needle lancing a boil.

She looked down at it, surprise quickly turning to pain. Her hands went to the gaping, bleeding wound in her torso. Then she transformed, shape-shifting from persona to persona so quickly, Mystique-style, that Reed could barely clock . . .

His mother's sharp face

Arno's deliberate knitting hands

Jo's spiky hair

Mr. Shaw's etched jaw

Rose's ponytails

cycling through endless mismatches before finally

landing on . . .

seafoam-green eyes

frizzy hair.

"Noa?"

The Green Bearer fell forward. Behind her stood the indisputably true Alejandra. She pulled her sword arm out of Noa's torso and wiped the blade on a corn-blue, homespun cotton dress with gold thread border.

"If you think this hurts, chica," Ale told the bleeding, gasping, crying Noa, "imagine what it will feel like in the waking world."

"What the . . ." Reed trailed off.

"You've been played, güey. How does it feel?" Ale's face showed no joy. "Now." She transformed her hands into sapphire cymbals and crashed them together. The echoing ring of 600 Hz shattered the dream nightmare.

Reed awoke in the chocolate and robin's-egg blue Airbnb bedroom. Ale stood over Noa, who knelt on the floor, clutching an invisible wound in her chest. Arno sat up in his bed. Jo appeared in the open doorway.

"I'm so, so sorry," Noa gasped.

"What the hell's going on?" Reed blinked, trying to make sense of it all. "Noa? Ale?"

"We have much to discuss. But primero lo primero. From now on"—the Blue Bearer's eyes flashed as sapphire as her Stone, which illuminated the entire room in its royal glow—"I am Xochitl."

— END OF BOOK V —

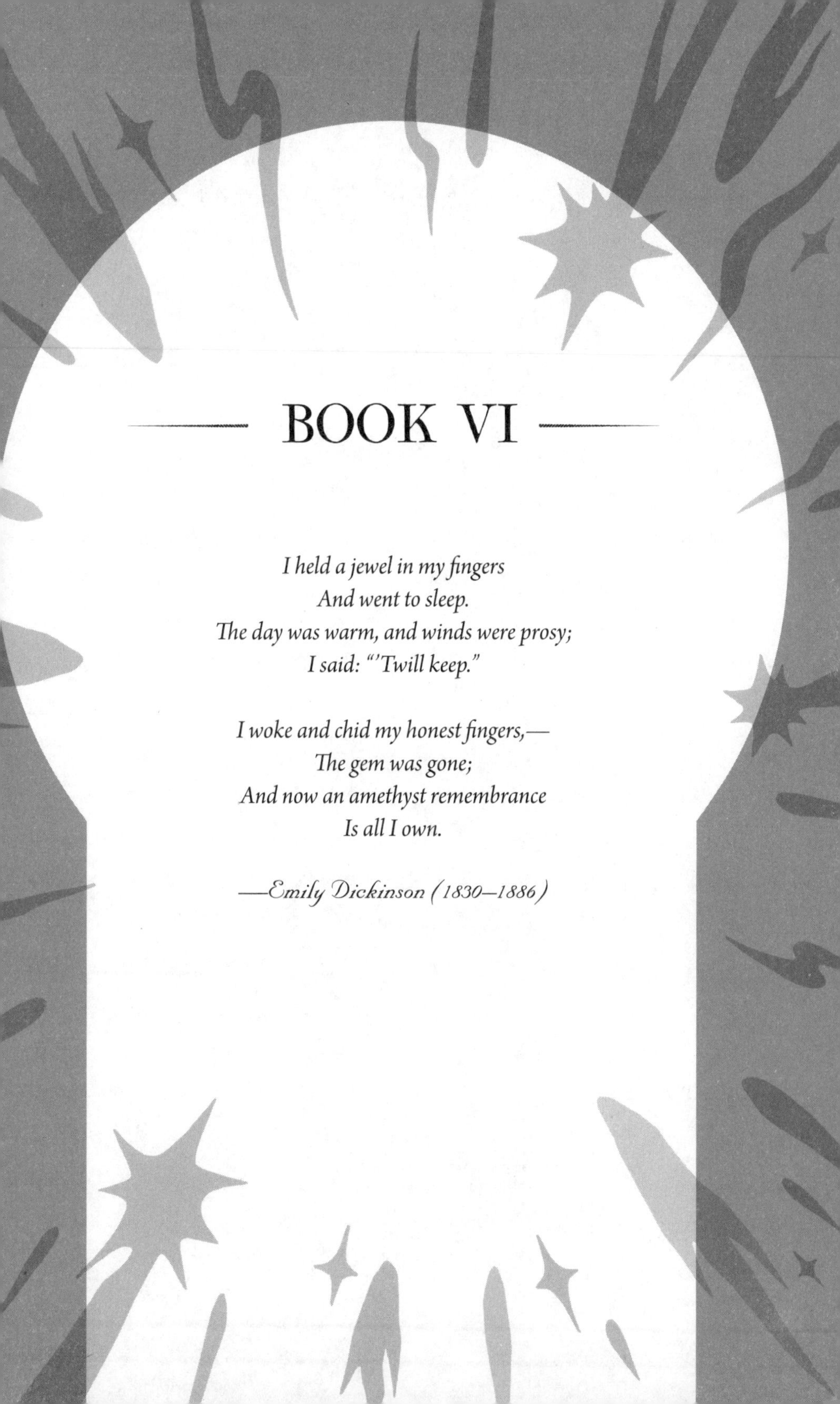

BOOK VI

I held a jewel in my fingers
And went to sleep.
The day was warm, and winds were prosy;
I said: "'Twill keep."

I woke and chid my honest fingers,—
The gem was gone;
And now an amethyst remembrance
Is all I own.

—Emily Dickinson (1830–1886)

CHAPTER 1

ALEJANDRA Y XOCHITL

As a child, I would climb up to the rooftop of my abuela's hacienda in Cuernavaca during storms, adorned in all her precious metals. I dared the lightning to strike me, so that I would be sent to the fourth house of death: the Mansion of the Moon, the Aztec paradise reserved for those who met their end at the mercy of the elements.

Perhaps that is why I knew I was in the Aztec underworld when I emerged from the square gateway that mi zafira had created on the corrugated cobalt tin shed in the industrial park after Reed had confessed his betrayal.

I did not leave him because I was hurt. I did not leave him because I was angry. I left him because if I had stayed, I would've wrung the life out of his miserable body.

But this was not the Mansion of the Moon. It was not even the Kingdom of the Sun, death's third mansion, reserved for those who died in battle or childbirth (these are, of course, the same thing).

Instead, I emerged in Mictlán, the first and most common of death's mansions, wearing the garb of an Aztec warrior: the quilted cotton of an ichcahuipilli, soaked in salt water to strengthen the fibers, over tunic and loincloth; sturdy leather sandals strapping my feet. I ran my fingers over the helmet atop my head and traced the sharpness of the teeth jutting down, just above my eyes. The warrior fangs of a jaguar.

I knew I would have to overcome many obstacles. The first was the great river Apanohuaya.

Swimming was impossible. I could not see the opposite shore and did not want to discover where the furious current would drag me. But then my pet from childhood, Cachucha, appeared at my side, with his smushed-in face and panting tongue. He grew until he was as large as a buffalo and invited me to climb upon his back. He would hold my salvation in his paws, for that is the job of the animal companion—the xoloitzcuintle. Mine was a pug, not a xolo, but I would do the best with what I had. What else can any of us do?

I held on as the currents crashed around us, threatening to rip me off his great bulk, threatening to drown me, until we arrived drenched on the opposite bank. I hugged him fiercely once I disembarked. I have always preferred animals to humans. Animals are loyal. Animals do not betray.

As Cachucha shrank to his original size, invisible spirits stripped me of my clothes. I knew this would happen, so I was not afraid. But they did not just take my clothing. They also stripped my memory of the Feats. With each article of clothing, part of my training disappeared from my mind, like sand dispersed by wind.

At first, I fought. My mind had been invaded enough. But I came to understand the spirits were aiding me. In this trial, I had to surrender. By the time I stood shivering in only my loincloth, I had let all the Feats go. They were, after all, only restraints. To evolve, you cannot walk someone else's path. You must forge your own, on your terms.

I left the shore of Apanohuaya. Was someone playing the drums? Or was I just hearing the stomp-stomp-stomp **stomp** *in my mind? I followed the sound to Tepetl Monamiclia and discovered two great mountains battling. I did not see how I could scurry between these giants. One misstep and I would be squashed, like an insect, inconsequential. An ignominious death.*

The drums saved me. They told me what to do. My father's people had danced the concheros for all eternity. I drew on my bloodline, back to pre-Hispanic times, and prehistoric times, and even further back. That power filled me and guided me through this epic battle.

stomp-stomp-stomp **stomp**
stomp-stomp-stomp **stomp**
stomp-stomp-stomp
stomp
*stomp-***stomp**
*stomp-***stomp**
One step right
One step left
One back
So that I may take
One great step forward

Finding and following my own rhythm was the only way a mote such as myself could survive these giants.

I arrived, unscathed, to the other side of the range, leaving the titans to continue their endless brawl. Theirs was not my battle.

Next, I journeyed over a hill strewn with flints and shards of Ilztepetl, much sharper than the metal of our European conquerors. But this was not ordinary obsidian, for it sliced even my sapphire feet. I left a trail of blood in my wake, my version of the German children's breadcrumbs.

I was vulnerable. I could bleed. But I persevered. Physical pain never scared me.

I endured Celhuecayan next, the eight frozen mountains wind-whipped with perpetual snow. Each step was a challenge through this arctic tundra. I transformed my hands into chimalli and used the circular shields to protect me. I made my way forward, one beleaguered step at a time. Sometimes, this is the only kind of progress we can hope for.

Did the visions come from hypothermia? Or were they sent to me? Or both?

In the sheer white faces of the mountain, I witnessed the profanity—a Bearer using their Potentia on another, as sacrilegious as receiving Communion without baptism. The irony was not lost on me.

Every episode eroded his will. Eroded him.

Bueno. Let him see what it is like to have your thoughts, your feelings, turned against you. He deserved it. And much worse. I would not save him. Not again.

Endless walking in the desert of Paniecatacoyan. Most of my four years in Mictlán were spent here, not knowing if I was traveling in circles, if I was making progress, if I was retreading already-taken paths. The most frightening mazes have no walls.

Without the companionship of Cachucha, my mind would not have survived the solitude. But he was always by my side, grinning his stupid grin, each breath drawn through that smushed-in face rasping like an old woman's snore, oblivious, innocent, as only creatures can be. This endless walk was where I allowed myself to mourn. I would not sentimentalize Hikaru in death, as so many do. I would honor him in all his complicated, problematic glory. His prowess. His entitlement. His joy. His arrogance. His sacrifice. It was the last thing I saw before I arrived here.

Then I allowed myself to mourn my friendship. I had trusted Reed the way I rarely trusted anyone. More than Timothée. More than Masuda. And he had betrayed me. I would never make that mistake again. Never let myself be vulnerable to another human being. Terminado.

A barrage of arrows fired by unseen hands greeted us when we finally emerged in Temiminaloyan. I planted my hands on Cachucha and sapphired us both. He wagged his tail like a puppy every time an arrow bounced off his jeweled form. No human has ever shown me such pure affection. Thankfully, the barrage was short, for the strain of transforming another made my blood run colder than ice, so cold I could not remember warmth.

In Tecoylenaloyan, a thousand fierce beasts devoured my heart. During their feast, I saw glimpses of the past. I suppose I should have been surprised to learn that the Provosts had been sacrificing Bearers to seal the Portal. But Señor Shaw and Father showed us what they were capable of. "Believe people when they show you who they are," my abuela used to say.

How did I survive a thousand fierce beasts dining on my heart? Easy. I had survived Reed's transgression. Physical pain is tangible. It is the body's way of communicating danger and threat. It serves a purpose. Unlike betrayal.

We tried to swim past the crocodile Xochilonal in the black waters of Apanuiayo, but he captured and consumed us. Inside him, more visions: of Tlaltecuhtli, the earth monster, mother of all living things, ripped in two by the rivals Quetzalcoatl and Tezcatlipoca. I saw her skin turn into fields of grass and flowers, her hair into trees and herbs, her eyes into springs and fountains, her nose into valleys, and her mouth into caves and rivers. Last, her shoulders turned into large mountain ranges, spanning the world, holding the heavens up and the earth down. A vision eventually showed me how to escape through the great crocodile's nostrils.

Finally, after four years and nine trials, Cachucha and I emerged to the lair of Mictlancihuatl and Mictlantecuhtli, the Lady and Lord of the Underworld. The skeletal monarchs sat on spider thrones, with bone headdresses like peacocks' plumes, and gems where their eyes should be. It was difficult to tell which was which. Like many cultures, the Aztecs did not conform to a gender binary. Besides, these figures were gods. They need not abide by our petty mortal categories.

One slowly swept a skeletal hand attached to a skeletal wrist. A bone owl swooped down from their shoulder, flapping its skeletal wings before speaking.

"When does the scarlet macaw turn into the raven?" The shoulder-perched owl blinked its saucer eyes twice. Just as they made Quetzalcoatl solve the riddle of the horn to repopulate the earth, I would have to answer if I wanted passage.

The two gods were terrifying, yes, but it was not death that scared me. It is something Christians have a hard time understanding, because the fear of death is baked deep in that religion, like barbacoa in the earth. But for many, death is not something to be feared. It simply is. Inevitable. Necessary. Freeing.

"When does the scarlet macaw turn into the raven?" the owl asked again. How did I know that the punishment for a wrong answer would be the obliteration that I feared. Worse than death. Erasure.

After all I had been through—Apanohuaya, the great river that tried to consume me; Tepetl Monamiclia, the dueling titans; Ilztepetl, the hills strewn with obsidian that sliced my feet; Celhuecayan, the eight arctic mountains of perpetual snow; endless walking in the desert Paniecatacoyan; a barrage of arrows in Temiminaloyan; a thousand fierce beasts feasting on my heart in Tecoylenaloyan; and finally, the crocodile Xochilonal, who devoured us in the black waters of Apanuiayo—I would not let a riddle best me.

"When does the scarlet macaw turn into the raven?" the skeletal owl asked one final time.

Scarlet. Red. Reed.

"Fire," I responded. "Death."

The Gods of Death swept their bony wrists with surprising grace. A gateway shimmered open in the air before me. It shone bright against the darkness. An invitation. The greatest reward: admission to the Mansion of the Moon, the fourth house of death, the paradise reserved for elemental deaths. A promise of an eternity of joy. The destination I had desired since I was a niña on my abuela's terrace in Cuernavaca, clad in all those precious metals, begging the storm to take me. The night my grandmothers got into their infamous dispute.

I took a step toward the brilliant gateway. Finally, freedom. From so many things. But most of all, an end to my broken, betrayed heart.

But Cachucha bit at my ankle, in the direction of another gateway, slitting open behind me. I tried to ignore it. But Cachucha would not let me.

This duller portal promised nothing but more pain. Even after years of traveling through this plane of death, after experiencing loyalty, surrender, strength, vulnerability, endurance, and companionship, I still hurt. I had not forgotten. I had not forgiven.

How could Reed have done that to me? I thought we were amigues.

Much to my surprise, I could not abandon him. It is not how I am made.

Cachucha was right. Another destiny awaited me.

I bid adiós to the Mansion of the Moon, to paradise, and stepped into this mundane world of chocolate brown and robin's-egg blue. To save my friend. My betrayer. To save Reed. Again.

⸻★⸻

"A valuable break from Cyclops, to interview the second round of candidates. I have narrowed successors to eight semifinalists, including our first female candidates, much to Father's distress. As much as he fights me on this break of tradition, the Muraqqa explicates that the selection of a successor is ultimately the Provost's decision."

Rupert Shaw
Provost, Pass Eleven

CHAPTER 2

EL REGRESO DE XOCHITL

"We could always kill her," I said.

"She's kidding, right?" A nervous laugh escaped from the frizzy-haired, green-eyed gorda with the cat eye glasses.

"Alejandra's kidding," the Purple Bearer assured her.

"She said her name is Xochitl," Reed jumped in.

"That's right, JoAnne." And I was not kidding.

"They go by Jo now," the Yellow Bearer corrected me.

It appears as if much had changed, and we all had much to learn.

When I emerged from Mictlán, I knew my name would be the Nahuatl word for flower. I knew it with the kind of simple, bone-strong conviction that Masuda and Timothée described liking boys. Some things just were. I had been Alejandra. Now I was Xochitl. Four years traveling through nine underworld realms changes you. Besides, why should we not all choose our own names upon entering adulthood, as they did in many ancient cultures? Why accept this inheritance from our parents, bequeathed before they knew whom we would become? I understood now. I was not part indigenous, part mestiza. I was simply many things. A descendant of a proud line of Aztec Jaguar warriors. And a descendant of Spanish colonists. Just as I was also a woman, and a fencer, and the Blue Bearer. A part cannot be the whole, but we are, all of us, vast enough to contain multitudes.

All five of us were still in the bedroom: Green kneeling on the meter-wide strip between the twin beds; Arno sitting up in his bed, entirely focused on Reed; Reed, in his bed, knees to his chest, staring off in the distance; Jo hovering by the door, consciously or not guarding the only exit; me, in front of the robin's-egg blue wall, where my square gateway had appeared.

Arno had introduced himself and then given me a brief synopsis. Three weeks since Baltimore. Ithaca. JoAnne: Jo, they/them, Purple, ally. Noa: Green, apparently a traitor. Señor Shaw and Father suspiciously absent. Two weeks till the Ikeda. My appearance in Reed's dream awoke him from over a day's slumber. Our very own Sleeping Beauty.

Even though Jo had assumed my guise in DC, I admired them. They were the only other Bearer with style: denim jacket over a lace bra and leather miniskirt. I suppose if I had her Potentia, I would always look like I had just stepped off a fashion shoot as well.

Or would I? Alejandra certainly would have. But what about Xochitl, who still wore the quilted cotton of the ichcahuipilli, layered over tunic and loincloth, strapped into sturdy leather sandals? Would I return to my previous wardrobe or continue dressing like an Aztec warrior from precolonial times? Would I trade high fashion for woven cottons, like my cousin Mariana, who had dropped out of college to live with an indigenous community in Oaxaca?

"Noa, I don't know Xochitl." Arno finally spoke, those dark eyes as deep as Mictlán taking in the whole room. "I can't tell you if she's kidding about killing you. From what I understand, though, none of us could stop her if she tried. Even if we wanted to." He clearly did not.

"Everybody chill out, okay?" Jo took a few steps into the room. "No one's killing anyone. I'm sure Xo—" Jo tripped on my name. If these gringos had a hard time with "Ale," I could only imagine how this would go.

"Xochitl," I offered. "So'-chee-təl." After much contemplation, I decided to go with what many considered to be the Spanishization of the Nahuatl word. I could have insisted on the most traditional pronunciation: "sho" instead of "so" for the first syllable, and a "tl" sound that was almost impossible for people who had not grown up with it, like the "Zh" in Mandarin, or the "eur" in French. But these gringos were trying, so I would meet them halfway. Besides, claiming the Nahuatl pronunciation felt performative.

They all took the opportunity to try to pronounce my name. The chorus of guttural sounds almost sent me back to Mictlán. "You can call me Xochi for short." Anything to stop this aural assault. "So'-chee."

"I'm sure Xochi," Jo started again with obvious relief, "is not going to kill anyone. None of us are."

"And why are you so sure of this?" It was important to challenge this kind of assertion early.

"Because that is what makes us different from the Shaws." They stated it simply, like a fact as obvious as the rising moon.

I nodded. This was different from the kind of bullshit Reed had tried to pull early on. This was simple reason. Besides, if I decided to kill Noa, a Glamour would not stop me.

Speaking of Reed. My fury flared the moment I saw him again. But without any fuel, it sputtered. Who could muster anything but pity for that pale, withered, discarded tamale husk of a human being? Three weeks should not have been enough time to deteriorate into whatever he was now.

His suffering did not forgive what he had done to me. Neither did the irony of his own victimization. But only a monster would not feel pity in the face of his assault. It is difficult, yes, to quantify these things. To put sin on a scale and weigh it against itself.

"Tell us everything." Reed looked at no one when he spoke. Soft focus.

"Okay, two weeks ago"—Green produced a smartphone from her matching set of faux silk pajamas and swiped through its calendar—"Principal Brendon-Hopper called me into her office and introduced me to Mr. Shaw and Father. They told me they knew all about the emerald and that I was . . ."

". . . destined to save the world?" Reed supplied.

Noa tapped her nose with her index finger.

We nodded. We understood. We had all fallen victim to a similar seduction.

"My first few meetings with them were at the school, which made it feel legit, you know?" Green leaned back against Arno's bed. "It sounds so stupid and obvious now, but at the time, they made me feel so special. Just like finding Green did."

Noa opened her hand to reveal Green, glowing, as if giving a performance.

La esmeralda was rectangular with angled corners. Rounder than my square sapphire, squarer than Jo's oval of an amethyst, longer than Reed's circular ruby, and narrower than Arno's teardrop topaz.

"Also, and I'm not expecting any of you to understand this, but I felt like they really saw me. From the very beginning." She pulled her hair back in a rubber band. "You get used to being written off when you're my size. But they just wanted to get to work. We started training. They taught me the Feats. No need for Locatio, obviously." She nodded at Jo. "So no Disjunctis. We whipped through Potentia,

Petrakinesis, and Teleportare. I'm a pro in all of them. I felt chosen. Special. Like I had real power. I'd never felt that way before."

"Tell us how your Potentia works," Jo commanded.

"The Feat of Dreamaturgy. Act One: I can travel into people's dreams. It helps if I have something of theirs. Something that has spent a lot of time on their body, something with sentimental value." She handed Reed a burgundy guitar pick. He placed it on his nightstand wordlessly.

"Father never let me visit his dreams," she continued. "So he trained me to power up on Mr. Shaw. Act Two: I can decode dreams. Uncover their truth. Think about what a powerful therapeutic tool it could be. Helping people confront their worst nightmares? Overcome phobias?"

"But that's not how you used it on Reed." Arno's words cut her reverie.

"You have to understand." Noa gesticulated when she spoke, like an Argentinean. "They told me you were evil. That you were going to destroy the world. And that I had to get you to Relinquo. And they predicted everything—when you would appear, what you would say to me. It made me trust them. You know how it's so easy to believe the first version of a story you hear?"

We all nodded our agreement. Except Arno.

"Dreamaturgy, Act Three: I can sculpt the dreamscapes that I visit. Tap into people's greatest fears, greatest desires."

"And your Price?" Jo asked.

"The time I spend Dreamaturging doesn't count as sleep. That's why I've been so tired all the time."

"When did you start turning my dreams against me?" Reed asked.

I looked at the spot on the wall where Reed was staring. Had I missed something so fascinating there that he could not bring himself to look away? No. Nada.

"A few days before you arrived." Noa's head hung low as she consulted her phone again.

"So, Asbury Park." Reed closed his eyes. "And here I was thinking I was going off the deep end because I was mourning one friend's death and self-flagellating for the inexcusable violation of another."

Having him name it, so that I did not have to, in public, for all to hear, was a beginning.

"But it turns out that someone had infiltrated my dreams and was twisting them against me as well!" Reed's delivery aimed for sarcastic/funny but struck closer to cynical/hurt. "Why me, Noa?"

"Mr. Shaw and Father decided the easiest way to unravel the group was to get you to Relinquo. They figured Arno would follow . . ."

Arno nodded. I appreciated his efficiency. He was not someone who spoke when he did not need to.

"And since they've figured out how to predict the appearance of a Stone," Noa continued, "they'd just find the new Red and Yellow Bearers and brainwash them."

"What about me?" Jo still hovered by the doorway.

"You're an anomaly, Jo." Noa perched on Arno's nightstand. "They still don't know what to make of you."

"What can I say?" Jo beamed.

"And me?" I asked.

"I don't know, TBH. They didn't tell me much. Especially once I started standing up to them. Because, once I actually met you, I figured out that what I was doing to Reed was wrong. And that you guys weren't evil." Noa wrapped her hair around her fingers. "Dysfunctional, sure. Complicated, no question. Totally ill-equipped to save the world, possibly—"

"We get it, Noa," Reed cut her off.

"But not evil. So I started questioning Father. That's when he changed. Fast. The threats started off small at first, but when Vershinin disappeared, I knew they weren't kidding."

"Who is Vershinin?" I asked.

"My dog," Noa replied. "My Pomeranian."

"They attacked your pet?" Fury seized me as an image of Cachucha, in all his smushed-in face innocence, appeared in my mind's eye. "They are even more depraved than I had imagined!"

"I don't care how good of an actor I am," Noa said, "having to lie, day in and day out, was killing me. And the exhaustion! After the second time I fell asleep at the wheel, I told Mr. Shaw and Father I was done.

"That's when my dad got accused of 'indecent behavior' at Cornell and put on an indefinite unpaid leave. No explanation. And a few days later, my mom was mugged in the parking garage downtown. Father told me if I questioned him again, worse things would happen. He made me check in with him every day, sometimes twice or three times. They hijacked my whole life. I wanted to stop, but I didn't know how!"

"You did the best you could," Jo told Noa. "Once someone like Father gets their claws into you, it's hard to get free."

"It was a good plan," Reed admitted. "And it would've worked, too, if Ale—" Reed corrected himself. "If Xochitl hadn't arrived."

"You held out longer than they expected." Noa Petrakinesised Green back into her pajama pocket. "Like, much longer. Which is why I think they were working on a Plan B. Those eye patches had something to do with it."

"Eye patches?" Arno tilted his head.

"Oh yeah—a few days ago, they just showed up sporting these eye patches." Noa put one hand over an eye to demonstrate. "They called it The Cyclops Strategem."

"Why didn't they just kill us?" Jo asked.

"When you Relinquo to someone, it's instantaneous. The person inherits the Stone immediately, like when Reed got Yellow from Hikaru. But when you kill a Bearer, the Stone disappears, and you can't predict how long it takes to choose the next Bearer. This close to the Ikeda's closest approach, they couldn't risk it."

"This close?" Reed asked. "We still have two weeks."

"Um . . ." Noa looked away. "About that."

"¿Si?" Something churned in my stomach.

"That was another lie." Noa wrung her hands. "The Pentacle Portal opens tomorrow."

"Due to the gravitational influence of celestial bodies—most notably, the Kuiper Belt objects and the Oort cloud objects—the Ikeda's orbit varies from approximately 37.4 years to 38.8 years in length. We believe that Pass Twelve will occur exactly 37.89 years after Pass Eleven, and I look forward to seeing which of the finalist candidates arrive at the same conclusion."

Broughton Shaw
Chancellor, Pass Eleven

CHAPTER 3

XOCHITL CONFRONTA

"Tomorrow?!" the four of us exclaimed in terrified unison.

"Yup." Noa nodded sheepishly. "Misinformation is a time-tested tool of fascism."

"This is what we do." Reed snapped out of his trance and into leadership mode. "Noa relinquishes immediately to one of us."

I saw the direction he was heading. "We create a list of possible Bearers . . ." I immediately began analyzing the strengths and weaknesses of Lucía, M., Timothée, and Masuda.

". . . Teleportare by noon . . ." Reed picked up and continued my train of thought.

". . . and teach them Feats essential by dinner," I concluded. Despite everything that had happened, how much we'd both changed, Reed and I slipped back into our rhythm with the greatest of ease.

"But then what?" Jo asked pointedly. "We still don't know what we're actually going to do when the Pentacle Portal opens."

"There is another option." Noa stood up. "I could remain in my role as the Green Bearer."

"You think we're going to trust you after what you did to Reed?" The vehemence in Arno's voice took me aback. "You could still be working for Father. This could all be part of the trap!"

"'If powers divine behold our human actions,'" Noa intoned, "'as they do, I doubt not then but innocence shall make false accusation blush.'" Despite her Target semisilk pajamas, blotchy cheeks, and frazzled hair, this Bearer gathered around her the simple regality of a queen. Or a king. Of a monarch. "Have Reed read me."

"It's not a bad idea," I conceded.

"You're the one who suggested we kill her!" The sun's earliest rays bent toward Arno as light danced beneath his olive skin.

"I already know the Feats," Noa said. "All the time you'd save finding a new Green Bearer could go to creating a plan."

Arno crossed his arms.

"I don't blame you for not trusting me." Noa removed her cat eye glasses and wiped them clean. "But I want to do this. As long as it means stopping Father and Mr. Shaw. I deserve the chance to get back at them for what they did to me. And my family. And Vershinin. So read me. I have nothing to hide."

Reed slowly pulled himself out of bed. He lined up his feet, shoulder-width, slightly angled out, as Señor Shaw had taught him, to perform his Potentia.

The Feats. They were funny to consider now. It is easy to follow someone else on the path they have discovered. It is a convenient way to travel. But to truly unlock your potential, you must find your own way. Intimate. Private. Mysterious. It is infinitely more difficult, stumbling through the wilderness. You will get lost. You will get cut as you traverse obsidian shards that slice even armored feet. But you will never forget the trail made in your own blood.

"It's easier if I touch you," Reed told her.

Noa guided his hands up to her face. Thumb and index finger on jaw, the rest splayed against her cheek.

Red lit up like a traffic light. Reed's eyes followed. He tilted his head forward. Noa mirrored him, and their foreheads met and their breathing synced as a hibiscus nimbus engulfed them.

They sat like that, locked, like lovers. Or adversaries.

It lasted only a few seconds.

"She's telling the truth. About everything." Reed dropped his hands from her face, and the hibiscus nimbus dissipated. "Except for that site-specific production of *The Three Sisters*. It looked awful."

"You had to be there," Noa insisted.

"She attacked one of our own. For weeks." Arno had drifted closer to Reed, protectively. The pull between them was so strong I feared for anything caught in between. "Just because she's telling the truth now doesn't mean we can trust her."

"You need a reason to trust me?" Noa walked into the middle of the room. "Okay. What if I told you I know how to resolve Disjunctis?"

"Impossible," Jo jumped in. "The Price for Locatio is Disjunctis, and that makes electricity go kablooey. That's a given."

"Think fast, Arno."

Arno barely caught the smartphone Noa tossed at him.

Disjunctis had become such an integral part of my life since becoming the Blue Bearer I had stopped questioning it. I had experienced it in many forms. Shorting the docks for the public bikes in Baltimore. The discharge that sent me hurling through the air like a cannonball when I sliced through the cables of Yellow's prison in the engine room of the towboat. And on and on and on.

But now, Arno held Noa's cell phone, and nothing sparked.

He gingerly pressed the screen. The opening chords to *Wicked* filled the room.

"What the . . ." Reed trailed off.

"Let me see!" Jo gingerly slid a finger over the cell phone screen. The volume to "Defying Gravity" increased.

Still no sparks.

"Does this mean I'm going to be able to surf the internet? Maybe even"—Jo dared to dream—"play the Xbox?"

"Okay, Noa." Arno placed the phone on the nightstand. "Explain."

"I just figured out what kind of electricity is compatible with magic." A touch of self-satisfaction crawled into Noa's voice. "No biggie."

We gathered around Noa, like children around a teacher.

"Remember that time that Zeb-un-Nissa used the compass in the Phantasmagoria?" The other Bearers nodded yes. "That's what got me thinking. Compasses rely on magnetism. And magnetism and electricity are just about the same thing—it's the reason they're called electromagnetic forces."

"Also why Storm could never defeat Magneto." Reed nodded.

"Or, for those of us who have studied actual science"—I shook my head—"a moving electric charge creates a magnetic field, a magnetic field induces a charge movement, which creates an electric current."

"Exactly!" Noa said. "So I asked myself: 'Noa, shouldn't that compass have sparked around Zeb-un-Nissa? Even a little?'" She leaped to her feet, playing both roles. "'Very interesting question, Noa. If our powers were truly incompatible with all electricity, the compass should've at least shocked her, and her Stone should've rendered the compass useless!'"

Reed, Arno, Jo, and I looked at one another, at Noa, at one another again, and then at the phone. None of us were used to being speechless.

"So I asked my dad"—Noa smiled in satisfaction—"who teaches renewable-energy sources, to explain it to me. This is how electricity traditionally works." Noa gesticulated. "First, you need to generate power: burn coal to heat water for steam, or build a dam to harness the force of rushing water, for example. You use that power to turn a turbine."

Jo wiggled their fingers, and a three-dimensional diagram of burning coal, heating water, floating steam, and spinning turbines appeared before them like an instructional video.

"Thanks, Jo!" Noa referenced the Glamour. "Next, the spinning turbine rotates the rotor shaft of a generator." The diagram expanded, adding another panel of a spinning cylinder with small lightning bolts to illustrate Noa's description. "The generator converts the mechanical energy into electrical energy, which is distributed by a power grid."

The diagram expanded to cover the entire room, lighting up with glowing, intersecting lines.

"That must be why the Shaws are so scared of the Portal opening!" Jo exclaimed. "They think that magic energy, unleashed in the world, would short the global power grid and send us back into a Dark Age."

"That makes sense," Arno said.

"So I asked Ezra." Noa nodded. "How is the electricity of a compass, say, different from a lamp I plug in?"

"Compasses use naturally occurring electricity. It's clean." This was freshman year stuff. "Anything that must be plugged in uses manufactured electricity. That electricity releases gas emissions, the leading cause of climate change. That is why it is called dirty electricity."

"Exactly!" Noa turned around, holding a single finger up in an "aha!" moment. "But there is an exception. Manufactured electricity that is clean and green."

"Like solar energy?" I guessed.

"Bingo," Noa responded. "No burning, no gas emissions, no climate change."

"Now we're moving into AP chem." I forced myself to stop tracing the slivers of sapphire on my neck and shoulders. How many more had appeared during my journey to the underworld? Certainly the three at the base of my skull were new. "1913, Bohr's model of the atom, right?"

"Pass Eight," Jo whispered.

"What?" Arno asked.

"Pass Eight," Jo repeated. "1913 was the year of Pass Eight."

All five of us held our breath for a collective moment.

"You think that's a coincidence?" Arno asked.

"I am starting to think," I replied slowly, "that there are fewer and fewer coincidences."

"The Bohr model of the atom!" Noa continued. "An atom's nucleus comprises protons and neutrons while the electrons rotate around it in concentric circles."

"Like a solar system." Arno's eyes glinted gold when he Petrakinesised his Stone into the center of the room. Yellow moved differently with a new Bearer. Cautiously, but with more deliberation.

"Using electromagnetic forces in place of gravity," Noa finished.

"We can work with this." Jo smiled like a child catching Santa Claus. They sent Purple into an orbit around Yellow. Soon, all the Stones were spinning around Yellow, electrons rotating around their nucleus.

"Solar energy uses silicon panels to absorb photons generated by the sun." Noa stepped into the model, making sure not to touch any of the Stones. "Those black panels use the photons to bounce electrons from one orbit to another. It's what makes solar different from other green energy, like hydroelectric and wind. Jo, do you mind if I . . . ?"

Jo gave Noa the curtest of nods, and she curled her index finger and flicked Purple, sending it from the innermost ring to the next. Like bumping Mercury into Venus's orbit. "The movement of the electron from one ring to another releases energy. The solar panel captures and converts that energy into DC electricity."

"As opposed to Marvel electricity?" Reed asked.

No one laughed.

"You know," Reed tried again, "'cause they're like the two major comic book lines?"

Still, no one laughed.

"Watching Zeb-un-Nissa and Sarmad use the compass made me think—what if Disjunctis didn't happen with *all* electricity," Noa concluded. "Maybe our magic is only incompatible with dirty electricity, the kind that's causing climate change. Maybe *the way* electricity is created affects *the nature* of the electricity itself. Maybe our powers are *perfectly compatible* with clean energy!"

"Okay," Reed conceded. "How would you test your theory?"

"I just did!" Noa declared, like a triumphant lawyer convincing a jury of her client's innocence. "I charged my cell phone using solar power. Totally clean energy. Sure, it took three days. But look at Arno. No sparky."

"No sparky," Jo agreed, gently poking the phone again. "And I haven't gotten that grody feeling inside my teeth every time I'm really close to a current."

"So what do you say?" Noa asked. "Have I earned my spot on the team?"

"This is impressive," Arno conceded. "But it doesn't change the fact that we still can't trust you, Noa, after what you did to Reed."

"Arno, I'm not sure," Jo started carefully, "that you're speaking for all of us. At least, not for me."

"Are you being serious, Jo?" Arno asked.

"I just don't think I would've acted differently in her place," they said. "Should we put it to a vote?"

"Anyone seconding Jo's proposal?" Reed asked.

"Are we seriously Robert's Rules'ing this?" I asked. "Everyone knows they are fundamentally problematic on a hegemonic level."

"Fine." Reed swallowed. "Let's try consensus, then."

"What do you think, Xochi?" Jo asked.

What did I think?

What she did to Reed was worse than what he did to me. And what he did to me was inexcusable.

But her loved ones were being threatened.

And she thought she was doing the right thing.

At least, at first.

When I left Reed, I told him I would never forgive his betrayal. But here we were in the same room again.

"I don't know about la gorda." That was the truth. I did not know.

"What's 'la gorda'?" Noa asked. "A Spanish term of endearment?"

"It means, 'the fat girl,'" I said.

"Uh, Xochitl," Reed started. "That's not exactly—"

"Oh, please," Noa cut him off. "*Fat* is not a bad word. We all have eyes. I'm fat, Reed's skinny, Arno's gonna be a balding otter by the time he graduates college, no one knows what the real Jo looks like 'cause they're always Glamoured up, and Xochitl is an Amazonian Wonder Woman Frida Kahlo goddess. Now, can we get back to saving the world?"

"I like her. You. I like you, Noa." I resisted the urge to raise my hand, as I would in a formal vote. Even after you reject the tools of oppression, you must force yourself to break their habits. "Noa is the best candidate to be the Green Bearer."

"Agreed." Jo manifested a big thumbs-up.

Two for.

"You attacked Reed! Deliberately! For weeks!" Arno shook with barely contained rage. "There's no way I could trust you. Hard stop."

One against.

Noa, to her credit, said nothing.

We all turned to Reed. What would happen when he pushed this to a tie?

"What you did to me was fucked beyond belief." Reed forced himself to look at Noa. To really take her in. To say the things he needed to say, as difficult as they may be. "But I'll get over it. Not just because you were also being victimized. Not just because it's the best thing for the team."

"Then why?" Noa asked him.

"Because I don't want to have to carry all that anger around with me." Reed stared into his ruby. "The Stone is burden enough. So it's the best thing for me, too."

How much of this was for my benefit?

Noa nodded and said nothing.

"Ideally, consensus is unanimous." My gaze has been described as persuasive. But Arno met it, resolute and unflinching. I respected him for that. He would not change his mind. "But as with a vote, a majority suffices. Bienvenida, Noa." I extended my hand to shake hers.

"I can't wait to kick some Mr. Shaw and Father butt!" Noa accepted my hand and then drew me in for a hug.

Without a word, Arno stormed out of the room and slammed the door behind him. It bounced back, hard, against the frame.

"I think he needs to be alone," Reed said.

"You understand so little about boys." Jo followed Arno out.

That left three of us in the room.

"I'm just going to—" Noa tiptoed toward the door. "You know, it's been so long since the two of you have had some real one-on-one QT, so why don't I go just in case you need some catch-up time. Call if you need anything okay have fun I'm outta here bye-bye!"

And then there were two.

"You can go if you want." Reed turned his back to me.

"I do not need your permission to leave." I could have stretched out a sapphire limb to make him turn back to me, but I resisted. Superpowers would not fix this.

"I know! I mean, of course I know that. I just . . ."

"You do not get to act the victim when you are the one who transgressed."

"She twisted my dreams, Xochitl. Into you!" He choked on the words. "You came to me over and over again. The things you said. The things you did. The way that version of you hurt me, again and again and again . . ." He punched his fist into the wooden headboard of the bed.

"Good." The ferocity of his feelings did not frighten me.

He continued punching.

Ithaca was waking up around us. Cars honked, dogs barked, neighbors greeted one another outside on the street. The smell of freshly brewed coffee downstairs awoke a longing in me that no time in the underworld would kill.

Reed punched and punched that innocent headboard.

I wanted to tell him he got what he deserved. I wanted to comfort him. I wanted to punch him the way he was punching that headboard. I wanted him to stop hurting himself. I wanted to hurt him. I did not trust myself to navigate all the impulses. So I said nothing. I pretended I was a statue, made of stone. Solid, stationary, silent.

"Hell, I guess this is as good a time as any." He wiped his runny nose on his bare forearm. "I know it's not worth much, I know it's just the beginning, I know I've got miles to go, but: I'm sorry. I'm really sorry." The anguish in his face almost moved me. "I should've never, ever done that to anyone. Especially you."

They were the right words. I nodded, acknowledging, but not accepting, his apology.

"You know that song, 'Are We Still Friends?' by Tyler, The Creator?" Reed asked. "It's built on an Al Green sample. E–E^7–A–Am–E–E^7–A–Am."

"¿Perdón?" What was he rambling on about?

"Sorry—was that out loud? I'm still having a hard time figuring out this whole reality thing." Reed laughed nervously. "But I mean, are we?"

"No." When a transgression was as great as his, a mere apology by itself does not fix it. But could I find it within myself to authentically give him anything more? "Not yet."

"Will we be good?" If he had been the least bit self-pitying, I would have struck him.

"You may have Orchestrated me to come, Reed. But I decided to stay. And I decided to come back. So I accept this beginning. But we both know a beginning means nothing without a middle and an end."

"Okay." He nodded.

What would happen now? How could we carry ourselves across the impossible chasm that faced us?

"So are we going to whip this group into shape, or what?" he asked me with a crooked smile. "Because God knows that's the only way we have a shot of succeeding tomorrow."

"But we do not even have a plan." Could I actually trust him again?

"Not yet!" That playful sparkle danced in his eyes, that thing that made him who he was. The thing that had let me love him. "But we're certainly not gonna come up with one like this. So wadda you say? Should I continue blubbering about how sorry I am, Xochitl, or shall we corral the Stone Bearers of Pass Eleven and save the world?"

If I had my choice, we would first establish trust before working together again. But life did not afford me that option. I would have to hope that working together would build that trust. I would have to have faith. In him. In me. In us.

Besides, against all odds, he had pronounced my name correctly.

So here we go.

Dios mío.

★

"The Noa Stratagem failed. Irrelevant. She was merely one of our many spinning plates."

Rupert Shaw
Provost, Pass Eleven

CHAPTER 4

XOCHITL Y LOS PORTADORES PRACTICAN LA CONTENCIÓN

Noa had, indeed, brewed a pot of coffee. Arno and Jo returned a half hour later. He still could not make eye contact with Noa, but at least he was here. That would have to suffice for now. He even made us breakfast sandwiches. I have traveled the world. Bacon, egg, and cheese was the only breakfast that could compare to true chilaquiles. We ate while we strategized. I started.

"We have four options." Half my sandwich stared back at me from my plate. My body was not accustomed to food. "One: do nothing. Two: attempt what they tried in Pass One. Three: seal the Portal, as Señor Shaw and Father would. Last, four: try something new."

Jo, conveniently, Glamoured my list in an elegant script above the circular breakfast table.

1. *Do Nothing*
2. *Repeat Pass One*
3. *Seal the Portal*
4. *Something New*

Reed shot his hand up as if he were in class. "I'm rejecting number three right off the bat."

"Why?" Arno clearly did not enjoy contradicting Reed. "I mean, they've been doing that for a few centuries, and the world hasn't ended yet."

"Whatever they want, we don't." Jo jumped in to agree with Reed. "Also, Terminatio is a suicide pact. I'm not saying I wouldn't sacrifice my life for the good of the world, but could we consider a plan where we didn't have to kick the bucket?"

"I mean, I'd rather not die," Noa offered. "All things being equal."

I gently swiped my finger through the third option on the list. Contact unraveled the Glamour.

1. Do Nothing
2. Repeat Pass One

4. Something New

"Should we consider number one?" Reed asked. "What would happen if we did nothing?"

"Let the Portal open, and instead of being in the Pentagon Chamber—what—go roller-skating?" Jo's surprise made it clear that in all the time they'd spent contemplating alternatives, they had never truly considered that possibility.

"My guess"—Noa took a sip of her second cup of coffee—"is that the bubbling magic you observed in the Pass Ten Phantasmagoria would flood the world. Disjunctis everywhere."

"Perhaps, before the industrial revolution, that would have been an option," I spoke up, "but imagine the collateral damage now."

"We'd be dooming the world to another Dark Age." Arno gathered the dirty plates and took them to the dishwasher. "The loss of life would be impossible to predict. For example . . ." He looked at Reed pointedly.

". . . Rose." Reed turned to the rest of us. "My sister's on a home ventilator."

"Also, doing nothing is the coward's path," Noa said with a vehemence that surprised me. "All the Germans who knew what was happening in World War II but did nothing to stop it, they were just as bad as the Nazis working the camps."

"Same as the Turks during the Armenian Genocide. 'Therefore to him that knoweth to do good, and doeth it not, to him it is sin.' James, chapter 4, verse 17," Arno quoted. "Like the people of Meroz who were cursed by an angel because they didn't help their brethren fight the Canaanites."

Whatever ill feelings Arno still harbored for Noa, they did not stop him from agreeing with her.

"We have a chance to help our *brethren*!" Noa exclaimed, leaning into the archaic word just enough to be funny without making fun of Arno.

Arno smiled, just a little.

Progress?

"We have an opportunity that no one else will ever have again." Sometime in the last minute, Reed's hand had crawled across the kitchen table and was resting on Arno's. Neither one of them acknowledged it, so we did not, either. "We have to take it. Because we know the world is going to end."

"We believe that because of Sarmad's True Dreams," Jo said. "But we don't *know* it, like, as a fact."

"I'm not talking about Sarmad. I'm talking about science," Reed insisted. "Noa—ask your phone how the world will end."

"Hey, Google," Noa spoke into her phone. "How's the world going to end?"

"Many possible scenarios of anthropogenic extinction have been proposed," a robotic voice informed us, "such as climate change, global nuclear annihilation, biological warfare, and ecological collapse."

"Okay, Google, what is the nearest and most probable cause of the end of the world?" Noa followed up.

"The United Nations General Assembly has warned that by the year 2030, the effect of climate change will be irreparable," the voice intoned with a robotic detachment.

"Hey, Google," Noa continued, "what are the consequences of climate change?"

"Global temperatures have gone up by two degrees Fahrenheit in the past one hundred years," the robotic voice continued unfeelingly. "Thawing the permafrost, destroying the villages built on it, releasing more greenhouse gases, unleashing potentially devastating microbes. The melting glaciers are raising water levels, contaminating drinking water, interfering with farming, threatening wildlife and forcing their relocation. Climate change also permits thousands of viruses to jump from species to species, increasing the chances of another devastating pandemic."

"Do we have any reason to believe that governments will unite to solve these problems in the next thirty-seven years?" Arno asked us.

None of us could answer hopefully, so we said nothing.

"So Reed's right," Arno continued. "Doing nothing is not an option, because some time in the last fifteen or fifty or 150 years, our relationship to the planet went from being symbiotic to parasitic. This is our chance to change that." Arno swiped his finger through that option, and it disappeared, leaving . . .

2. Repeat Pass One

4. Something New

"So what about Sarmad and Zeb-un-Nissa's plan from Pass One?" I said. "We use the power of the Portal to supercharge our Stones and make the change we want."

"The definition of insanity is doing the same thing over and over again and expecting different results," Noa countered. "If their plan didn't work, then I don't know why we should try it again."

"Repeat Pass One" disappeared from the list. A single option remained, hovering in front of us in all its intimidating glory.

4. Something New

"Isn't coming up with ideas your thing, Reed?" I asked. He had been talking about leading since we met. Time to see if he could dance the dance.

Four sets of eyes turned to him.

"A little something has been scratching at me." Thought and mischievousness danced in his eyes. For a moment, he looked like the chico I first met all those weeks ago in Washington, DC. Innocent. Playful. Authentic.

"And when were you planning on sharing with the class?" Noa inquired.

"We'll need one more Phantasmagoria to really figure it out," Reed answered.

"But we rejected the Pass One approach," Jo said.

"That doesn't mean we can't learn from their failure." There was no defensiveness in Reed's voice. "This seed of a plan hinges on how the Pass One Bearers were going to power up their Stones."

Noa insisted that we perform the Synergia in the cavern behind the waterfall. I was grateful for the change in location. We walked in silence, led by Noa. Hopefully, it wasn't a trap.

"You sure you're up for it?" Jo asked Reed when we arrived.

"No," he said. "But you know what would really help?"

Jo rolled their eyes. "Whenever you're ready, dweeb. Phan—"

"—tas—" Arno increased his volume.

"—ma—" Noa held her arms up very dramatically.

"—gor—" I joined in.

"—ia!" we all screamed together.

Red and Purple turned the cavern magenta.

"Thank God this is the last time we're gonna have to do that," Jo drawled just before the Phantasmagoria swept over the craggy walls and transformed them into Zeb-un-Nissa's chamber.

"The initial Price of Cyclops comes as no surprise. The first sacrifice has been made. The second awaits."

Broughton Shaw
Chancellor, Pass Eleven

CHAPTER 5

ZEB-UN-NISSA MAKES A PACT

Zeb-un-Nissa stands with the other Bearers of Pass One around her fireplace. The fire roars, like an inferno. Is it the heat or their exertion that makes them sweat? Their Stones connect around the dancing flames, connecting the Bearers as well. She feels their presences. Their thoughts. Their desires.

"Now that our Stones are one, they must channel the fire's energy," Sarmad instructs as his ruby sends a crimson conduit into the heart of the flames. "This is what I have seen in my True Dreams. This is how we will harness the awesome power of the Pentacle Portal tomorrow."

Zeb-un-Nissa is already shifting between asanas, searching for the ones that will help her perform this Feat. Sarmad can just do these things, but she needs movements to help her focus, help her achieve what appears effortless for him. She stifles another yawn. For three days, they have practiced every morning before the sun rises, when it was safest for all the Bearers to be in her chambers.

When the aquamarine bridge connects Blue to the heart of the fire, her whole body thrills with the rush. *If this is what a mere flame feels like, how will we possibly survive the Portal tomorrow?*

It takes Belawadi, the Yellow Bearer, three attempts. The Purple Bearer, Imtiaz, a mere two. But Henry's conduits turn to pistachio wisps every time he tries to draw the flame's energy into his dull emerald.

"Hurry up, Henry." Belawadi's teardrop topaz flickers and flashes saffron.

"I'm trying." Blotches discolor Henry's pale skin, as pink as his striped doublet.

"Enough!" Sarmad commands.

The Sphere vanishes. Sarmad recalls his Stone. The other Bearers follow suit.

"Henry, if you cannot master a simple fire today, how will you fare tomorrow in the face of the Portal itself?" Sarmad barely whispers the words, but they wither more than any yelled reprimand. "And not even I can predict how the walls of the Chamber, connected to all the precious stones in the earth's crust, will affect our Stones."

"Sorry, Leader," Henry whimpers.

"Leader?" Zeb-un-Nissa turns and adjusts the dupatta to hide the frown spreading on her face.

"Didn't you know?" The Purple Bearer fidgets with the many rings on her elegant, long fingers. "That's how we are to refer to the ruby Bearer now."

Zeb-un-Nissa turns to face Sarmad. "That is enough."

"Henry must succeed once before we can depart." Any other boy giving orders while disguised as a servant girl would appear comical. But Sarmad's sincerity and passion transcend his attire. "I have seen it in my True Dreams."

Zeb-un-Nissa bites her tongue. She and Sarmad rarely disagree in front of the others. Better to project a united front. This time.

She gives the slightest of nods, and they begin, again, in silence. The Bearers return their Stones to the fire's edge. Sarmad's ruby connects to her sapphire, her sapphire to Belawadi's topaz, the topaz to Henry's emerald, the emerald to Imtiaz's amethyst. The circle completes when the amethyst connects back to Sarmad's ruby, then rotates in rainbow arcs until it forms a sphere. Much to everyone's surprise, Henry is first to connect to the flame.

"Success. That is enough for today, *Leader*." Zeb-un-Nissa walks the fine line of using Sarmad's self-appointed title and mocking it. "Belawadi, Henry, Imtiaz, the best thing we can do now is rest."

"We will return to practice," Sarmad intones, "at noon, one last time."

"But I must perform for the emissary of the exiled king and Vakhtang, Lord of Mukhrani." The Purple Bearer slips her oval Stone into a fold of her flowing skirt. "Don't you remember?"

"Of course he remembers, Imtiaz." Zeb-un-Nissa smiles. "He meant to say sunset."

"Sunset," Sarmad repeats. "Of course."

"If we are quiet, may we sneak out of the zenana?" Belawadi holds her teardrop topaz to the light.

"Too dangerous." Zeb-un-Nissa shakes her head.

"Henry, will you transport us back?" Imtiaz bats her moons of eyes.

"The last time I Traveled with another, I was bedridden for half a day," Henry whines.

"But Color Walking exhausts me," Imtiaz snaps as if she had not been flirting with him just a moment ago.

"It is good practice, since we must Color Walk to the Chamber tomorrow," Zeb-un-Nissa mediates. "And we will want Henry at full strength."

Imtiaz mutters something under her breath about royalty and princesses and orders. Zeb-un-Nissa pretends not to hear as she unlatches the inlaid ivory chest that contains their dyed muslin curtains.

The other three Bearers hang their fabrics on the wall opposite the fireplace.

"Asalamualaikum." Zeb-un-Nissa places her hand to her heart.

"Cheers." Henry waves goodbye.

"Allah Hafiz." Imtiaz puts her hands to her face and bows.

"Namaste." Belawadi bows her head.

A moment later, they Color Walk through the curtains and are gone.

"'Leader'?" Zeb-un-Nissa puts her hands on her hips.

"It inspires them." Sarmad has a faraway look in his eyes. "See how Henry overcame his timidity?"

The apricot sun peeks above the horizon. It will be morning soon.

"How will the power of the Portal compare with this fire?" She squelches the flames with a bucket of water. "Are you sure this is the path?"

"Do not lose faith in me now, Princess."

Zeb-un-Nissa flinches when he refers to her by her title. Perhaps he is right. Perhaps the world would be better without all this formality. "We could wait. We could research. And then when the Ikeda returns in thirty-seven years . . ."

"We have no idea what will transpire between now and then." He slowly hangs up his damask muslin curtain. "We have no guarantee that we will even be alive. What if the next Bearers are not blessed with our benevolence? What if they use the Stones' Blessings for their own selfish gain?"

"If we must act now, how do we know this is the righteous path? What will be the Price when . . ." She trails off, and again he says nothing. "You struggle to remember, Sarmad."

"I struggle with nothing."

"Just yesterday, you spoke to Belawadi as if you had never met her. And the day before, I received a report that you were found naked, outside the mahal, with no memory of who you were. The bribes to ensure the guards' discretion could have supported the widows and orphans of our city for a season." She speaks without judgment, as if detailing a celestial object's journey through the skies. "You confuse noon with sunset. Your True Dreams, they come with a Price. As do all things."

"And what is your Price?"

"I am not eager to discover my Blessing. Nor convinced that it is the right name for it." Zeb-un-Nissa wraps her dupatta tighter around her. It will be a cold day.

"In Ancient Greek, the same word is used for 'blessing' and 'curse.' As in Hebrew."

"Let it not be said that the Jews do not appreciate irony." Zeb-un-Nissa smiles. "But are not the Armenians known for their negotiating skills? Who would enter a contract without first knowing its terms? I can sense the limitations of our jewels. They are not meant to be used like this."

"We must do something to save the earth from its impending doom!" Sarmad insists. "We are obligated."

"Is that not takabbur?"

"You accuse me, a peasant, of hubris?" Sarmad raises his voice, then remembers himself. "A vow, then." He holds up his hand. "Should we believe, when we are in the Chamber tomorrow, that we've embarked on a dangerous course, we shall use our Sphere to seal the Portal instead."

"A vow." She puts her hand up to his, close, but not so close that they are touching. "Swear it."

Sarmad kneels. "By the God of Judaism, Christianity, and Islam." He repeats the vow three times. "Just as bridegroom and bride do, in the Armenian wedding ceremony."

"Truly? It is an Islamic tradition as well." She smooths his damask curtain. "Now go. Who knows when the mahaldar will awaken. And we have much to do before tomorrow."

"I worry about Rupert's lingering attachment to the children, a helpful reminder for future Passes of why the Provost should and must maintain a healthy distance."

Broughton Shaw
Chancellor, Pass Eleven

CHAPTER 6

REED AND THE PLAN

"So I know there are, like," Reed addressed the rest of the Bearers in the cavern as the Phantasmagoria disappeared, "a whole lotta variables and unknowns—"

"—that's the same thing," Jo slipped in.

Reed repressed the urge to shoot them some serious side-eye. "—but now we have a seed of a plan. Or, I guess I should say, the seed of a fragment of an idea that might blossom into our plan with everyone's help, which this idea so clearly needs."

He waited as patiently as he could while the other Bearers erupted in a chorus of protests that echoed around the cave behind the waterfall.

"I still don't understand . . ." Noa raised her hand.

"Have you even considered . . . ," Jo started.

"What did you mean when you said . . ." Arno consulted his yellow notepad.

"Claro, of course there are many questions." Xochitl waited for the cacophony to die down before she sauntered over to Reed and stood next to the rock he was using as a stool. "But does anyone have a different idea?" The sound of the waterfall outside filled the cavern. "We do not have much time, and we only have one plan. So why not see if we can make it work, together, as a team?"

If Reed had said those exact words, and even used Xochi's surprisingly diplomatic tone, they would not have had the same effect. But because it wasn't him, because it was someone else, the gesture had significantly more weight.

He watched in something akin to awe as she led the process by which the Bearers examined, criticized, and ultimately grew the germ of a plan into The Plan.

"Arno, have you been taking notes?" Xochitl asked.

Arno nodded yes.

"One at a time, then," Xochi instructed.

"All right." Arno flipped through the pages of his yellow notebook. "I think this is the easiest way to organize them . . ."

They spent the next hour analyzing every crevice, nook, and undiscovered corner of the idea. Noa asked the same question three times. For reasons inscrutable to Reed, she finally accepted his third response, even though he could've sworn it was identical to the first two.

Jo had one of their episodes and needed ten crucial minutes of the discussion to be repeated for them. Rather than do that himself, Reed asked Arno to reiterate the missed points, using his furiously scribbled notes. This not only saved Reed the chore of doing it, but it also let him listen, which, in turn, allowed him to see two potential holes that had previously avoided scrutiny. It also let him admire Arno, who bore as little resemblance to the sophomore who mumbled his final humanities presentation as 2006 Taylor Swift did to present-day Taylor.

Arno spent most of his time asking questions of clarification. At first, Reed interpreted these questions as criticisms. But when he actually listened, he could hear that Arno was simply asking for a level of detail that Reed assumed was unnecessary. Going deeper, slowing down, making sure everything was accounted for, simply strengthened The Plan.

It certainly took more time than it would've taken Reed to iron out all the variables (and unknowns, which were similar but not identical things) by himself. Noa insisted on taking five-minute breaks every fifty-five minutes, and by the third break, Reed wondered if they were ever going to come to a conclusion, or if they would still be in this never-ending meeting when the Portal opened tomorrow.

Xochitl paced while she moderated the session. For reasons Reed couldn't entirely articulate, her methodical walking around the perimeter of the cave unnerved the hell out of him. But he didn't say anything. It was his problem, not hers.

At times, Reed wanted to scream: *Why can't you just say, "Yes! Let's do it!" It's not like any of you have a different idea, so why not give this one a fucking whirl?* What catastrophic, prehistoric event made our species so suspicious, so reluctant, so scared to try something new? Especially something someone else had come up with? It was like every initiative Reed had ever proposed, on the GSA, to the Student Council, even to his band, Ragna Rock. Always greeted with hostility first. But this time, instead of barreling forward, he took his time.

God, it was hard. Especially because now, time was their most precious resource.

I swore never to Orchestrate someone else, but maybe I could use my Potentia on myself? What would it be like if I had the power to force myself to chill?

He breathed, deeply. And again. And again. He didn't just need to give the other Bearers the time and space they needed to make the plan their own. He needed them to grow it, from the melody he offered, into a song, with structure, chords, and tempo. As he witnessed Arno's considerations, Noa's exclamations, Xochitl's examinations, and Jo's investigations, he got it.

It wasn't about handing them a perfected finished plan, fully formed, like Moses presenting the stone tablets of the Ten Commandments. That might have been the idea of leadership that Reed had inherited. But it wasn't how actual consensus was formed. Collaboration was about believing, genuinely, that whatever they came up with together was better than anything he could come up with on his own. That the multitude of perspectives could achieve a greatness that surpassed any individual vision. He had to live in the precarious space of both having answers to the questions being lobbed at him, but also being genuinely interested in the other Bearers' solutions to those questions. He needed to have ideas, but be open. He had to allow for the possibility of being surprised.

The process might take more time. It might be less efficient. It might require repetition and compromise. And more repetition. And, believe it or not, even more repetition. But without faith that the end result would ultimately be superior, what was the point of being part of a team?

"With a Little Help from My Friends."

With all due respect to that British quartet, the Joe Cocker version, thank you very much, that turned a 2:45 track into a 5:12 masterpiece, changing the signature from 4/4 to 6/8 and adding backing vocals to make a simple ditty into a gritty, soulful masterpiece.

Each Bearer contributed in their own way. Jo's knowledge of the Chamber and the Portal, Noa's familiarity with the Feats, Arno's expertise with his Stone, and Xochi's strategical prowess unfolded corners of The Plan that Reed would've never been able to consider, let alone solve. As the Bearers' contributions were incorporated into The Plan, Reed realized it wasn't just the product that benefited. The collaborative process allowed each of them to fulfill their unique needs so that when the final Plan emerged, they were all invested in it. They had buy-in. Ownership. That had an empirical worth more valuable than all their Stones put together. Especially for a Plan with this many variables. And unknowns.

"Reed," Arno asked gently, "have you thought about Rose?"

“Of course.” Reed winced. Would he have much preferred a plan that didn’t potentially endanger the technology responsible for his sister’s life? Duh. But no plan was perfect. Besides, if they could come up with this in a few hours, they could figure something out for the future. “We’ll have thirty-seven years to figure that out, give or take. Along with everything else.”

“Okay.” Arno nodded.

Reed kept waiting for someone to bring it to a vote, or at least initiate the final consensus discussion. But at a certain indefinable moment, it became clear: this was what they were going to do tomorrow, when the Pentacle Portal opened and the fate of the world lay in their young adult hands.

They practiced the Sphere of Containment on a campfire, just as the Pass One Bearers had. When they felt somewhat sorta confident about their rate of success, they returned to the basement of their Airbnb to practice the Feat of Teleportare.

“What would you say about our odds?” Jo asked.

“I hate this game.” Xochitl stomped, and Blue flew into the lapis patch in front of her.

“But if you had to?” Noa placed both hands over her head, elbows at angles.

“Fifty-fifty.” Why did Reed have to discover his mentor was evil before he learned this Feat? Why did it work for Noa and not for him?

“I was going to go with sixty-forty.” Arno was as close to Reed as he could be without being in physical contact.

“And if we really worked together?” Noa pushed. Green expanded on the painted wall into a gateway. She stepped through and appeared on the other side of the room.

“Forty-sixty,” Reed quipped.

“That’s not funny.” The corners of Xochitl’s mouth stifled a smile as her Stone expanded into a square gateway.

“I wish we had weeks to practice. Months, even.” Reed’s shoulder blades ached from all the time he’d spent in the Feat, staring at the red patch in front of him, willing his Stone to transform into a fourth dimension-defying gateway. So far, it wasn’t cooperating.

“It’s just like rehearsal.” Noa called Green back to her. “Regardless of how much time you have, it’s always less than you want.”

After two hours of Noa’s help, and some rather impressive cursing, Reed was finally able to Teleportare with some meager consistency. “Let’s keep our fingers crossed for tomorrow morning." He swayed as his feet hit the carpet on the other side of the basement, barely catching Red.

Noa ordered in Thai. Arno insisted they set the dinner table with utensils and napkins, and eat the meal in as civilized a manner as possible.

"Am I the only one feeling Last Supper vibes right now?" Noa asked.

"You want to take the Judas pose, Noa?" Arno offered her a cup of tom yum soup.

"Sick burn." Jo laughed.

"Fair 'nuff." Noa accepted the plastic to-go container.

"Should we keep watch tonight?" Xochi barely touched her gluten-free Pad Thai. "In case Señor Shaw and Father try something?"

"Yes! This is the last chance they'll have." Jo blew on their steaming tom yum. "Once we're in the Pentagon Chamber, we're in the clear."

"What if they figure out another way to enter?" Noa asked.

"It's buried thousands of miles deep in the earth's surface." A bout of laughter seized Jo. "Under the Chicxulub crater in the Yucatán Peninsula, formed by the asteroid that killed all the dinosaurs."

"How do you know that?" Reed asked.

"I don't know how." Jo giggled again. "I just do."

"Noa"—Xochi poured hot sauce on her mango salad—"can you . . . spy on their dreams?"

"I can"—Noa fidgeted for a moment—"but I'm not going to."

"Why not?" Arno asked.

"I know it doesn't mean much, but that's what I decided after . . . after what I did to you, Reed." Noa reached out and squeezed his hand. "I'm only going to use my powers with absolute consent to help people."

"I hear that." Reed stole a shrimp from Noa's soup.

"Why don't we just Teleportare there now and wait?" Arno asked. "We can take pillows and sleeping bags."

"The Stones get jumpy in the Chamber. Something about the walls and how they're connected to all the precious stones in the earth's crust. You'll feel it when we're there tomorrow." Jo giggled staccato. "Not safe for us to be there any longer than we have to."

"Have any of you given any thought to what you'll do?" Noa asked the group. "If we make it?"

"There's so much of this new world to explore." Jo was deadly serious now. "Especially once the Ikeda has moved on, our powers are gone, and I can use all things electrical."

"I would give anything to play another gig with Ragna Rock." Reed's hands fiddled with a phantom guitar. "Just to shred on my Maple Electric again, to get to that amazing place where you're playing but also taking in what everyone else is doing around you."

"I'm not going home." Arno picked at his fried rice.

"Ever?" Reed asked.

"Ever. Doesn't matter what happens tomorrow. I'm going to be on my own from now on." Arno spoke with a simple clarity. "I see that now—see everything that I can do by myself."

"You're sixteen, Arno," Noa scoffed. "You can't live on your own."

"Watch me." He put his rice dish down.

"This may sound trivial, but I just want my normal life. To party with M. and Lucía. Fence." Xochitl traced the sapphire slivers on her neck. "Just to live."

"What about you, Noa?"

"Tech for *Hamlet* starts on Monday." She wrung her hands. "You think we'll be back on time, or should I tell my director to put the understudy on standby?"

"Having spent my life studying the Stones, the Bearers, and the Feats, I am still surprised by how much I have learned in the last few days. A helpful reminder that there is no substitute for doing something, actually experiencing it, firsthand. The lived experience is king."

Rupert Shaw
Provost, Pass Eleven

CHAPTER 7
ARNO LISTENS

Arno lingered when Reed offered to clean up for the group. Noa's very specific instructions about which of their garbage should be separated into recyclable, compostable, and unrecyclable waste made it at least a two-person job. But the environment wasn't his only motivation.

"I got those." Arno dumped the uneaten food into the compost.

"You don't have to—" Reed said.

"—I know," Arno overlapped.

Why was it that sometimes, when they were alone, they could talk with the ease of best friends, but other times, like now, every word was a trial?

They separated, tossed, organized, and salvaged for a few minutes of silence that hummed between comfortable and awkward.

"Is everything okay, Reed?" Arno finally asked.

"I want to tell you . . ."

"Yes?" Arno's hand trembled as he snapped the cap on the soy sauce bottle.

"If we get through this . . ." Reed tossed the greasy brown paper bag of used condiments into the garbage.

"When we get through it."

"*If/when* we get through it"—Reed smiled crookedly, compromising—"I'll tell you all about what the last few weeks have been like for me. How fucked it is when your psyche's been assaulted and you don't trust your own thoughts and feelings. How that makes you doubt everything that you believed."

"Everything?" Arno groaned as some nam jim sauce stained his shorts. He still had no idea what he was going to wear tomorrow. What do you wear to save the world?

"Almost everything." Reed continued scraping food off plates. "But you stuck with me, Arno, through all of it. I would've lost my way without you."

The urge to redirect was great. So very great. Arno's favorite tactic. He imagined his double from the crystal world, smiling at him, giving him strength. "I'm only here for you."

"I think that was true at first." Reed wrung out a wet towel and looped it through the oven handle. "But now?"

The question surprised Arno. "You're right, Reed." He contemplated for a few moments before responding. "I understand, now, what a gift we've been given."

"And burden."

"We have the chance to do something really important. So thanks. For believing that I could do this, because—" Arno suddenly felt the need to tell Reed everything—about how important he was to him, about how this might be their last day together, and night, and how he couldn't let that time pass without making up for all the time they'd lost together, all the time they were supposed to have been together, all the time he hadn't been courageous enough to be honest about his feelings.

"Because?"

All the feelings bubbled up inside Arno, a pot of simmering sauce suddenly turned up to rapid boil, threatening to spill over and make a mess everywhere. He was going to do it. He was going to tell Reed everything.

"Because I want to tell you . . ."

Do it!

"Tell you that . . ."

Grab me!

But what if Reed pulled away, rejected him,

Take me in your arms!

the way he'd been rejected before, and left alone,

Kiss me!

as he would probably be for the rest of his life?

"Yes?" Reed asked.

But he couldn't.

Arno's insides collapsed and sank, like the *Titanic*, snapped in half, dragged down to the bottom of the ocean floor under its own machinery, taking its crew and passengers with it.

"I need to tell you that what we're doing is the most important thing we'll ever do"—he stumbled over the last word—"together."

Contradict me!

"That's what I was going to say, too." Reed nodded, visibly relieved.

Arno couldn't form words, so he just nodded back. He knew he looked stupid, but he didn't want to say something that wasn't true.

He had disappointed himself. He would always be a coward. Scared to talk in front of the class without bumbling like a fool. Scared to tell the boy he liked how he felt. Scared to have true faith.

Besides, that wasn't important now.

It was a relief of sorts, actually. At least now he could focus on the Portal. And wasn't that the important thing?

"I'll leave a light on for you." Arno left Reed and climbed the stairs alone.

Arno stood at the doorway of the bedroom a few minutes before 2 AM, supposedly listening for any signs of Father or Mr. Shaw. But really, he only had ears for Reed.

Jo had taken the first shift. Arno's was about to come to an end. Noa had volunteered to take the next one, the worst one, in the middle of the night. Arno was impressed: her Jewish guilt rivaled his Armenian.

He didn't know he wouldn't be going home, should they survive the Pentacle Portal, until he heard himself says those words. But their truth was unassailable. What had surprised him most about becoming the Yellow Bearer was how easily he had adjusted to it. It wasn't the power, or the mission, or even the group that had changed him. It was having purpose. Now that he'd tasted that holy wine, he thirsted for more.

He didn't need a Stone. He didn't need powers. He didn't even need a team. He could do good all by himself.

Noa's alarm beeped three times, loud, from her room down the hall, before launching into "Defying Gravity." The song cut out abruptly when Noa turned off her alarm. His shift was over.

Arno got into bed, sliding under the sheets for the last time. Theoretically, he could go to sleep now.

Theoretically.

If not for . . .

When he was around Reed, Arno's heart still skipped beats, like the percussionist from Ragna Rock who got kicked out. Arno would never forgive himself for chickening out earlier that evening. The world deserved someone braver to save it. Between having to tell Reed how he felt and facing off with Mr. Shaw and Father, he would choose the latter any day.

Just thinking their names sent rage coursing through his rigid body. He willed his fists to unclench. They left sweaty trails on the bedsheets. The moonbeam slanting in from a half-raised blind bent toward him before he realized he was charging up. He'd been doing this more and more lately—subconsciously cataloging all natural light sources in case of a surprise attack. That background tension took its toll. Like having to be on the lookout whenever he and Reed held hands on their boardwalk strolls way back when. Would there ever be a place where he and Reed could do that without worrying? Would he and Reed ever do that again, period?

The only part of his old life that he missed—that he'd almost give it all back for—was that day he walked along the Asbury Park shore, holding Reed's hand, kissing and being kissed by him for the first time.

He kept the moonlight. Let Mr. Shaw and Father try something tonight. He'd show them what happened to anyone who dared to hurt his Reed. Which, of course, made him think of . . .

Noa. He still held her accountable. She could've told them the truth. She could've gone to the authorities. It might not have worked, it might've endangered her family, but she still could've done those things. Should've.

And yet, and yet, and yet. He, of all people, knew how hard it could be to stand up for yourself. Holding on to these feelings wasn't going to help the team. Or him. As much as he coated it in moral righteousness, when he was being really honest with himself, Arno knew the thing he couldn't forgive was that he didn't detect it. That he let Reed down. Arno prayed to find the compassion in his heart, to forgive Noa and himself.

The strained breaths escaping Reed changed into anguished gasps, as if a snake had wrapped itself around his neck. Arno knew it was nothing to be truly worried about—Mr. Shaw and Father couldn't have figured out some way to emulate Noa's power, could they? It was just a bad dream, he told himself, a nightmare, a nonsupernatural event that people everywhere endured nightly.

And yet. It physically hurt him to see Reed in pain. Reed's pain became Arno's, like there were no boundaries between them, like the lines blurred where Arno ended and Reed began. To see him squirming, tossing, turning. To hear him moaning. He knew he shouldn't risk going over there and gently waking him up, seeing if he needed a glass of water, or just to talk. He knew he shouldn't.

"Reed?" Arno found himself sitting on Reed's bed, gently caressing his face. "Are you okay?"

"Arno?" Reed rubbed the sleepiness out of his blue, blue eyes.

"I'm here." Arno didn't know that Reed had gone to bed shirtless.

"I was having the most intense dreams." Reed stared straight up at the ceiling.

"But not like Dreamaturgy-intense, right?"

"Thank God, no." Red sparkled bright, and Arno saw Reed was actually blushing. "Pass One. The night before their Ikeda approach."

"Just like us."

"Just like us." Reed faltered for a moment. "They were . . ."

Red continued to sparkle mischievously.

"Would it help to talk about it?" Arno asked.

A neighborhood dog barked at a real or imagined intruder.

"Can I just . . ." Reed trailed off. "Can I show you?"

Arno nodded.

A second dog responded to the first, setting off a canine chorus.

Reed sat up, resting his bare back against the headboard. The moonlight shadowed his face.

"It'll be easier if . . . ," Reed started. "Do you mind . . . ?"

Arno scooted closer. He closed his eyes and felt Reed's hands on his face: thumbs on his jaw, index fingers next to his nose, remaining fingers splayed across his temple. His eyes remained closed, but suddenly, he saw two curtains: one damask and one chartreuse, flapping on the wall opposite the fireplace in Zeb-un-Nissa's quarters.

Sarmad's servant-girl robes are haphazardly discarded around the chambers. He wears only his white smallclothes. Henry is fully dressed, in doublet and britches.

They kiss. Like, a lot.

Was it wrong to spy on this remembrance of things past? Is that why Arno was also blushing? Or was it just being this close to Reed while watching two guys . . .

"Is it wrong"—Henry pulls away—"for us to do this?"

"Why?" Sarmad asks unabashedly. "Because of what the Bible says?"

"That's not what I meant!" Henry giggles. "I meant, is it wrong what we're planning on the morrow in the Pentagon Chamber."

Sarmad shoves Henry away and stands up. "I knew it!"

Arno marveled at Sarmad's comfort with his seminudity. For Sarmad, it was not a transition state, to be glided through as quickly as possible. For Sarmad, it was a place to luxuriate and spend some time.

Reed's hands slipped off Arno's face. He blinked, suddenly back on the edge of Reed's bed. Were they closer than they had been before?

"So not a nightmare?" Arno squawked.

"Not quite."

Yellow hovered between them, glowing with the light of a single candle.

"Do you want . . ." Reed trailed off.

Arno nodded in what he hoped was not too obvious a way. When Reed hesitated, Arno placed Reed's hands back on his face.

"I knew you could not accomplish this!" Sarmad exclaims. "I told Zeb-un-Nissa!"

"I would do anything for you, Sarmad. Anything." Henry declares his devotion with a pilgrim's passion. "Just tell me it's the right thing to do."

"It's the right thing to do, Henry." Sarmad speaks slowly, giving each word emphasis. "As is this." He pulls Henry back in for a kiss.

"Don't," Arno squeaked when he felt Reed start to pull away. He put his hands on Reed's just before he felt Reed's lips on his own.

Arno's eyes popped open, but he did not pull back. He drew Reed closer to him, with days, weeks, months, years of desire.

The kiss was simple and strong and unapologetic, like a practical gift.

Sarmad undresses Henry slowly, as if performing a holy ritual. He slips Henry's doublet over his head, then unlaces his britches as Arno gently placed the tip of his finger on Red. Reed moaned as if it were his body that Arno was caressing.

"Is this all right?" Arno asked Reed.

"Is this all right?" Sarmad asks Henry.

Henry nods as Reed nodded, neither trusting themselves to make sound.

"I have desired you since we met," Arno and Henry tell Reed and Sarmad.

As soon as Arno has uttered the words, a crushing weight he did not know he was carrying disappeared. It's funny how some secrets weigh you down, while others release you to soar like an angel.

"You need not desire the thing you can have." Sarmad smiles.

Reed's fingers reached for Arno's as their Stones found each other. "With all these unknowns . . ."

"And variables." Arno smiled.

"You are the only constant, Arno." Reed squeezed his hand. "I feel safe with you."

A Teleportare doorway shimmers in the cobalt curtain as Zeb-un-Nissa enters her chambers. Sarmad and Henry pull away quickly, as if caught doing something they shouldn't. But she does not flinch.

"The zenana is especially active this evening. Anyone could enter my chambers, at any time, unannounced. But I can make you safe. Watch." Her eyes flash true blue, and a perfect cube envelops them in its chamfered magnificence.

"Your Blessing!" Sarmad places a hand against the protective casing. He pushes against it, but it does not budge. He thrusts at it with a dagger. The tip of the blade bends before snapping off. "Indestructible," he exclaims. "Just like you!"

Zeb-un-Nissa smiles, then wills their private chamber opaque, and sends it to the far side of her chambers. She draws the curtain for extra privacy before stepping outside.

The Post Cognition of Pass One fades away as Yellow and Red burn like the lanterns in Zeb-un-Nissa's chamber. Their light comingled, creating marigold burst after marigold burst, filling Arno and Reed's bedroom until it sparkled like the night sky.

"Intimacy between Bearers is discouraged at all costs."

Broughton Shaw
Chancellor, Pass Eleven

CHAPTER 8

ARNO AND REED, TOGETHER, FINALLY

Would it be different if they were not Bearers?

Or if Reed had unlocked a different Potentia?

Or is this what the first time is always like? Arno wondered.

When love and sex synergize, like two precious Stones.

"Bloom" by Troye Sivan.

Just for you.

"This is certainly not how I planned to be spending the day before the opening of the Pentacle Portal. But here it is. A successor has been chosen. Since neither Father nor I will be able to mentor her, we have had to tap an unlikely option to act as the next Chancellor. Unlikely, but inevitable. Isn't that always the case with siblings? I trust in the provisions we have made and the resources we have invested to ensure their success in thirty-seven years."

Rupert Shaw
Provost, Pass Eleven

CHAPTER 9

REED, THE MORNING AFTER

Reed heard the doorknob turn a moment too late. He jumped out of bed, roused Arno, and willed Red to his side, only then realizing he was still naked.

How did Mr. Shaw and Father get past Xochitl?

He'd sworn never to Orchestrate again, but now that Arno's well-being was at stake, he was willing to do anything . . .

But it was not Mr. Shaw or Father who dared disturb their peace.

"Wake up, sleepyheads!" Noa barged into the bedroom, with Xochitl and Jo close behind.

"Oh!" Noa stopped abruptly when she saw a naked Reed crouching between the beds and an equally naked Arno slowly awakening under the sheets. "Ow!" she exclaimed when Xochitl banged into her and they both went tumbling down.

"Watch out, world," Jo drawled, barely sidestepping the pileup. "The clumsy Bearers are here to save you!"

Reed yanked a sheet off the empty bed and wrapped it around himself. "We're going to need a few minutes."

"At least." Arno smiled lazily.

"Sure yes of course." Noa unwound herself from Xochitl.

"What's the big deal?" Xochitl asked her.

Jo and Noa each whispered in her ear.

"Their first time?!" Xochitl exclaimed.

"At least we're not going to have to watch them moon over each other anymore." Jo headed out of the room, gesturing for Xochitl and Noa to follow.

"But not our last." Arno grinned unabashedly and kissed Reed's bare shoulder.

"It's so cute how you think we're going to live after today." Reed stroked his hair.

"What makes you think I'm not talking about today?" Arno tugged Reed back into bed.

"We'll meet you downstairs, okay?" Reed laughed as he landed on top of Arno.

"Take your time." Noa blushed.

"And happy Pride!" Jo added as they left.

"Is it really?" Arno exclaimed.

"I'd forgotten!" Reed exclaimed. "Last Sunday in June!"

"Pride or no Pride, hurry up." Xochitl headed out.

"Xochi's right," Jo added from the hallway. "The Ikeda waits for no one."

"Time to save the world," Noa called over her shoulder, "bitches."

★

END OF BOOK VI

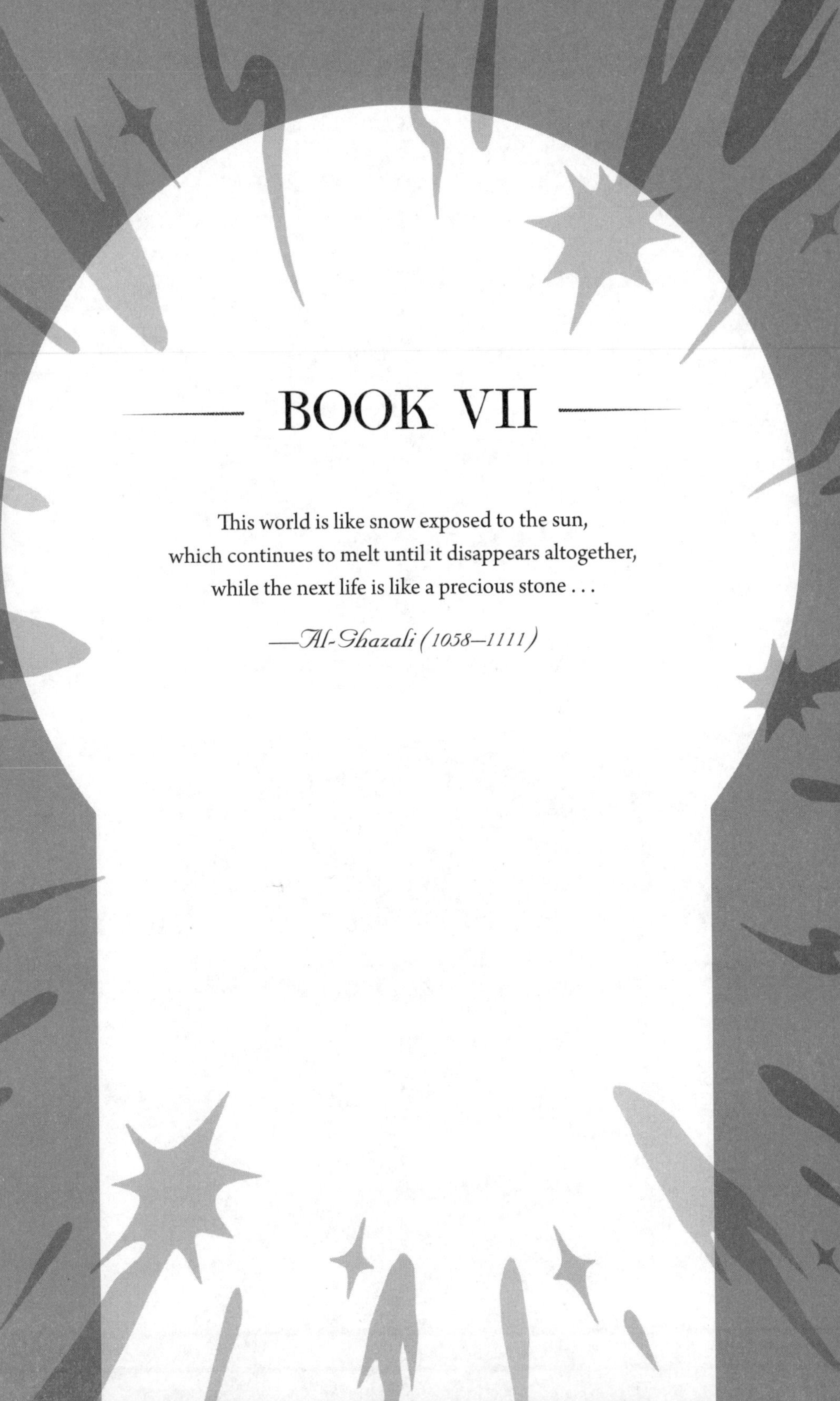

BOOK VII

This world is like snow exposed to the sun,
which continues to melt until it disappears altogether,
while the next life is like a precious stone . . .

—Al-Ghazali (1058–1111)

CHAPTER 1

REED AND THE BEARERS IN THE PENTAGON CHAMBER

The Feat of Teleportare was a slippery fish that flopped this way and that way and lots of other impossible, mind-bending, maddening ways all designed to elude Reed's grasp. Thank God he'd helped come up with The Plan. At least he wasn't totally useless. But seeing the ease with which the other Bearers turned their Stones into teleportation gateways that morning was all the proof he needed. He didn't realize how easily everything else had come to him until Reed found himself as the remedial student in the class of Pass Eleven Bearers. Was this how Marlon Jackson felt as he marveled at the vocal and dancing ability of his brothers Jackie, Tito, Jermaine, and, of course, Michael?

This might very well be the last day of Reed's life, and although he mourned everything he might never get to do—see another sunrise, celebrate a proper Pride in New York City, say goodbye to his mom or Rose, allow whatever he and Arno had finally discovered to grow—this was what he chose to fixate on. Accepting Noa's offer to stay behind to help him was one of the more humiliating moments in his life.

Enough self-indulgence, Reed. Don't make it about you.

He finally managed to wrestle that slippery fish down, and he was rewarded with a round ruby gateway. He stumbled into the Pentagon Chamber a disorienting moment later, fighting lightheadedness to stay standing.

He leaned back against the ruby wall to steady himself. Fainting would be an inauspicious way to begin this final leg of the adventure. Besides, Jo would never let him live it down. He was finally able to take in the splendor of the Pentagon Chamber.

Each of the five jeweled walls of the Chamber loomed so high it was impossible to see where, or even if, they reached a ceiling. He appreciated Jo's warning against arriving any earlier than absolutely necessary. Red vibrated like an amp throbbing with feedback, its energy coursing through Reed in unexpected loops and pulses. The entire Chamber purred with power.

Even though he'd seen the Pentagon Chamber in the Pass Ten Phantasmagoria, Reed was in no way prepared for the intensity of actually being there. Like the difference between listening to Lil Nas X on Spotify and then actually seeing him in concert. Of course, the spectacle of the concert added to the soul-exploding experience of the event. But it wasn't just the costumes and pyrotechnics. It was being in the actual space with other people, breathing the same air, and sharing the music with them in actual time. It was live. It was real. No recording could capture or compete with that. That music had a soul of its own. Just like the Chamber.

He placed a hand on the ruby wall. It was smooth and cool and whispered things that he did not understand. He removed his hand. Enough mysteries for one day.

Xochitl warmed up in front of the sapphire wall, to his left. Continuing her tradition of saving the world while looking fabulous, she found a way to marry Ale's fashionista taste with Xochitl's rustic attire. She still wore those leather sandals but had traded the loincloth and tunic for an A-line sleeveless princess dress embroidered with geometric patterns that were almost as mysterious as how she'd been able to procure that outfit.

Reed wanted to survive today for many reasons. Proving himself to Xochitl was high on that list.

Arno was next, sitting cross-legged with his back to the Chamber, both hands pressed against the topaz wall. T-shirt too large, jeans rolled up, the red/blue/yellow scarf knotted around his neck. Reed decided against reaching out to him through the link that had fused them since last night. Always feeling Arno's soothing presence was all he needed.

Noa had stayed to help Reed—she should be appearing any moment now in front of the emerald wall. Finally, to Reed's right, Jo lay on the ground in front of the amethyst wall of the Chamber, asleep, unconscious, or resting.

The air tasted metallic, like a furnace was overheating.

Reed was still climbing his way out of the vertigo when Arno reached out to him through their new bond. Warmth sliced through the haze of dizziness, spreading through his body, through all his extremities, and his face flushed with the memory of last night. And this morning.

Reed had been as gentle as he could with Arno last night. Doing his best to give Arno the first time Reed wished he'd had was its own reward. He couldn't predict that being with Arno would also stitch together something inside him that had been ripped apart. Didn't know that it could be like that. Didn't know how being with someone you loved could heal.

Their oneness remained, as if they were extensions of each other now, countries that could decide at any moment that the border separating them meant nothing and simply unite. Their eyes found each other for a stolen moment of intimacy. *I'd give the world for another night with you.* Reed wasn't sure if he'd transmitted that thought or received it. Nor did it matter.

A moment later, a rectangular doorway grew in the emerald wall, and Noa twirled through, velvet cloak swirling behind her. "'O brave new world/That hath such people in it!'" Her rich voice echoed up the Chamber.

"'Has,' not 'hath.'" Jo slowly got up from the floor. "Do you have to make everything more pretentious than it already is?" They were an Annie Lennox vision today: white button-down, black blazer, crocus tie slimly knotted, capped with a periwinkle pixie cut.

"No glasses today, Noa?" Xochitl asked.

"Contacts on show days." Noa performed a small flourish.

Reed slipped on his burgundy sequined jacket. It was jankier now than it had been when Versa handed it to him in Paradise. But it still sparkled.

"Bejeweled" by Taylor Swift. Chorus: C–Dm^7–Am–Gsus^4. Like many of her songs, complex in its simplicity. Reed didn't know if he still polished up real nice, but it didn't matter.

His sneakered foot slid against the surprisingly smooth floor of the Chamber, which subtly angled down to the center of the room, where the Portal would appear.

"Still no Father, right?" Noa asked anxiously.

"The Portal will be obstacle enough," Jo intoned ominously.

"Then places, everyone!" Noa called out.

"Thank you places," Reed responded as earnestly as he could. "Or is it, 'Thank you, places'?"

"O Reed," Noa British-accented, "you can be so droll."

The sound of howling wind echoed throughout the Chamber.

"Do you feel it?" Jo looked up, as if they could see into the ether above. "The Ikeda is near."

"Just as we practiced, Bearers," Xochitl barked over the howling.

The Five Bearers of Pass Eleven stood in front of their respective walls. Reed pulled back into his practiced Spider-Man crouch. Red floated to his heart.

Xochitl drew herself into an en garde stance. Blue flew out of her dress, like a dart landing in an invisible opponent. No acceleration. No deceleration. Just motion. It settled in front of her core.

Yellow spiraled around Arno, ascending an invisible circular staircase, arriving in front of his forehead, a dazzling third eye.

Noa opened her hands and released Green from her palms like a bird. It hovered at her throat.

"Anyone else feeling déjà vu?" Jo unbuttoned their jacket as Purple leaped out in a cavalcade of carnations. It settled above their head, the centerpiece of a floral crown.

The Pass Eleven Bearers stood at attention.

"Do we know how much time we have?" Xochitl asked.

"You have some place to be?" Reed asked. "Because—"

It started so small Reed would've missed it if Jo hadn't gestured for him to shut up. A midnight black that grew into a star at eye level in the very center of the Chamber. It warped time, space, and light around it. Lightning sparked out of its five arms.

A ripple behind Reed flickered at his concentration. The look on Arno's face told him to turn around.

A circular Teleportare gateway appeared in the ruby wall. It rippled once, twice, and then finally a third time before another Reed fell through. Almost simultaneously, a second, distressed Jo emerged from an oval gateway in the amethyst wall.

"The fuck?" Both Reeds swore.

CHAPTER 2

ARNO

Is it really too much to ask for, Arno wondered, *for one day without surprises?* Once all five of them arrived in the Pentagon Chamber, he had thought they'd be in the clear. Foolish, foolish him.

Another Jo? Another Reed? What other unforeseeable events would they need to overcome?

Arno abandoned his position in front of the topaz wall when Jo—their Jo, not this new Jo—fell to the ground and curled themself into the fetal position. He scampered around the perimeter of the Chamber, along the emerald wall, to avoid the spinning star.

"Jo? You okay?" They shooed his hands away before he could touch them.

"Two too much," they moaned, rocking back and forth. "Two too two too much."

Apparently, the sight of another version of themself was more than they could handle. And really, who could blame them? Seeing a second Reed unsettled Arno—he could only imagine what the experience must be like in first person.

Reed was faring better than Jo, Arno sensed through their bond, the special one that had formed last night. After.

Last night. This morning. *Please, God,* Arno prayed. *Let us survive so that we can do more of that.*

But now.

Focus.

Arno couldn't do anything to help Jo. He joined the other three Bearers, plus the two new visitors, huddled in a circle in front of the ruby wall.

"Let me get this right." His Reed arched a skeptical eyebrow at new Reed, who was dressed identically, minus the burgundy sequined jacket. "You're from thirty minutes in the future. You tried The Plan, it failed, and you managed to Teleportare *through time* to come back and warn us to seal the Portal instead?" He shook his head. "This sounds very *Avengers: Endgame*."

"Just don't get me started on the holes in their time-travel logic." Future Reed looked identical to their Reed, down to his adorable cowlick. "Or multiverse, for that matter."

"He does sound like you," Xochitl conceded.

"What happened to the rest of us?" Noa asked Future Jo.

"We don't think . . ." Future Jo choked up. "We don't think that Arno or Noa made it."

"Xochitl managed to Teleportare," Future Reed added, "so hopefully she'll emerge at any moment."

"Or not," Xochitl responded characteristically unsentimental.

"You're going to understand if we need to talk this out, right?" Reed looked at Future Reed and Future Jo pointedly. "Without you."

"How much time," Future Jo eyed the growing star, "do you think we have?"

XOCHITL

I did not like this in the least. "I do not like this in the least. Teleportare through time? It smells of horseshit." I spared a glance at the two allegedly Future Bearers, who had gone to the amethyst wall to tend to Present Jo. What I would give for a problem I could slash through.

"Xochi, you spent four years traveling through the Aztec underworld," Noa reminded me. "Jumping back in time a half hour requires much less suspension of my disbelief."

"Did you read Future You and Jo?" I asked Reed.

He nodded.

"And?"

"It's hard to get a clear take. I think there's something Future Reed isn't telling us?" Reed squinted. "Maybe he's using his Potentia to hide it from me? But it could just be Red's confusion at trying to read itself—myself?" Sweat beaded

Reed's upper lip. "And I'm sure you're all feeling how the Chamber is amplifying and distorting our powers. So, basically, I have nothing useful to report."

"Their Stones must be authentic, right?" Arno asked. "Otherwise, they wouldn't have been able to Teleportare in here."

"Can you Petrakinesis his Red, Reed?" If this new Reed was capable of Orchestrations, like ours, how could we guarantee that we had not already been compromised?

"Oh, that's a good idea," Arno agreed.

Reed scrunched his eyes, but Future Reed's Stone didn't budge. "Nothing. It feels like a genuine precious Stone. Not identical to Red, but certainly of the same ilk."

"The same *ilk*?" Noa muttered. "And they call me the pretentious one."

"What can you ask him that only you would know?" Arno eyed the ever-growing star.

ARNO

"Rose's favorite color is pink. Her birthday is November 30. Mom is planning to buy herself a convertible Tesla for her fiftieth birthday and giving me—us—her Audi." Future Reed smoothed his hand over his stubborn cowlick. "I'm sorry we don't have a sister who died ice-skating or some equally rando detail, but do we pass? Can we try saving the world now?"

The spinning star in the middle of the Chamber had grown to the size of one of the incense holders used in the Orthodox Armenian services. A few more minutes, Arno guessed, before the Pentacle Portal reached full size and opened. Every time he gazed into it, time lost meaning. The black of this star was darker, richer, more beautiful than any color he had ever seen. It was not from this planet, maybe even not from this plane. The more it grew, the faster it spun, the more its two dimensions felt like three. Arno forced his attention back to the Future Bearers.

"I believe them," Present Reed exclaimed.

Arno checked in with Xochi and Noa. All three nodded their agreement.

"Tell us everything, as quickly as possible," Xochitl instructed. "What happened? What went wrong? What can we do differently?"

Future Reed and Future Jo described the failure of The Plan. Within a few days, they guessed, their power grid would crumble and their world would be doomed for another Dark Age. The End.

"We don't know exactly how much damage we caused, but we're pretty sure it's just a matter of time before civilization collapses and"—Future Reed faltered under the weight of his guilt—"you know, worst-case apocalypse scenario."

"But there is some good news!" Future Jo exclaimed. "We believe the two of us can seal the Portal. Which means . . ."

"We're off the hook?" Present Reed asked. "Really?"

"A sacrifice must be made," Future Reed responded. "And it's not like the two of us have any place in this timeline anyway. Who knows what temporal paradoxes we're risking by being here. It is the only way."

XOCHITL

Part of me was relieved. I was not confident that The Plan was going to work. Maybe closing the Portal was the best thing to do. Even if it's what Señor Shaw and Father wanted. Just because they were evil didn't mean closing the Portal was wrong.

The other part of me mourned, mourned that we would not have the opportunity to see if we could actually execute The Plan. But taking the risk after being forewarned by messengers from the future would be just foolhardy.

"Let's do it." I mustered enthusiasm. Life did not have to be like the movies.

The star was almost as large as one of the Teleportare gateways we had conjured to enter the Chamber. Shortly, it would reach its full size. Then it would open and become the Pentacle Portal.

ARNO

I get to live! Was it wrong to take a moment to celebrate that? *Reed and I can be together!*

"We'll create the Sphere with Arno, Xochi, and Jo," Future Reed said. "Reed and Jo from this timeline can stay on the lookout in case Father and Mr. Shaw try to crash this party. The moment the Sphere is complete, all five of you Teleportare yourselves out of here. We'll take it from there."

We nodded.

"It's showtime!" Noa barked.

The Reeds almost bumped into each other as they stepped into position.

"You sure there's nothing else for me to do?" Present Reed asked his counterpart.

"I know what you're thinking." Future Reed smiled wearily. "But don't offer yourself. This is your time, not mine."

Present Reed nodded with obvious relief.

Arno lingered between them. He squeezed Present Reed's hand and kissed him on the lips. "See you on the other side, okay?"

"You can count on it."

Arno turned and found himself face-to-face with Future Reed. Should he kiss him, too? Or would that be adultery? Or is it not cheating if you do it with a future version of the same person? Too much to consider now.

He settled on leaning in to kiss Future Reed on the cheek.

Future Reed jerked back violently.

A younger Arno would have crumbled. Every interaction with Reed had been calculated before and analyzed after. Each glance. Every word. Every moment of contact. They had meant the world to Arno. They had been his world.

But Arno, too, had changed.

"Change of plan, everybody," Arno announced with absolute conviction as the light in the Chamber rushed into him. "That's not Reed."

CHAPTER 3

ARNO

Realizing his Potentia had never been more necessary for Arno, or tasted more delicious. He welcomed the light of the Chamber into him. He didn't know what was going on—Glamour, impersonator, multiverse evil version—but it didn't matter. He was going to show whoever they really were what happened when someone messed with his Reed.

Flush with the hypercharged light of the Portal, Arno could now see the shimmering seams of overlapping swirls of light surrounding the Reed impostor, like . . .

Arno unwove the Glamour, just as he had unwoven Jo's Camouflage on the beach in Asbury Park. The Ikeda's proximity made his power jumpy, like an Armenian in a Turkish market.

The stitches of the Glamour pulled apart,

Unraveling

Unknitting

Revealing . . .

A glittering onyx, tapering to points on either end in a perfect mandorla, sat where Mr. Shaw's right eye had been.

With a speed that surprised everybody, Present Jo rolled onto the balls of their feet. "You know, part of me was hoping we'd just be able to do this thing without you crashing our party." Their Purple dispelled the Glamour covering Future Jo. "But another part was hoping you'd try something."

A shining, tapering diamond, identical in shape to Mr. Shaw's double-pointed onyx, had replaced Father's left eye.

XOCHITL

"I knew they smelled of horseshit." I hated being right. All. The. Time.

"The Cyclops Stratagem!" Noa wrung her hands nervously. "A little on the nose, if you ask me."

"Or on the eye?" Reed quipped.

"Enough." The diamond in Father's eye socket gleamed like the button on an Apple product.

"We come in peace." Señor Shaw held his hands open, palms up.

A laugh I did not know I had in me escaped from the cage of my chest. "Is that what you told Hikaru?"

"We don't have much time," silver-haired Father cut in crisply. "Although you've seen through our ruse, our offer still stands. We've fabricated two Stones powerful enough to seal the Portal. We are willing to sacrifice our lives. Which means that you can go free. Go home—or wherever you want, for that matter. Just turn your back and be done with it all. We absolve you."

I looked at the other Bearers while they regarded one another. Were they thinking what I was thinking?

It wasn't an unattractive offer.

ARNO

The light from the Chamber hummed inside him, intoxicating Arno with its power. He believed Father and Mr. Shaw were telling the truth. About the Stones and the Portal, at least. And yet, the truth could be just as slippery as a lie. *You may walk with the devil,* as the Armenian proverb went, *but you can never let go of his tail.*

"Your Stones will remain charged for another few weeks, or even months. Think of all you'll be able to do!" Father's posh accent made his words sound maddeningly reasonable. "Noa, Dreamaturg into every major head of state and get them to pass legislation banning fossil fuels. Jo—have you even tried to locate your parents? Regina is still alive. Think what joy you could bring her. We're offering you all a way out."

This is the power of Satan's temptations, Arno realized. Of course you tell yourself that you will resist him when he comes to you. But then he tempts you with the thing you want most. The thing you might not even realize you desire. And you must reckon with yourself.

Time.

Life.

Reed.

Was it wrong to be tempted? To let his imagination indulge in the fantasy of a life after today? A life with Reed?

Arno let it all play out in his head. They leave. Father and Mr. Shaw use their unholy Stones to seal the Portal, the way the Portal has been sealed for centuries. The Bearers survive. Reed and Arno get to be together. They live—well, "happily ever after" might be a bit naive—but that didn't stop Arno from believing they'd end up happy together forever. Maybe raise a family. They would use their lives to better the world. He didn't know quite how yet, but he was sure they'd figure it out. And the world would go on.

And on. And on.

It was so very tempting.

"The Portal is about to open." Reed eyed the rotating, decelerating star in the middle of the room. "We don't have much time."

How many kids would he and Reed have? What would be their names? Would they be boys, girls, gender-fluid? Arno couldn't control his dream, and it sprouted forward with unexpected details and nuance.

But what world would their children inherit? Most probably, sometime during their kids' lifetime, one of the top ten most likely ways for the world to end would come to fruition. Maybe not necessarily a total extinction-level event. Maybe just 90 percent of the population. Or, just as likely, the world would slowly twist its way into an even more dystopic version of itself. Gradually, imperceptibly, turning into a living hell.

Climate change.

Water shortage and food insecurity.

Economic and racial disparities.

Forced refugee displacement.

The Four New Equestrians of the Apocalypse.

“I agree with Reed.” Father spoke with the conviction of someone who’d never suffered from impostor syndrome. Probably didn’t even understand what it was. “We do not have much time.”

The Bearers regarded one another.

All the while, Arno would live with the knowledge that he could’ve stopped it. That for the briefest of windows, he had the chance to perform something miracle-level. And that he didn’t. That he abdicated his responsibility because it was the easier thing to do.

He would have to live with that.

The easier thing was so very tempting. That didn’t make it right.

“I have all the time I need.” Arno paused so that he wouldn’t have to talk over the sudden screeching of the Portal. “And I’m not going anywhere, Father. There’s an opportunity here. To not take it, to not do good, is as evil as evil itself. As evil as you.”

Conviction, his armor, fortified Arno. But he didn’t speak for the group. They would have to make their own choices.

“‘Whither he goest, there will I go,’” Reed quoted. “Or some biblical shit like that.”

Xochitl looked Father up and down. “You don’t scare me, viejo.”

“This is for Rahalleh, Vlad, Nalja,” Jo recited with great reverence, “and Efrat. For the Pass Ten Bearers and all the Bearers from all the Passes who have been betrayed by Chancellors and Provosts for hundreds of years.”

All eyes turned to Noa.

“I think,” she started, faltered, then started again. “I think that’s your exit cue.”

“‘Resist the devil, and he will flee from you.’” Arno turned and faced Mr. Shaw and Father, on the other side of the Chamber. “So flee your sorry asses out of here.” He quickly added, “Pardon my language.”

The Bearers horseshoed Father and Mr. Shaw against the purple wall.

“Won’t you at least consider . . . ,” Father started.

“Enough talking,” Xochilt cut him off. “Váyase.”

“I can admit when I have been defeated.” Father regarded the Bearers with a degree of dignity. “For all our sakes, I hope you’re right, Pass Eleven Bearers. The fate of the world depends on it. Let’s go, Rupert.”

Mr. Shaw walked to the amethyst wall as his eye-shaped onyx melted into a Teleportare gateway.

But just before he stepped through, Father’s diamond flashed rust, as did his remaining eye. “Begone!” he whispered to Jo.

Arno watched helplessly as Jo, compelled by Father's Orchestration, hurled themself through the open gateway.

"I'll be back," Jo promised the other Bearers just before the gateway shrank back down to the onyx, sealing itself shut behind them.

Jo's amethyst, severed from its Bearer, dropped to the floor with a leaden thud.

"Where are they?" Arno yelled. "Where did you send Jo?"

"Does it matter?" The rust faded from Father's diamond, and it returned to its austere white. "The rest of you can surrender now. She was the only one among you who was truly a threat."

"You misgendering son of a puta!" Xochitl yelled. "Bring them back!"

"Or what?" Father asked.

"Enough talking." Arno quivered with light. It was time to stand up to this monster.

"Agreed." Father's diamond flashed acid yellow as he leached the light out of Arno and sent lightning-like tendrils at the group. Arno could barely hear his own yelling over that of the other Bearers as his nerve endings fried like bacon.

"Father, you promised!" Mr. Shaw protested. "No more violence!"

"Rupert, it's time for you to make me proud," Father commanded, "for once."

"Forgive me, Bearers. I am not my own man." Mr. Shaw charged Xochitl.

She easily spun out of the way as Reed joined her to corner Mr. Shaw.

Arno maneuvered Yellow just in time to absorb Father's next lightning attack.

"You and me, Noa." Arno hoped he sounded more confident than he and his still-sizzling nerves felt. "Ready?"

Noa sort of nodded.

"The problem with children"—Father drew himself back in an unrecognizable Feat—"is that they always make things more difficult than they have to."

The battle commenced.

CHAPTER 4

REED

"Back me up, Reed." Xochitl's arms stretched into swords of jagged shards as she charged Mr. Shaw.

"Is this really worth it, Alejandra?" Mr. Shaw's onyx glimmered navy, and his hands joined into an inky, two-handed monster of a blade that sliced down at her.

"My name"—she caught his sword in hers and threw him off—"is Xochitl."

They danced on the balls of their feet as blades met.

"You see that you have aligned yourself with the archvillain, right?" Reed's probe of Mr. Shaw's mind revealed only deafening static. "Like Saruman to Sauron. Or Kylo Ren to Snoke. Or Catra to Hordak. Or . . ."

"Point made, Reed." Mr. Shaw dodged under one of Xochitl's swipes. "But blood is thicker than water."

"It's bad enough you betrayed us." Reed continued to probe for weaknesses in Mr. Shaw's psychic defenses. "Do you really have to inflict your terrible proverbs on us as well?"

Xochitl dodged his leg sweep, leaped through the air, and transformed her blades back into hands to land the roll.

Keep him talking, Reed thought to himself. *Anything that might distract him and give Xochitl an advantage.*

ARNO

"Keep your distance!" Arno called to Noa as Father's diamond fists came swinging at her.

"Don't worry!" Noa rolled backward. "I have three years of stage combat!"

Arno hurled Yellow at Father. He dodged the topaz, but he didn't anticipate Arno's Stone boomeranging back to flash-bomb him. Father's temporary blindness bought Arno and Noa a few precious seconds to retreat.

But losing his sight didn't slow Father down nearly as much as Arno had hoped it would.

"You've been very naughty, Noa." Father assumed a boxer's stance. "Maybe that's what we'll call you from now on." His indestructible fists dented the topaz wall where Noa's head had been a split second earlier. "Naughty Noa."

Chunks of the topaz wall cracked and broke under Father's onslaught.

"How could you do that to me? To my family? To Vershinin!" Tears brimmed in Noa's eyes. "How could you make me do that to Reed?"

"Another problem with children"—Father's forearm extended, and he open-palmed Noa across her face, drawing blood—"is that they refuse to take responsibility for their actions."

XOCHITL

My Body Fortification. Jo's Glamours. Arno's Photo Alchemy. It appeared that the onyx and the diamond mimicked our Potentias. Typical. The Shaws could not even come up with anything original. I could not imagine, however, that the artificial Stone granted Señor Shaw fighting prowess. Which meant he had spent his life training with the blade. He must have, to be able to match me.

But I was used to fighting men. Fencing was one of the few sports where any body type could excel.

We lunged. We swiped. We angulated. We flicked. We counterattacked each other's counterattacks.

I let him think he was gaining ground, and when he came in for a finishing blow, I deflected his sword with mine and sliced his exposed side with my dagger. His blood was my reward. I moved in for the kill.

His onyx flashed eggplant, and then he was gone.

"He's using Jo's Camouflaging trick." Reed scanned the area with Red. "Behind you!"

I sensed him the moment before an invisible fist punched my kidney. I buckled and back-swung, but all I met was air. At least it was a flesh fist and not an onyx blade that had struck me, which meant . . .

"They can only use one power at a time!" Reed shouted.

The celebration of that revelation was cut short when Señor Shaw's invisible fist uppercut me. My feet left the ground before I landed hard on the surprisingly smooth granite floor.

"Cannot fight what I cannot see, Reed." I elongated my dagger into a second sword and windmilled my blades, hoping to land a lucky blow, or at least force Señor Shaw to keep his distance. As long as parts of my body remained flesh, I was vulnerable.

"See through me." Reed sent Red between my eyes. As if I had donned ruby sunglasses, a rose sheen swept over my vision. Just in time to spot Señor Shaw's gray silhouette and evade his kick.

Señor Shaw was not the only thing I could see when Reed shared his power with me. The sharing connected me with Reed as well. Would I have believed how genuinely he regretted what he'd done to me otherwise? The profound and complete nature of his repentance? How he would have done anything, *anything*, to make it up to me?

Could I have found true forgiveness without such assurance? How did others?

I caught Señor Shaw's extended foot and threw him backward.

ARNO

"I have a pretty good guess about what you desire." Noa held one hand to her bleeding nose, and verdant tendrils wisped out of the other. "But what do you fear?"

"I'm the one who trained you, girl." Father swatted her tendrils away as if they were bothersome flies. "Even if I were asleep, you wouldn't be able to penetrate my psyche."

With reflexes that astounded Arno, Father slapped Yellow out of the air and into the center of the room. Arno barely Petrakinesised his Stone back against the gravitational pull of the ever-expanding star, threatening to open into the Pentacle Portal at any moment.

Now that Father's sight was fully restored, he easily knocked Noa down. He raised his diamond fist over her cowering body.

Arno risked the velvet black rainbow light of the swirling star in the middle of the room. He churned its magnificent power into a kaleidoscope cone around Father. A psychedelic rainbow enveloped him.

Father swayed, hypnotized, lulled into a stupor.

"Noa. Try again! Quickly!" The star's light popped and crackled through Arno. It was infinitely more powerful, infinitely more dangerous, than any light he'd alchemied before.

Noa rolled over, twirling her hands around Green. Her voice echoed deep and powerful. "What. Do. You. Fear?!"

★

REED

"Xochi!" Reed yelled too late. "Look out!"

The Cone of Mesmerism Arno had projected to stop Father inadvertently captured Xochitl in its sway.

A blow from an invisible Mr. Shaw doubled her over. A second dropped her. Reed ran to her prone body, swinging wildly.

"I'm sorry, Reed. Truly. For all of it." Mr. Shaw did look genuinely apologetic as he wavered back into visibility a few feet away. His onyx glowed with a sickly acidity, and a laser leaped out of his open palm.

Time slowed down as Reed stared down at the energy projectile about to end his life.

Never learning who his father was. No more gigs with Ragna Rock. Mom. Rose. Arno, of course.

What he hated with every part of his sixteen-year-old body was that it would be for nothing.

The raw energy zigzagged to him like Darkseid's Omega Beams.

"The End," by The Doors, closed just about every bar mitzvah and sweet sixteen that Reed had ever attended. Appropriate enough, then, that the C–D–G chord progression was the last thing that Reed would hear just before . . .

Goodbye, Arno.

. . . just before the energy bolt bounced off his sequined jacket harmlessly, in a rainbow refraction.

"Not bad, Rojo." The light show snapped Xochi out of her stupor.

"Does this count as me saving you once?" Reed popped the collar of his bedazzled jacket. "So that we're closer to even?"

"There is no debt"—she punched his bicep so hard he winced—"between amigues."

★

ARNO

Arno would've given anything to see what Father feared. He was also relieved he couldn't.

"No! No!" Father howled as the wrinkles on his leathery face contorted. "Avaunt, ye evil thing!"

"That's for my family." Noa twisted her wrists, sending chartreuse tendrils into Father's eye, ears, and mouth. "And that's for Vershinin!" His body lifted off the ground, enmeshed in her Dreamaturgy.

Arno risked a glance at Reed, who was shielding Xochitl with his sequined jacket. If Father's moans of anguish were the result of just a few moments of Noa's power, what had Reed endured night after night?

Silence swept over the Chamber as the howling winds and rumbling cut out. The spinning star in the middle of the room abruptly came to a halt. It settled parallel to the floor, like a well. The cosmic rainbow black of outer space filled its insides, twinkling with stars.

The Pentacle Portal had opened.

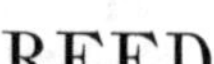

REED

The Portal was open.

If they didn't form the Sphere of Containment soon, it would all be for naught.

Placement time.

Reed shook his head to clear his mind, from the flickering Pass One visions, from his memory of Arno, last night, this morning. He needed to focus.

Red pierced the nearest star limb like a thumbtack pinning a banner to a corkboard.

A wave of heat erupted from the Portal, throwing everyone back. Reed broke the fall with his wrist. Hopefully, the swelling was a sprain, not a break. No matter. Nothing mattered but keeping his Stone in the Portal.

The star's flailing appendage did its best to free itself, thrashing and whipping against his ruby with all its might.

ARNO

The wave of heat threw Noa and Arno against the emerald wall. His bruised body landed with a thud. He rubbed his head. The bump was already forming. At least he was getting up, unlike Noa.

A quick scan of the room: Reed holding the first arm of the Portal in place, Xochitl guarding him. Mr. Shaw rising to his feet in front of the amethyst wall. Noa, still crumpled at the emerald wall. Father, staggering out of his fugue state in the topaz/emerald corner. This was Arno's chance.

His chance to kill Father.

He'd been preparing himself for this, for the possibility of taking someone else's life. It would require knowingly breaking one of the Ten Commandments. If there were any circumstances in which murder was justified, this was it.

A simple laser to the jugular would do it. It was a small price to pay for victory.

His index fingertip sparked and sizzled.

The Price of their Potentias had been made conveniently clear. But what was the Price for compromising his beliefs? How long was that recovery period?

On the other hand, what if they lost because Arno wasn't man enough to do what had to be done?

It didn't matter, ultimately. Because now that he was confronted by it, now that the option was staring him down in all its lethal possibility, Arno knew he didn't have it in him to kill. Not even in these circumstances.

He put his index finger down as a puce Glamour swept over Father, rendering him invisible. Arno cursed himself—if he hadn't spent these invaluable seconds contemplating his moral conundrum, he could've subdued Father, taken him out of play. Instead, he was on the defensive again, squinting for the seams in Father's Camouflage. Too many power swirls, too much interference from the now-open Pentacle Portal. He abandoned Father and ran over to make sure Noa was all right.

Pulse, check. Thank God. He gently slapped her face into consciousness.

"'If it be thus to dream,'" she muttered, "'still let me sleep.'"

"No can do, Noa." Arno helped her up.

"What are we even going to do without Jo?" Noa asked.

"We have to attempt Containment without them," Arno said. "We can't let Mr. Shaw and Father take control of the Portal."

"All right then." Noa shook off her dizziness.

Arno blinked, fighting off the blinding white dancing on the perimeter of his vision. He prayed for a few more minutes of sight.

XOCHITL

I did not know how much power I had left, but I was draining my tank quickly.

I turned back to flesh, except, of course, for the parts that never did. Last night, I traced over fifty shards on my body, hard and rigid, like scales. On my limbs. In the crooks of my elbows and knees. On my feet, my hands. Slicing through my abdomen and torso. I didn't have the courage to look at the ones on my shoulders and back in the mirror. I just ran my fingers over the parts where skin turned to Stone turned back to skin.

I do not know when I stopped thinking about if my body would return to "normal" after the Ikeda passed. It seemed like a luxury, compared with simple survival. I had made my peace. Or, maybe, I had just come to understand that there was no "normal."

Father and Señor Shaw were both Camouflaged invisible. Regrouping? Strategizing?

Arno and Noa arrived in front of the red wall. I could not tell if he was supporting her or vice versa. The left side of her face puffed with discoloration, and he limped, wincing with every step.

"What do we do?" Arno asked.

"I think we have to assume that Jo is out of play for good." Reed grunted under the strain of keeping his Stone in place.

"We can still try The Plan." I kept my voice low so that Señor Shaw and Father couldn't hear us. "Make the Sphere of Containment with the four of us."

"That's what I was just saying!" Arno exclaimed.

"Focus on Placement." I recalled mi zafira to me. "C'est moi."

Just in time.

I sent Blue the moment I saw Father's diamond move to the second ray of the Portal. The two Stones darted in and around the Pentacle Portal's second arm, two ice hockey players jockeying for position.

Every time the Stones clashed, I flinched. Contact with his unholy Stone was more of a violation than when someone touched Blue. I needed to end this. I charged through the center of the room, sliding under the Portal like a baseball player stealing a base, my hand elongating into a lance.

Father dodged counterclockwise to the topaz wall. Its light poured into him. I flattened my other hand into a mirror shield. Let him try to blast through that.

But I was not his target.

His evil platinum lightning arced at Reed.

ARNO

"Watch out!" Arno stepped in front of Reed, using his body to shield him.

Is that rancid smell my burning hair?

His limbs spasmed uncontrollably when the onslaught doubled as Mr. Shaw shimmered out of Camouflage and his lightning joined Father's.

Arno's teeth rattled. A molar cracked against another in an especially violent twitch. But he forced his mind to retreat from the pain, as it had all those years he sat on stiff wooden pews in church, wondering how a religion founded on love could alienate so many. He sought refuge in his crystal world.

For the brief, infinite, shining moment he was back there, his double showed him what to do.

Then he returned to the Chamber. But he wasn't in pain anymore.

Because the attacks were made of light.

He understood light. He always had. In all its forms. Arno was many things. Armenian. Queer. Sixteen. Chubby. Scared. In love. But right now, most of all, Arno Sarkisian was the Yellow Bearer, photo-alchemist.

He opened his arms wide and looked up, like he could see straight into the heavens. He'd never absorbed so much before, nor in such a potent form.

Mr. Shaw and Father doubled down, drawing so much that the Chamber itself darkened, a theater dimming before the main event.

The more they attacked, the more Arno took in. Everything in him opened to accept the onslaught. He would be dead if he tried to fight it. So he surrendered. Absorbed. Accepted.

"Jo," Arno choked up. "Jo taught me all kinds of ways to access the Stone's Blessing. And without your dogma to unlearn, I am capable of things you will never understand. For the only thing you believe in is yourself."

His blood, a living current, sizzled. The pores on his skin tingled. He understood his body on a molecular, then atomic, then subatomic level.

"What trial did you endure to inherit your Potentias?" Arno asked. "Did you survive yourselves?"

He blazed with the intensity of a supernova.

Their attacks sputtered like a car engine stalling. Father faltered first, with Mr. Shaw close behind. The impulse to lash out at them with his godlike power tempted Arno. But he would not let himself be corrupted as they had been, not by all the power in the world. This was his chance to show them how true power could be wielded.

The living photon emerged from his body slowly, like spilled ink spreading over a page.

"What foulness is this?" Father backed away when he saw he was its target. He pivoted to the right, but the blanket of photosynthetic energy was there, having leaped the remaining distance without any regard to the dimension of space.

He turned to the left, but the barricade of light had already curved its way there. When the cage domed up and around him, Father's diamond fell out of the air.

XOCHITL

I had to look away from the solar cage that Arno had conjured to trap Father. It made my retinas ache, like staring at an eclipse, threatening permanent damage. I would not have dared, even in full plate, to pass through it. More important, Arno had given me my chance. With Father's diamond out of play, Blue easily lodged into the Portal's second arm.

The beads of sweat clinging to my upper lip and forehead turned to frost as the Portal released an arctic blast.

NOA

Noa's lungs ached from the frozen air as she spied Mr. Shaw inching his way to Father's diamond.

Oh no you don't! I'll show you what this gorda can do.

She launched into a full run, barreling into his unaware body, checking him back to the amethyst wall, then smacking the diamond out of his reach. In her brief moment of contact with Father's Stone, she felt something—a foulness—an evil—a transgression—something even wronger than being late to rehearsal.

ARNO

Mr. Shaw recovered from Noa's cannonball, dodged her second attempt to keep him down, and rushed Arno. He tackled him like a football player.

"Release Father," Mr. Shaw insisted.

"Or what?" Every word caused a small cloud of dewy condensation in front of

Arno's mouth. Arno wasn't strong enough to throw Mr. Shaw off him, nor could he divert any of his power without compromising Father's cage.

Mr. Shaw raised his fist. Arno turned his head away. It was not the first time he'd taken a hit. At least, this time, it would be for something he did, not just for who he was.

Father's solar cage flickered when Mr. Shaw's fist struck Arno's face the first time. Were the dizzying stars a result of being struck or the beginning of his Price? By the third strike, the cage had disappeared. Did all blood taste metallic?

"I'm pretty sure striking a student is against school policy." Reed leaped onto Mr. Shaw's back, kicking, punching, and scratching.

Mr. Shaw tried to throw Reed off, but he clung on like a rabid marsupial. Their former college counselor settled for back-slamming Reed against the emerald wall. Reed's body crumpled to the ground.

"With the Ikeda this close, I'm feeling all kinds of things possible that I didn't before." Noa had sneaked up on Mr. Shaw during his scuffle with Reed. "For example." Her eyes flashed as shamrock tendrils extended from her Stone. *"Sleep."* The tendrils entered Mr. Shaw through every orifice. *"Sleep."*

Mr. Shaw swayed once. Twice. Then his eyes dropped like curtains, and he crumpled next to Reed.

"Eyes on Father, everyone." Arno bid his light cage adieu. White spider cracks fractured his field of vision as he willed his topaz into the third limb. It spiraled up and over, like one of the dried maple copter seed pods he'd launch into the air so he could watch it helicopter down to marvel at nature's simple glory.

The last thing Arno saw was Father's diamond slam into his topaz like a vicious croquet ball. He didn't need sight to keep his Stone in place. Father's diamond bounced off his Stone harmlessly.

★

XOCHITL

The violence of the Portal's thrashing made me wonder whether we were even doing the right thing. It reacted to our Stones as if they were assailants.

Perhaps it was pointless to consider these points now. We had crossed the Rubicon. Only the Rubicon was fighting back. Sparks erupted from the Pentacle Portal when Yellow was placed in its third arm. The ones that landed on the sapphire parts of me fizzled harmlessly. The ones that landed on my skin burned. Let them. Not enough power left to expend on these nuisances.

Then I charged Father. I had to keep him occupied long enough for Noa to complete her Placement.

I could not believe it was so difficult to land a strike on a viejo like him. But he danced around me and my sword and my dagger, moving with a bullfighter's grace.

I guess that made me the bull.

He said some things to me, horrible things. They do not bear repeating.

Men had been trying my entire life to make me think I was less. That I was not qualified. That I needed their permission.

They had not succeeded.

Neither would Father.

NOA

"Whatta to-do to die today." Noa used her favorite tongue twister vocal warm-up to gather all her strength. "At a minute or two 'til two." She centered herself between the unfurling fourth limb and the emerald wall. "A thing distinctly hard to say . . ."

Green floated out of her hands.

". . . and harder still . . ."

It traveled, tentatively, to the Portal.

". . . to do!" Green landed in the star's fourth limb.

A sickly wave of nausea filled the Chamber.

XOCHITL

When Green locked into place, the Portal responded by leaching the strength out of my limbs. I could barely remain standing. Luckily, Father felt it, too. He stumbled, finally, and I drew first blood as my jagged blade grazed his side. I turned fast, using the momentum to go for his neck.

I had prepared myself to kill today. All warriors must. I had already been judged. Let us see to which mansion of death he would be delivered.

What should have been a finishing blow turned into a mild rebuke when my arm reverted to its natural form before it struck his chest. No more Potentia left. I was empty. Depleted. Nada. Father grabbed my now-flesh hand before I could withdraw and twisted it behind my back. He landed a flurry of open-handed blows to my exposed face, chest, and back. I crumpled to the ground like a leaf just as Father's diamond pinned the final limb.

Five Stones had completed Placement. Just not the five any of us had imagined.

REED

Reed watched helplessly as Father's diamond took position in the final limb of the Pentacle Portal.

"What happens now?" Noa asked.

"Four versus one." Arno's white-glazed eyes looked straight into the heart of the opening Portal. "We can do this!"

Magic erupted out of the Pentacle Portal's open heart. Pure, potent, uncontrollable. It flamed up, the firebrands floating to the top of the Chamber. A fountain of fire, bending time and space around it. The Portal made the aurora borealis look like a science fair project.

Reed initiated the Synergia of the Sphere of Containment by sending an arc from Red to Blue.

"You've failed, Father." Despite the throbbing from his wrist, Reed was delirious with joy. "You're not strong enough to wrest control of the Portal from all four of us."

"Oh, child. There are many ways to vanquish this bitter conquest," Father scoffed. "Awake, Rupert, and do what must be done."

Mr. Shaw sat up violently, like a marionette. "But Father . . . ," he began.

"We do not have time for this." Father's diamond blurred rusty. "Obey."

Around the Portal, Red's arc reached Blue. Bearer connected to Bearer as Stone connected to Stone.

"Arno!" Reed's warning came too late for Arno to evade Mr. Shaw's punch. Or the next one. Or the next one.

Blue arced to Yellow.

Mr. Shaw hurled Arno against the topaz wall. He fell to the ground, and a moment later, Yellow fell out of the Portal.

"Arno!" Reed went to tend to Arno's limp body.

"Reed, no!" Xochitl yelled. "You can't leave the circle!"

"But—" Reed started to protest, but he knew Xochitl was right. The consequences of abandoning now could be catastrophic. He settled for reaching out to Arno through their link.

I'm okay, Reed, Arno assured him.

That would have to be good enough for now.

The onyx pounced into the star's third limb, catching Blue's arc just as it arrived.

More and more molten magic spewed out of the Portal's open heart.

Onyx arced to Green, Green to diamond, and diamond back to Red. The circle spun on its own axis in every possible angle, forming the Sphere of Containment.

The Chamber wavered, like a Phantasmagoria.

ZEB-UN-NISSA

Zeb-un-Nissa is here, in the Chamber. But she is also flying through the galaxy, a ball of ice and cosmic dust and fire and light, speeding through space at a blinding velocity.

Pure magic leaps forth from the heart of the Pentacle Portal, like the famed hot springs of the Nubra Valley, just as the Sphere forms around it.

Zeb-un-Nissa braces, using the rough floor beneath her feet.

She is connected to the other Bearers now. She can hear their thoughts, feel their longings: Sarmad's burgundy hunger. Belawadi's golden determination. Henry's viridian fear. Imtiaz's violet thrill.

Can they feel me now? My indigo hopes? My cobalt concerns?

They work in concert, all five as one, like a herd of gazelles leaping through the underbrush. Their Stones connect to the Portal and harness its pure magic.

"It's working!" Sarmad's crimson excitement thrills them through their bond.

XOCHITL

The Synergia we knew as the Sphere of Containment connected us. I understood now, without a doubt, that the diamond and the onyx were things that were not meant to be. Part of me was curious how Father and Señor Shaw were able to create those Stones, let alone bond with them. But not all mysteries would be solved today.

Father and Señor Shaw wrested control of the Sphere of Containment as easily as a parent takes a toy from a child. They used the Sphere to shrink the Portal down just as every generation of Bearers had done. As it shrank, it tugged us into the center of the Chamber, toward its open heart. We were powerless in the face of its awesome power.

When I met my parents in New York City for Holy Week, my father surprised me with a Zero G experience. Everyone loved the twenty seconds we spent hovering without weight atop the Boeing 737's steep parabolas. But I preferred the double gravity that weighed us down as the plane reached its parabolic apex and prepared for its next swoop. The pull from the Portal was like that, to the nth degree.

"Try again!" Reed yelled.

Reed, Noa, and I coordinated our efforts to wrest control of the Sphere again. To no avail.

"Stupid children," Father muttered. "Now you die for naught. What a waste."

ZEB-UN-NISSA

I knew we could do this together! Sarmad's voice whispers in Zeb-un-Nissa's mind, as if his lips are perched at her ear. *Can you feel it?*

I can.

Zeb-un-Nissa marvels as the power of the Portal succumbs to them. She allows herself a brief fantasy: the look on her father's face when she shows him all she can now do. The power she lends the empire, the good she shares with her people, the poverty she eradicates, the education she affords. This is worth the risk, is it not?

REED

They were mere feet from the Portal's heart. It would consume them and their Stones any moment now.

"You see all the drama you caused? All the unnecessary suffering?" Father sneered. "All for what? There's a reason things must be done the way they always have been."

Everything Reed and the other Bearers had endured, everything they had survived, would be for nothing.

The Shaws would win.

The world would continue spinning in its irrevocable ways.

All because they'd failed.

The Sphere of Containment had shrunk the Portal to the size of a modest campfire. Reed was so close he could peer into its infinity.

You have to have faith, Arno's whisper of consciousness told Reed.

"Do you see now the futility of resistance?" Father resumed. "You're just children, after all. What did you possibly hope to accomplish?"

"Could somebody please"—Reed released a lifetime of resentment of authority figures into his response—"shut this queen up?"

"Your wish, Reed," Jo's voice boomed throughout the Chamber, "is my command."

Purple lifted itself up, as if by its own accord. The forgotten amethyst spun through the air, a Frisbee with all the time in the world.

"Angle shot, corner pocket." Jo's disembodied voice echoed in the Chamber as Purple arced around diamond, then struck it like a billiard ball. The diamond flew straight into the open Portal as the amethyst took its place in the Sphere.

"How is this even possible?" Father stumbled forward toward his lost diamond and the Portal's heart.

"You think you can get rid of me that easily?" Jo emerged from Purple like a djinni from a lamp.

The Bearers hollered with joy.

"Now that's what I call an entrance!" Noa cheered.

"I'll make you pay for your disrespect, you . . . you . . . you radical!" Father spat out like a curse, while desperately trying to find leverage on the smooth floor. The Portal tugged him closer and closer, until his legs dangled at its gaping mouth. "Rupert!"

"Go-Go-Gadget arm." Mr. Shaw extended an onyxed limb to Father, who grabbed it with both hands.

"Pull me forward, you dolt," Father hissed. "Why must everything be such a grind with you?"

The reprimand stung Mr. Shaw and created the crevice in his defenses that Reed was waiting for. In the second before it sealed itself back up, Reed slipped into Mr. Shaw's psyche.

Quiet. Gray. Fog. A place where time had no meaning.

His defenses were gone. Everything was gone from his ashen mental landscape except for the two of them.

"You will never get it," Reed told Mr. Shaw.

"Get what?" Mr. Shaw asked.

"His approval." Reed understood, now, the gaping hole he'd seen when he'd previously deep-dived into Mr. Shaw. Its desperation. Its eagerness. Its futility. It was a chasm that the unconditional love of Reed's mother ensured he would never know.

"I know." Mr. Shaw nodded sadly.

"But you should still save him."

"You think so?" Mr. Shaw asked. "You continue to surprise me, Reed."

"I mean, I'm not saying you should let him stop us. But you don't have to let him die. He's just doing what he thinks is right. Sure, his tactics are impressively toxic. But you have to find it in your heart to forgive him. The way Xochi forgave me. The way I forgive you."

"I wish I could take it all back, Reed." Mr. Shaw's face crumpled, crestfallen. "In the moment, it seemed inevitable. Every choice leading to its next logical conclusion. But then you stop and look back and wonder how you could possibly have strayed so far. For whatever it's worth, I would do it very differently, given the chance."

"That's impossible, of course." Reed shrugged. "But failure is necessary for growth, so the only real question is: what have you learned and do you have what it takes to make it right?"

"I think so." Mr. Shaw looked up, into the slate sky of his psychic plane. "But the proof is, as the saying goes, in the pudding."

The gray landscape dissipated, and they returned to the corporeal world.

"I'm sorry, Father. For everything." Mr. Shaw rescinded his jeweled limb out of Father's grasp. "Truly."

"Rupert! How dare you . . ." The shocked snarl stayed on Father's face as the gaping-open Portal swallowed him.

Mr. Shaw relinquished control of the Portal to the Bearers. They immediately used the Sphere to stabilize the Portal before it shrank any further.

ZEB-UN-NISSA

Once again, the image of another set of Bearers flashes before Zeb-un-Nissa. She blinks them and their outlandish costumes away. She must focus.

"Just as I foresaw," Sarmad intones as the magic from the Portal fills their Stones.

REED

"What took you so long, Jo?" Reed asked with a nonchalance he most certainly did not feel.

"Aw, you missed me!" Jo gushed. "But if you think that was awesome, check this out." Something inside Purple released. Opened. Welcomed. "I think this is how they did it in Pass One."

The bubbling magic geyser of the Portal poured into their amethyst.

Xochitl, true to character, got it on her first try. Noa took a few seconds to translate Jo's action into a Feat. Reed imitated it successfully on his third go.

"You're attempting the failed sin of Pass One?" Mr. Shaw asked incredulously. "Zeb-un-Nissa explicitly warns against this in the Muraqqa. She wrote that the very delivery of the Muraqqa is proof that supercharging the Stones with the Portal risks destruction. And that was before Disjunctis!"

"Can you trust us?" Reed asked. "The way I trusted you?"

Mr. Shaw's onyx opened and accepted the Portal's power.

ZEB-UN-NISSA

The connection between Stones and Bearers is profound. The heart of the Portal sings to Zeb-un-Nissa, a bewitching melody of tanburs and rebabs: deep, resonant, sympathetic.

The Portal is a hookah; its magic, smoke; her Stone, the mouthpiece. She inhales.

XOCHITL

I saw the Pass One Bearers as clearly as if they were in the Chamber with us. I copied Zeb-un-Nissa, my new ancestor, first Blue. Pure black cosmic magic, richer than a perfectly ripe zapote negro, moved from the Portal, into my Stone, and finally, into me. I understood, immediately, why the Pass One Plan could never work.

ZEB-UN-NISSA

Sarmad, something's amiss.

Discord vibrates in Zeb-un-Nissa's soul.

The power makes me tremble. Like too-hot tea poured into a glass carafe, just before it shatters into a thousand shards.

He doesn't respond.

Sarmad?

REED

The magic of the cosmos, black and glittering and shining with tiny stars, filled Reed like power chords rocking an auditorium.

"Under Pressure" by David Bowie. *The Magicians* remake, naturally.

ZEB-UN-NISSA

"Sarmad, we took an oath!" Zeb-un-Nissa yells across the room.

"You fear power," Sarmad intones. "You fear yourself."

She knows that mere mortals are insufficient containers for the Portal's powerful elixir. Sarmad's Plan will not work. She knows it intrinsically, intuitively, the same way she knows it is wrong that her brothers can be emperor but she cannot.

"Belawadi? Henry? Imtiaz? Surely, you feel it, too." Three sets of cold eyes meet her entreaties. "Certain disaster awaits us. We cannot continue!"

"Leader prepared us for your betrayal." Beads of sweat dot Belawadi's face.

"Just like a princess"—Imtiaz scowls—"to issue commands."

Henry, pale as a ghoul, looks away.

Zeb-un-Nissa, Jewel of Womankind, the Hidden One, knows what she must do.

ARNO

Arno gently touched his swollen face.

Ow. Ow. Ow. Ow everywhere.

He cracked his eyes open. A curtain of blinding opaque white.

He drew himself up using the broken notches in the topaz wall as handholds.

ZEB-UN-NISSA

"This is exactly as I have foreseen it, Princess." Sarmad luxuriates in the power filling him. "All is happening as it did in my True Dreams. We have nothing to fear."

"Sarmad, I want to believe you." Zeb-un-Nissa knows that wanting something does not make it so. "But I cannot, because . . . I know you are lying."

"How?"

"Your tell," Zeb-un-Nissa says sadly. "You are touching your face."

Sarmad stops scratching his nose.

"This whole time, you have been peppering your True Dreams with lies to achieve your end." Zeb-un-Nissa can taste the truth of her words as they leave her mouth. "You claim that you have seen all this, but you do not know what will happen any more than we do. What damage we may be wreaking on the world. Because surely, that is the destination where this nefarious path will lead us." It is difficult to say these words, to reveal him like this in front of the rest. But it must be done. "You are no seer. You are a charlatan."

"Ignore her," Sarmad instructs the other Bearers. "She is hysterical."

Knowing what she must do does not make it any easier.

Her first cobalt chamfered cage snaps shut around Sarmad's Stone, like a steel trap around prey.

"You dare?" he bellows.

XOCHITL

We mere mortals were not meant to hold such power. That is why the Pass One Bearers failed. That is why we, the Pass Eleven Bearers, came up with The Plan.

When I could not take it anymore, when I felt like I would explode like a volcano, I opened another channel. An escape hatch. So that all that power could be routed somewhere. Straight to the sapphire wall behind me. I became a transformer, slowing down the magic, converting it into something that could be harnessed. Channeled. Distributed. It conquered my body, colonizing every cell in my being, before continuing on its path. From Portal, to Stone, through me, up the sapphire wall, and finally, into the earth's mantle.

ZEB-UN-NISSA

Three more chamfered sapphire cages enclose each of the remaining jewels.

"Even if you stop us now, how can you guarantee what will happen when the Ikeda returns?" Sarmad speaks calmly, but his ruby batters against its cage like a rabid strawberry finch.

"I cannot. That is why"—the concentration required to keep all four Stones captive makes speaking difficult—"I have taken measures."

"What measures?" Sarmad furrows his forehead.

"I have entered a contract with the exiled King of Great Britain." Zeb-un-Nissa hopes against hope that this, if nothing else, will persuade Sarmad to relent. "Charles II has committed an illegitimate branch of his family to mentor future generations of Bearers. James de la Shaw and his offspring will be our shepherds. The Muraqqa, along with a handsome payment in trade goods, will be en route to him tomorrow, unless I intercede."

"You foolish woman, what have you done?" Sarmad curses.

ARNO

Still no sight. Arno fumbled to his feet. *That's okay.*

The current of power flowed into Mr. Shaw's onyx, then into Mr. Shaw, and back into the topaz wall. But unlike the other walls that lit up like billboards, the topaz wall flickered and faltered. Mr. Shaw howled as the power accumulated inside his body. It would obliterate him soon.

Even moving carefully, Arno stumbled on the rubble at the base of the topaz wall, the fragments broken off by Father and his diamond fists.

But if a blessing can be a curse, then a curse can be a blessing, too. As Arno slowly got up from the topaz rubble, he gleaned the clue he needed. He placed both palms against the topaz wall and drew in the magic light spewing out of the Portal.

He patched the topaz wall with that magic, delving into the lattice of the crystals themselves, knitting the prismatic pyramids back together, loop after loop, gartering, stockinetting, reverse gartering, cabling, seeding, and ribbing on an atomic level, where energy and matter were one.

New patches of aureate geodes filled the crevices of the topaz wall.

Arno couldn't see the wall light up like the most glorious Christmas tree. But he certainly felt it.

REED

Reed cheered when Arno healed the topaz wall.

If only he could figure out how to connect to the molten power gathering inside his Stone. Everyone else just seemed to intuit how to do it. Even Mr. Shaw. Why couldn't he? And how much time did he have, before . . .

"Um, guys?" Their Sphere of Containment shimmered once.

"Hurry up, Reed!" Xochitl vibrated with the Portal's power.

The Sphere shimmered again. After the third shimmer, it disappeared in wisps.

Without the Sphere to contain it, the Portal twisted and warped like melted glass. It yanked the Bearers so close to its heart that Reed was face-to-face with it, peering into the infinity of the cosmos.

ZEB-UN-NISSA

"It is not too late for us, now, to find an alternative," she yells over the sound of the Portal. "If we work together."

"I do not believe you are capable of it, Princess," Sarmad sneers. "I do not believe you will betray your fellow Bearers. That you will betray me."

Zeb-un-Nissa calculates quickly: the unstable Portal, the Bearers' cold eyes, the time remaining. She does not have nearly as much information as she would like. But she is sure that if they proceed, the magic will destroy them and the Stones and then, unchecked, wreak havoc on the world, even worse than the fate Sarmad has foretold.

Sometimes, one must simply act. Sometimes, to do nothing is the sin.

"Goodbye." As if pushing a boulder, she wills all four jewels into the Portal's heart.

XOCHITL

Quien saltar quiere lejos, debe medir la distancia.

"One must step back to take a great leap."

Reed had not yet completed his part of The Plan. Could not.

The unstable Portal would collapse on itself.

On some level, I think I always knew this moment would come. Emotions, light, dreams, and Glamours can accomplish only so much.

I understood why Father sounded giddy when he had talked about making the ultimate sacrifice. When you commit to that decision, everything falls away. The scale of your contemplation shrinks the world.

Had I had enough time to recharge?

Only one way to find out.

The transformation started in my core, in the part of my body I contracted just before a lunge. My blood chilled as it spread down my thighs, up my torso, down my arms, up my neck, down my knees and calves. My hands and feet changed just before my chin, my mouth, my nose, ears, and eyes. It crawled up my back, sweeping over my face like a cowl.

This time, it went deeper. Into my blood, my muscles, my tendons, the fasciculus that connected them. Then deeper. Into my bones, my marrow. My organs turned last.

Full sapphire. Truly. Mi destino.

I took a step back.

I thought about indulging myself for one moment: to say goodbye to Masuda, to Timothée, to Lucía, to M., to my parents, to my grandmother's hacienda in Cuernavaca, to fencing, to all my social media followers, to everyone.

Then I decided against it. I had never been sentimental. Why start now.

I took the great leap.

ZEB-UN-NISSA

The heart of the Portal pulls the Stones into it, like a whirlpool.

Their Bearers fight in vain.

Sarmad's eyes flash crimson, and he sees something the rest of us cannot.

REED

After trying, time and time and time again to return to his ruby crystal world, suddenly Reed found himself there.

But instead of his mirror double, he discovered Sarmad sitting cross-legged, across from him, in the crimson canyon.

You feel that power, do you not?

Reed nodded.

Let me help you.

"Yes, please," Reed responded.

Sarmad held two fingers up. Reed mirrored him.

Reed was in that world and in this one, at the same time, realities converging and overlapping. In the ruby crystal world, he and Sarmad sat opposite each other, index and middle fingers lightly pressed together. In this world, the dam around his mind burst open, and the accumulated power of the Portal rushed into him.

It threatened to tear him apart, eradicate every physical trace of him from the earth, burn him to a crisp like newspaper in a furnace, without even ash as proof that he'd ever been.

He felt for the towering magnificence of the ruby wall behind him.

No! Sarmad's eyes flashed open. *Keep it. The power. For yourself. Use it to make the world in your image.*

"But that isn't The Plan." Reed found his fingers magnetized in place, against Sarmad's.

Do you trust the people of your world to save themselves? Sarmad scoffed. *They are ruled by their pettiness. They need a great leader. A ruler, like you.*

Reed's hesitation was all Sarmad needed. He opened his hand. Against his judgment, Reed opened his as well. All five fingers met.

XOCHITL

Holding the Portal open was like trying to keep a dragon's jaw from snapping shut. The sheer power of it humbled me, its radiance searing over the polished surfaces of my sapphire body. If not for this invulnerable form, the lavalike magic would've burned me out of existence.

Did the Ikeda await on the other side? Or some other world, some plane, like Tlalocán? Or did it lead nowhere? Or was this world, our world, the only one?

Maybe that was why we continued to fight for it.

The Portal contracted and warped around me. I jammed my back against one side and my feet into the other.

"Reed! ¡Vamos!"

But he was somewhere else.

REED

It was tempting.

After all, Sarmad told him, *there is a reason that Reds are Leaders. Let me show you.*

Image after image appeared.

"Unstoppable" by The Score. Em–Am–C–Am.

Reed becoming Student Council president of Asbury Park High.

Then Rutgers University.

Reed getting elected to City Council.

Then mayor.

The House of Representatives.

The Senate.

As Vice President.

Then our country's first gay president.

Or, at least, the first out one.

Reed passing the kind of legislation our country needed, protecting LGBTQIA+ youth, finally enacting gun control, supporting racial equality, reining in climate change, ensuring abortion rights.

Reed giving speeches.

Reed getting applause.

Reed standing up for the things he believed in.

Reed inspiring others.

Reed having purpose.

Reed leading.

ARNO

"Come back to us, Reed."

When he didn't respond, Arno reached out to him using their link, that special rapport that had opened up between them last night.

Reed, where are you?

Still nothing.

Reed?

REED

Ignore him, Sarmad instructed. *We must focus on the greater good.*

XOCHITL

I saw it all.

Reed.

Sarmad.

I would not let him betray me. Not again.

"Reed, this is where you choose. ¿Comprendes?" I did not need to yell.

"This is where you show us—me—yourself—what you are made of. This is it, amigue."

REED

Ignore her as well. Sarmad spoke with an oracle's conviction. *She does not know what leadership is.*

But Xochitl could not be ignored. What was he made of?

He had come so far since he'd found Red on the shores of Asbury Park Beach. If he could, would he give it all back? All the adventure, all the power, all the wisdom, all the experience?

Until just now, he would've said yes. He would trade it all in a second to save himself from the pain, the betrayal he'd endured, the betrayal he'd inflicted, the hurt, the damage, the loss.

One time, his mother had asked him—if he could, would he choose to be straight?

At times, he'd have said yes. Why intentionally choose the harder path? Why open yourself up to the hate of strangers? Why opt for a life where every time he wanted to hold Arno's hand in public, he'd have to weigh the dangers? Why endure the microaggressions, the internal calculus of figuring out how to subtly out himself without making anyone uncomfortable, and then wondering, when he was not able to find such a way, if it was just the actualization of an internalized self-hatred? Not to mention having to navigate the normal-size and macro aggressions.

Life was tough enough.

But now, staring into Sarmad's eyes and the heart of the Portal, Reed understood. He wouldn't choose to be gay despite the hardships. He would choose it because of them. Overcoming those obstacles on his own terms strengthened him. Like the calluses on his fingertips, earned from months and years of guitar. It didn't stop there. Those experiences didn't just make him stronger. They also made him better. They watered the garden where perspectives could grow and flower into empathy.

He couldn't turn back time (A–Asus^4–A–D–Dsus^4–D–Bm–E, thank you, Cher) any more than he could rewire himself. But why bother? He was born this wa-ay.

Reed would do the best with what he had. He would alchemy everything he'd endured—all the pain and agony and terror and disappointment—and turn it into something fabulous.

It wasn't about power. Anyone could be good, if they chose to.

But choosing good was only intention. Experience was the transformer that converted intention into action.

Experience led to pain. The worst part wasn't your hurt. It was the hurt you inflicted on others, on loved ones, intentionally and unintentionally. Inevitability didn't soften its sting.

If you could emerge from all that pain, though, without succumbing to cynicism, you'd be rewarded with empathy. Empathy was the only path to real good. Not that Golden Rule bullshit. Treating someone the way you wanted to be treated wasn't that hard. But treating them the way *they* wanted to be treated, on their own terms—that took imagination. That was a real feat.

You had to use yourself to overcome yourself. You were your greatest obstacle and your only tool. Everyone, everything else, was just an illusion.

Not that there was anything wrong with illusions, Reed smiled, invoking Jo and all their Glamourousness.

Reed didn't need to overcome Sarmad. He only needed to overcome himself.

"Fight Song" by Rachel Platten. G–D–Em^7–Cadd^9.

He still had a lot of fight left in him. More than he would've ever imagined.

None of them understand true leadership, Sarmad continued. *You will show them! We will show them what it means to rule!*

"Thanks, but no thanks, Sarmad. That's not leadership." Reed understood it now. Understood it all. From the beginning to the end, the alpha and the omega, the hamza and the ye, the whole thing, with a singular, undeniable clarity. "True leadership is service."

You are a fool, like the rest of them. You could have been king!

"Every king is a fool." Reed pulled the rest of his calloused fingertips away. "And maybe this queen doesn't need to be king."

Time to get back to work.

Reed blinked his way back to the Chamber. He surrendered the power to the ruby wall behind him.

The current entered and exited him, splitting him in half from the inside. How could anything hurt so much and still be so glorious?

ZEB-UN-NISSA

Sarmad's final curse wounds Zeb-un-Nissa. But she knows that leadership is not for the faint of heart. Her father taught her that.

Besides, her work isn't done. The Portal demands one last offering.

Even with her eyes closed, Zeb-un-Nissa sees it all: the Chamber with its five jeweled walls, the Pentacle Portal spewing magic not native to this world. She doubts if she has the will to do what is needed. But the Portal does the work, drawing her closer and closer. All she has to do is release. To stop fighting. To surrender to the great powers, as one surrenders to the tide.

XOCHITL

I wish I could describe to you what I saw there, in the magic world of the black cosmos, through the heart of the Portal. Such beauty. Such power. Things that no mortal was ever meant to witness. Or perhaps, it was our birthright. Perhaps, if everyone could see it, could see the grandiosity of the universe, we would understand our role. We would be free.

Like so many things, the Portal was not good or evil. It just was.

Reed had completed his part. But too late. At least, for me.

The Portal closed around me, drawing me into it like a mother welcoming a child back to its womb.

PONG.

I embraced death, as it had embraced me.

ZEB-UN-NISSA

Her last thought is of the letter she left her father, hidden in the secret drawer of her inlaid desk. An apology. A goodbye. And also a plan: feign conflict between them. To explain her absence, claim she is sequestered. Better that than have the court suffer the scandal of her disappearance.

She wishes she could see him one last time. She fears what he will become without her.

XOCHITL

His hand locked around my elbow.

"You're not getting away from me that easy, amigue." Reed reached in and yanked me out of the Portal. Out of death's embrace.

I let him save me. I let myself be saved. But like all things, it came with a Price. Reed and I fell to the ground. His hand clanked against the smooth floor.

The ruby, sapphire, topaz, emerald, and amethyst walls dazzled like the Zócalo on Mexican Independence Day as the light traveled up and up and up, revealing the Chamber to be hundreds of meters high. The walls, leaning into one another imperceptibly, culminated at a single point on top.

The five colors met at the obelisk's capital. They converged at the very top before erupting in all directions, infusing the earth's mantle with their magic. In my new form, I could feel the energy enhancing and imbuing the precious stones. Like long-lost lovers, reunited.

The Portal disappeared in a single blip.

Our Stones landed with a clunk on the smooth floor.

CHAPTER 5

REED

"What did you do?" Mr. Shaw dropped to the ground, gasping and wheezing.

"We infused all the precious stones in the earth's crust with the Portal's magic." Reed inspected his right hand, the one that pulled Xochi out of the Portal, in its new, transformed sapphire state. Impossibly, sensation still extended into the previously calloused fingertips. But moving a finger, even a fraction of an inch, required herculean exertion.

"That means . . ." Mr. Shaw trailed off, trying to wrap his imagination around the implications.

"That for the next few weeks, hundreds, maybe even thousands of people will become Bearers." Noa swished her cape behind her. "That'll be all the proof the world needs that the Stones are real."

"And it will prepare everybody because . . ." Jo trailed off.

". . . in approximately thirty-seven years, when the Ikeda returns . . . ," Reed continued.

". . . we'll have another few hundred Bearers," Arno concluded. "Or a few thousand? We're not really sure."

"And anything that still runs on the dirty electricity of fossil fuels will be rubbish," Mr. Shaw finished. "You've initiated the greatest act of ecoterrorism the world will ever know."

"And hopefully, saved it in the process." Xochi's voice rang metallic through her fully sapphire form.

"Everyone says we're 'almost out of time' to save the environment." Noa wiped her brow with the edge of her cape. "But at a certain point 'almost out of time' becomes 'out of time.' It's our home. Nobody else is going to take care of it."

"So what do we do with him?" Xochi looked down at Mr. Shaw.

"We could really use his family connections to help us accomplish everything we need to get done before Pass Twelve." Reed weighed each word carefully. "If we think we can trust him."

"As much as I appreciate the gesture," Mr. Shaw dry-wheezed, "I'm afraid you'll have to do without me. Someone like me was never meant to wield one of these precious Stones." The black fire started in the eye socket that housed the onyx. "I knew what the Price would be when I initiated Cyclops." The combustion slowly spread over his body.

"Is there any way . . ." Reed trailed off, unable to say the words.

"I am, unfortunately, out of time." Coughs and spasms racked Mr. Shaw's body. "But because of what you've done today, hopefully, our world will not be."

A younger Reed would've wailed or protested or tried something impossibly heroic and equally futile. But this Reed knew when to accept the inevitable. He took Mr. Shaw's hand in his own. Mr. Shaw lifted his head to address all the Bearers.

"I have faith in you, young people. Now, Reed, may I impose one final request?"

How did Reed know exactly what Mr. Shaw was going to ask? He yanked the onyx out of Mr. Shaw's eye socket. His body immediately disintegrated into ash.

"Probably for the best," Jo interrupted the moment of mourning. "No way in hell I was gonna work with that loser."

ARNO

Arno waited apart from the group, in the topaz/sapphire corner, where Reed found him.

"I still can't see," Arno whispered.

"It'll come back in time." Reed gently nuzzled his nose against Arno's neck. "You'll see."

"I don't think so, Reed." Arno turned to him.

Reed did a double take. Arno's eyes—iris, cornea, lens, pupil, everything—had turned entirely, opaquely, yellow-brick-road yellow. Could Arno sense the tears that jumped to Reed's eyes?

"I'm never going to see again." Arno shrugged. "Is it weird that I don't really mind?"

"Boys Don't Cry" by The Cure.

Until they do.

"How come?" Reed kept his sobs silent.

"I finally feel like I can truly see now."

"See what?"

"Almost everything is an illusion, really. And the few things that aren't, that are true and real, like our love, are clearer than they ever have been." Arno smiled. "Life is going to be so wonderful now that we know what to do with it."

"I want you to know"—Reed kissed Arno's hand—"you can count on me."

"Bruno Mars, right? I love that song!" Arno's hand found Reed's. "Just don't say anything to the Bearers, okay? At least for now."

"Why not?"

"I don't want them to worry."

Reed pulled Arno in close, and their bodies swayed to a song only they could hear. He didn't trust himself with words, especially through the tears. But for another few weeks, at least, he wouldn't need them. He opened himself to Arno.

This is me, Arno. All of me.

He let Arno in, let Arno see all of him: the ugly, the proud, the shy, the confident, the insecure, the snarky, the curious.

"Oh—oh!" Arno's golden eyes shimmered. "What a beautiful song."

XOCHITL

I placed a hand on the sapphire wall. I could feel the magic infusing the Stones of the earth's crust, weaving into their lattices, enchanting them, augmenting them, making them like ours. I did not want to leave the wall. In many ways, I had more in common with it than with the other Bearers now.

"If you change back, Xochi, you'll recharge sooner." Jo had been uncharacteristically silent since the battle had ended.

"There is no changing back," I announced. "This is me."

"But even if that's true," Noa said, "once the Ikeda moves out of closest approach . . ."

"The transformation is complete, permanent, and immutable." I felt like I could just step into the wall behind me and become one with it. If only there weren't so much work still to do. "At least this world will have to accept that we are real. I will be living proof of the new reality."

"Thank you for saving us." Reed leaned on Arno as they joined us in the center of the room.

"Again?" I tried to smile. My new face barely accommodated the gesture.

"Again." He addressed the group. "Good job, everyone. I'm putting you on a thirty-seven-year hiatus. Rest up. Because before we know it, it'll be time to mentor the Pass Twelve Bearers."

"And what makes you think"—I stepped forward—"that you are the most qualified for the job?"

"Nothing," Reed answered. "That's why I'm hoping you'll let me help you do it."

Reed, assisting me. Finally, something that made sense.

"Okay, bitches." Noa swept her cloak behind her and staggered up from the floor. "Curtain call's over. Time to go home."

"Agreed," Arno said.

"Um, guys?" Jo peered into their Stone. "I don't think I'm coming with you."

"It'll get real boring here real fast by yourself." Noa arched an eyebrow.

"I think I figured out how I was able to return after Father Orchestrated me through the Teleportare gateway." Jo expanded, growing, filling the space in the Chamber. "And how I managed to return to Pass Eleven in the first place."

"You gonna share with the class?" Reed raised his sapphire hand as if he were waiting to be called on. "'Cause I would love that mystery wrapped up before the adventure's over."

"It's simple, really." The visage of Jo shifted through all the colors of the rainbow, as the Portal had just done, sparkling with the stars of the night sky. "I'm not Jo."

"You're not?" Arno pivoted his head in their direction.

I marveled as the Aztec constellations swirled within the star pattern sparkling throughout Jo's ever-expanding self.

"I'm just an illusion."

The Bird, pierced with a bone, in the same vicinity as Taurus.

"Don't say 'just.'" Arno pulled away from Reed. "Everything has its own worth, Jo. You taught me that."

Jo continued expanding, filling the Chamber. The Frog. The Butterfly.

"I don't mean it like that, you cornball." Jo's voice grew as they did. Stereo.

"Something happened to me inside Purple, between the Passes. I'm Jo, but I'm also all the Purple Bearers from all the Passes. There's so much I see now, so much I finally understand . . ." They shimmered, like one of their Glamours on the verge of disappearance.

"Don't go, Jo." Arno, a Jonah engulfed by the whale, pleaded.

". . . but it's going to have to wait. See you at Pass Twelve, suckers!"

Jo imploded into Purple, which emitted a supernova's blinding intensity before it disappeared.

The rest of the Bearers cried. If I could have, I would have joined them. But Stone does not weep.

CHAPTER 6

REED RETURNS HOME

Reed stood outside the front door to his house in Asbury Park, New Jersey.

Could it really have been only six measly weeks?

He almost knocked on the door before remembering he didn't have to.

It took a moment to fish the spare key out from under the fake rock by the welcome mat. Everything took an extra moment when you couldn't really move what used to be your dominant hand. He'd never pick strings again, of course. But then again, he'd never need to look for a pick, either. There were worse fates than playing rhythm guitar.

Rose lay barefoot on the sofa in a simple, azalea-patterned summer dress. She slowly removed the nasal mask that connected her to the ventilator perched on its rolling base.

Reed fought the impulse to run up and hug her. She'd need time to take him in.

She sat up and turned to him.

He waited for her to exclaim, to scream, to come running over to him, to hug him, to welcome him back.

A Stone as pink as his sister's namesake flower twirled and twinkled above the sofa, as if winking at Reed. Rose cocked one of her asymmetrical eyes. "You are in so much trouble."

★

Dear Pass Twelve Bearers,

We have xmailed you each copies of the Muraqqa, as well as the agenda for our first meeting next week, during which we will establish community guidelines and consent/safety protocols. We look forward to helping you become a light for future generations.

Reed de Vries, *Secretary of the Provosts' Council*
Pass Twelve

EPÍLOGO

The first time I shared this story in its entirety, with the Pass Twelve Bearers, I had the luxury of telling it with Reed and Arno and Jo. Noa was gone, but that is a tale for another time. Arno was still alive for Pass Thirteen, but by that point, he could only contribute so much. He never quite recovered after Reed. I suppose neither did I. Then it was just me and Jo, until they, too, were finally released. Only I remain. The subsequent volumes of the Muraqqa chronicle all the Passes, but I continue to tell the story of Pass Eleven because it was the essential Pass. The one in which we took responsibility for the Stones, the Portals, and ourselves.

Our story might sound trivial now, all these years decades centuries later. Insignificante. But it is not just our story. It is your story, too, and you needed to hear it. If you do not know where you come from, how can you know who you are, let alone where you may go?

What will you do with your Potentia? There are endless possibilities, but only one path that will finally heal our broken planet. Nuestro planeta roto. I will do my best, as I have always, manifestation after manifestation, Portal after Portal, Pass after Pass. But I have not been part of this world for so very long that now it feels alien to me. And I to it. Besides, it will fall to you to do the actual work. As it always has. Do not blame me for this. Blame the Stones. They have always chosen their own destiny. Just as they have chosen you.

So forge your path. Do not let the knowledge that survival is dependent on your success deter you. Because this is our last chance to get it right. Such is your burden, the burden of the final Keepers of the Stones and Stars.

— END OF BOOK —

AUTHOR'S NOTE

Thank you for reading my book. Can you believe I have the chutzpah to ask you to read more? There are, however, a few things I feel you should know, dear reader:

✡ Princess Zeb-un-Nissa is very much a historical character. This is the first paragraph of her Wikipedia entry*:

- Zeb-un-Nissa (15 February 1638–26 May 1702) was a Mughal princess and the eldest child of Emperor Aurangzeb and his chief consort, Dilras Banu Begum. She was also a poet, who wrote under the pseudonym of "Makhfi" ("Hidden, Disguised, Concealed One").

The poem she is writing when we meet her, in Interlude A, is a real poem that the historical character composed. To read more of her beautiful poetry, I recommend *The Diwan of Zeb-un-Nissa*.

✡ We know much less about Sarmad Kashani, who was also a historical figure. Wiki tells us**:

- Sarmad Kashani, or simply Sarmad (ca. 1590–1661) was a Persian-speaking Armenian mystic and poet who traveled to and made the Indian subcontinent his permanent home during the 17th century . . . The reputation as a poet and mystic he had acquired during the time the two traveled together, caused the Mughal crown prince Dara Shikoh to invite Sarmad to his father's court.

There is no reason to believe that Zeb-un-Nissa and Sarmad ever met, and the circumstances of their relationship are entirely imagined.

---

* Wikipedia, s.v. "Zeb-un-Nissa," last modified September 28, 2023, https://en.wikipedia.org/wiki/Zeb-un-Nissa

** Wikipedia, s.v. "Sarmad Kashani," last modified October 4, 2023, https://en.wikipedia.org/wiki/Sarmad_Kashani

- The nine levels of the Aztec underworld through which Ale/Xochitl travels, Mictlán, is the underworld of Aztec mythology.

- Many of Ale/Xochitl's views on Mexico's relationship to indigeneity were taken from "An Homage to Our Roots? Undue Cultural Appropriation in Mexico," by Yásnaya Elena A. Gil, translated by John Pluecker.

- Everything else I made up.

ACKNOWLEDGMENTS

It takes a village, people. I am lucky to belong to a village with these incredible folx.

Josh Adams, gentleman agent, who believed in this story from the moment I pitched it to him over a decade ago.

Trisha de Guzman, editor extraordinaire, who shepherded this book with infinite grace, intelligence, curiosity, and insight.

Joy Peskin, who told me I could write.

Linsay Firman, Samuel Buggeln, Suzanne Agins, Rosemary Andress, and Sarah Braunstein: Story Whisperers All.

The Writing Excuses Podcast (and especially Mary Robinette Kowal), for providing me eighteen seasons of company and instruction.

MaryBeth Bunge, who taught me how to knit, the importance of consensus leadership, and many other things.

The cafés: Sullivan Street Bakery on Forty-Seventh between Tenth and Eleventh; Aficionado on Fifty-Third and Eleventh; The Last Bite Café in High Falls, New York; The Crafted Kup in Poughkeepsie, New York; the Toks of Mexico City and Acapulco; and all the cafés of San Miguel de Allende.

Liz Duffy Adam and Aryn Kyle's 9 AM Writing Group.

Gabriela Narro Loris and her daughter, Tonalli Narro Loris, who were kind and generous enough to endure my clumsy Spanish as they taught me about their time with indigenous cultures in Mexico.

John Phillips, who spent a night teaching me everything I ever wanted to know about electricity.

Naira Mirza, FSG's editorial intern, whom I've never met, but whose insights were pure gold.

Bob Proehl, author of *Nobody/Somebody People* duology, who helped me with the anatomy of action sequences.

The legion of authenticity readers: Ollie Hennis, Alejandra Oliva, Darius Anthony Harper, Scarlett Stitt, Mylos Gaffney, and Zebunisa Jilani. (Zebunisa refused payment for her services, so I offered instead to include the information for her charity, the Swat Relief Initiative, which seeks to support the Swat Valley in Pakistan, and restore girls' schools destroyed by the Taliban: https://swatreliefinitiative.org/.)

Libby Appel, who generously allowed me to use her translation of *The Three Sisters* in Book V, Chapter 7.

One Ring, a now defunct Ithacan doughnut joint in Ithaca, whose deliciousness got me through some tough times.

Officer Graham Campbell, who was kind enough to review the police scene.

Shelley and Ron Cooper, for providing me the space to write and access to their garden.

Linsay Firman, Suzanne Agins, Russell Sprague, Ryan Migge, and Dustin Chinn, who role-played the final sequence.

Christopher Guild, who DMed the final sequences session with a true D&D aficionado's panache and attention to detail.

Bill Reeves Jr., was also in that role-playing session, but I'm giving him his very own special thanks because we've been discussing this genre passionately and with some regularity for our forty-plus years of friendship, and also because I shamelessly stole the stratagem he employed in said session.

The Extraordinary League of Alpha Readers who read the first draft and whose feedback made the book 100,000 percent better: Connor Bryant, Hunter Herbert, Jamie Wells, Jessi Bond, Christopher Guild, William J. McGinn, John Phillips, Ani Panikian, Poppy Peabody, Aimee Ouellette, Bee, Sonia Saxena, Rafael Ascencio, Addyson Wells, Poppy O'Neill, Faith Huff, Socks Carter, Kamarria Grigsby. Y mi suegra favorita, Margarita Almada Navarro.

The Extraordinary League of Beta Readers who read a later draft and whose feedback made the book another 100,000 percent better: MaryBeth Bunge, Emmaline Keddy-Hector, Ross Haarstad, Samuel Buggeln, Amineh Helalian, Nicole Synn Vassallo, Jimmy Kenna, Mackenzie Trowbridge, Jamie Wells,** Maggie Murtha, Lucas Robinson, Rose Chadwick, Julianna Gonzalez, Linsay Firman, Poppy O'Neill,*

* The asterisk indicates readers brave/foolish/wonderful enough to read the manuscript twice!

** Jamie Wells wins for being the only reader to read the manuscript ALL THREE ROUNDS.

Lizzy Miller, Caryn Zambelli Cushman, Sally Stewart, Stephen Bel Davies, and Jared Brendon Hopper.

The Extraordinary League of Gamma Readers (I know, can you believe I inflicted this text on more innocents?) who read the penultimate draft and whose feedback made the book a final 100,000 percent better, with a special shout-out to the asterisked lovelies who had already read it: Xanny, Connor Bryant,* Michelle Adelewitz, Joshua Nichols, Tilly Garnett, Nicole Synn Vassallo,* Gabriela Palmer, Mackenzie Trowbridge,* Amineh Helalian,* Julianna Gonzalez,* John Phillips,* Jamie Wells, Lizzy Miller,* Ross Haarstad,* Rafael Ascencio,* Satvi Haber, Ani Panikian,* Luka Tomasevic, William J. McGinn,* Miriam Crowe, and Russell Sprague.

Mi familia politica, who welcomed me to Mexico and their family.

My Mexican culture/Spanish consultant and husband, Rafael Eduardo Ascencio Almada. If you want to know what love looks like, it's reading an early draft of a 550-page book in a genre in which you have no interest, just because your husband wrote it. Twice.

And Glen de Vries, who always made time for his friends. See you in space, buddy.